HOYT'S CHILD

Other fiction by R. V. Cassill

THE GOSS WOMEN

DOCTOR COBB'S GAME

LA VIE PASSIONNÉE OF RODNEY BUCKTHORNE

THE HAPPY MARRIAGE AND OTHER STORIES

THE FATHER AND OTHER STORIES

THE PRESIDENT

PRETTY LESLIE

CLEM ANDERSON

XV × III

THE EAGLE ON THE COIN

R. V. Cassill

HOYT'S CHILD

1 9 7 6

DOUBLEDAY & COMPANY, INC., GARDEN CITY, NEW YORK

All of the characters in this book
are fictitious, and any resemblance
to actual persons, living or dead,
is purely coincidental.

ISBN: 0-385-09675-5
Library of Congress Catalog Card Number: 75-21218
Copyright © 1976 by R. V. Cassill
All Rights Reserved
Printed in the United States of America
First Edition

For Erica, who wrote me a letter.

Money is human happiness in the abstract: he, then, who is no longer capable of enjoying human happiness in the concrete devotes himself utterly to money.

Schopenhauer

And what to say of him God knows.
Such violence. And such repose.

Richard Wilbur, "Tywater"

BOOK I

I

The American girl who called herself Victoria and no longer answered to a last name followed two armed men down a shale slope in the Guerrero mountains. Behind her was another American. He was a few years older than the girl, but his fluffy, pale beard made him look younger than he was. The two men ahead of them were darker. One of them was nearly the color of the Indians native to this state. The weapons they were carrying were U.S. M-16s, stolen eighteen months ago from a National Guard armory in San Diego.

A bird whistled twice out of the jungle on their right and the bearded American looked up for it with wide-eyed curiosity. None of the others paid any attention to its call.

The girl was dressed in a fatigue jacket and cutoff denims. Her skin was the color of smoked honey. Her long hair was naturally a light brown, but the sun had bleached tawny streaks in it, like the stripes of a very old battle flag seen through imperfect glass. She had put tennis shoes on her bare feet when the four of them left the dust-colored VW bus parked on the lane above the slope.

They came down to the level of a dry stream bed. From here they could look out through an opening between the green mountains onto the hammock sag of the jungle farther down, still vivid with the colors of the sinking sun. There were gaudy evening clouds in the sky, edged with shining yellows and pinks.

The man called León stopped. He whipped the stock of his M-16 to his shoulder and playfully swung its muzzle across the

long flank of the ridge opposite them. He lowered the gun,
savoring the feel of its stock and forestock in his palms. Blithely
he said, "I like them more than the Russian AK-47." Then, to
make sure this did not sound like praise of the country from
which they had come, he said, "The best weapon is the weapon
of your enemy."

"They still look like toys to me," Victoria said. Three hours before, she and her boyish-looking friend had wheeled their VW
into the barnyard of the mountain farm where León's people
were waiting for them. From a rendezvous north of Guadalajara
they had brought two suitcases full of smuggled parts that
were supposed to make the M-16s usable, since the guns had
not been stored in the San Diego armory in firing condition.
Full of the importance of their mission, Victoria had been
stunned with disillusion to see the stolen rifles cached in León's
barn looking like futuristic plastic imitations intended for small
boys at Christmas. She had expected immense and brutal machines of destruction. At least she had expected something that
looked more damaging than the expensive hunting rifles or over-
and-under shotguns she had been allowed to handle by well-to-
do boy friends. "They don't look like they could kill *anything*,"
she said now with uncertainty and anxiety.

Her naïveté was pleasing to León. He snapped a clip of ammunition into his weapon and said, "Since the *señorita* was so
helpful in this matter, she will be the first to try." To Bunny Stewart he explained, "We have had the cartridges since before
Christmas, but my friends, too, think the toy bullets will not
make big holes. Only Raúl and I have experience with them."

Victoria pushed back her sunglasses so they sat atop her sun-
streaked hair. Then the steel-and-plastic gun was in her hands
and León's fingers were close to her breast as he illustrated how
the first cartridge was brought into the firing chamber and how
the lever was positioned for full automatic fire.

"No," he decided, returning the lever to the other position.
"Fire only single shots. Two or three, as you like. We are too
near the village. If we are heard it should seem to be hunters.
Tomorrow my friends and I will go farther back in the mountains to begin training where we will not be heard."

Victoria nodded breathlessly. She put the gun to her shoulder, grinning like an embarrassed child whose turn has come in a violin recital.

Her first shot threw a small, chill-colored puff of dust from a patch of shale on the mountain ahead of them. Echoes clattered in diminishing volume and rhythm. The flare of pride in her face was like something stamped on a bright coin. "I always *liked* guns," she insisted, to no one in particular. She fired again and a third time without waiting for the echoes to quiet. Then her thumb flicked the lever León had told her to leave alone. Her finger convulsed on the trigger as she fired a burst of perhaps eight shots. They came too quick to count. A quarter of a mile away several dust puffs in a line sprang from the shale while echoes piled frantically.

"Yes!" she said with a triumphant exhalation of breath. When she handed the gun back to León she put both her tingling hands in her armpits and squeezed down hard. The pupils of her dark-blue eyes were contracted to the diameter of nail points. "Yes! Oh, yes, yes!"

"Hey, you weren't supposed to," Bunny Stewart said. He had had the jitters badly for the two days they had the smuggled gun parts with them in the VW. "Do you think anyone heard?" he asked León.

"Don't turn into a creep," Victoria said.

León reassured him with the fatherly laugh of a veteran.

That night Victoria and Bunny slept on the floor of their VW bus as they had most nights since they bought it in Veracruz. Tonight it was parked alongside one of the barnyard sheds where León's men were sheltered.

From her sleeping bag she whispered, "It was only you that bitched me about the shooting. They didn't care. They don't think like us."

"They're the real thing," he admitted. He did not suppose he was the real thing but he had done what was required of him. For something he believed in. He had seen it through without asking too many anxious questions to mark him as an amateur of the revolutionary movement, and now that he had finished his task he was ready to be proud of himself. "You've been great," he said. "We've lucked through this far. Tomorrow we'll be out of here. I want to find a beach and lie and count my toes."

She made a sound of disagreement.

"Then we'll count your toes," he said with that upsurge of elation that a man rightly feels when he has slipped past danger without being struck. "I've been too strung out to count any of your parts to see what's missing." He put a tentatively exploring hand on her arm near her breast.

She was in no mood to be fondled by him. She was kindled to a passion that would be degraded by caresses. "I mean, I don't want to leave here yet."

She was in no mood to slip back into the minor excitement of sex with him, but suddenly she was astride him almost before he identified the sound of the zipper on her sleeping bag. Straddling his chest and pinning his arms within the folds of his own bag, she caught his head in her fine, quick fingers and shook it with her fiercer love.

"Don't you see?" she begged. "Now I know what I could be good for. I want to stay with them."

She had listened to him faithfully before this day to learn what she was good for. He had been her instructor in college, and she had believed enough to follow him beyond that. She was a girl with a swift and irrevocable capacity for belief. Now, in Mexico, she believed that their coming to this farm with the gun parts was the least they could do for a just and worldwide revolutionary design. He had prepared her to believe this. Following him she had learned to believe in the torture scars of escaped Chilean and Paraguayan political prisoners on display in the apartments of sympathizers in Boston, Rio and Havana. In Cuba, where she and Bunny had spent six weeks before Christmas, she had believed in the mass meetings—the smell of the crowd's arousal softening her vigorous young body like wax getting ready to burn—and the eerie, hot sleeplessness of fertility in the tropic nights they had spent outside Havana with the cane-field workers.

The months of travel with him had changed her. She had been a selfish petty college girl when they became lovers. Now she felt prepared for a destiny in which personality and self would

not matter at all, a brutal destiny. He had excited her imagination more than he had ever stirred her senses in their sex routines, and by now sometimes she thought her body hardly mattered any more than her personality. But no intoxication of faith
in what he called "the Movement" had ever matched what she
had felt in the jungle twilight with the sound and shock of the
gun startling her into a glimpse of what she might be as she fired
into the rocks. Then the crescendo of shattering echoes had
faded into the green mountain slopes, leaving her forlorn again.
Again uncertain of who she was.

"Can't we stay with them?" she pleaded.

2

Ten days later they wheeled their old VW through the entrance gateway of one of the largest, gaudiest, newest of the luxury resorts on the whole west coast of Mexico. El Dorado.

Bob Pardon was one of those who watched their arrival. Bob
was a man who belonged there, as they so obviously didn't. A
man near sixty with bandy legs left him from a childhood bout
with polio, a hard-working man—who liked to do his work amid
sensory delights.

So when the girl drove into his life with her bearded consort,
Bob was set up with his paper work spread around him on an
awning-shaded balcony three stories above the landscaped gar-
dens of El Dorado. The awning above him was ivory and green
and it did lovely things to the light of the late-winter afternoon
slanting in from the Pacific. His balcony overlooked the main
parking lot. With more amusement than shock, he watched the
VW bus with its sun-crazed and now almost colorless paint come
timidly among the palms below the gate and maneuver for parking space among the Cadillacs, Continentals, Mercedes and rental
cars of the paying guests. The VW settled to a stop between a
chartreuse Cadillac and a flame-colored Porsche.

Bob saw the driver was a young man with a beard so fluffy,
soft and full it made him think of the stuffing of a nursery toy or
the seeded head of a dandelion. He had no impression of the girl

riding beside this preposterous beard until she stepped down onto the asphalt of the lot.

He saw her then as being dressed for defiance. She wore a scuffy jacket and raveling shorts. There was a hostile stiffness in the way she stood scanning the ostentatious luxury of El Dorado's buildings.

She made a half pivot on her bare feet, her long shadow seeming not to move at all, as her eyes swept restlessly over the balcony from which he watched. He could not really make out her face at this distance and from this height, but he sensed the derision with which she took him in along with the pleasure boats and sunbathers and forty million dollars of sparkling new real estate.

Then she walked around in front of the VW to join hands with the bearded young fellow, who had come down from the driver's seat. With their linked hands swinging they ambled out of Bob's sight, presumably heading for the lobby and main desk on the ground floor beneath him.

Bob would tell himself later that if Charlotte Keefe had been with him to witness this arrival, her canny Irish eye would have read the storm warnings in the appearance of these young Americans the way an experienced sailor reads the flags over a Coast Guard station. He was the brake on Hoyt's exuberant notions of financial glory, but Charlotte was quick. Her years as Hoyt's mistress—or partner; she was anything but a kept woman—had taught her to size up situations with the speed of a dealer in a big-time casino.

"We're a good team," quick Charlotte said to him. Truly they were, but this afternoon she had skipped out on him—God knows where—and left him with unfinished business, decisions he needed her help in making.

The guest list—to which Charlotte had added so many notes, asterisks in red ink, check marks in mauve—absorbed him again, but he saw that he would have to wait for her comment in deciphering the amendments she had made.

Einar Carsten
Céci Chaumont
Countess Vivien Conti

Diedrich and Elizabeth Dahl
R. B. Hals and niece Gudrun Hals
Jill Hatch
Jean-Louis and Candy Heaulmière

By rumor and gossip, as well as from personal contact, he knew a substantial fraction of these people. Even Charlotte did not know all of them. But in any case he read a different message than she from these nearly four hundred names of the glamorous, the super-glamorous and the sub-glamorous who were being invited to the belated grand opening of El Dorado.

Inescapably he had to see it as among a number of business documents he kept under review. This resort, in which so much of Cooley Hoyt's money and credit was tied up, had been open for business more than a year. The results were, to put the matter discreetly, "disappointing." To put it in Cooley's own terms: "I'm bleeding at every pore."

But the spectacle of his own losses—of blood or anything else— was a signal for Cooley to abandon all caution, and in an upswing of hope he declared the resort was going to be saved by new infusions of money. "We need a firestorm of publicity. We got to make El Dorado a household word."

"I thought it was already a battered cliché," Bob had said. But his grumbling had never slowed Cooley in the panic of inspiration.

"Yeah, sure," he said enthusiastically. "It clicks in people's ears. What I have in mind is a second grand opening. Get Charlotte's friends up here and bring in the media to watch them change their string bikinis. We were underfinanced. I'm willing to raise another million and blow it all on the party. A firestorm of publicity!"

"I neglected it before," Charlotte said. "I shan't this time if we must make a go of it. Though my friends have a little more to show than their bikinis, love."

In any event, her friends were apt to be more useful for publicity than Cooley's. He swore he would invite the Shah of Iran to set the pace and tone of his festival. But some of Charlotte's friends and admirers—nearly as glamorous—could be counted on to actually show up, if things were managed right. The guest list of celebrities was mainly her contribution.

Rico López
Semura Okeido
Marichen Brenner
Elizabeth Gunn-Tewksbury
Hink Vanderheufel
Maette Mornay (one red asterisk; three mauve check marks)
Like some splendid, illiterate novelist, Charlotte knew all their
stories. While she had been working here with him before lunch,
she had diverted him with gossip about every third or fourth
name.

"Maette Mornay? Bob, you may not take my meaning but the
Suwes travel with her this season. They'll not come to our shindig without her. Not even if Cooley had really got the Shah and
Farah to say they would be here. Did you know Cooley *tried* to
call? Got through to a man in the Iranian Secret Service who
says security's too great a problem. Yes, she travels with Inge
and Helmut everywhere."

"Travels?"

"One must draw what interpretations he wishes. It's not me
own word for what they do, them three. I have it from Jovan
Kovacs that young Mlle. Mornay travels where they do."

"She travels both of them?"

"Ah, I couldn't say as to that. Nor if it's worth it to them, since
I've never laid eyes on the piece. All the same, we have to house
them accordingly while they're our guests. They require a king-
size bed in their suite."

For an old man, Bob thought, for a man who needs to drive
himself hard for his soul's sake, but likes the pleasures of the eye
and the spices of civilization, dialogue like his with Charlotte
was among the things that justified his existence and made it tolerable to work as hard as he did for an offshore pirate like Hoyt.

Urbane, wicked, shrewd, yet somehow innocent because she
stopped short of judgments on those she probed and exposed—
within the next two hours Bob would feel keenly again how
much more at home he was with women like Charlotte,
Charlotte's age, than with the intolerant morality of the young.

As he was savoring her meditations on the Mornay girl,

breathing the air turgid with the smell of cultivated herbage and tranquil ocean, the manager's secretary broke his contentment.

"Señor Pardon?"

The man was standing at the back of the balcony with a telephone in his hand. He beckoned with a discreet jerk of his head. The call was from the clerk at the desk.

"Why are you bothering me with this?" Bob asked. "Can't Greer or the assistant manager handle this sort of thing?"

The clerk was quick and profuse in his apologies. Greer, the manager, could not be located. It was thought he had left the grounds with Señorita Keefe and Señor Fentress, the decorator. The assistant manager had, in fact, been the one to suggest that, in a matter of such delicacy, it would be appropriate to refer this to someone of Señor Pardon's authority.

"There is a young lady, sir. With her companion. They don't wish to pay for their accommodations."

Irritably Bob said, "You mean they're trying to skip their . . ."

He stopped. The gale warnings he had neglected before seemed to be flapping their semaphore message at the backs of his eyeballs.

When I saw them get out of that damned two-hundred-dollar Volkswagen I should have known, he thought. When I saw that girl stiffen her neck and look at this place like it was a *barrio* full of unemployed sexist, racist, agist, Wasp lepers . . .

"They wish to stay without payment," the clerk said. "The young lady declares she has a document that would entitle her. I have asked to examine it, but she will not show me and wished to discuss only with someone of authority."

"Yes," Bob said, feeling every year of his age and still not feeling ready for the encounter about to take place.

"She declares herself to be the daughter of Señor Cooley Hoyt."

"Yes," Bob said. "Send her up."

3

For him there was always a choice of whether to reveal at once to people he met that he was crippled. As the secretaries showed the girl through the manager's office and onto his balcony he remained seated behind the table where the promotional material was spread with the guest lists.

"I'm Victoria," she said. She folded her hands into her armpits in case he had been tempted to greet her with a handshake.

"Welcome to El Dorado, Miss Hoyt."

"Victoria," she repeated.

He grinned very slightly at this inverted formality of hers. Like her shabby clothes, it was evidently part of a discipline she had elected and which she meant to enforce on all comers. She did not respond to his grin.

"My friend and I were kind of looking for a beach where we could lie and count our toes," she said.

"That's permitted on the beach here."

"Well, we thought we might stay over. Couple of days."

"I told you you're welcome, Victoria. Stay as long as you want. We have—I'm sorry to say—quite a number of empty rooms. Suites. Or cottages."

"Well. It looks like . . . It's kind of funny to find a place this fancy out in the middle of nowhere."

"You haven't seen anything yet. You haven't had time for a look at the grounds, the boathouses. The yacht anchorage. We even have a zoo." He had been about to call it a children's zoo and mention the aardvark and the tortoises, but he said, "A campy little zoo and a swinging discotheque. Shops . . ."

"It looks all right," she conceded. "But there's a problem."

The problem was that she wanted to be coaxed, wheedled on her own terms, he thought.

Certainly her problem was not in proving to him she was Cooley Hoyt's child. She had her father's eyes, dark blue, looking black when she narrowed her lids. In the way she rested her big-shouldered frame on widespread bare feet she communicated some air of the roistering swaggerer, the small-town bully, he was used to in her father. In the girl it was more touching and more attractive than in the forty-seven-year-old man.

"My friend and I don't seem to have any money," Victoria said. "Not like seventy-five-dollars-a-night money. Is that honestly the cheapest room in the place? That's why they sent me up from the desk to see the manager. I mean, my father actually invited me to come to his opening party or whatever it is and meet the celebrities."

"That's not for several weeks yet. But I'm sure your father would be unhappy if you didn't stay. Now that you've come all the way down here."

"Provided I can prove I'm his daughter? You want to see my invitation?"

Bob shook his head.

"You might not even know he had a daughter," she suggested. Her fingers played with the flap of her jacket pocket above her left breast. He felt she wanted encouragement to show the letter she had mentioned.

"Daughter, Victoria Evelyn," he said. "I've signed a lot of checks to you, though we have not, I think, had the pleasure of acknowledgment, except for your signature on the back of them."

"Oh. You're *that* Robert Partner," she said, with her own grin now answering his. "I thought you were just the manager here. I'm not much of a letter writer."

"Like your father."

"I suppose when someone keeps you supplied with money you ought to write once in a while and say thank you or at least 'I got it,' huh?"

Bob was not going to be drawn into comment on the etiquette of corresponding with a father who had deserted you. As far as Bob knew, Cooley hadn't seen this girl standing here now since she was five, but even in the worst times, when there were screaming creditors on all sides demanding the last cash in the Hoyt International account, a check for a thousand dollars had gone each month to this girl who had now showed up here in clothes that might have cost in the neighborhood of two dollars at the Salvation Army.

"Acknowledging receipt never occurred to me," Bob said. "But since it's only been ten days since we sent a check to your Cambridge address, your father and I thought . . ."

"Yeah," she said. "I guess he thinks I'm still in college this year. And that's another reason I suppose we shouldn't turn up and disillusion him. We only wanted a couple of days to lie around and count our toes. Look, the checks always catch up to me. I told you we weren't entirely *out* of money. I guess we could come up with a hundred fifty for a couple of nights."

"I won't take your money. I told you we had rooms. If you've changed your mind and are determined you have to pay, you can call your father in Cuernavaca and dicker with him. He'd like to hear from you. I know you can reach him. I talked to him this morning."

"No!"

He would find that she had a habit of enigmatic exclamations. She pumped a hell of a lot of breath into a single syllable, as if emphasis alone was her main resource of communication.

"See, it's true he invited me." She fished a folded letter from the jacket pocket now. "I wasn't about to show this to the dude down at the desk." Quickly she scanned the letter again and decided against showing it to Bob as well. "What my father actually suggested was for me to bring a *girl* friend along and . . ."

"I saw you drive in," Bob said with all the gentleness and patience he could muster. "Did you think I didn't realize you were traveling with a man? And doesn't it occur to you that if I can sign your father's checks for him I might be in a position to decide whether you kids can have a bed for a while? If you don't want him to know you've been here, I can promise he won't find out. Can't you trust me for that?"

She wasn't going to trust anything he said. And in that, also, he recognized her as Cooley Hoyt's child. Hoyts were sign readers. Cooley paid attention to words. Occasionally he could make sense out of a profit-and-loss statement, though mostly he relied on Bob or his accountants for translation. But when he made up his mind to go for broke he watched the mouths from which promises came, the movement of the neck, the steadfastness of an eye meeting his own in a showdown of insincerity.

And here was his daughter—unpersuadable until Bob stood up and she saw he was a cripple.

"Let's go find your friend and see if he finds the place amusing," he said.

She wasn't listening, and she wasn't going to let her friend make the decision for her. She saw Bob's bandy legs and aban-

doned her resistance. He could sense her yielding as he hobbled
off ahead of her and he thought it a bad sign. It was as if she
recognized his visible deformity as the reflection of something
twisted in herself which she must always give in to.

                                4

He would have wanted her to be amused by the red-and-pink-
striped jeep in which he drove them around the El Dorado compound. It was a frivolous vehicle, the color of a lollipop. White
tassels jiggled from its sunshade. But, if anything, she was scornful of its capricious decoration. She rode in it reluctantly, stiff as
a matron inspecting the wards of an insane asylum.

In his good nature he wanted to provide a haven where an
outcast princess could gambol thoughtlessly with her prince. Ah
yes—that was Bob's friendly impulse, but Bunny Stewart was
hard to cast as a prince. He might be one or two degrees less
stiff-necked than Victoria. But he introduced himself as an "academic renegade" and in their introductory small talk chuckled
smug ironies about having been fired from Victoria's college.
"They charged *me* with radicalizing the girls. Ha! They don't
seem to realize even girls can have minds of their own. Right,
Victoria?"

"Right!" she echoed grimly—squinting disdainfully as the jeep
ambled up and down cobblestone lanes lush with flowers, past
literally dozens of small courts, arcades and flowered culs-de-sac
from which opened the doors of rooms, suites and cottages as
capriciously adorned as the jeep.

Bob parked to take them out on the breakwater whose great
boulders hooked around the yacht basin. The afternoon was
vivid with the color and movement of water sports. A dozen
catamarans with red, white and green sails skimmed the bronze
and blue roll of waters in the bay. Paddleboats nipped in and
out from the beach dotted with sunbathers.

He had seen all of this many times but still his eye was
soothed and enchanted by it. Surely some part of it should have
softened the girl's ironclad puritanism. But with curling lip she

said, "It's so . . . so . . . so . . ." Her tone expressed the distaste
for which she could not find a word.

"We call it Disneyland South," Bob said, willing to mock if
that would put him on her wavelength.

"Such a waste," she said.

Bunny said, "It *is* pretty shocking to come out of the mountains where there's such intense poverty among the Indians. And
suddenly confront this."

"Indian villages where they don't have anything. Maybe one
red, white and blue Pepsi-Cola cooler in the middle of the bamboo shanties," Victoria said, so passionately Bob felt she was
blaming all social injustice on him personally.

"We look forward to the day when all this will belong to the
workers and peasants," he said. She gave no sign she recognized
this as a joke. Bunny, at least, grinned and winked.

He said, "Got to take your blessings where you find them. Actually, when the college fired me—and Victoria decided to come
along—they did us a real favor. We've seen a whole world down
here."

"Poverty . . . ?" Bob prompted, keeping his irony at a low
pitch.

Bunny was easing up. He said, "Not just that. We've nibbled
the high life. Had some time at Can Cun and Acapulco. Counted
toes on the beaches there. I must say we've never yet come
across a place quite as . . . *showy* as this. Victoria, your old man
is ahead of his time."

"El Dor*ado!*" she said, pronouncing the syllables like a nonsense phrase concocted merely for derision. "What a yuck
name."

"Well," Bob said. "Well, now. Your father's got a little more
sophistication than that may sound like. He's a pretty clever
business head. You know, Mencken once pointed out that no one
ever went broke underestimating the intelligence of the American people. With forty million dollars invested here, we need a
yucky name to lure the noncollegiate crowd, you might say."

He thought the girl flinched ever so lightly at the mention of
forty million dollars. Just enough to hint that under her tough,
consistent pose and New Left slogans she was still Hoyt's daugh-

ter. The mention of big money touched a particular nerve in Hoyts. The smell of smoke to purebred firehorses.

"That's a pretty reckless investment in times like these," Bunny Stewart said.

"Oh, it's reckless."

"For a place as isolated from the tourist mainstream as you are."

Now it was Bob's turn to flinch. The young man was right—and that was why they were being driven to desperate measures to attract attention. "Ah, we're aiming to correct that isolation. Listen! Hear the bulldozers over the ridge? They're rushing to extend our local airstrip. Once that's done, we'll jet them in from all over the world. The strip's going to be finished for our—well, our *official* grand opening. You young folks ought to hang around—or come back—for that."

"I've heard about it," Victoria said. "Dripping with glamour. Flesh and flimflam."

"Literally dripping," Bob said, holding on gamely against all her belittling, stifling the impulse to shake her and tell her to straighten her young head up to take the world as it offered itself. "The Shah of Iran will not be coming, though he was asked. Oh yes, we asked him. We're not bashful, since we're inclined to protect our initial investment. But the President of the Republic will be here. Fly-past of jets. All that. Tourism is a serious business for Mexico. Stick around for the gala and you'll see Ortiz Rosio anchor his yacht right there."

"The *dictator?*" Victoria asked, as if her worst suspicions had been confirmed.

"He's not," Bunny said. Showing the precision of the academic soul. "He's not actually a . . ."

"Not even the dictator before the present one," Bob said. "Though he's been accused of bad things. As rich men are when they grab their money out of a poor country and run to Europe with it."

"*His* money?" Victoria grinned. "Anyway there's a lot of political prisoners in his country. He's the one they call the Butcher. Didn't I read that?"

"You'd like him," Bob teased.

"I would *not*."

"You'd feel a daughterly affection for him," Bob went on gravely. "In the flesh he's a little banty rooster of a man with a passion for beating *norteamericanos* at golf. People aren't always like the impressions you get from the papers."

He had wanted to tease her about dictators, butchers, swindlers and the uncomfortable bigotry of scorning what you're unwilling to learn about. But you didn't tease this girl. You didn't get away with it. She might have been technically wrong in calling Rosio a dictator. Being caught in the wrong only made her more fierce and, a few minutes later when their talk had swung back to her father and his showplace here, she burst out to declare: "He's a fascist, too!"

Bob wanted to slap her for that. Spank her. Cuddle her. Croon to her. Because he wasn't fooled. He saw her slitted eyes as those of a shamed and yearning child, contrarily pleading to be shown that what she is afraid of is all a mistake, a bad dream from which she can waken.

So again he kept patience with the thought that a few days of water sports and idleness here would make it possible to talk to her like a human. With that in mind he took the trouble of leading them to one of his favorite retreats on the premises.

It had been Charlotte's idea to make a sort of aerie in the rocks that went up to the massive retaining wall against the hillside. There was a cozy little poolside bar up there in the two-story building that arabesqued above the terrace. From the café tables one could look down at all the pools of El Dorado—thirty-seven of them, including the main one, a hundred yards long and shaped like the fallen petal of an immense flower.

Beyond these and beyond the silhouette of buildings and palms the ocean spread in a kind of royal calm. It would take an unbelievable puritanism not to be seduced by this natural and man-made panorama of delights.

The daiquiris served to them by a lithe Indian boy in snow-white uniform were just as good as what met the eye.

"Okay," Bunny Stewart said, making a show of liquefying all his bones in total surrender. "I have tasted the lotus and it works. I have tasted the truth serum and am ready to testify. I believe I'd like another. Victoria?"

"Stick to it," Bob said. "Just sign your chits. I'll arrange at the desk for them to check you into a room. And now if you'll excuse me. I have work to finish. But I'll see you again. Maybe this evening at the discotheque. I'm a bug for dancing. . . ."

With that, he hauled himself onto his crippled legs and was about to leave them. But as he moved to the stairs at the edge of the terrace he saw a truck pull into the central courtyard below in the circle of boutiques and luggage shops. There was a bulging canvas tarpaulin over its load, hiding its shape, but when he saw Charlotte Keefe and Page Fentress step down from the driver's cab, at least he remembered why Charlotte had deserted him for the afternoon.

Fentress, the decorator Charlotte had "stolen" from a project of the Aga Khan's in Corsica, had discovered an antique revolutionary monument in one of the small towns up the coast. It was Fentress's whim that it would make a stunning contrast to the chrome-and-glass façades of the shops. But before he trucked it in he had wanted Charlotte's approval. It was astonishing how many things here had grown to their present opulence by way of Charlotte's approval.

Seeing her, Bob made a serious tactical mistake. "Someone here I want you to meet," he called back to Victoria and Bunny.

But hard-eyed Victoria had seen the arrivals, too. "Is that her?" she asked.

"Charlotte Keefe," he said. "A friend of your father's." That seemed an inoffensive way of putting the matter. After all, the girl had spoken of her bearded lover as her "friend." Surely the word was current—no more, but no less frank than most of the vocabulary of Victoria's generation.

"I know about her," Victoria said. To Bunny she explained, "I met her once." She had no explanations at all left for Bob Pardon. "Come on, Bunny. Let's hit the road. I didn't think she'd be here."

"Oh *no!*" Bob protested. Bunny gave a shrug of bewilderment. Victoria acted as if she hadn't heard.

Still, her abrupt decision to run had not been intended to strike at him. Probably no one who got in the path of her anger was ever precisely the target she intended. Maybe she was only afraid that Charlotte would tell her father she had been shacked up here with Bunny.

But mournfully she left one message with Bob. "Look, when his great party is all over and done with, you tell my dad I saw what he built here." If that could be construed as a wishful expression of tender feeling, she quickly took it back. "Tell him this kind of thing isn't for me. If he ever wants to see me, it won't be in a brothel like this. Just let him know that someday."

Ah, she had intended that harsh, theatrical pronouncement to stand as her definitive repudiation of El Dorado. But, like her father, Victoria was a victim of her swiftly changing impulses. Like him, she seemed to leave loose threads dangling as she darted hither and yon.

She had refused to show Bob her letter of invitation when they had met on the balcony. But somehow she had failed to get it back in the jacket pocket from which she had taken it. He found it lying unobtrusively among his notes.

He read it after dinner that night. He had no compunction about reading it because it was his habit—almost his life's work, he thought ruefully—to follow after one Hoyt or another and tie up the loose ends they couldn't help leaving.

This letter was in Cooley's familiar, boisterous scrawl:

> Dear Vicky,
>
> Well, it's been another five years since I last saw you, and that surely was a ridiculous misunderstanding, so there is no need to remember it.
>
> I'm writing because of an impulse. Some of the best things, along with not so good things, have come to me in life by acting on impulse. I have always thought that someday you and I would get together and have a chance to get acquainted.
>
> So I thought that a good chance might be this spring, in March, to be exact. You may or may not have heard that for the last five years I have been building a superfantastic and fabulous hotel at Mandanas Bay on the Western Coast of Mexico. It is nearly finished now, and everyone who has seen it seems to agree it is "fairyland." You may not re-

member when you were very young and we lived in a place
called Skelton Duchy, which was the same sort of fabulous
place, though I believe we have outdone it here.

It was remembering you in that place where you seemed
to be in your element that gave me the impulse to ask if you
would come to El Dorado (as we call it) when we have our
gala grand opening in March. Extensive publicity before
then, and all the jet-set "beautiful people" we can round up
to be guests for ten glamorous days, and that is plenty. It
will be the news event of the world resort season and here-
after a synonym for glamour.

Baby, it would be such a thrill for me if you could show
up for it and we could patch things up at last. You could
bring a friend from college. (Or three or four!) I promise
they'll all be dazzled and have plenty to talk about afterward. There are some things I do up right and this is one of
them.

Well, let me know as soon as you can. Will you be having
spring vacation about then? It doesn't matter, does it? It
would do you good to get a little time off from the grind of
studying and see what life is like South of the Border.

Your,
Dad

P.S. Let me know if you need money or anything arranged.

II

1

Strong, voluptuous, immaculately tanned and supine, the body of Charlotte Keefe would never betray the irritations that might be crackling in her mind. She lay on the cushions of a beach chair beside the magnificent main pool at El Dorado with an elbow in the air, her forearm dangling to the white phone into which she was speaking. Her immense sunglasses kept Bob Pardon from seeing whether or not her eyes had narrowed at what she heard.

Then with the amusement that kept him sane in his employment he heard her say—like any wife getting bad financial news from her man—"What happened to the million and three you said was coming from the Indonesian government?"

Here we go again, he thought. The roller coaster of Hoyt International on another of its thrilling plunges. . . .

He listened hard to hear if Cooley Hoyt had *any* answer to a question like that. He heard no words—only a faint, rhythmic sibilance that must be Cooley's heavy breathing.

Charlotte put the phone back in its cradle and beckoned to one of the pool attendants to take it away.

For a couple of minutes she did a little heavy breathing of her own, then sat up and said to Bob, "We better get down to Cuernavaca. Can we fly down this afternoon? The man's in a snit. Bad off. He'll need some straightening up."

"What's he done?"

"It's not what he's done. Well . . . for one thing he apparently had a grand donnybrook with John Halvorsen in Mexico City and broke the option, so there's no chance of money from there. The worst of it's his mental state. You know what he said? He wants to call our party off. *Now!* Ah, we must get to him fast."

"Yes," Bob agreed. Alas, Cooley Hoyt's mood was *not* the worst current factor in the financial situation. Alas, there were no discernible rails under the wheels of the roller-coaster car.

"He was depressed that the Toronto Exchange is going to drop its listing of his IMTF. Something about divesting—or not divesting—himself of everything left over from ADC."

"Yes," Bob said. The miracle was that the Toronto Exchange had been gullible or tolerant this long.

Charlotte peeled off her sunglasses. Her beautiful, naked eyes were neither angry nor alarmed and, indeed, there was just the faintest trace of an adventurer's smile on her lips. "Can you just tell me in one word if we're broke or not? He'll never level with me. Always having a game with me."

"No one knows," Bob said.

"Oh, now," she protested. "You're all so clever with the paper work. Surely . . ."

"No one knows," he repeated. "No one at all."

"But that's crazy," she said. With a forefinger she traced the curve of her golden shoulder—as if verifying the reality of a beauty so much more reasonable than the monetary antics that supported it.

"Absolutely crazy," he said with full solemnity.

How could you look at Charlotte in her element and still believe there was sanity in using up your cunning to balance cash flow with the flight of time?

2

While he had been on the phone with Charlotte, Cooley Hoyt was also beside a swimming pool. This one was small and homely and it had a permanently musty smell, like rotting wood. Overhead the old trees of the courtyard were alive with small birds whose names he would never know and the tall, stuccoed walls enclosing the court were flagged with flowers whose colors he merely noticed as bright.

He liked this rented villa in Cuernavaca—as much as he had liked most of the rented châteaux, apartments, villas and summer houses from which he had conducted his business around the world in the fifteen years past. It was comfortable enough for him. Handy. Showy enough, at least, to impress his visitors that he was still traveling first-class.

And it was safe. The iron gate and the high wall kept people from getting at him.

As usual—as always—he had just given Charlotte a fraction of his troubles. For the last three days an American had been prowling the street outside trying to serve a subpoena on him. He already had a subpoena commanding him to appear before the First District Court of New York. His lawyers had advised him over and over again there was no way short of kidnapping that any U.S. marshals could force him back into the United States. Nevertheless, he was in contempt of court for refusing to comply and someday—*someday* when the political climate was right again—he meant to go home where he belonged and square everything up.

If things in general had been going well, the appearance of this new process server would not have worked on his nerves as it had. But he feared bad luck because he thought it brought bad luck. To know someone was stalking him, lurking outside the wall, got to the worst of his multitudinous superstitions.

And things were very bad. By now he needed a yearly cash flow of one point five million to service his debt structure. ADC was in a bail-out situation and, while there was enough Chinese paper in the IMTF to bat it around another year to eighteen months from one jurisdiction to another, the Canadian ruling would make the untracking of subsidiaries much easier for the prosecutor in New York. If the British got off their ass for a hard look at prior dividending of the ADC . . .

"Riordan!" he called. His muscle-bound bodyguard was snoozing on the far side of the pool in an untidy circle of *Oui* and *Penthouse* magazines. Damn fool seemed to have an erection, or the good beginning of one. And in a mixture of envy, contempt and kindness, Cooley let him go on sleeping, though he had just taken the notion of sending him out into the street to find the American and put a few bumps on him.

He had to make a move! For the last three days it had been dawning on him that if he couldn't come up with a good one he was going to lose El Dorado along with everything else that was crumbling away into wastepaper in his rotting corporations. And as the gloom got deeper, his superstitions convinced him if he lost the resort he would lose Charlotte in the same wipe-out.

Yet in some topsy-turvy way it was for the sake of her investments of love and gaiety that he had quarreled with John Halvorsen and made the prospects even worse. Halvorsen—who called himself "the Sun King," no less, because he was board chairman of a great string of resort hotels girdling the world— had been interested in El Dorado from the time the first ground was broken for building. Earlier his corporation had made two offers of outright purchase. The option to buy had helped Cooley keep his credit so far.

But . . . the son of a bitch was still a beach boy at heart. No class at all. If he got control of the place he'd make it into an expensive Howard Johnson's. Which is just about what Cooley had told him at their disastrous meeting in Mexico City. So the fucker canceled his option and left saying he would pick up the pieces when Cooley had to drop them.

Six years ago everyone had agreed that the new resort, unnamed then, was a genius conception, the best Cooley ever had. The land was a bargain. The site was unbelievably, hauntingly beautiful. The point in choosing so remote a site had been, he and Bob Pardon told each other then, obvious to anyone who knew how to read maps. The tide of American tourists was bulging down from Mazatlán and Puerto Vallarta. And the movement out from the squeezed playgrounds of Europe had already inflated Acapulco out of range of the venture capital Hoyt International had always been obliged to scrape precariously together for any enterprise.

But . . . four years ago Cooley's accountants had told him he ought to unload. They advised selling the land he had picked up so cheap and the uncompleted buildings. He could have taken a fine profit then, because other investors were catching on to what he had dared begin. Many negotiations had been started on the accountants' advice. The Mexican government seemed on the verge of subsidizing a consortium of nationals who liked the bay and the offshore islands and the Babylonian gaudiness of the architecture Cooley and Charlotte had dreamed up between them. "If we can't do it bigger and better than anyone else, what's the point?" they said. And though Bob Pardon had wanted to sell out then, Charlotte wanted to hold on.

Two years ago Bob had announced flatly to Cooley that he would be money ahead if he simply abandoned El Dorado. "Walk out. Throw the key in the ocean. Let the lizards have it back again." There had been architectural changes by then. Uneconomical buildings added. Extravagances recommended by Charlotte's architects and her friend Page Fentress, who wanted the new resort to outshine the Aga Khan's Costa Smeralda and everything else rumored to be abuilding in the New World or the Mediterranean littoral.

But Bob was cool and Charlotte was passionate. She listened to part of the financial threats. And said, "We've almost finished it now. Let's open it, at least, and see what we have got." Yet, from the time they opened it a year ago it was obvious they had made one awful mistake. They had failed to see that a bigger, better airstrip was a necessity. They simply had to bring in the kind of guests who intended to fly from wherever they were happy to where they might be happier. So another seven hundred thousand dollars was being pushed into the gorges by bulldozers enlarging the airstrip. The government promised a tax credit to cover a lot of this expense. So far there was no final settlement on that.

Just now on the phone he had weakened enough to tell Charlotte they might have to call off the grand plans for their reopening festivities. The truth—and he faced it a little more often with himself than in talking to any other living soul—was that there was nothing to gain in calling it off, either. Neither small economies nor huge economies would help.

Why had he got into this quicksand? Probably to show Charlotte he could still pull rabbits out of the hat and make the drab world sparkle for her. To show . . . well, he still hoped his daughter might appear for the festivities, though she had not answered his letter.

Now, sitting in a black depression, scraping the bottom of the barrel for some clever maneuver, it came to him that he might as well take the chance of phoning his daughter in Massachusetts. He needed a pickup. If she said she was coming . . . if she was friendly enough to say she *wanted* to come . . . well, then, hell, he would find a way to tide the whole thing over. Other men drank when they were down. He thirsted for signs that his luck might change.

He reached down to pick up the phone from the mossy tiles at his feet.

He had just put his finger in the dial when Riordan hit him with a ferocious body block and knocked him out of his chair.

Riordan would say later that he hadn't been asleep at all. Just squinting. Just relaxing to save his strength.

At any rate, as a bodyguard should, he had seen the flat brief-case come sailing over the wall. He would say later, when Cooley complained of various scratches and scrapes and a sore shoulder from having been dumped on the courtyard tiles, that he had realized it must be a bomb.

So when the briefcase lay there unexploded and inert as a dead flounder on a beach, he yelled, "Don't touch it, boss," and again attempted to dump Cooley out of harm's way. Riordan's reflexes were good. It was just the rest of his nervous system that was slow.

What the briefcase actually contained, it turned out, was the subpoena that directed Cooley Hoyt to appear forthwith as a witness in the bribery trial of his old friend Ben Hogben, formerly governor of the state in which Cooley had first incorporated his ADC investment company before taking it overseas. Good old wheezing, bottom-pinching Ben Hogben caught in the flood of prosecution after the dam broke at Watergate.

The discovery of the briefcase's actual contents was made later. At first, even though Cooley doubted it was an attempt to assassinate him in any literal or physical way, he had no intention of touching it. In a minute he had seen the two prongs of a ladder poking above the stuccoed wall. And on the ladder was a man, plainly American, with his camera held in front of his face, at the ready.

It was the process server, despairing at last of everything except going home with a photo of Cooley Hoyt picking up the briefcase and thus, *pro forma*, accepting the subpoena served upon him by the Commonwealth.

Good God, what had the American legal system come to when it stooped to infantile tricks like this? It was shabby. It embarrassed him for the country he loved, though he was in exile.

Very loudly Cooley said, "Riordan, get out there and break that son of a bitch's neck."

Suddenly the camera, the head behind it and then the ladder itself disappeared with a swoop as Riordan ran bellowing toward the gate.

3

You lick a lot of sandy pisspots to put a business conglomerate together out of nothing. You get down under where they sweat on you, and you grovel and suck and yelp how much you like the screwing they give you. And you wait through mornings, weeks, months of anxiety lonelier than anything else on earth, knowing how many clever individuals, ruthless corporate giants and meat-grinding governments are sitting by with pruning knives sharpened for your balls.

Thinking . . . there is always a string hanging loose somewhere. If you are just sleepless and quick enough to grab it, the whole bag will unravel. The digits, the coin, the green stuff will fall on you like sweet rain.

Even in the blackness of his present depression Cooley Hoyt believed this. For one almighty reason. It had happened to him. More than once.

There were miracles.

They probably weren't worth what you had to put out to make them happen. When he was ninety he would still be too young to understand if they were or were not.

But once you were addicted to them—as once he had been addicted to alcohol—nothing else competed with your thirst for them. He had cut out the booze. Totally. Maybe the truth was he had given up alcohol in a direct exchange for the deeper intoxication of money. Maybe when he was ninety he would know if that was how it worked.

For the rest of that day he felt it come on him again, the bright warm tingling in the veins and at the base of the skull that brought the illusion that he was different from other men. Born with a secret and a trick that would always turn disasters right around.

Probably the delirious upswing of his confidence began when he heard his own loud voice commanding Riordan to demolish the process server. For he had a voice meant to command. A freak of nature. A gift he had been born with, to take the place of brains and even courage. The voice had courage, many times, when Cooley felt like a trapped mouse.

But even with that voice commanding him, Riordan didn't catch the process server. After all, he couldn't run down the hill toward the center of town barefoot and shirtless—as he had been at the moment of crisis. Some bodyguard!

He came back in a few minutes, sheepishly carrying the ladder abandoned by the intruder. "Sonbitch jumped in a car," he said. "What you want me to do with his ladder?"

"You can keep it," Cooley said. He rubbed his sprained shoulder. He was feeling better already. "Keep it. You can never tell when it will come in handy."

"There's another guy hanging out in the street. Another American, looks like. Want me to run him off, too?"

"You can't run people off the streets. It's a free country."

"I think he wants to see you."

"Did he say so?"

"That's what he said."

"Then he wants to see me," Cooley said. "Get back out there and find out who he is and what he wants."

After putting on his shoes and shirt, Riordan was up to that. He came back again after a hostile interrogation to report that the visitor *said* he was a retired U. S. Air Force officer, living up near Lake Chapala. "Looks harmless. An old guy. Big, though. Looks like an army guy. Trim. I ask him why he doesn't call he wants an appointment. He laughs and says that's a good question. He didn't give me much. Want me to get rid of him?"

Cooley—needing the lift he would get from hearing his own voice in persuasive conversation, believing in the loose string that would start the unraveling he had to have—said, "What the hell, show the old guy in."

If Colonel Harold ("they call me Bull") Timmerman had looked as harmless to Cooley as to Riordan, Cooley would have spent a lot less time with him. Which was not to say that Bull Timmerman came on breathing menace or hinting at intrigues. His china-blue eyes and his huge, well-manicured hands gave no signals at all. He had no questions, and he was in no hurry about anything—certainly not in a hurry to explain why he was here. He had no credentials except his word and his appearance. Evidently he was used to needing no more. He still looked like a man who had done well for twenty years in the Air Force and enjoyed the physical fitness that had become a habit. Very clean and clean-cut. His short hair was gray, with the faintest touch of pink to it.

"I think you and I may have met once in Bangkok," he said. "I was military attaché there with the Embassy before the Vietnam thing got sticky. If we didn't meet, I knew who you were. You were selling for some Japanese company then, weren't you?"

That much was correct. You felt the colonel had all his facts right and in good order and wasn't straining to push beyond them. By the time Cooley asked him to stay for a bit of lunch outside by the musty swimming pool, Colonel Timmerman had indicated that intelligence was really his military specialty. "No cloak-and-dagger stuff. With my appearance, I'm a little too easy to recognize, wouldn't you think? Chairborne for fifteen years after Korea. Can't say I regret any of it, or the friends I made in so many parts of the world. It's useful. Lets me be helpful to a lot of people, and I like to be that, when I can. I still drift around quite a bit. I've got friends all over. Just as you have. You've spread yourself around the world pretty thin, Cooley."

They were enjoying cigars in the calm, dense tranquillity of the courtyard, under the motionless big trees where even the birds were observing siesta, when the colonel indicated he was trying to help some young friends of his now. "Pilots," he said. "This one guy is maybe the greatest natural pilot I've ever known.

It's more than skill. Temperament. The guy would have been a Francis Drake in another time. A buccaneer. You'd like him."

Well, then, this likable young fellow and his friend had themselves a couple of World War II B-25s, which they flew around the Caribbean and Latin America generally. They'd been in a few scrapes. It wasn't exactly commercial aviation as that is generally understood. "I have the suspicion they've probably taken a few cargoes—and people—a few places that weren't ever reported on their flight plans. Well, what are they going to do?"

"Find the openings," Cooley agreed. He was beginning to see a pattern developing. The colonel was here on business.

"Find the openings. Right. I wouldn't swear to it that they haven't nipped into the U.S. of A. now and then. Come in under the radar. Little fields in Georgia. Texas. In and out. The southern border is like a sieve. You know drugs are going in on a human wave. Hundreds, thousands of young people—the operators call them *mules*—students, tourists, airline stewardesses, immigrants—bring the stuff in. They get pretty clever about it. Soak their clothes in a cocaine solution and then wet it down and wring it out in a bathtub in L.A. or Dallas. How about that?"

"But your friends?"

The colonel's unwrinkled forehead creased a little now. "Are in a bind right now. They seem to need money to make sense out of their operation. The way I hear it, they may not even need investment capital as much as they need a way of getting the money out—getting it nicely laundered. Sifting it into corporate bookkeeping, huh?"

"I guess that's done," Cooley said blithely. "I've never touched that kind of money."

"Of course not," the colonel said. "Why should you? You've got things lined up right, everything paying off for you, there's no reason to monkey with it. No, indeed. I was only explaining why my friends are unhappy now. They were doing nicely until they somehow ran afoul of Rosio."

"Ortiz Rosio?"

"You know him? Of course you would."

"He's invested in my enterprises. In years past," Cooley said. It wasn't quite like that, but this was as close to the truth as he chose to come. When he'd said he'd never laundered money through his corporate bookkeeping, he had omitted counting the money Rosio had secretly transferred from his country to a Swiss bank, a great deal of it going in the briefcases of Cooley's representatives in the South American territories.

"Yes. Rosio has done pretty well in the legitimate side of his investment. Pretty well. But, according to my friends, his is the big money in the big drug deals and he's frozen them out. They're nickel-diming around just when they're ready to go for the big time—and know how to do it."

"Things are tough all over," Cooley said.

"Oh, not for all of us. I'm content with what I've got. And you're riding high. I've been hearing about the big shindig you're planning over on the coast."

"Rosio will be there."

"Yes, I know."

"And your friends thought if they had a representative to go between them and Rosio . . . ?"

"I don't know what they thought. Or what they think," the colonel said genially. "I only mentioned that in passing. What I really came to see you about is this. I told you I had friends all over the world. Including some Arab friends. With money to invest. I know you hold land up and down the coast from El Dorado, and I'm just here to get some notion of whether I can put them in touch with your people. . . ."

There were no Arabs. Or—of course there *were* Arabs. Out there somewhere there were Arabs, not only dripping with wealth, but conceivably disposed to invest it in lovely shoreline properties. But Bull Timmerman was not really here to convince Cooley that he knew any of them well enough to be in a position to advise them what to do with their money. He didn't really try.

He had delivered what he came to deliver when he mentioned his underemployed flying friends with a talent for finding abandoned airfields in the southern United States. Confirmed the point of his mission when he said, "Yes, I know" Rosio would be at El Dorado soon.

The colonel was an errand boy, supplementing his retirement pay, to be sure. To be sure he was not a principal in any deal.

But he was canny, and he got the notion that Cooley meant him to have, that he had come with his feelers to the wrong man.

Cooley never had and never would get involved with drug smuggling or playing hide-and-go-seek with the money that came from it.

For one reason—he might think of others if he had to—Bob Pardon would blow the whistle on him if he tried, and it was just inconceivable that any money could flow through their accounts now without Bob's learning of it pretty quickly.

And yet when the colonel was gone, he was bucked up by the feeling that there were a few steps still left on the ladder *below* the bottom rung he seemed to have reached. Desperate men have been shoved back to honesty by reminders that outright crime is at least *conceivable* as a resort beyond the last resorts of the business world.

And he felt as if the back of his fingers had been lightly brushed by the string that could unravel his problems—while he had been taking a siesta beside his pool and dreaming that a hefty angel with china-blue eyes had told him stories.

4

So when Charlotte and Bob arrived by plane to cheer him up that evening, they found he didn't need it. He wanted to cheer them.

He was dressed like a grandee in a ruffled shirt and a fawn-colored jacket with gold embroidery to the elbows. His black beard jutted like the beak of an arrogant bird. His teeth gleamed in the candlelight of the dining table he had asked the servants to set up for a feast in the courtyard.

While Bob and Charlotte had cocktails and narrowed their eyes in bewilderment at what had come over him, he insisted on reading them "very funny" bits from the subpoena that had been so grotesquely hurled in at him.

"Of course I feel sorry for Ben Hogben," he said in his majestic, rolling voice, the voice of a prophet standing above the troubles of his tribe. "A man in our time can't do much of anything without breaking one law. Or another. Of one country. Or another. Of God. Or man. Outdated laws that have never been scrubbed from the books. I imagine Ben Hogben may have trespassed some *statutes* in his time. But *this*"—he waved the subpoena on high—"is just a grandstand play. My name's well known. Going to be better known when we hit the press with our grand opening. They drag it in—one way or another—and it gives them extra clout with the jury.

"I pray for Ben Hogben and I'm halfway tempted to go up there and give my testimony and . . . fight for him!"

"I wouldn't," Bob said, beckoning the serving girl for another cocktail. It occurred to him that if there was a god of dishonesty, he would lie to mortals in a voice about like Cooley Hoyt's.

The astonished Charlotte demanded, "Did the Indonesians come through with that money since I talked to you this morning?"

Cooley took her hand and kissed it. "I'm sorry for the way I sounded. Momentary depression."

"There's reason for it to be permanent," Bob said. "On the way down I made a list of things you've got to do. The one thing that makes sense is for you to get on the plane, touch all the bases from Hong Kong to Beirut and liquidate every damn thing that can be liquidated. I mean everything. So we can shore up El Dorado until we get a decent offer."

"Now, I don't know about that. And I'm not so sure we can't hold on to El Dorado. Charlotte's invested so much love in the place . . ."

"I must point that out to our creditors," Bob said.

"We'll do whatever we have to," Charlotte said. "I'd hate it, but . . . Now, Cooley, listen. We came down here determined to talk turkey. I'm willing to do what I can do. Give up anything. Start again. Whisht! What does it matter? But let's don't say things we can't make good on."

Now Cooley looked hurt. Didn't they trust him? Hadn't he pulled off impossible zigzags of financing before? Whatever it looked like right now on the books . . . hell, bookkeeping was never the whole story. There was . . . faith. Cooley Hoyt would keep the faith.

"Let's review," he said magisterially as the first course was served and he poured wine into their glasses. He shook a forefinger at the shadows dancing in the leaves above the candle flames. "Full utilization of what's available. With all the wonderful people coming to our party—to Charlotte's party"—he toasted her with his glass of Fresca—"and many very rich people among them . . ."

"Right," Bob said. "It's the perfect setting for Hoyt salesmanship. But what have we got to sell them? Dazzle them, sure. Then they look at the books."

Cooley was undaunted now. Patient. "I meditated this afternoon. Right here. I won't say I have a perfect solution, but . . . The key to it all is Ortiz Rosio."

Bob choked on a bit of crayfish. "He's the sharpest of them all. You're not going to sell him anything."

"I've done business with him before," Cooley said.

"What kind?"

"I have some projects to go into with him." Cooley was getting edgy. "All right, Bob. If I can get Ortiz interested in investing in the hotel, even—and holding still awhile—or in the condominiums we've got on the drawing board . . . Whatever. It will make it look better to the others."

"If he comes," Charlotte said dolefully.

"What?"

"I said, 'If he comes.' You know he's on his yacht in Florida right now. Jovan's in the party." Jovan Kovacs was Charlotte's oldest and best friend, from before the time of her connection with Cooley. "I talked to her after you called this morning. She'll be there, of course. But she says Ortiz keeps changing his mind. None of those in his party know what his plan is from one day to the next. Jovan thinks it's political. There's talk of another upset in the government, and he may go back home."

"Well. Shit," Cooley said.

"There's no use talking as if Rosio was the key to anything. Yes, he's news, but we're going to get all the publicity we want anyhow," Bob said.

"Shit. He's a criminal anyway. Goddamn fascist oppressor. Nobody hated more in all Latin America. Who needs him?" Cooley said, showing the first crack of the evening in his confidence.

They had settled on no substantial plan by bedtime. After his unreasonable disappointment at Charlotte's comment about Rosio, Cooley began to get morose. He was determined to talk as grandly and optimistically as before, but he showed his state of mind by yawning, by acting befuddled, as if he, and not the other two, was heartily drinking the good wine. By ten-thirty he had gone altogether silent and Charlotte said they must turn in.

As she was undressing in front of the dim light from the closet off the bedroom she asked, "I thought you didn't want to go into it in front of Bob, but is it really that crucial that Ortiz Rosio appear at El Dorado? It's true we've many other celebrities coming."

"What if it is?"

"Why, then, we must make sure he does. I'll fly to Miami and keep after him until we get there. I could trade places with Jovan. She can come to El Dorado to welcome the first guests."

"He hasn't asked you."

"I get what I want," she said simply. "He likes me. He'll have me on and be glad."

"I don't know."

"Stop *worrying*. There's nothing worth it."

To enforce her command, she turned, fully naked, and advanced on him, already sprawled in the bed. And it seemed then that the greatest of her many gifts was the talent for producing hard-ons. She was good with hard-ons because she valued them so much and knew so well what to do with them. She fondled them and fought them, praised and teased them, made them her own without robbery. She made them seem everlasting, even while she squeezed and rode them down to throbbing and glorified softness.

Afterward, while the charm lasted, it was impossible and unnecessary to be dishonest with her because of the great honesty bestowed from her body. The best kind, because, for a while at least, it shamed his thoughts into imitating it.

As he lay there in the utter tranquillity and in the zone of protection she gave him against all threats and enemies, he said quietly, "Bob's right about one thing. I've got to make a big trip before our grand opening. See how all my boys are doing here or there. There's still some in various places who believe in the organization. Who will come through for me. One way or another, I think."

And she, who had just re-created him with such consummate skill, said wonderfully, "Handle them the way you handle me!"

In the morning, dripping with optimism about his coming trip, Cooley said, "My father always told me that to make good you needed a big hard-on for the world."

"*What?* He said WHAT? What's that?" Bob Pardon said, pretending a *great* outrage and feeling outrage on a familiar scale. "Your play has got to be defensive. At every stop. It calls for pencil work. The closest calculation."

"Oh, sure," Cooley said. "That, too."

III

The freewheeling days were over. In peak times, when the Vietnam War was keeping things lively, Cooley flew to consult his far-flung representatives in his own jet. For this present trip he had to go by commercial airlines. The Moroccans had impounded his Lear a year ago when he sent Godell there to negotiate a closing of the African Development Corporation (ADC), to get out of Africa once and for all.

Cooley made the whole twelve-day swing without an accountant, considering it best to take only his bodyguard. Riordan provided a constant, slow drain on his nerves and morale. Cooley told himself he adored the Irish, but he must have meant only Charlotte, his Irish Kid, his lucky piece, who had sent him out to win one more for the Gipper.

Win? Well, he was doing his best—which in this case meant little more than pep talks for a number of Hoyt Enterprise representatives who still had some stake in pushing stock for him or stood on shaky scaffolds set up to keep one or another government from crowding him until things got better. To such representatives he said, "The man who will win is the man who can stick it out *in the third hour of the bombardment.*" He wanted them to believe that though Hoyt Enterprises was being heavily shelled, he would stick to the command post, unflinching.

Most of the ones still left with attachments to one or another of the companies he had incorporated in the Antilles and Curaçao, for tax purposes, went on believing him. For two reasons: (1) they trusted his slipperiness, having seen it pay off before, and (2) they no longer had a choice, being too deeply committed.

Liquidating—or pulling the rug out from under your own representatives, to put it harshly—was a sorry business. But in general Cooley's mood remained upbeat, for he was doing it with the old adroitness. The only real pang came on him in Hong Kong. While there he got news from Nigeria that a former bond salesman for ADC had been beheaded and otherwise mutilated in a public street of a small Nigerian city by indignant bond owners. Cooley could not be sure he remembered the poor guy, but thought he might have shaken his hand at a sales conference in Geneva, soon after ADC went public. He had a memory of brown-blue lips stretched in a wonderful smile, and of the trust in honest brown eyes. The thought of the beheading and the uncertain memory of that face haunted him all the way across the Arctic on the Tokyo–Lisbon leg of his journey.

Yet he knew that now, as always, the success he had led so many underlings to in years past depended on his own confidence. And these days, as he flew, he beefed that up by thinking how—as a last-ditch maneuver, mind you—he might go in with Rosio for a killing in drugs. In quick and out quick . . . and he must not let Bob Pardon know he was fooling with that kind of thing at all . . . and, lo, there might be money for a heavy infusion into his corporations. To redeem all the promises he was making as he flew.

He didn't *mean* to let anyone down.

But the loose dreams set off by what Colonel Timmerman started in his head were not the only stimulus that kept him going. In Rome—where he had always been lucky—the wild goose he was chasing laid an egg that might turn out to be golden. His old friend George Seip wanted to put another layer of paper between the German shareholders of UMD (Uganda Mining Development) and the heavy positions he had built up in Dutch precious-metals issues. A company that Cooley's lawyers had incorporated in Curaçao to cover his retreat from the Angolan oil venture had been dormant awhile with listed assets of no more than two hundred thousand dollars. He turned over

voting rights and five-year warrants to buy the remainder of the
stock in return for an unsecured loan of two hundred million lire.
Of course, the loan he got was not cash. It was warrants and
debentures validated by Seip's WWF (Worldwide Financial).

Not cash—but the sort of paper that might look good in Mexico. Might look good to any of the potential investors who would
be turning up for the party at El Dorado.

Let professors of economics and lawyers debate about what
was real money and what was not. Cooley had learned a
different kind of lesson from being in the thick of things, licking
the sandy pisspots and offering his own to be licked in turn. He
knew money was people. Money was faith. . . .

George Seip had put him on to an old lady in Rome who had
lost her faith in the Italian economy. She was unloading the family jewels.

Therefore, as he flew west toward home, there was an emerald
necklace for Charlotte to prove his trip had been successful. The
necklace rode in Riordan's left jacket pocket, since Riordan had
a sensitive left armpit and, of course, could not wear a shoulder
holster on a commercial flight.

"Riordan?"

Riordan gave him a big, stupid grin and pumped his left arm
three times against his barrel chest to show the jewels were safe
there, all right, and everything was rosy.

2

Ditching Riordan in Cuernavaca, Cooley flew very early on
Sunday morning to El Dorado, alone with the pilot of his chartered Cessna. They flew straight west to the coast and followed
it a few miles out on the chance they might spot the *Evita* with
Charlotte aboard. Rosio's yacht was due in today. Some of the
smaller fry were already at the resort, of course, already slopping
up the booze of their teetotaling host.

"There she is," the pilot called.

Cooley snapped his briefcase shut and scanned the emerald
and cerulean stretches of the morning ocean. As far as the horizon slow-moving piles of cumulus cloud were ranked in soft per-

spectives. From the closer ones shadows floated like immense lily pads in a garden pool. The white yacht moved among them like the sharpened tip of the arrow formed by its wake. It seemed irritatingly motionless to Cooley.

"Buzz it," he ordered. "Can you get them on your radio?"

"I can try that," the pilot said, already banking and diving in what would be an S curve in three dimensions.

"Never mind. It's too early," Cooley said, laying a hedge against possible disappointment.

The shadow of the plane crossed the wake lines of the vessel, closing fast like a submerged hunter. They passed the starboard side of the *Evita* at an altitude of less than two hundred feet. No one was on deck except a few crewmen and the first officer on the bridge. The officer waved, perhaps recognizing the plane or its red insignia. The crewmen flapped their arms and grinned.

"Buzz them once more for luck," Cooley ordered. But all the flower-colored deck chairs around the pool on the rear deck remained painfully neat and empty. "Let's go home," he said.

In twenty minutes they saw the multicolored turrets of El Dorado against row after row of green mountains. In twenty-six minutes they were over it. Five skinny old men were on the beach in white uniforms, sweeping the sand with wide push brooms.

On the airstrip a tank truck was refueling one of the chartered DC-9s. The newly graded strip still looked crude and raw. Never mind. It was out of sight of the hotel buildings.

There were seven planes below them as they came in to land after a descending swoop down a mountainside. The Learjet bore on its wings a gaudy orange pattern like an enlarged segment of a Japanese flag. That meant the Sun King had come down after all from Orange County, but of John Halvorsen himself or any of the other significant guests there was no sign as Cooley drove a jeep into the hotel compound and up to his and Charlotte's suite.

Even Bob Pardon was still not stirring, he was told by Oriente, the assistant manager, who had been on the lookout for him. Oriente came trotting with a bellboy to help Cooley bring in his luggage and golf clubs.

"Did Bob stay up to see everyone tucked in?" Cooley asked. He began to strip as soon as he got inside his door. With his shirttails dangling comfortably he scratched with both hands at the hair on his chest.

"That's not been so easy. We've had a wild three days getting them settled as they come in." Oriente laughed. "I believe everyone is happy. Can't tell while they're asleep, can you? I believe Page Fentress was the main problem last night. He was much distressed—I quote him in part—at the room we had assigned him when he expected a suite." He was not only partly quoting Fentress, he was subtly mimicking the regal faggot arrogance that Fentress could display if he thought himself belittled. "*Muy gravedad.*" Oriente chuckled. "Protocol had to be reviewed on the spot, I'll tell you."

Beyond the concerns of protocol and self-esteem, Fentress would have been eager to be housed in quarters that showed off his distinctive styling, the blending of Art Deco with furry tassels and Second Empire. After all, he was here partly on business, as many of the other guests would be, hoping to meet and entertain new clients. Page would demonstrate even to the hopelessly heterosexual how to inhabit his interiors graciously.

"There were other toughies," Oriente said. "We could have handled most of them diplomatically from the office. We've done our homework on them. Bob's a good coach. The real ball buster was John Halvorsen. As I understood it finally, he was expecting Minette Reeves to have a room of her own. And we'd put her in with another starlet, you see . . ."

"And Big John already had a cunt in his room, so he couldn't bring Minette there. It figures," Cooley said. He understood the imperatives of studship with the same sympathy he had for compulsive boozers, though he no longer touched the stuff himself.

"The way I handle John when he gets boisterous . . ." Cooley began.

Oriente did not want him to think they had bungled anything without his personal guidance. "Bob offered his rooms to that other girl, but as I understand it, Mr. Halvorsen was eventually led to the idea that Miss Reeves's roommate wouldn't mind . . ."

"If he took them two at a time," Cooley said. "That's what

I'd've recommended. Knowing John as I think I do. Keep everyone happy, huh?"

The bellboy was anxiously looking for a place to stash the golf clubs without marring the Page Fentress effect of what was called the Monarch Suite, with no joke intended. "Lie 'em against the wall," Cooley said with a yawn. "I got to take me a good crap. Giorgio," he said to Oriente, "I can never manage on a plane. I've had the habit since I was a Boy Scout and I read in the handbook you should do it every day. I've been on planes for two weeks. . . ."

Giorgio Oriente was not greatly interested in his bowel habits. He left briskly, only saying that Bob Pardon wanted Cooley to pay attention to the mail laid out for him on the chrome-and-glass table.

He was not greatly interested in mail. There was the usual volume of it, he noted, and what was on top looked like it might constipate him all over again.

With his shirt hanging loose he went out on his balcony patio. The enchantment of air, sun and sea and all these walls he had reared up amid them hit him with sudden intoxication.

He was always under pressure, and the pressure allowed him very little leeway to notice the beauties of morning coastlines, mountains or cities. Even when he caught sight of El Dorado from the air he felt less of a lift than most casual tourists did at their first glimpse of it.

But now here he was inside of it—like a lucky bee deep in the throat of a succulent and gorgeous flower.

By God, he thought, *it's mine*. And for just that little while he stood there, bowel-purged and triumphant, all the rich and beautiful people still sleeping within his walls seemed to him like his own livestock, housed in his barn.

Up here, above his domain, his creation, he stood on a pedestal built out of the refined abstraction called money—thinner than the honeyed air in his mouth and lungs, but miraculously buoyant.

Too damn much to stand.

The pure soar of such feelings upset him too much. He knew

he needed a drink or to get his nuts off to sober back down onto the ground.

Hastily he went inside and drank two full glasses of water from the bottle in the faggoty bathroom. That helped, but he still felt dazed. He felt his pulse, timing it with the absolute accuracy of his quartz watch and finding nothing unusual about it.

He unwrapped the emerald necklace and laid it out carefully in a circle just in the middle of the monogrammed spread on the bed, exactly where he meant to put Charlotte's fine huggable, pinchable, stretchable, electric and expensive ass down as soon as the *Evita* hove to anchor and he could get her off.

The empty circle of the necklace on the coverlet was a poor thing to stand gawking at, so he went back onto the balcony. His mouth already felt dry again.

This time his eye caught a single figure on the beach, though a few early risers were beginning to straggle to the main pool on his right.

Against the surf he saw the slender, hesitant figure of a girl. And now for the first time since he left Cuernavaca a thought came that made him go back at the mail laid out for him. He turned over every envelope.

The sight of the girl on the beach, the unfamiliar relaxation of the moment, had allowed him to hope there might be word from his daughter. She might be coming. Hell, surely for a girl her age the temptation ought to be irresistible, whatever she had been taught to feel about him by now.

Nothing. With an angry exhalation he went back to the balcony. He saw a great, feathery, brilliant loop of foam swirl about the wading figure of the girl down there. His mind performed a typical somersault of faith and hope.

By God, that slender girl, so lovely at a distance in the morning light, *could be* Victoria—come to surprise him. She was a poor letter writer.

Nothing was impossible. Not here. Not this morning.

Shit, it was foolish to think it could be his daughter. It wouldn't be the first foolish thing he had done to rush down and see.

Breathing excitedly—faithful to the promise of the lovely morning, if nothing else—he hurried into his swimming trunks and robe. Barefoot, he hastened down the cobblestone path to the manicured sand of the beach.

3

The girl said her name was Maette Mornay. She had to spell the first name for him. It was French colonial, she said. It didn't mean anything. "Do you theenk eet's a pretty name?"

He thought *she* was pretty. She was prettier than any kid of his would have been, he thought, remembering the brief glimpse he'd had of Victoria at fifteen and remembering her mother. This one was luscious. The boobs held up the halter. There was just enough coral cloth to cover her pubic hair and the cheeks of her ass were not encumbered at all by the strap up the back. The face was meaningless pretty, but she didn't intend to come across facewise. Bait for John Halvorsen.

He didn't tell her his name. The monogram on his cotton beach robe meant nothing to her, though she had scanned it when he approached and said hello.

It was enough for her that she had some company. "I was in blue mood when I wake zees morning," she confided.

"Aren't you having a good time?"

"Lovely! You are not danceeng last night over the yacht's basin? In the discotheque?"

He admitted missing that.

"Was very gay," she explained to him. "Was like . . . fairyland! When ze lights are on"—her girlish fingers flickered aloft to illustrate for him the swaying of searchlight beams and the multitude of lanterns among the palms or around the platform built over part of the yacht basin for dancing. "Zere are so many danceeng I might not have seen you. Oh. And on ze golf course. Down zere is a tent. *Du cirque.* Cir-cuss. Fortunetellers. Such amuseeng things zey tell me!"

She collapsed to a sitting position on the sand, going down with the boneless grace of a ribbon dropped from languid fingers and recomposing its curves by the caprice that ribbons have. He sat down stiffly beside her, and she clapped her hand confidentially on his knee.

"Zey tell me I weel meet a man, dark like you, weez a beard like you. Ha-ha. No. Zey don't tell me zat. I won' tell you wat zey tell me, for zen eet weel not come true. Even in fairyland! But what zey say is so much fun. Also zere is a man, so veegorous, so much *fun*. He is rideeng ze elephant on eets head in ze *cirque—*cir-*cuss*. Also on ze golf course. He grab up two girls and take zem for an elephant gallop. Gallop?"

"Gallop," Cooley said with glum politeness. Maybe the girl would shut up if he suggested a swim.

"An elephant gallop! All ze world is laughing so much at heem! Also later when zere is so much—so man-ee—danceeng over the water and zere is the *son et lumière* on all the yachts and on ze walls, like a *véritable* fairyland . . . fireworks as well . . . zere is zees *same man* who makes so much fun for all the world. All the photographers, the televisions, zey are watching heem, following heem for what he will zink of next. He ees ze Sun Keeng. . . ."

"John Halvorsen," Cooley pronounced the name dismally to himself, knowing he had been upstaged and dispossessed from his own kingdom by that California prick.

"Yes!" Maette Mornay exclaimed. "He has push two, three, I don't know how many couples eento ze pool. So much laughing. Zey are all so *bien coiffé*, dress up. *Zut!* Eento ze pool. I don't know eef I laugh so much ees why I have blue mood zees morn-eeng. Yes?"

"It shouldn't work that way. Everybody should be happy here."

"Een Europe *les hommes d'affaires*, beenissmen, are all so cautious. So *propre*. I have seen zem. Just sit on zere doffs. But Sun Keeng is meelionaire many times over. Yet so *vibrant*. Full of veegor, like John F. Kennedy, wheech you do not see over zere. Eet ees new world. Eet ees fairyland!"

Cooley kept nodding to the girl's flavorless enthusiasm, getting angrier at Halvorsen. Between them they were spoiling his first morning here.

"Oooooo, loooook!" she cried. From the open doors of caves the morning crew of workmen was bringing out the catamarans and lining them up on the sand. The new sails looked like enor-mous artificial flowers set up in a giant sandbox. "Also zere is a breeze," Maette told him. "We are ze first earlee birds. We weel go in ze boats while others sleep!"

It occurred to him for a minute that he and this long-limbed adventurer might go out to meet the *Evita* on a yellow catamaran. Somewhere down the coast they would come bobbing alongside, and surely in that case Charlotte would be among those lined up at the yacht rail laughing at what the sea had tossed up.

Dammit, foolishness like that would please her and show her he was up for the spirit of her party here. ("Don't be so afraid to let yourself go when you're with people having a gay time. Kick your heels. You know you're Cooley Hoyt.") She would think he had showed the Rosio gang he was as lively as any of them, and she was always squarely on his side when he "showed them." Showed anyone he was quicker and trickier than they.

But he knew he was not going to do any such thing. It was too much like a caper John Halvorsen might pull. Worse, if he and Maette got beyond range of scrutiny from the shore, she might expect him to come through. And she might tell people if he didn't. And boffing her would be like eating a piece of waxed fruit. He wasn't game for that.

4

So he waited for Charlotte's arrival in the Monarch Suite. He took the emerald necklace from the bed and hid it in a drawer when he came in. Then he tended to his mail.

Between ten and eleven his phone began to ring. Pérez, the bullfight idol of the fifties, wanted to challenge him to golf—if the absurd circus tent had been removed from the sixth fairway.

Hector Avidibian simply wanted to present his sincere felicitations and declare that El Dorado was truly a fairyland. Hector had come down from fishing at Cabo San Lucas, which was also a fairyland, but of nature merely, while El Dorado was a work of nature *and* art. He wanted to congratulate Cooley on the cuisine. (Cooley remembered at last that he was hungry; he called for toast and coffee.)

Céci Chaumont, Kate Lammers and the Countess Vivien all called on the mistaken assumption that Charlotte had arrived with him. Only Céci wanted any conversation with him. She wanted him to know there were too many photographers sneaking out of the shrubbery. She had come here hoping to enjoy her friends. One of her friends had already been embarrassed by *paparazzi* of an odious stripe. The unspeakable John Halvorsen must *absolutely* be induced to go back among his own kind before all of Céci's kind were disgusted with his antics.

Her diatribe against Halvorsen was his one miniature piece of good luck all morning. It prepared him to be cool when Halvorsen got him on the phone.

"Done!" Halvorsen shouted. "I'll buy your dump if you keep it stocked with cunt."

"Take it easy and enjoy your blessings."

"I know. You're a big softy, Coo. You built the mother just so Charlotte could have her coming-out party here. That's this week, and you haven't done so bad. But you'll lose your ass in the hotel business. I could tell you already where the bite is going to come. Fucking staff is a bunch of peasants. It'll be five years before you have a first-class hotel. You can't stand the drain. I'll still probably give you half of what you put into it. Someone lost his head with that stupid zoo and you must have hocked your teeth to build that airstrip. The thing is . . . my money is real in case you're building up a retirement fund."

"Glad to hear you're doing so well, John."

"Huh?" There was an interruption, a sound like scuffling, and then the Sun King bellowed, "I said 'eat it,' you bitch." The sound effects he employed in negotiation were a real caution.

"Cooley? Sorry, I got interrupted here. Like I mentioned, the service is frightful. I've got to go to Acapulco this evening. Don't piss your pants. I'll be back. Get your books laid out and we can have a real eyeball-to-eyeball. I'm serious. This time it's firm, Coo."

"Get yourself a fried-chicken concession, John."

"Easy! I've already talked to Bob and he says it's not out of the question. Put on the old thinking cap! Give my love to the adorable Charlotte. See you."

After that assault Cooley drank another full glass of water and went back out on his patio. Nothing was as beautiful as it had looked when he first stepped out here this morning. But, with a taste of sand in his mouth, he congratulated himself that his investment in the opening here was going to pay off.

IV

1

"It's Victoria," the breathless voice on the phone said.

"Victoria Hoyt?" Bob Pardon asked. The guest list included a starlet named Victoria Ali, whom he had chosen to lodge with Minette Reeves, and it would not surprise him if she had a complaint today.

"Victoria," the voice repeated, with the militant impatience that made her identity unmistakable.

"So you came back after all. Are you having troubles with the desk clerk again?"

"I'm right across the bay. I can see you," she said. "I can see all the boats and everything, but I wanted to call before we came over. I suppose it's too late."

"Don't be shy. Come on."

"All your rooms must be full, aren't they?"

"Busting at the seams. But we'll find a place for you. And your friend. Your dad's here. I guess you haven't spoken to him yet."

"No! Could you . . . give us a room just tonight but not tell my father right away?"

"I'll let you tell him. I'll put the room in your name. Just tell the guard at the gate and the man at the desk that you're Victoria *Hoyt*, please. I'm afraid you'll have to use your last name."

"Well . . ." She was consulting her absurd, stiff principles again, and he felt his patience waning. Then quickly she yielded. "Sure. I've got *some* clothes in the bus. It's a real fashion show over there, I'll bet."

"It's not a problem. Nearly everyone is naked, to tell the truth. Come as you are."

"I can't come in a bathing suit. Is there any way we can slip in without too many people spotting us, I mean? A back way? Servants' entrance, you know."

There were several, but Bob refused to play along further with her whims. "You'll have to check in like anyone else. I have too many obligations today to come and meet you."

"Mmmmmmmm . . . Is that Rosio who just arrived?"

From this he could guess her relative location. She was close enough to have a full view of the bay, where the *Evita* had dropped anchor less than half an hour before.

"It's his yacht. Can you see all the little boats going out to greet it? Your dad's out there, I think. Charlotte Keefe came in on it."

"Oh, her. Yes."

"Rosio didn't come."

"You sure?"

"Now, Victoria. You didn't come back to see him. There's lots more interesting types here. Come and see. I've got to hang up now."

Still she made him wait while she conferred with someone who seemed to be standing outside her phone booth. Bob could hear only the vowel sounds of a male voice. Then she said, "Look, you've been good. We sure thank you. Just be sure there's a room saved. We'll try to check in before night. If not, thanks."

He had the distinct impression that once again Victoria had refused the bait her father had tempted her with. He was not particularly amused with the idea that the girl might be in range of sight from his balcony. She had taken selfish advantage. He had kept his promise not to tell her father of her previous hit-and-run visit. If she came in now there would have to be explanations of his silence on that matter. If she didn't show, the trouble of arranging for a room would be wasted.

Nevertheless, once again, he played his part in good faith. He called instructions to the manager's office to have a room available for her as quickly as possible.

He saw, in the dancing water alongside the *Evita,* not only a swarm of catamarans and rubber rafts and canoes but also the sturdy fishing boat Karen Steiglitz had commandeered for her cameramen and other journalists. He should be on the fishing boat at this moment, for now that the festivities had begun, the news people were his central responsibility.

Karen and her three-man crew were here to videotape a story for the Nick Sanders show. The inflection they gave it was a matter of genuine concern.

"You know we don't do fashion stuff, travel and resort news," Karen said, leveling with him from the moment of her arrival. "Nick just wouldn't be interested in a lot of skin shots. Not even the over-age studs snapping the elastic bikinis."

No, if El Dorado got any favorable publicity on the Nick Sanders show it would have to be earned the hard way. "Nick's after *him,*" Karen said—meaning Cooley Hoyt, implying clearly that the objective of the taping was to show him off to the American public as a crook and an asshole, an embezzler and a fugitive from the post-Watergate Morality, a slick promoter squandering other people's money on this stupendous frivolity while the unemployment rolls mounted across the United States. "Now that his name has come up in connection with the Hogben trial, Nick wants us to get enough footage for possibly a half hour. If Hogben's convicted you may get the leadoff on the show."

There was not much chance of persuading someone as shrewd and experienced as Karen that Cooley was a misunderstood public benefactor. The play was for point spread, not victory. Bob's task—which he rather enjoyed—was to keep maneuvering Karen's subconscious sympathies little by little—like a lawyer who knows he cannot hope for acquittal but hopes for recommendations of mercy.

In this he was helped by the fact he liked Karen and she liked him. "What's an honest, upright, shrewd man like you doing working for such a turd?" she demanded while he was regaling her with tequila sours.

And yet this was not a direct expression of scorn or hostility. It carried a note of regret about the rules of the game they were committed to—as if she had really asked: What's a good woman like me doing working for a turd like Nick Sanders?

So he had tried to draw the picture for her. At least give her an inkling of why he had shepherded Cooley and his business acrobatics so many years. "I have to admit that I like being on the outside. Neither the Harvard Business School nor the polio quite managed to take my balls off, though they wrecked me from there down. And Cooley's got to play the outsider game because the big boys won't let him play inside. The first time I ever met him he let me know his father had ridden with Pancho Villa. How about that? There's a backwoods, outlaw streak in him that they've mostly rubbed out of business in the States. Nobody knows for sure, but I'll bet one Hoyt or another has been fighting the government since the Whiskey Rebellion. Now they're offshore. . . ."

"I like that," Karen said. "I like his father riding with Pancho Villa."

It was fine she liked that detail. Fine that it happened to be true—in just the same sense that everything uttered on the Nick Sanders show was true. It was verifiable as fact, comically misrepresentative of the dense tangle of personal history it was supposed to represent.

So were his tidbits about Charlotte. "She was bumming around Europe before she picked up with Cooley. Living the hippie life, the flower-child life. She called herself a dancer. Floating with some high-priced people. But going nowhere. Zip —along comes Cooley Hoyt with some money—well, he's turned over plenty in the last fifteen years—and said, 'I'm a ladder. Climb me.' When you meet her you'll see what she's made of the opportunities he gave her."

Son of Pancho Villa and Irish Flower Child? These labels for Cooley and Charlotte were not untrue. Better than Fascist Bastard and Lion-Hunting Cunt.

"It's worth the trip to watch her in operation among the beautiful folk we've got here. Her and her friend Jovan Kovacs. Charlotte plays on people instead of a harp. Charlotte the Harp. She plays on being Irish, too. You'll hear her accent come and go, according to the occasion. She's a genius in her own element. And a very stately young woman."

"So she's described in *Women's Wear Daily*," Karen said with a tone that warned him not to oversell his product.

"Oh, you'll see. That's what you're here for. And make up your own mind about the spectacle."

Though . . . not if he could help it.

As the launch carried him out among the bobbing small craft in the yacht basin, he caught sight of Karen standing atop the cabin of the fishing boat. She was watching the activity on the decks of the *Evita*, as a good newshawk should.

But as he came closer he saw that she was wearing a replica of the thong bathing suit that Jovan Kovacs had impressed on her mind. Bless her heart, she looked good in it. Bless his heart, he would certainly tell her so.

She was not impervious to the messages that El Dorado was created to broadcast to the seducible world.

She hopped down from the cabin roof as he was helped clumsily aboard by a couple of other journalists who liked him. "At least it's a gorgeous day," she said. "At least it's *gorgeous*. My boys are taping everything just because it's so pretty."

He would not be distracted from admiring her thong bathing suit. "Forget Kovacs!" he boomed. "You do it with no help from cosmetic surgery."

"Hush!" she said. "You're the most devious flack I've run into yet."

She didn't mean a word of it. As Cooley Hoyt said—"Everyone trusts Bob Pardon." That, Cooley insisted, was what made Bob indispensable to all his enterprises.

2

It was high noon and the knife-winged birds were circling in the flawless sky when the *Evita* paid out her anchor chain and sagged beautifully to rest in the yacht basin. At a hundred and thirty feet she was the biggest boat there, a dowager empress among the sloops, yawls and motor cruisers anchored around her.

After all, Cooley had gone out to meet her. The launch had taken him out as soon as she hove in sight beyond the mouth of the bay.

Now he and Charlotte stood with arms around each other's waists waving and smiling to all their friends as the crowd swarmed toward them in paddleboats, rafts or catamarans. Cooley was wearing a yachtsman's cap Charlotte had commandeered for him. Now and then he waved it in an exuberant salute.

Then, overhead, a yellow para-kite swooped toward the ladder on the *Evita's* side, towed by a motorboat invisible on the other side of the breakwater. The splendidly bronzed man riding beneath the yellow silk blew a kiss. "It's Page!" Charlotte shouted. "Page! Come join us."

Everyone else was converging on her and Cooley in their hour of beatitude. It was like being exiled royalty welcomed home by their joyful subjects, and with Charlotte there where he could claim her and show her off, Cooley forgot the loneliness of his journeying. He waved his cap like a victorious college athlete and sent his big voice booming out over the water in welcoming cries.

The ladder was aswarm with bikinis and hairy-chested sportsmen from the boats bouncing gaudily below the spot on deck where he and Charlotte were hugging, kissing or shaking hands with all comers.

But Page Fentress, at the end of a nylon towrope, was soaring up, up and away under his wind-bulged silk.

A pallid, middle-aged American paused on the yacht's ladder to watch Page mount into the blue sky like someone who made his home there. To the woman whose passage he blocked, the American said, "I told you they called them that because they actually flew."

"Call who what?" she demanded with an impatient giggle.

"Spitfires. Saucers. Squirrels," he said. *"Fairies!"*

"Oh," she said. "Anyway he looks brave." In the pageantry of the moment all the men looked brave and all the women beautiful. Even the blue sky looked expensive and fashionable.

The woman's gaze approved it all. Then she pushed on up the ladder to throw her arms around Charlotte and cry, "Now I know it's begun. You're here."

It was uproars like this that made it worthwhile to be Cooley Hoyt. While it lasted he was determined to give no thought to what it cost. He was determined not to be shaken by the word that Rosio had left his yacht in Panama, though Charlotte had taken him belowdecks to greet him with that information the moment he boarded.

"I promised I'd deliver him," she wailed.

"Unimportant. Everything else is clicking."

He told himself grandly that he needed neither Rosio nor anyone else. He renounced the pipe dreams of poppies blowing in the fields of Chihuahua and of killings in the heroin market. Ugly stuff, anyhow, and here all was pure to the eye. Happy. Wonderful.

But she had to give him her accounting, because the manner of Rosio's departure had not smelled right to her. "It was nasty how they took him off. I think it's got to do with politics. There's talk that the old crowd in his country might stage a coup. It's possible he'll go back in with them."

"Took him off?"

"So it appeared. We were so long at anchor after we'd come through the Canal. Stinking hot. Then a Coast Guard boat drew alongside. Two Americans came aboard. Do you suppose they were CIA? They were with him in his cabin ever so long. He left with them on their launch. I wouldn't say they were menacing. Yet it was all a bit furtive."

"Maybe he'll be along in a day or two."

"He didn't say as he left. Cooley, he's a sly one. He's sly and I think you might use him. For one thing or another. He'd never talk business with a woman, but I did my best. Told him how well you were managing. All our prospects here."

Sure he needed Rosio. Never mind the specifics. The yacht itself with its sleek passageways and elegant cabins reeked of money, and the suggestive secrecy of the waxed doors on either side of the carpeted corridor leading to her cabin had roused him mightily.

Caught in this mixed passion that felt so much like blind physical lust, he could not believe that Rosio would be long delayed. The rich old man was tantalizing him. It was as if the fellow might be working him up deliberately—and that surely meant there was action possible.

"What are you grinning at?" Charlotte asked. "I'm very disappointed."

He showed her what he was grinning about. Guilelessly he un-
zipped his yachting pants and let her behold the readiness of his
erection. Lord—he wanted to hump this costly, secretive boat itself if someone would tell him where to put it in.

"I see you're ready for the party to begin," Charlotte said
slyly. With consummate, cool grace she bent to kiss his offering.

Somehow it was like the kiss of a teacher thanking a pupil for
the apple he has brought her. Not perfunctory. Not conde-
scending. But . . . reserved. Like sly old Rosio, she understood
he would be all the keener for being put off.

She rezipped him deftly and patted the hard bulge with a
promise that in the orgiastic days now beginning he would not
be cheated. Everything in good time. He must trust her, as mistress of the revels, to orchestrate the excitements on ship and
shore.

"Our friend Rosio said to give you hugs and kisses. Don't
worry about him. He spoke most cheerfully to Maria and me as
he was getting on their launch. Still, the men who took him off
. . . I could have given them a foot in the balls for keeping us
idle in such heat. There's so much fiddle-faddle these days. And
now we'll have our own hands full without worrying what such
chaps are up to."

3

Splendid for her age, wearing waterproof makeup and a man's
panama with a band of Peruvian cotton, a waist-wrapped T-top
to show breasts that budded in Wally Simpson's generation, the
Countess Vivien Conti was one of the few people who got to oc-
cupy a deck chair on the swarming deck of the *Evita*. Her companion Tino Grünherz was holding the honeydew-green chair
beside her for Charlotte Keefe. Charlotte had promised to come
for a moment's chat with her best friend as soon as she'd spared
a hug for Jovan Kovacs. Jovan, the Countess saw, had just come
up the ladder and stepped on deck in a shirtwaist bikini, a swirl
of diaphanous shawls flaring from her shoulders.

Tino reclined in the honeydew chair, quite motionless except
for the fluttering just below his hairless rib cage that showed the

accelerated beating of his heart. His eyes were too nearly closed for anyone to notice the hatred with which he glared out of a contemptuous private world at the milling, pampered bodies pattering in masses about the deck like rodents in search of blood.

Blood! Actually Tino saw it gather and drip from the periphery of his field of vision. From the blurred flower stems of his eyelashes. From the varnished masts and lines of rigging. All these red mouths, opened for speech, laughter or the smirks of conviviality, seemed thirsting for the viscous crawling of blood on the yardarms.

In the swimming pool visible between his pedicured toes, three ludicrous females splashed around the paunchy, hairy man he despised. They were moiling a pool of blood and threatening to contaminate the toad's drink. The toad protected it with one hand, while he fended their dripping hands away with his elbows.

This was the American boor who had called Page Fentress a *fairy.*

"Tino!" Countess Vivien whispered. "My book!"

He fumbled in his shoulder bag for it and opened it to her place mark before he laid it in her hands. *L'Après-midi d'un Faune.* Her bony finger searched down the page. She frowned unbecomingly as she began to read.

Tino rolled back into the comfort of his own sweat on the plastic of the deck chair, clasping his hands on his breast this time, like the figure of an idealized boyish knight on a tomb. Now, through the slits of his eyelids he watched the black circling birds. Vultures perhaps. Carrion birds or birds of prey. But so clean compared to this human rabble.

Sombre lys! Ténébreuse allusion des cieux . . .

Tino found himself reading along with the Countess, inside her fastidious mind as she veered upward on the soaring language. He closed altogether those blue eyes that the tropic sky reflected so inadequately. Against the roseate backdrop of his lids he watched the spectacle of Page Fentress, lithe as Icarus himself and bronze except for the loincloth that matched the booming yellow silk of the para-kite. Vaulting into the empyrean . . .

How little it *mattered* to anyone except American boors that such an exquisite body might have known caresses. Winging from the sordidness of lust, beauty knew—Page Fentress knew—how to transform the flesh into pure imagination. Tino was learning that. The Countess was his teacher. Her fleshly requirements of him had never been excessive. An initiation, no more. She had elicited from him hardly more than a ritual acknowledgment of the orifices and powdered crannies of a body that would never grow slack with age. By night he slept beside her in the same fleshless harmony he felt now when she was reading Valéry beside him. They slept like mother and child in even-breathing warmth. When he woke beside her in the darkness of luxurious bedclothes, even her snoring was one of the myriad delicious little secrets they had come to share. The proximity of her spirit alone had the power to soothe him back to sleep. It was a magnificence that made him immune to the viciousness of the mob.

"Tino!"

"*Ja?*"

"She's coming now."

The Countess had psychic gifts. Even when absorbed by Valéry she had an uncanny faculty for noting the disposition and movements of people around her. So—even before Charlotte Keefe and Cooley Hoyt began to ease their way back through the pack of guests between the cabins and the starboard rail, the Countess's sensibilities had registered the shock wave of deference and attention that preceded them.

Tino waved to Charlotte through the thicket of shoulders and soft scarves that might have hidden the Countess from her. He pointed down to indicate that he had faithfully kept a place for her.

He saw that Charlotte's glass was empty and snapped his fingers at one of the deck stewards. He remembered that Hoyt did not drink hard liquor. It was the only redeeming thing he could remember about the boor.

As Tino stood up from the honeydew chair, a fat young man with bulging red trunks rolled into it. Dripping wet. "Hey," he said to the Countess, "I paid my own plane fare down here for an interview with the Butcher. Now they tell me he jumped ship in Panama. You're the Countess Vivien, huh? You're supposed to be a buddy of his from the world-famous spas of Europe, right? You know why this mysterious change of plans?"

"Butch . . . er?" the Countess asked, keeping her place in *L'Après-midi* with her finger. She had never known a butcher.

"Please!" Tino said, standing at Prussian attention beside the revolting intruder. He did not want to do anything that would seem ungraceful to the Countess, but he wanted to go for the beast's eyes with his fingernails.

"*Bitte,*" he said. "*Plizz.*" He stamped his bare foot.

The fat boy rolled his eyes in his direction and then gave him the finger.

"What's the trouble?" Cooley Hoyt said.

Struggling with tears, Tino began, "This person has . . ."

"He is looking for a butcher," Countess Vivien said unbelievingly.

"I came down here—paid my own way—to get an interview with Ripper Rosio, Butcher of the Pampas. I'm told he's a no-show. You Hoyt? Maybe you heard the army revolted and they're flying him to a border town to stand by for the take-over? I'm the *Rolling Stone* correspondent," he said, lowering the volume of his voice.

Charlotte Keefe laughed and crouched beside the fat boy. She gave him a happy wink and broadened her brogue. "Begad, thir's nothing to what yuv heard. Meself, I saw him last evening in Panama. 'Twas doctor's orders he remain there a day or more."

Cooley said, "We asked the press not to come aboard the *Evita.* Jill Hatch is going to sing tonight. You're welcome to come to the fireworks. There's a press boat out there somewhere." He jerked an angry shoulder toward the rail.

"Butcher?" Countess Vivien asked, a little more plaintively.

"I know," the fat boy said. "I swam over from it."

"Swim back," Cooley said.

"Please!" Tino said. He did not stamp his foot this time—perhaps because he thought Mr. Hoyt was about to fling the fat boy over the rail. Mr. Hoyt's eyes were pretty ominous.

"You want a break in the press, stay cool, Hoyt," the fat boy said.

"And who is not cool, pray?" asked Charlotte. "Look me up tonight and I'll make sure you get time with Jill Hatch. After she has sung. After the fireworks. Eleven-thirty? Come to my table then?"

"Git!" Cooley said.

The fat boy scratched his crotch. Then he got up and made his way slowly to the rail. He made a fairly nice dive from the *Evita's* brassworks. There was a mocking cheer from the press boat. The happy people on the *Evita* echoed it a little more good-naturedly.

"I understand nothing," Countess Vivien said. "Tino, a small Bacardi."

"It was a reporter from *Rolling Stone*," Charlotte said soothingly. She eased into the chair Tino had held for her and finally accepted the drink the deck steward had been holding for her. "I adore your hat, my love. Have you seen Jovan's print fichu?"

"He was a reporter," Countess Vivien said, as if coming out of a trance and repeating to herself the oracular voices she had heard while it lasted. "He wanted to know why Ortiz Rosio did not come here on the *Evita*." Now she smiled at Charlotte, the faithless smile of those who are very old and very wise. "Dear Jovan showed me all her clothes yesterday. There are no surprises. Thank you, Tino," she said, accepting her Bacardi as he crouched beside her to listen.

"I have predicted everything that is to happen here." Her emaciated hand groped for Charlotte's. She clutched Charlotte's wrist as if to comfort her while she passed on tragic news. "I know you think you humor me when you listen. All of you. However, in my letter to Anne-Marie, posted two weeks ago—was it not, Tino?—I warned her we should not expect to see Ortiz here. You may ask her to show you the letter written in my own hand, Charlotte. It is just as I say now. Ortiz, I wrote, is a man of feints. Never, I wrote, is one to think he will arrive at the destination he declares. Never! I who have known him since his youth could have told you he would not arrive here, Charlotte. Well . . . it is all in my letter to Anne-Marie."

"Where is he?" Cooley asked.

The Countess turned to him with a slight irritation at being interrupted. "Evidently he is not here. That is exactly as I predicted. If you don't believe, ask Anne-Marie. She is in her room."

"I don't need to ask her," Cooley said. "Tough luck! I like old Ortiz. We'd have shown him the time of his life."

"He was looking forward to the fishing," Charlotte said.

"Fishing!" Countess Vivien said scornfully. "Charlotte, no. He deceived you, too. It is part of his careful plan to deceive. In my letter I wrote, 'The plans of Ortiz are inscrutable.' You will find those precise words when you see the letter. I insist you see it."

"I'll certainly take the time to do that," Cooley promised.

On the fishing boat that Karen Steiglitz had claimed for the press, Bob Pardon and the man from *Grazia* helped the fat boy climb over the side when he had swum back.

"There aren't many rules here," Bob said. "Still, I've found you always luck out better if you ease along with the traffic. I thought you guys all knew it was agreed only guests would board the *Evita* for Miss Keefe's arrival."

Seeing no response of comprehension on the boy's round face —and not recognizing him except as one of the people on the fishing boat when the beach crew rowed him out—Bob tried again, "*Nous n'avons pas beaucoup des règles, chez nous, mais . . .*"

"Gotcha, Pop," the boy said.

"Then can you tell me why you swam over there? Tell me whom you want to interview and I'll make it easy," Bob said severely.

"I'm the man from *Rolling Stone*."

"Or I'll make it tough. I haven't seen your press card, have I?" More than that, Bob remembered there had been no response to the invitation sent to the magazine in question.

"Do I carry it in my swimming trunks?"

"What room are you in, young fellow?" Bob was keeping his voice down. Only the man from *Grazia* seemed to be following the conversation with any interest.

The boy met his eyes for a long moment, then rolled his

tongue around his teeth, bulging his wet cheeks. "Okay, Dad. I came in over the wall. I'm staying in a fleabag the other side of the bay. But it's no joke I'm writing you up for *Rolling Stone*. I've got a letter from them."

"Writing it on spec?"

"We all got to start somewhere."

"I'll buy that," Bob said, "but . . ."

"You better check with Miss Keefe before you bounce my ass out of here. And Hoyt. They promised me an interview with Jill Hatch tonight."

"I'll check it out. And tell them you came in over the wall." The fat boy shrugged to concede defeat. "Gotcha twice, old-timer. So I'll swim in and silently fade away. Just one thing. Nobody's going to rough me up if I try to walk out the main gate? Fair enough?"

"Nobody gets roughed up here," Bob promised. "I've got a walkie-talkie. We'll give you a ride back to where you're staying if you want."

"Man, no, thanks. But, thanks. You know . . ." He was going quietly, but he wanted to leave one more barb planted. "You know, I don't blame Rosio for not showing up here unless he brought more goons along than it looks like. Your security stinks. I came right off the main road and down the retaining wall. Mighty pretty, but it's got stones like a ladder. Just a tip."

"We're grateful for all suggestions," Bob said.

"You look like you're about to be sick," Karen Steiglitz told him. "What was our fat friend all about?" She had evidently been watching the exchange from the prow, where her camera-man was filming the small boat traffic by the *Evita*'s ladder.

"That boy," he said, mopping his brow.

"Gate crasher?"

He nodded. "I expect we'll have some more. I hope the others try to come in at least by the main gate." He blinked and wiped his domed forehead. He cleaned the sweat from his glasses. "I hope that boy never knows how lucky he is not to have a bullet in him. He's doing a piece on spec for *Rolling Stone*."

"Who'd harm anyone simple-minded enough to do that?" she asked. "But you'll look after us all, won't you?"

"That's what I'm paid for," he said. "We don't want anything that would damage the image of idle voluptuousness."

"Mustn't give money a bad name."

"That above all," he said lightly.

V

1

The fireworks frightened the shorebirds.

When the first percussion of explosions high in the air sent a lattice of red, white and green parabolas radiating above the bay, the birds began to desert the beaches and the crannies of the breakwater. They were conditioned to accept the noise of motors and the yelps of water sportsmen. They were only mildly curious about the band or the amplified electric guitar that backed up Jill Hatch in her act. But as the overhead blasting went on and increased in tempo, waves of pressure traveled the dense air. Whether the birds took the sound and dazzle of fireworks for the arrival of a storm, or whether the compression waves unnaturally disoriented their nervous systems, at each pause they hesitated only briefly before moving farther out on the water or farther around the curve of the shore.

To jack up the emotional effect of the cannonading overhead, the band was playing "The Virgin of the Maccarena" for the whole crowd of guests assembled on the platform extending into the yacht anchorage.

When the noise of the fireworks and the band was at a maximum, Bob heard the first exchanges of small-arms fire.

Heard them without recognizing them yet. Later he would suppose that his nervous system refused to organize the pattering of shots into a meaningful signal because of the chattering bullshit of the journalists around him. He had about twenty-five

of them on his hands tonight. They were clustered in a gazebo
overlooking the tables around the dancing area. Supposedly it
was a vantage point from which they could watch the antics and
costumes of the guests. The party tonight was organized on an
Art Deco theme. From the trunks of the women, at least, there
had been an outpouring of junky treasures—sequins and cloches
and feather ropes and chromium jewelry.

All this, plus the fireworks, seemed to be going over big with
the crowd below them. But the news people only quieted while
the amplifications of Jill Hatch's voice and guitars drowned out
their quips or the boom of fireworks shut them up. For most of
the day they had been showing off for each other. It always happened when you got too many of them together. They were com-
peting with one-liners.

"Chaumont may travel with a vibrator, but Marichen raises
dogs."

"Are you sure Ron Ziegler got his start this way?"

"Cornfeld may have invented it, but Hoyt does it topless."

"Her tits are insured, but only for collision."

"Arabs have never been out of style. Whe she first set out
from Transylvania to see the world she showed up in London
wearing rubies from what was then Transjordan . . ."

"Crossing the bar with a hairline scar."

". . . and the Sheik said, look, you want them? *Dive* for them
then, he said. Dive for them."

Only the correspondent for *Der Spiegel* was reflecting on the
costly spectacle, and he was just now finding a moral lesson in it.
"A miracle of self-hypnosis and obedience," he was saying to
Karen Steiglitz. "Self-hypnosis—that if they devoutly pay attention to what would amuse a child . . . that if they watch the
bright lights and clap to the music, the world will not fall from
under their feet." The German was a short, blocky man with an
intense stare, in which he placed great confidence. All day, Bob
had noticed, the man had been placing himself to stare squarely
into Karen's eyes while he analyzed each detail, from the flora
and fauna to the quality of brass on the *Evita*'s rails (not up to
German standards). "The delight of the eternal bourgeoisie who
know nothing of history . . ."

"All the same," Karen said with defensive hysteria, "Cooley
Hoyt got his start with Pancho Villa. No, it was his father, wasn't

it, Bob? The *older* Mr. Villa. *Sancho.* Oh, look at that one scatter! As Oswald Spengler said to Karl Marx—enjoy."

Bob was glad she had been talking.

Otherwise, this time, she would have heard what he knew to be gunfire. Not from the direction of the golf course. He had thought the first shots—which he now admitted could have been nothing else—had come from down there. These seemed to come from the jungle up on the ridge. Perhaps a mile away. An irregular musketry that he guessed to be from the guns of the local police.

"Karen, dearest," Bob said. "Will you see that everyone here has enough to eat and drink and that Oswald Spengler is not belittled in my absence? I'll try to catch up with you all a little later."

A ripple of explosions crossed an arc of sky. The last parachuted fountains of fire drifted down toward their reflections in the dulcet water. The crowd hushed again and then responded with a many-throated sigh of delighted appreciation, dying out as languidly as the burning colors slipped to extinction.

He thought she was irked with him for leaving her to fend off the German's portentous lectures, so he said, "Linger a little while? The bonus will be in your slipper, Cinderella."

He was careful to hobble slowly down the stone steps from the gazebo and across the flagstones of the court. He crossed the rope suspension bridge over the pool. At the far end he waved back in case anyone was watching him go. It was only in the shadows of the palmettos beyond the pool that he permitted himself to break into the grotesque lunging surges that would have to serve for running.

He was sure the reporters had not identified the sound of gunfire, and he heard no more of it as he ran.

2

Nevertheless, Karen caught up with him just as he came to his jeep in the staff parking lot. "Hell, then, come on," he said bitterly. He could not spare the time to distract her.

Turning onto the slope up to the main gate, the tires shrieked on the cobblestones. Karen grabbed the frame of the windshield as they went pitching and bouncing up the hill. A flashlight bloomed directly into their eyes, a pulsing bull's-eye of light within concentric rings. Bob braked to a stop under the looming arch that enclosed the gatehouse. As the afterimage of light faded they saw the single guard on duty was holding a carbine in one hand, the probing flashlight in the other. His walkie-talkie was on the ground, leaning against the wall of the gatehouse. Just beyond the gate in the middle of the turnaround a police van sat with its doors all swung open from hasty disembarkment.

The walkie-talkie came on with an urgent squawk. The guard picked it up and acknowledged the call. There was a rapid exchange and the guard said, "They have caught one on the golf course. Maybe there is one, two more who have slipped through between there and here. Others up there, I think." With the beam of his flashlight he touched the dense, solid-seeming foliage beyond the turnaround, with a kind of fearful delicacy rummaging the paths that entered it like the mouths of caves running into the stone of the ridge itself.

"And the police went up after them? Did you see anyone go up there?" When the guard shook his head, Bob said, "Give me that," and took the walkie-talkie. He called the main office and spoke rapidly to Harold Freeman. "Get the boathouse gang strung out along the beach at the end of the golf course. Is Sergeant Santiago there? Tell him we've got the main gate covered, and if he can stop his people from hosing down the whole damn jungle with the burp guns . . ."

While he was still talking, Karen saw the white-jacketed figures converging on them out of the dimness of the grounds, coming at a run up the slope which she and Bob had climbed in the jeep, but converging from many points among the buildings, like swift moths bearing on an irresistible point of flame.

She recognized a busboy from the breakfast room and another who gave out towels by the poolside as they jolted past her. One or two at a time they entered the guardroom and came out with carbines, diverging again with the same swiftness to take their places down the wall that separated the El Dorado grounds from the road and the jungle beyond, disappearing again into the pockets of dark between the ornamented lampposts on top of the wall.

"Get the number-three crew up in the lobby and make sure the big door on the vault is secure," Bob said into the mike before he tossed the slender black cube into the guard's hands again. He was already revving the jeep motor when he ordered, "Stay here, Karen," saw that she would not and took the longer, roundabout road toward the golf course.

"You're organized like a fort," she said. She felt an unexpected, somehow horrifying gaiety at being swept into whatever was happening, a mindless commitment transforming her as the busboys and menials had been transformed into a small army by the sheer momentum of running to their posts.

"Lot of jewels in the safe," he called back against the rush of black wind.

But then she saw the first of the other police vans parked or still arriving along the highway. She counted five—she may have counted short—before Bob swung into the gate by the golf course and they saw half a dozen more parked or abandoned hastily around a dark sedan.

"It's an army," she said.

"You don't understand this country," he said shortly.

Bob hobbled straight to the sedan. The overhead light was on above the back seat. A dark man with a heavy mustache was talking into the mike in the back of the seat. At first this was the only vehicle to show a light except for those on Bob's jeep. But presently the back door of an ambulance was swung open, and by the light coming from inside it she watched a loaded stretcher and what appeared to be a weapon passed in.

It was only minutes before Bob came back to her. While she waited she saw one last, off-schedule flurry of fireworks down in front of the El Dorado compound. She counted to three before the sound of the explosions reached her. She remembered Bob's anxiety in the afternoon at the prospect of the fat writer's being shot, so her tone was grave when she said, on his return, "Is he dead?"

"Not the one we saw them loading. There's one dead, yes, but this fellow isn't seriously hurt. They think there's another one wounded out in the grove. Some of them may have got across the highway back into the mountains. Or into the water. They've radioed for patrol boats from Manzanillo."

"It was a trap, wasn't it?"

"A stupid one. Stupid all around. I don't know what they were up to. If they'd let us know in advance . . ." He left it to her to understand that the festivities of the night should have been called off.

They had to wait in the lane while the ambulance with the dead man and the wounded one swung around and drove away before them. Then, from the direction of the highway, another pair of headlights approached.

It was a taxi that turned out to contain Tino Grünherz. When two burly police approached from one side of the cab, Tino tried to scramble out the other door. Bob got there in time to prevent such foolishness. He pushed Tino back in and slammed the door tight to keep him safe.

"Please," Tino said. "It can be explained. I have no money. I can get money." He was trying to squeeze himself into a small ball as his eyes held fast to the gleam of a pistol in a policeman's hand.

"Take it easy, young fellow," Bob said. To the police he identified Tino as one of the El Dorado guests. He advised the taxi driver that the other road in from the highway was still open. But by the time the driver had backed and turned, one more vehicle was choking movement in the lane.

It would seem to Bob he recognized the VW bus the way he had recognized it when he first saw it below his balcony—not by color or license plate, but by some sheer incongruity in its appearance in these circumstances, like the intrusion of a living dinosaur into the make-believe of a children's theatrical.

Of course it was Victoria and her friend Bunny. Of course Victoria could only show up in the midst of one kind of carnage or another, he thought. But he still believed then that the unpredictable couple might have checked into the room he had saved for them sometime during the day, and that, like Tino Grünherz, they had been diverted from the fireworks by some other attraction. It crossed his mind that there were drugs available in the city across the bay and that these two as well as Tino might have been directed there by someone on the hotel staff.

As he hobbled toward the VW he saw that Victoria was dressed for the evening party. At least her shoulders were bare above the white top of her dress. Her hair was handsomely swept up into a knot at the top of her head. He still thought of drugs when he saw the ghastly blankness of her face that he would remember when other details of the night were lost. A girl's face empty and fixed as that of a figurehead on an old frigate . . .

"I told you we'd come," she said to him. "We would have been here earlier. . . . What's happened?"

"A little disturbance."

"Accident?"

"No. If you'll go back to the end of the lane, take a right; then the first right and follow it more than a mile to the gate. I'm going back soon. You can wait and follow me."

"We came in this way the other time," she said petulantly.

"I don't think so," Bunny Stewart said. He did not sound high on drugs or anything else. He sounded as if he wished he were. "Turn around, Victoria. Thanks, Mr. Pardon. Back to the highway?"

"I knew those were police vans on the highway. So many," she said. To no one.

"Let's go now," Bunny Stewart said. "We'll find our way, Mr. Pardon."

"What's that?" Victoria squeaked. At the periphery of grass, flower beds and shrubbery lit by the crossed beams of headlights, her eye had caught the passage of a group of uniformed men. These four were carrying a stretcher. There was evidently a body on it, the face covered by a blanket.

"Something awful's happened," she said. "We didn't make it." Her mouth, pale with lipstick, did not tremble. It was fixed slightly open in wonder. In the bad light it could have been an expression of a spoiled child's disappointment.

"Let me drive," Bunny Stewart said. He sounded as rattled as Tino Grünherz had been. There a quick flurry as he changed seats with the girl. He got the VW started promptly but managed to stall the motor twice before he reversed its direction in the lane. "See you at the hotel," he called to Bob with a patently false suggestion that the normal routines still prevailed.

Before they got away, the VW was stopped by yet another squad of armed police, who had just come out of the brush on the golf course onto the lane. Again Bob hobbled to intervene. "Guests of the hotel," he bawled into the face of the corporal. The corporal shook his head. "The daughter of Señor Hoyt," Bob said. "Let them pass, if you please." But this corporal, at least, did not give a damn for the name of Hoyt and would accept Bob's word for nothing until he had checked with the mustache in the sedan. When the corporal was finally satisfied Bob said to Bunny Stewart, "Get up there as fast as you can. Get off the road. You're registered, aren't you? Baggage in your room? Oh, *hell.* Well, get it done before you do anything else. Wait. Tell them to register you at five this afternoon. Tell them I said so. Move!"

But he was still watching their taillights creep meekly back toward the highway when Karen said beside him, "You didn't tell me Hoyt had a daughter here. She looks like she's *still* riding with Pancho Villa."

"Ha! You didn't get a good look behind the beard. Would you believe the guy she's with is her teacher at college?"

"And they're in Mexico on an archaeological dig. Yes. I'll believe anything you tell me. But you have to tell me or I won't know what to believe, will I?"

3

He would assume until morning that Bunny Stewart had followed his precautionary instructions, had been scared enough to do exactly what he was told—particularly if the VW was loaded with hash or mescaline or whatever else had delayed their arrival from across the bay for so many hours.

He would make his way over a number of tissue-paper assumptions for most of the rest of the night.

He ditched Karen in her room with the promise that he would get back to her before he talked to any of the other reporters about the fracas on the golf course. He would knock at her door before he slept. But in the meantime he had to make sure that none of the other news hounds went poking around where they might get shot. That the army of busboys and janitors did not start firing at approaching headlights or low-flying helicopters. That the jewels in the manager's safe had not been heisted under cover of a feinted attack. That Cooley Hoyt did not blow a blood vessel or get hold of a gun himself to join in the rumpus.

He needn't have worried about Cooley's joining the shooting—though he found Cooley had been on the phone and was summoning Riordan to come up from Cuernavaca this very night, bringing whatever guns he could lay his hands on.

Cooley was on the phone a good deal for the rest of the night —for already the story was spreading among the news people, and those of the guests and staff who realized anything special had happened, that the terrorists had been after Ortiz Rosio. It was the sort of story whose truth builds like a snowdrift or a sandbar forming underwater, one drifting grain at a time.

Nevertheless, in these times and circumstances, it seemed more probable than any other explanation. Seizing on it, Cooley was also seized by the realization that now Ortiz—his great good friend—was unlikely ever to set foot on the beach here. And all at once it had become an important setback for him.

He was on the phone for hours, trying here and there on both sides of the Atlantic to piece together some notion of Rosio's present whereabouts. "I got to get ahold of him. Tell him all's secure here. Nothing to be afraid of. Hell, this *proves* how well we got it under control."

Between dissuading Cooley from his telephone counterattack and soothing police and journalists, Bob endured the night and even, at its end, kept his promise of getting back to Karen. But it was nearly five o'clock before he tapped on her door.

She gave him a drink, badly needed by then. Before it made him sleepy, she let him know that she had been on the phone as well.

"They seem to know something about this in New York already."

"Big news?" He was skeptical of that. He saw that she had

picked up something—directly or indirectly—that she was reluctant to spill to him.

"Of course not. No, it isn't big big."

"Only people without names got shot."

"It would have been bigger if they'd actually hit Rosio," she said with a sad laugh that partly apologized for the ruthlessness of her profession.

"Nick Sanders told you the gang came for Rosio? They know that in New York already?"

"Wasn't that the point of the shooting?" she asked uneasily.

"It *seems* to be. I'm the only one on the premises who doesn't have a theory. Except I think most of the guests don't know anything but fireworks went off."

"I woke Nick," she said. "In case I haven't indicated it before, he's a real bastard."

"It's good to be loyal to them that pay us."

"No. Listen." He saw she had decided to tell him what was bothering her. Or, more likely, part of it. Censorship and self-censorship are always matters of degree. She said, "That bastard Nick knew it was coming up. Now I'm pretty sure that's why I was really sent down here with my crew. I mean, someone told him—it must have been weeks, at least several days ago—that they would try to hit Rosio here."

"They?"

"Oh, I certainly wasn't told who *they* are. But you've got to believe that Nick is wired into some high-level international politics. That's the way it is now."

So here, at the end of the night, he had a glimpse of the monster—not a dragon, not a demon, but the terrific tangle of almost passionless disorder that rises when it is too easy to send voices instantaneously from climate to climate and from one power to another that has to pretend to understand.

He felt an artery throbbing painfully in his temple as he visualized the magnitude of confusion made possible by the ingenuity of those who imagined or said they were spreading light.

"Well, piss on the electronic kingdom," he said wearily.

"I'm not happy about it. I've been tricked, too," she said. "Bob, really, if I'd known I'd've told you. Surely there would have been some way to head off the bloodshed."

"Not if Nick Sanders needs it for his television show. Wait. I know that's not fair. He only knew about it, you say. I guess you have to blame those who take the guns in their hands."

"Does no good to blame anyone."

"And that's what we've come to!" he said, with his last bitter rebellion against the absurdity of this night. "No one to blame. No one. Just *it*. The Tower of Babel we've erected, and which we serve."

She had been troubled and this break in his façade of patience and coolness troubled her more. She came across the room to kiss his forehead.

"Okay, old man. I guess we do need someone to blame to make it human again. But that can wait until tomorrow. Can't you sleep now? I've got some dandy pills I'd be glad to share. . . ."

"Generous," he said. "I don't need pills."

"What?"

"Ah. That's what I've never known. Religion? No. Trust in my fellow man? Now that is what I'd like to have, and times come when it is very hard."

In his own room at last he meant to crawl into bed and sleep. He was sick about the killings of the evening, but there was nothing he could do now.

He only sat in his easy chair to tug his shoes off. Yet he had fallen asleep there before he could summon energy for that enormous task.

So when the phone rang he was sitting upright, and it was within his reach. Through his glass doors he could see the sun was rising.

"Who?" he said groggily. "Victoria? Oh, yes."

Through the kaleidoscope of waking images he remembered she was calling from that phone booth across the bay from which El Dorado looked so gay and arrogant in the noonday sun.

"You old motherfucker," she said. "You old crippled motherfucker. You got some of our people last night. You old murderer. Don't you think you're through with us! We'll be back. And you

tell that pig Hoyt we're going to take everything he's got and
. . . and . . . and . . . You'll see!"

The mixture of childish tantrum and grim, unlimited menace
was too incongruous to draw any kind of response from him at
all. It paralyzed the emotions, so that for as long as he held the
phone he could feel neither pity nor outrage at what she seemed
to be telling him. And she seemed to be saying she belonged
with the men who had made the attack.

He did not mind being cursed. What he minded was not being
able to pity her for the irretrievable isolation into which she had
cast herself, as if all her cunning had been concentrated in making herself venomous to those who might have caught and held
her before she was utterly lost.

Worst of all, he minded the silence after the phone went dead.
He put the instrument back in its cradle with a numb, cautious
hand, as if it had become a fragile glass vial of high explosive.

"Goddammit *all*," he said. Then he was on his feet. He forgot
he was tired—being only aware of a dull anger at the wide, inco-
herent spaces separating those who were born to know and care
for each other.

VI

1

"Nor can I fathom why the child should call you instead of her father," Charlotte said. She was wearing her oversized sunglasses against the tropical morning light, the glasses tinted so that the colors projected on the fine skin of her face were like those coming through stained glass onto chapel statuary.

She poured them all more coffee from the massive silver pot. She was breakfasting with Cooley and Bob on the high patio in front of the Monarch Suite. Of the three, she was the only one who had got a reasonable night's sleep. The Lord knew what time Cooley had come rolling in. Bob had nicked himself shaving and his eyes were pink.

"I fail to see any sense in the whole thing," she said.

"Because no one knows where it all begins or what's the boundary of it," Bob said. Beyond that inevitable mystification, no one was telling all he knew. Or, like him, they were shading and editing their reports. He had stopped well short of suggesting Victoria might have come to help the raiding party.

"Victoria and I made friends—I thought we did—when she and her young man dropped in before," he said.

"People trust Bob," Cooley said. He offered this now almost as an apology. A few minutes before, he had been lashing out because no one had told him his child was anywhere but safe in college in Cambridge, Massachusetts.

"I might've been told she was invited at all," Charlotte said. There were ruffling accusations enough to go around, if it came to that. Nothing to be gained from them, she felt. "It would've been sweet if she could've come with her friend and had the best of it. Last night went off so well. Ever so many people told me what a wonderful day it had been, and they love the spirit of it all."

"What's she doing driving around Mexico with a *man?*" Cooley said in torment. "I never thought her mother would allow *that.*" He was going to find someone to blame for his betrayals if he had to range all the way back to the hypocritical prudishness of the woman who had been his wife. Yes, there were those who cried "Shame" at him, and all the while, secretly, they were conspiring at depravities he did not allow himself to think of.

"Don't be righteous," Charlotte said. "Your girl's not an infant now."

"Not a tramp, either," Cooley groaned. "Not a . . ." He could find no other word he even wanted to pronounce against her. But his disappointment was great, though he was far from knowing all the truth.

"She's doing what she thinks is right," Bob said, with no assurance except what he was making up on the spot. "What else can any of us do? I liked the young man she was with."

"You were going to let them shack up? Both *in one room* here?"

"Quit it," Charlotte said. "He was if they wanted to. It's the times we live in and we must make the best of them. Now she's disappeared again."

She was trying to commiserate with Cooley and at the same time keep him from lunging to extremes. She had got a good sleep while he was uselessly phoning half around the world. She had not known until Bob came this morning that there had been an attack.

But Cooley was too raw to be checked. Suddenly he bellowed, "Why should I give a shit about Victoria? Hell with her." He saw a hummingbird among the flowers on the wall behind Bob and threw a papaya at it, savagely, with intent to maim. It paid no attention to him. "Burn this crummy place down to the ground! Pity those jokers didn't get in and blow us up. Tell the sailors to come ashore and drink up what's left. Rape the bitches!"

During the night a destroyer of the Mexican Navy had come up from the base at Manzanillo. From where they sat they had a full view of it, circling dead slow beyond the motionless elegance of the *Evita*. In fact, it had brought marines to comb the offshore islands for the escaped terrorists while the police went the other way into the jungle. But its presence seemed to satisfy Cooley's grim inner visions of wrath and wholesale carnage. "Rape the bitches!" he said again, as if pronouncing sentence on any or all women.

"If it's rape you need you might come home at nights instead of wasting all on the foolish telephone. You learned nothing," she chided him mildly. "Buck up, man. Our party is going better than we could have hoped. Nothing like it, ever, they all was saying to me last night."

She knew the mood and mentality of their guests. She was sure the little fracas on the golf course need not interrupt the orgiastic idyll they had begun. Page Fentress had already phoned to say they must incorporate the destroyer in a pageant of a sea battle. "I'll lead an assault of para-kites against their guns. We'll have a kamikaze charge of para-kites!"

Anything could be accommodated if you gave it the right tone. Anything.

So she was nibbling her roll and enjoying the rich brew of her coffee when Jovan yoo-hooed from the lane below. Jovan climbed to join them up a circular stairway walled with flowering vines. Against such a backdrop she looked as glamorous as ever, but she had come with worries.

"There's a dreadful rumor about this morning," she said, addressing herself of course to Charlotte, as if men were of no help in crisis.

"And all quite true," Charlotte said airily. "We were besieged. That's it, isn't it?"

Jovan nodded. "And Tino Grünherz killed. Or at least fired on."

"Not true," Bob said.

"Who'd waste a shot on the wee thing?" Charlotte chuckled. "No one and nothing was killed, darling. See the Navy?" She pointed out to the destroyer. "We're overprotected and Page is already panting to go ravish 'im a sailor. We were just laughing at all the stir there was."

Bob cleared his throat. "Two of the attackers were killed."

"Poor devils," Charlotte put in hastily. "I meant, none of ours was even menaced."

"Barbara Noailles has the story," Jovan said. "The Countess is very upset about Tino. Barbara said as a fact they'd be leaving this morning. She told me they would fly Tino's body back to Munich, but . . . Still, Barbara means to take her people to Acapulco this afternoon."

"I'll handle it. Never mind," Charlotte said. "Barbara'll never go to Acapulco if Marichen and Elizabeth go with us to the island this morning. You'll ask them, love?"

"I'll get them," Jovan promised.

"Mind, the boats will be leaving right on schedule. Everything's going as planned," Charlotte said.

"Barbara is telling the *Women's Wear* person that John Halvorsen won't be back," Jovan went on, ticking the points that needed to be covered.

"Big John's got himself trouble in Los Angeles," Cooley put in with a triumphant snarl. "One of his girls OD'd in his mansion and the press is investigating his 'harem.'" His spree of international phoning in the night had yielded at least this much incidental good news. "They'll sandpaper him down. You tell the *Women's Wear* chick that Noisy Barbara sucks lemons."

"You mind the police and I'll mind the women," Charlotte said. "I can handle Barbara. And must get myself dressed now. Your thong suit, Jovan?"

Of course not. "Everyone's copied it now. I saw one of the press in something like it yesterday."

Whatever turmoils were still building in his mind Cooley was not going to expose any of them in front of Jovan. "Go on and have your fun like nothing has happened. Bob and I will have the police off our backs by evening and we'll get shed of that damned gunboat, too. Just keep 'em all laughing. We can't afford to have anyone start running out on us."

Charlotte knelt astride his legs and burrowed under his beard to kiss his neck. "It's you who needs the fun. Let's take him off to the island, Jovan."

"How I'd go for that!" he boomed. "My day will come! No, but I'll see you tonight. I brought you something from Rome I haven't had a chance to give you yet."

Charlotte squinted charmingly. "Tell me what it is or I shan't sleep all the afternoon."

"Guess," he commanded.

"Oh-oh," she said, turning to their henchmen with the leer of a burlesque queen. She trusted them to do their duty as she would do hers. Her show of bawdy and brainless good cheer was offered as a pledge that the team could count on her.

"Get old Escobar's wife, too," she instructed Jovan. "We'll keep them all happy."

The day was high and blue and fair. It was a lovely stage on which, once again, the make-believe of success and happiness could be acted out. If they acted it well enough, all the mysteries and threats of the night would, surely, be proved untrue.

2

A string of offshore islands lay in a gentle half circle six miles seaward from El Dorado. In the summer they were often invisible from the mainland, but in this perfect and seasonable weather even the tiniest one could be seen from the hotel balconies without field glasses.

The middle-sized one—less than five acres altogether at high tide—was called Los Colombes. It had a perfect miniature mountain in the center, complete with waterfalls that ran for a few hours at least after heavy rains. The tiny mountain showed a few colorful rock faces. The palms and thickets at its foot gave shade to more than a dozen exquisite coves, the best of them opening back toward the beaches of El Dorado. The tawny beach that girdled the island was barely path-wide when the tide came in, and in storms the waves from the Pacific sometimes dashed all the way across among the palm trunks. At low tide the shallows could be waded half a mile back into the bay. There was a stone reef that fish loved. Rumor had it that one of the last saddleback tortoises from the Galápagos had been spotted by this reef since construction began on the resort buildings, but Charlotte had never glimpsed anything that exotic.

They had developed Los Colombes to be the ultimate retreat beyond the extravagant threshold on the mainland. There were no obviously modern structures here. A few cone-shaped shelters of bamboo and elegant thatching were scattered where the land rose toward the foot of the little mountain. The chocolate color of the thatch looked like the work of a chic *modiste*, and in fact all the island had now a feminine grace and smartness. "Calypso's isle," Page Fentress called it. He adored it, though none of the styling and decor was his.

Two of the larger thatched shelters had been fitted as bathhouses. Another one was equipped with a bar and coin-operated gambling devices and pinball games of 1930 vintage. There was a big brass pan of nickels and dimes laid out for the players.

A buffet had been set up near the bar. Three small pigs were roasting on a spit. The table was rainbowed with native fruit and a long display of iced seafood.

Few showed much interest in the pinball machines. They were here to explore the well-groomed paths and rough overlooks. Among the anchored flotilla of launches and catamarans swimmers went snorkeling or scuba diving along the reef. Beyond them the shabby destroyer idled back and forth, giving the sad sailors a tantalizing glimpse of paradise.

Charlotte herself had been totally truthful when she said she was coming out here to sleep. It was her great talent for battle to be able to drop out of the midst of tension, sleeping while Cooley wound himself tight as a banjo string. Many insiders of Hoyt International, over the years, had remarked that she and Cooley lived and schemed on an emotional seesaw. In the proxy fight that led on to the contracts for base building in Vietnam (certainly Cooley's most profitable years) she had slept through Tulsa, Oklahoma. She remembered it later only as a hotel suite, "posh but tasteless," with air conditioning suitable for the Sahara.

Riding their emotional seesaw, they were dangerous to anyone who assumed they were splitting apart because they were headed in different directions. Ortiz Rosio had believed that when she joined the party on the *Evita* in Florida.

"Cooley's time is over. Your time with him is up," the old man had said, unzipping to let his limp cock dangle, teasing her gallantly with intimations of how much he could promise if she stooped to stiffen it for him. "You mustn't waste all your youth on a lost cause."

Well, she knew how to give back intimation for intimation. She had stiffened his cock for him—without giving him what he more and more wanted—and he followed the stiff cock like a compass needle leading him right where Cooley had wanted him delivered. Until those bothersome chaps had warned him off in Panama. (She had no doubt now that someone had tipped him assassins were going to strike at him here.)

Too bad it hadn't worked. But she had the satisfaction of knowing she had done her part. For Cooley.

Ah, they were worse than married after these ten years, she thought, worse linked to each other than a couple of murderers who both feared the other might peach on him. Churches didn't make such unions as they had, nor sex neither, for sex was of the body and both she and Cooley could use their bodies like the topmost of a pile of corpses to climb on for what they set their minds to. A fond priest had told her before she was twelve, "Some are called to the Church and some are called to the World, child. Yer not fer the Church whatever yer thoughts may be now or what they've told you."

Had she ever, even then, wished to be a nun? A Mother Superior, more likely. More likely counted the advantages than wished, too, if it came to that.

There had been a time when she was grabbing the ropes that would swing her out of Ireland when she had thought "the World" meant sex. She was very naïve about money and power in those days and evidently almost as naïve about the limits of bodily pleasure. The first rich man who fucked her in Paris could have had her as long as he liked for the sweetness of it, for her delight in the delight she gave him. The Marquis de Noailles. An uncle or so of that bitch Barbara. Like Barbara only in the elegance of his body, conditioned even in his sixties like a prized stallion with irreplaceable bloodlines. Sex with him had been so good, so disciplined to fit with the other elegances he gave her a taste of, she might have followed it like a mirage to the end of her days, far off, through all the downgradings and disappointments of fucking all the others.

Though by the time she took up with Cooley in Zurich she guessed that the main thing the old man had taught her was how to make it as sweet for others as he had shown her it could be. Marquis Jacques was dead in a light-plane crash in Egypt by that time. He had kept her on the most delicate and finespun of tethers in the five years before his death. She saw him at Cannes and Monaco and occasionally at an après-ski in Switzerland, at the Costa Smeralda and Acapulco once each, but she never slept with him again after the first two years, except for the Easter weekend when he summoned her and Jovan to his estate in Normandy. She remembered a walk alone with him over the greening pasture where his colts ran and into an orchard where every apple tree was perfect with bloom. He had let her know on that walk that he was going to die soon—and perhaps the plane crash had been a suicide; she thought that probable; he would not let the treasure of his cherished body cheapen with age, he joked. He had let her know he was well pleased with her. He would leave her no money. Surely she understood what his legacy had been. . . .

From Paris, London, Tel Aviv, New York, Stockholm, he had written her many letters. (She sent him only cables and an occasional present—wine or the odd, rare jewel she could afford.) He had advised her gently and drolly. From all the letters she got no hint at all that he was being fatherly. She thought he was defining the World for her, and repeating with more sophistication what she had heard from the priest she had loved so hopelessly from nine to twelve. Jacques de Noailles knew the People of the World and without cynicism he guided her knowledge of what she could offer them and what she could take.

While she was young, still so young, her offerings would, *bien sûr*, be of the body and its promises and its appearances to a large extent. That was a law of civilization as of nature. The spiritual values of all the civilization that had flowered down from Greece had opened from the beautifully budding flesh of youth.

Had she read Plato? No? Good. She must trust her friend when he passed along to her the distillation of Platonic wisdom or of La France in its magnificent seventeenth century: That culture begins in the body, the gesture, the diet, the physiology. . . . What work and exertion in the service of beauty of many generations was made visible in the beauty of young women! Beauty was never an accident. It was the link between the exertions of the great race and the taste which, then, in its turn furnished a principle for selecting company, place, dress, sexual satisfaction. . . .

While she was young—"while as an artist you are still young," he said wryly—not all the encounters her appearance and dress led to would be delightful. Not all the world was as sweet as the blossoming in Normandy at Eastertide, or as the Irish hayfields where they had ambled once in their first April. And in making her offerings to the world there would be plenty of downright doggishness and ugliness. He had every confidence that she would outlive them without complaint. *"Il est indigne des grands coeurs de répandre le trouble qu'ils ressentent."* He trusted her great heart not to pour out the confusion that, *naturellement*, went with taking on all the people she was fucking at the end of his civilized tether.

"So many," she said, while the scent of apple blossoms and the breeze from the Channel made her grave confessions almost another delight.

No matter. He had taught her a fastidiousness in the midst of lust and grunting that would see her through "the confusions." A fastidiousness that might, in the long run, incorporate doggishness itself into the service of that civilization he was proud to serve as aging *chevalier*.

Besides, a very big gob of the men and women she had fucked since he took her over were People whose company he had recommended to her, either by letter or by obvious personal appreciation. There were jewels in the foreheads of toads, he had taught her, and the fastidious senses focused on the jewels. . . .

And come to think of it, there were not so many toads, either, among the people he had put her on to. It was not as if she ever had an aversion to aging men, or any low American prejudices about color. Or to novelties, either, such as women or combinations, though if her preference were asked she would say of the women that it was far sweeter with the committed dykes than those who were trying it for a fling.

It was all all right in those days before Cooley. All right and a good bit better. The Marquis's legacy of Platonic and seventeenth-century wisdom seemed to go right along with the inspirations that made her chuck poor old Ireland. Different words for a happiness with her body that was familiar before she ever heard them and went on when she forgot the most of them. "I took to it like a duck to the pond," she said to Jacques, explaining to him how far he was from finding her a virgin, virginal as she might have looked at nineteen. "I'll tell you the first time if you must hear, but I'll hide me face to keep from laughing."

When she lay down to sleep, she often pulled the trick of dropping off by summoning that healthy, private laughter.

This afternoon—in a cove that looked like it had been spooned from the shore of Los Colombes with a jolly big ice-cream dipper; with the faithful Jovan sprawled topless beside her, still jabbering and fretting; with Nancy Escobar polishing her monocle as she frowned at the bay and the nuisance of the watchdog destroyer; with Dr. Okeido squatting a little farther off, explaining to Marichen Brenner and Elizabeth Conti why they muss nevah, nevah, nevah soomitt delica tissues da face to massage of machine—naw de troat, no, no; with faithful Gosta and faithful Edo dying for their turn to tell her what had befallen Ari and Werner and Einar and Rico. . . .

Charlotte sniffed the miraculous odors of the afternoon, dusted sand from her elbow and went to sleep.

She was going to have a good one, the sleep she deserved. This fancy little island was her dream beyond the coarser dream of El Dorado and all the cunning or work she had devoted to it these last years.

Feeling the moist warmth of the cove-side sand, she had a sense, a certainty, that she had waited all her life for this afternoon. It was not going to be grabbed from her easily.

Another thing that helped her sleep was believing she deserved it. Cooley was on to most of her tricks and matched them with his own as they rode their seesaw. That was how they loved each other, if you called it love, and why not? Even he did not quite fathom all her dervish turns to get this place completed, to hold him steady among the financial ice floes where his instinct was to skip when any of them threatened to sink under his feet.

It was satisfyingly her own decision that so damned much money had kept being committed to El Dorado.

And what for?

What really for?

Why . . . for this *moment*. The moment she, Charlotte Keefe, from county Cork, could put her merry, conniving head down and say what a great race she'd run while it lasted. She wasn't sure that anyone at all in his right mind would say that El Dorado was a great work of art. Or even this miraculous little island. Which might have been just as sweet a haven if no money at all had been spent to doll it up with the chic thatched huts and paths.

But the dear angels—and maybe even Jacques de Noailles— would call a work of art what she'd made of her own life and Cooley's. And what was money for if not to use just so? A couple of backcountry farmers with not a pot to piss in for beginners had come this far. Let the marking angels drive a stake right in the side of the world and let's see who else could climb so far.

Nothing had to come after a work of art was achieved. Not according to anything she'd ever heard from Jacques de Noailles.

If she'd come all this way with Cooley, she'd *gone* all the way with him as well. From the beginning he'd scared her more than any other man she'd ever put out for. There was a need in him— she still had no name for it, unless she went back to the language of Mother Church, and God forbid—a need like some devil poking up in her trying to fetch out a soul to use for the one he'd lost. Trying to tear the Irish balls off her as if his own big ones were never enough for what he had in mind.

Afraid of him right enough, but sticking with him through times when all she could think was what a crud he was, what a seamy, selfish pig rooting in her like she was the sty for him and that's all. Tender sometimes, careful not to hurt her—and tearing at her some ways like those never had who put their teeth in her clit or banged her with belts and hairbrushes. The body healed.

The clit healed and the belt marks on her good Irish ass had done it no lasting damage.

Where souls were involved there was no healing. You stayed with the damaged ones and kissed them from the damage in yourself. She would never say a word to a person about Cooley's soul, but leave the mumbo jumbo about religion to him, when he saw fit to bring it up. Still, if the union between her and Cooley had nothing to do with souls, it had something to do with those huge, dark, empty places where souls disappeared without a trace when you forgot the Church, or denied it, as she had.

The first week they were together he had terrified her when he told her why he had quit the drink.

He told her he thought he had killed someone by night on a drunken drive from Atlanta to Tallahassee. He had been a salesman then for Southern Utilities and was driving from binge to binge about the Southland of his own country.

He had wakened this night at the steering wheel to find himself turning in at a farmhouse drive. He had stumbled into the parlor of that place in the country and collapsed on the sofa without waking anyone. He believed the farmer and his family must have been asleep upstairs; he never knew. In the first of the predawn light he had roused enough to go into the yard, where his car was sitting with one door blocked by a lilac bush. He remembered the sound of branches scraping the paint as he brought the car to a bucking halt.

Then he saw a human hand clinging to his front bumper, still oozing blood from the shreds of skin and bone at the wrist. He went back in and slept a while longer on the farmer's sofa. Again he roused without a sound to show there was anyone else in the house with him. This time when he went out to his car, the hand was gone.

"I don't know if the dogs had come and got it," he said earnestly.

He got in his car and finished the drive to Tallahassee. When he checked into a motel in Tallahassee, he could make out the dust-caked outline of a hand still printed on the chromium. "So I drank some more. I was drunk in that motel a week," he said. "By the end of the week there were hands hanging all over the room and in the shower. I never touched alcohol again."

She had been young and shocked enough then to respond by saying, "For all you know, every bit of it was hallucination." Later she knew that at least part of his story was a lie. He had not quit drinking for good until three or four years later when he broke up with his wife. By then Charlotte knew him well enough to see it made no difference whether the severed hand was a real one or a hallucination. He had committed some atrocity of the soul for which he could not imagine forgiveness.

She was never sure whether he might have committed such an atrocity on his wife, Mary, or if he thought that the abandonment of their two children was of the same order of importance as the possible manslaughter on the road when he had been drinking. "Mary and I never quarreled," Cooley had said to her in a voice husky with reverence. "It was an ideal marriage. In that way. I married her too young. She didn't know what she wanted yet. She grew up her way and it wasn't mine. She was an intellectual. I married her before she got to college. But we never quarreled."

"Charlotte, Charlotte!" It was her aunt's voice waking her to tell her that her father had been thrown by his mare and the neighbors were bringing him home dead.

It was Jovan Kovacs saying, "Charlotte, you cried out. Bad dream?"

"No dream," Charlotte said, and then tricked herself back to sleep.

But surely Jovan's suggestion, made in a moment when she had not her wits to defend her, brought on a whole series of dreams. One following the other in quick succession.

She dreamed: That she was lying on the sand of this cove beside a stone figure with breasts exactly like Jovan's. There were sounds of living water from the spring that tumbled among the boulders not far from her head. She could smell apple blossoms and hay.

She dreamed: That a child of hers and Cooley's had wakened and was watching her from a crib swathed in yards of dusty lace. The babe watched her with one terrible eye wide open and said, I am hungry. Why didn't you feed me?

She tried to answer that there was no milk in her breasts, but her breasts were gushing.

No, the child said, I can't eat that, it's *pain*.

She dreamed: That whatever had happened last night on the golf course was happening to her right now. She lay in darkness with her arms and legs tightly bound. The fireworks over the bay was a real bombardment by English gunboats. The arching rockets and many-colored flames were looking for her, coming closer. Armed men were closing in.

She dreamed: That there was a huge hummingbird hovering in front of a mass of flowering vines. It disdained the flowers and came straight for the palm of her hand, which she was unable to close. Its beak penetrated her hand and when it was withdrawn her hand was puckered and dead white and shrunk to half its normal size.

This time she recognized Jovan's voice, for the last dream had warned her that she must get her wits about her quickly, quickly.

"Charlotte, the boys have brought us tequila sours. I've taken one for you."

Perhaps, she thought, Jovan had touched the palm of her hand with the cold glass, supposing that her sleep was sham. But she still heard the menacing hum of the bird.

Wouldn't you know? There was a speedboat trailing a pair of water skiers across the blue eyeball of the bay.

"For the Irish," she said with a groggy effort to sound gay. Her fingers closed on the glass Jovan offered. The tequila tasted like the flowers in her dream.

"For the Irish, what?"

"For the Irish, dreams are too easy to explain."

"Want to tell me yours?" Jovan asked. "I'll interpret."

"Nah. You've learned shrink language. You'd tell me money is shit."

"Are you worried about money then? Is that what you dreamed?"

"When did I worry about money?"

"I was frantic this morning, when I first heard of the shooting," Jovan said. "Now it seems fifty years ago. The sun does that. Is Bob Hope coming tomorrow?"

"That's not settled. Have you told folk he was?"

"Certainly," Jovan said. "How about Tiny Fred?"

Charlotte nodded. "But not the Grateful Dead."

"I told no one they were. They were never mentioned to me."

"You can check the guest list with Bob again. It changes every day. And will to the end." The scheduled end of all this carnival was still nine days off. Christ might make his Second Coming here before then, with all the surprising changes. No, that was blasphemous to think, and Charlotte was superstitious about blasphemy. "I wish we could have brought the Shah. Rosio had nothing like the standing, even should his people call him home in their troubles."

"Worry, worry. Wish, wish."

"I'm not. I was dreaming about the ideal marriage," she said as the boy came around again with a fresh tray of sours.

"That's it!" Jovan said. "You and Cooley get married now. That'll stun everyone here. It should make the news wires as well."

"They'd remember Eva Braun."

"What a *vile* thing to say!"

"It's been said to my face," Charlotte said. "I fixed the bitch, to be sure. I have that comfort. Yet, there it is to be said, if the divils want to shit on the man. Some always do."

"You *must* have had a bad dream. Awful," Jovan said. Her eyes were anxious, at least. She cared a great deal for Charlotte, and not just for the sake of what they'd been through together. It was rare that she had to pick up Charlotte's spirits. Charlotte was great for that herself. But who could defend themselves against dreams?

Now searching for a means to help her friend over the blue moment, she said, more solemnly than she often sounded, "You and Coo trust each other. Trust is the ideal marriage. No doubt the reason I've never reproduced is I would never trust a child of mine. Not that I trusted my husbands either, as you know, but with men you know where you are. You can always estimate where you stand, I believe." After Jovan's three marriages, she stood exactly where she wanted with each of her former husbands. "The ideal marriage is not ideal," she summed up now.

Her *mot* pleased Charlotte so much she was still chuckling from it when Page Fentress waded in to them. He had stopped among the group in her cove for a few minutes before she went to sleep. But he was full of energy, as always, and most of the others had been then, as now, nearly as torpid as lizards. She had last glimpsed him ambling away on one of the paths with Helene Brunner and the son of the Bauxite King.

Now he came to them dripping from a swim. Somewhere in the water he had put off his crimson *cache-sexe*.

If anyone in the party deserved to be totally nude it was Page. His splendidly controlled tan was even on his whole stunning body except for the red and white penis and scrotum, vivid against his fig-leaf shape of pubic hair. He was no more self-conscious at their display than at the display of his high jumper's legs. Yet his emergence naked from the deeper water was a bit theatrical, intentionally so. Nancy Escobar fitted her monocle swiftly under her brow and stared agape.

He came to stand among the tequila drinkers, shaking himself like a magnificent dog and showering them with drops. His teeth shone in his bronze face like something he had found by diving along the reef—treasure not quite human. A beauty that ought to belong only to the dreamless flesh pulsing within its armored shell far under the foam of the surf.

His torso, his buttocks and his sex offered indescribable—almost imperceptible—responses to the gazes of the whole group. His merry eyes at last fixed on Jovan, reclining a few feet away.

Gracefully he knelt to her. With the deliberation of a figure in a dream, a faun uncovering a couchant Venus, he lifted the knit shawl from her breasts.

"MAHH-vlsss AHN-MLL!" The breath in his words was theatrical as the sound of leaves in the eucalyptus above their bower, as the lisping of the wavelets.

Jovan smiled, very faintly, stonily. She made no move besides to stop or encourage him. She did not tremble at the caress of the sliding fabric of her shawl as he swooped it behind him in the twirl of a bullfighter's cape.

He put his lips reverently to the nipple of her left breast. It was a kiss of adoration. A pilgrim's homage to a statue in a shrine at the far side of a desert.

The touch of art needed to set a signature on this island of dreams.

Perfection.

3

Charlotte would remember the perfection of that tableau when she became the withered, tough old woman she had every intention of becoming. She would remember it as something done *for* her—but also as something done *by* her.

For an instant she had seen with her own living eyes an image of that living beauty Jacques de Noailles had promised her she *could* see—at a price.

And as she was dressing in the Monarch Suite for cocktails and dinner toward eight o'clock that evening, she told herself, a little tipsily, that she would never have seen it if she had not fallen into dreams on that island, bad as they were. . . .

From the bidet and shower she came into the dressing room and still half in a trance began selecting clothes. Tonight under her Givenchy gown she knew she must wear a proper foundation garment. Since her hips were in such good shape and only her breasts and midriff required the tiniest disciplining, it was proper to choose a chemise-top bra and corselet combination with fluffy ribbons dangling to buckles for her stockings.

Cooley loved all types of corseting, whether she needed them or not, and she had him lightly in mind as she fastened the snaps behind her back and saw her good legs prance below the reflection of fluffy lavender silk in the mirrors around her. Legs as good as Page's, she thought.

She heard the door open and close in the bedroom beyond. Surely it was the hairdresser come to set her hair. The girl was a bit late, but she didn't mind. The masseuses and hairdressers were being run ragged here, and Nancy Escobar, for one, needed Maria's attentions far worse than she. She put on only a robe over the foundation garment before she slipped into the bedroom.

It was Cooley she had heard. He had stashed his golf bag

against the antique prie-dieu and was slumped, sweaty and red-faced, in a yellow chair. His beard was tucked pathetically against his chest under his bowed head.

"You've come from playing with Pérez?" she asked as soothingly as she could.

"With Burton Tilly."

"Ah. Y'had a good talk with him? Or no time for it?"

"He's as gutless as the rest!" Cooley got his head up, but it was plainly an impulse of anger that gave him strength to raise it.

"I'm sorry. You mean . . ."

She thought Cooley's eyes must have been bright red, but they were so nearly closed she only could be sure of their rage.

"The fart is quitting. He's 'got a pittance tucked away.' We're dropping ass first into a depression! The old guy's going to hole up somewhere in the Caribbean and write a book. He's pulling out of business. I wanted to ask him . . ." Cooley's hands jabbed at the corners of the universe, angrily pointing out all the possibilities for corporate maneuver which he had meant to ask the Englishman to share with him. "He's got his island all picked out."

But Cooley's disturbance was too great for her to believe that any disappointment with Tilly had generated it. It was not just Tilly who was putting him on.

"Is it Victoria?" she guessed. "Is there any more word of her?"

"No," he said. "No. But I've been trying all the damn day to figure what she's up to. If she'd called me instead of Bob . . . If I could have heard her voice, maybe I could understand."

The hairdresser knocked then and Charlotte sent her away. After her day of satisfaction, out of the fatalistic peace it had brought her, Charlotte wanted to pay her debts to the restless anguish in him that could not find a voice.

He seemed to understand her concern, at least, and to appreciate her giving him the opening to spill his secret thoughts in private.

"Now there's no point in any of this," he said.

"Of what?"

"This place. This party. All these bastards swilling it up."

Slowly and rather coolly she said, "Don't spoil it by saying too much. Just because you're tired. Go have your shower and we'll have a lovely evening. There may be some bastards about, but there are those who care about us."

He was not warned by her coolness. He had started to say what was in his heart and the rest of it came out recklessly. "There's no point in it if she can't see what I've done."

"You were singing a different tune this morning."

"It's that damn man who's got hold of her. I don't know what they've done to her."

Charlotte had given him the chance to fish his real bitterness out of the depths—to speak—and he had gone too far. Suddenly they both knew it.

"Well," she said. "There's things I can help and things I cannot. If you're bound to be maudlin about the child, I can understand. But for heaven's sake there's nothing I can see to be done. So let's be on with it. There'll be people waiting."

She rose then to finish her dressing. "I must say her behavior suggests she's one of them on drugs, as so many are. Americans. Perhaps we'll know one day." She intended to put a little spite in her suggestion. Enough to shock him back into the role he must go on playing.

Abruptly she shucked off her robe. In the angled mirrors on the walls she saw her sleek legs and his bagging, sweated slacks. She saw the dark flash of her bush of pubic hair as she crossed to find underwear and stockings from the drawers.

So did he. He grabbed her in the middle of the room. He called her name with a painful groan as he hugged her, rasping her neck with his beard. She felt his hand seeking in her crotch. "God, I need it," he moaned.

In that first onrush she felt the crudeness of his need. Not of her. Of *it*, the mere relief, the mere distraction from his pain. And the crudeness sent a flame through her, a coursing rush of need that matched his strangely. But it frightened her as well. He wanted *it*. He wanted her to be whore to that ugly, despairing necessity. And if she yielded, neither of them would have the strength to put on again the appearances that protected them from all those others they had assembled around them. Her body was not unwilling. Her body wanted to go down straight onto the floor, pulling him into her and giving him release, and it seemed she was again sacrificing her body and its need for his sake when she struggled and pushed him away.

"Am I the only son of a bitch in this place can't get a decent screw?" he bawled.

What had been a mixture of pity, shock and shameless desire swept without a pause into anger. She hit him with all her strength. The hard heel of her hand connected with his temple. It rocked him back without quite dislodging the grip of his arm around her shoulders.

"Sorry," he said quietly. But then she felt him tremble with a new spasm of resentment and rebellion. With a snarl he said, "Hope they can't smell my sweat on you."

She hit him again for that, just as hard as before. "Shower and get dressed," she told him savagely. "If you've got any balls you'll walk out among them with me and let them see who you are. You'd knuckle under to them before me."

He let her roll back in the angle of his arm. He was staring at her as if in new-found admiration. As if she had caught him just in time and kept him from sliding down into the quicksands of truth.

She was ready before him and went to stand outside, leaning over the railing to absorb the sounds, the smells and the lights of the place beginning to purr the promises of the evening's gaiety and glamour. Lights artfully concealed amid the shrubbery of the walks and lanes gave a unity to this little world they had created out of the salvage of a brawling, imperfect universe. Being here at this hour, she felt, was like being on the inside of a jewel, where all the paths and stairways were refashioned from the common light outside, and the men and women she could see moving here and there below her in their exquisite clothes were just as miraculously transformed as the stones they glided over and the walls that marked the boundaries of this perfected place.

Yet it was as if amid the smell of flowers her nostrils held the stink of Cooley's trouble, like the smell of his sweat but not to be washed away so easily. And from beyond the rising music and the musical merriment of voices scattering unintelligible words into the evening air, she thought she heard the silence of the ocean. It was one vast complaint of emptiness, like the voice of the baby in her dream that had rebuked her for denying its hunger.

Then Cooley came out to join her. He looked elegant and imperial. His broad, strong face with its jutting beard was the mask of a conqueror, a king made generous by his triumphs, fit to sit at the head of the table and dispense bounties of food and drink to his subjects. Sure as she might be of her own appearance and charm, she had sometimes envied him the quickness and ease with which he could assume the role demanded by this occasion or that.

But then, just before they took their stately walk to join the party in the main dining room, he snapped his fingers and ran back into the suite.

He came out with the necklace he had brought her from Rome. Then and there he fastened it around her throat.

She wished she had not understood so perfectly what this gesture at this moment meant. It was an appeal of utter beggary, a pleading far more shameless than his crude clutch at her body.

The touch of the stones on her throat made her shudder. They were terribly cold, unnaturally cold in the mellow warmth of all that surrounded her in the twilight. She thought if she looked down at them she would see a necklace of tiny, amputated hands like those he had seen in a drunken hallucination.

Nevertheless, she gave him a quick kiss to thank him. She would wear whatever he hung on her. She was a woman who kept her bargains.

VII

All day the damn sun had been in the wrong place. Sneaking up on him. The part of Cooley that couldn't be fooled knew that. The part he had to use for thinking was fooled and baffled by damn near everything he saw and heard.

The sun was not merely farther west than it should have been at any given hour; it kept slithering around to pounce out at him from behind the top of a palm tree or bother his eyes with a reflection from the bay or fresh-water pools bounced at an angle impossible for either the time of day or the time of year.

The sun, like a big cat, was going to take him in its own sweet time. He knew that, just as he knew—as he had known since he first learned of the attack last night—that the shadowy gunmen on the golf course had been coming for him.

Rosio? What would they want him for? That could be explained. Hell, explanations were flying around like a swarm of bees. But Cooley knew what guilts he was wanted for, what injuries he would have to pay for when they got him. He might not yet be willing to say them even to himself, but in the part of him that couldn't be fooled the sums of guilt were already added up.

Once in the late morning he had said ominously to Bob Pardon, "Chickens coming home to roost."

No. Neither chicken nor vulture. The rush and roar over their heads was a DC-9 coming in to land at the airstrip, approaching low over the bay and making the voluptuous palm leaves tremble as it passed three hundred feet above the central building of the El Dorado compound.

They had learned before lunchtime where Rosio was. Safe in New York and resting, the captain of the *Evita* said. Messages flickered on the airwaves and telephone lines. All of them needing translation; all of them producing ten riddles for every answer they gave.

"Scared off," said Cooley. Before Captain Da Costa brought word about where Rosio was holed up, he had clung to his notion that "in a day or two" Rosio would arrive to be dazzled by the charms of this lotusland. But Da Costa understood from his employer that soon he would fly back to Paris, even more remote from both the charms and the dangers of Latin America.

"Very few will be," Bob said. The DC-9 was bringing in the party of Canadians who were in dead earnest about putting high-rise condominiums on the lovely coast just north of here. In the baggage compartment they brought a scale model of the structures they proposed. It would, by evening, be installed in the main lobby, while the Canadians were installed around the pool with fruity iced drinks in their hands.

"If I could only have got them face to face with Ortiz," Cooley lamented. "Play them off against each other. Get that prick Halvorsen in for the wild card in the deal. . . ."

But while he talked in the old way about the arrangements he might have made, his head ached with the dismal mystery of his daughter's whereabouts. The sun cast a sharp black shadow of his gesturing arm against a tall ceramic urn, the shadow moving where it had no right to be.

"I've been with the press people. We're under control in that quarter," Bob said. "Only Karen Steiglitz wants to know when you and Charlotte are going to have a block of time for her. I told her not today. You better be thinking what you're going to say about Governor Hogben in front of the cameras."

"I'll give her a peek up his rectum!"

"Yes. And you and I will have to have a late lunch with Lieutenant Encerros. The concern there is that since the President is coming Friday we want no question about security."

"If the President of Mexico isn't afraid to be here . . . I can't understand Rosio chickening out. He could have sat here safe—at my table—and . . . no one was touched. Why is he up in cold New York?"

"There are a lot of questions we'll never have the answer for. That's nothing new. Anyway, I think it's a good idea to show the lieutenant we appreciate his gallant defense."

"We'll butter him up. He's not going to ask any questions, is he? It's pretty cut and dried those goons meant to hold Rosio for ransom. . . ."

"Nothing is cut and dried. I'm sure he'll have questions. Our move is to listen carefully."

"I'm a good listener. Listen for what?"

"I won't know until I hear it," Bob said, sounding a touch irritable. "What I'm afraid of is I won't know it *when* I hear it."

Out on the bay a random wave caught the absolute radiance of the sun and flashed it into Cooley's throbbing eyes. It looked like the white blast from the muzzle of a cannon.

"I wish he could tell me where that damn kid of mine has gone," he said.

The thing Cooley resented most about Lieutenant Encerros was the importance he had been given by last night's fracas down on the golf course. There you were with cops. Cops of any kind. They fattened, they swelled like bullfrogs at mating time when you let them in on your troubles. Better to handle all your affairs by six-gun law. . . . That was one of the few things Cooley had learned from his father, and he did not need Bob's caution to listen instead of volunteering either information or giveaway questions to the lieutenant. The thing to do was give him good food and drink and then figure afterward what *he* had unintentionally given away.

Encerros's skin was pure Indian. It was close to the color of the holster under his dark-blue jacket. His mustache and the bridge of cartilage in his nose were like his badges of authority, the old Spanish ruthlessness showing through the pudginess of his Indian face. Obsidian eyes looked out from a nearly feminine fringe of eyelashes. His long hair curled at his collar line.

His table manners were studied. He broke his roll with a minimum of shattering—a man who didn't care to make crumbs. His napkin was often at his lips—a man who didn't want you studying the expression of his mouth when he spoke. He smiled a good deal, but his smile was very slow to break and very faint.

They were eating outside on a balcony, and as he chewed Encerros mostly looked down from under the green-and-ivory-striped awning as if his main concern might be the handsome, hardly clothed figures of guests drowsing in the palm shadows around the pool. As if he knew how much they owed him and was basking in this sense of his importance.

It was clear from the moment they shook hands and sat down at the lunch table that he was not going to push. No. His questioning had been directed elsewhere. But he had some new information to share; if they wished to cooperate with him in interpreting it, that would please him.

"It is this morning we have searched the *Evita*," he said, "with the fine assistance of Captain Da Costa." He implied that the captain understood so well the gravity of the situation.

"There's no doubt the raiding party was after Rosio?" Bob asked.

Lieutenant Encerros allowed his lids to close over his black eyes. When he raised them again, he said, "Very little." He broke a roll with much care not to shatter its crust and buttered its tip.

"Now none," he said. "On the *Evita*, in one of the storage lockers we have discovered a container full of explosives. Yes! A metal can which is labeled that it contains wax. Wax for the furniture and the interior decks."

"Wow," Cooley said.

Yes, he might well say "Wow." For it could not have been put aboard since the *Evita* came here. Perhaps it had been placed there in Miami or even in Barcelona before the yacht began its westward cruise. At any rate, it suggested, if it did not make clear, that the plotters had "international connections." He himself, Lieutenant Encerros, had fortunately received information that the raiders would come from the sea, but he had received no information that they were more than locals or displaced people from Rosio's country. "They might have taken him and other hostages and demanded the release of political prisoners. They might have got to the airstrip and taken a plane to Cuba. That we knew. It is why we took also precautions at the airstrip."

"You did a splendid job," Cooley said in organ tones. Sunlight flashed on his knife as he moved it to carve the meat on his plate. "If there are international connections, you can't blame Rosio for scampering home, can you, Bob?"

"We do not understand the explosive on board the *Evita*," Lieutenant Encerros said. "It is in an ordinary can such as might contain wax. How will it be exploded? This is not a matter for me to answer. I only have to report to the federal government in Mexico City."

"You've done such a great job I think the President can feel perfectly safe coming here," Cooley said. "Perfectly safe."

"If he comes he will be safe. There will be federal security assessment. No doubt troops. Already there are security people with your staff." Encerros, if he was not a modest man, was a man who concerned himself with the tasks appropriate to his level of command—not looking above except for instructions or the appropriate praise due a man who took care of his assigned responsibilities.

"Just before I joined you I am informed of this—a detonator of Cuban manufacture was found by the highway this morning. A truck driver has found it. After his report, agents were sent to examine the area. Here and there along the highway they have found two grenades and a revolver."

"On the highway to Guadalajara?" Bob asked. "I'm surprised you didn't have a roadblock on it last night."

The lieutenant looked pained. At least he blinked again, holding his heavy lids closed longer than before. With his eyes closed he must have realized he did not need to justify his strategy to them.

"In case the vehicle was of the staff or even of some among your guests, I would like my men to make inquiries. To check your records. To see if any of the guests have parted in the night."

"I don't think you have to question guests," Cooley protested.

Bob said, "Of course you can check the records. It oughtn't be too hard to ask in the staff to see if anyone is missing."

"Good," Lieutenant Encerros said. "My concern has been to alarm none of your guests, Señor Hoyt. No, no, no. It should not be necessary. It would be well to know who has gone. After all, there was traffic on the road. Not much at that hour."

"We'll cooperate to the hilt," Cooley promised him. "I want to get this cleared up and cleaned up. You think some international connection was bringing the detonator here to blow up that stuff on the *Evita*? Imagine that, Bob! All that explosive hidden all this time. Charlotte could have been killed. Good God, I wouldn't want to be in Rosio's shoes if they want him that bad. . . ."

That was his response in front of Encerros. Later he asked Bob fretfully, "Did you hear what you expected?"

Bob puffed his cheeks, nodded miserably. "Part of it."

"What? You know it could be anybody after him. The CIA. Why not? And they could have detonated that stuff from a submarine."

"It could have been anybody . . . and maybe it was you they were after—are after—instead of Rosio. What you've got to worry about is Victoria. And that when she called she said they'd be back. For you."

"Aw, now. Aw!"

Cooley's refusal to believe had some touching dignity to it and Bob hated to disintegrate it further. Yet he went on firmly. "First of all I reasoned that her call came from Guadalajara or somewhere near there. Now Encerros tells us about the stuff dumped along the road. The detonator of Cuban make. Your girl and her friend must have chucked it."

"Aw, she didn't say they were . . . she was . . . after me? What for? Me?"

"But I don't *think* we have to worry about that threat. Not from her. For the fun of it, I checked flights out of Guadalajara this morning, the ones heading for the States. Victoria and this man Stewart are on board a flight to Los Angeles. With any luck she should be safe home in a couple of hours and whatever she's been into I guess she'll have sense enough not to do it again."

"That's completely wrong," Cooley said. "She wouldn't . . ."

He stopped in bafflement, realizing he knew nothing at all about what his daughter had been up to for three quarters of her young life. "You're making all this up," he said.

"I hope so."

Aspirin helped temporarily. So did the shower he took before he joined Burton Tilly on the golf course. So did his notion that Tilly and he might team up on something profitable now that Rosio's appearance had become indefinite. In Rome, George Seip had not only regaled him with reminiscences of the way Tilly had torn chunks out of Bernie Cornfeld's disintegrating Fund of Funds before Vesco grabbed the lion's share but followed this with drooling envy for Tilly's present ventures in Abu Dhabi. So Cooley was smelling like a rose and whistling Dixie when he and Tilly rode out onto the exuberant greenery of the golf course. The surrey fringe on top of the cart was waving gaily over their heads as they bumped lazily along through the mellow air.

But then first he had to listen to Tilly's emphatic assertions that he was through with finance. Absolutely! Had seen the handwriting on the wall. "You and I, Hoyt, were creatures of a unique and freak historical situation. Must read more history, my boy." Then the wrinkled old Englishman had followed up with incomprehensible and pompous reflections on how he meant to end his days writing meditations on the Psalms. "I've found myself a wee speck of a Caribbean island, a house with a view—no mod cons, but I shall endure it—but I shall dwell with my books, making a book as Sir Francis says one should."

When Cooley interrupted these reveries to mention George Seip, Tilly laughed in his face. "Stop!" he bellowed jovially. "I know all about Seip's UMD. The rogue approached me in Rome hardly more than a fortnight ago. Literally begging me on bended knee to intervene, however temporarily, to prevent the attachment of some utterly dubious holdings in metal. I say, you haven't put your foot in his quagmire, have you?"

"No," Cooley said, feeling the aspirin fail him with unnatural suddenness.

"For if you have, you're jolly well asking for trouble."

It was just about that time that Cooley—feeling threatened by sunstroke and seasickness from the swaying of the golf cart—spotted four people walking more or less parallel to them, though sixty yards off in the direction of the coconut grove bordering the planned landscape. Before he recognized them, Cooley thought they might be reporters. One of the men and one of the women had cameras and camera bags slung over their shoulders.

This was the area where the men had been shot last night. He had been told this, though he had seen no point in coming down to inspect it himself. But it would be like idiot reporters to come tramp the turf after the shooting just so they could say they had been there. Damn, he hated them and the falsity they spread from the facts they fed on.

He recognized one of the men as his bodyguard Riordan. He remembered then that in his marathon phoning last night he had called the idiot to come up from Cuernavaca. Then he had had some notion of answering bullets with bullets, and Riordan at least must understand how to do that.

With Riordan, Cooley recognized Helmut and Inge Suwe. Both of them had cameras. Wouldn't they, though? Show a Kraut a scene where blood had been shed and he would want to go take a picture of it.

The lithe girl, tagging along behind them on her beautiful girlish legs, was the one he'd met on the beach all alone. Riordan seemed to have attached himself to her.

And would probably make out. Shove the muscle to her because women always were ready to put it out for a man with no troubles on his mind.

It was sheer moral revulsion that made Cooley snatch a golf ball from the container and rifle it at the sightseeing foursome as the cart trundled past them.

If he was aiming at anything specific, it was at Riordan's innocent grin.

These irritations had served to distract him for a while from thinking about Bob's unacceptable suggestions about Victoria—the impossible theory Bob had put together. He didn't have to believe it yet. So he would not. Nevertheless, when he left the golf course he hurried in search of Bob.

He found him at the bar that curved its thatched roof around a bit of the main pool. He was with a group of cool, relaxed gentlemen who seemed to be the Canadian delegation. Bob made an attempt to introduce them, but Cooley waved it awkwardly—no doubt offensively—away. Ignoring them, he blurted, "Any word?"

"They're on the ground," Bob said, and the Canadians pricked up their ears at this cryptic signal, as if wary it might have something to do with their mission.

"On the ground," Cooley said—and felt some grisly stiffness inside himself let go. His grin must have convinced the Canadians that Bob's coded signal meant that the contract of the century had been agreed to.

"Great!" he shouted. He threw back his head as if to laugh in the face of the sun.

And at the moment of purging relief when he thought that his child was safe, the sun flashed blindingly in his eyes.

Because it struck him then that she was safe *from him*. She was safe *back there*. In that other country he had given up for this. It struck him then that there had never been a chance for things to add up otherwise.

It was to find escape from that melancholy that he had set on Charlotte. And she had not failed him. Bless her. When she hit him in the head he had welcomed the blows. Once again she had done the right thing at the right time for him.

She could hit hard. There was a jingling in his head—like the happy tumble of a few coins from a pinball machine after he had pumped dollar after dollar into it.

VIII

"Ah ahm combahn da sculptah widda sujjun," Dr. Okeido announced with his usual quiet immodesty.

"That's good," Cooley said.

"Wow," said Jill Hatch—whose boyish figure needed the help of neither a sculptor nor a surgeon.

At dinner in the main dining room, Cooley was seated royally between them at the head of the table. Presiding over a roomful of lovely and talented people. People on top.

Dr. Semura Okeido had whittled tiny slices from some of the world's most celebrated women and sewed them up again with exquisite stitches. With his merry Japanese eyes he studied your face and your earlobes to see how much could be whittled off to achieve his sculptural ideal. And how much you might be willing to pay for it.

Jill, of course, was a lot easier to talk to. Between Okeido's infrequent oracular pronouncements she was entertaining Cooley with comment on the art and economics of her trade. In her next film she would play a woman who walked out on her dull husband, a "money man," and then "bunked around" with rock musicians who helped her begin her musical career, a career that largely paralleled the career of Jill Hatch. "Except I never married anyone."

"Wohman ess lakh tahrtle," Dr. Okeido said with a suggestive laugh.

Like a pool player who calculates the lie of each ball after every shot, Jill had estimated her image and bankability after this film was released. She talked as impersonally about herself as Cooley might have talked to the Canadians about the prospects of land development. He strained to memorize some pointers that might be useful. He always tried to learn from top people.

"Wohman ess lakh tahrtle. On der bahk put'm. Mahny tahrtles heah."

"Right," Cooley said.

"I go to them and say I want this much front money. I want approval of the story and I want approval of the group that backs me up. I want approval of . . ."

Then the waiter whispered in Cooley's ear. Lieutenant Encerros wanted to see him in the manager's office.

It would have been smoother, it would have been more in keeping with the behavior of top people, if Cooley had sent back word that he was occupied at the moment. But he was already on his feet before he remembered this.

"Right on!" he said to Jill Hatch. He gave a smile of confident complicity to Dr. Okeido and hurried out. Around him, as he went grinning and bowing among the tables lit by wavering candlelight, the violinists were playing the music of heartbreak. Always helpful to the appetite and the digestion.

He saw Charlotte turn with a questioning look and he gave her a cheerful wink.

Wind yourself up to deal with clever people—people smarter than you are—and you're an easy mark for the stupid.

Encerros!

Or if he wasn't stupid, suppose he was just worn out by a long day spent among people whose ways and language he neither appreciated nor found informative. Whatever it was, at the day's end he was left with only a sullen spite.

He was in shirt sleeves when Cooley arrived. The composite picture of the cop kept after hours and yearning to sweep the last untidiness under the rug so he could head for home. Against his sweated pale-blue shirt his shoulder holster and snub-nosed revolver looked somehow like the eye patch of a blind man, strapped diagonally across a wan face. His long hair shone greasily in the lamplight.

He thanked Señor Cooley for having come to him. There was one matter of some delicacy on which he wished a consultation. He understood—ah, very well—the annoyance it might be if he were to interrogate the guests. Even those who arrived on the *Evita*. He had tried to spare them out of courtesy.

By now, he said, it was almost a matter of the cut and dried that the assassination attempt on Señor Rosio had been political. At first, on the basis of information available to him, he had considered that the attack might have the objective of taking the rich man and holding him for ransom. "Though they are said to be a political group, there are Communists who hope for gain, no?" He had even to consider that there might be personal motives of someone who might have enlisted the bandits to accomplish his revenge. "A crime of passion, no?"

No, it was almost perfectly clear that the condition of politics in Señor Rosio's country and in the world must explain what had happened. Did the inexplicable detail of the explosives not point to a worldwide conspiracy? Not very effective, in his opinion. The Communists were not so clever as they were reputed to be. In any case, the political ramifications were not his responsibility. He would turn the matter over to the federals for investigation of what was international. They might be in a position to investigate Barcelona, which was full of radicals. Like Guadalajara, from which many troubles came. Like Mexico City. Like all big cities.

Yes, Lieutenant Encerros was winding up his part in the disgusting matter. However, there remained one question that had arisen from the interrogation of the crew. On it, perhaps, Señor Hoyt had an opinion.

"Señorita Keefe. She joined the party of the yacht in Miami, yes?"

"Sort of at the last minute that was arranged. Not the last minute, you see, but . . ."

"Why?"

"That's a little hard to explain," Cooley said. "To be with her friends. Miss Keefe moves around a lot. Here. There. She has more invitations than she can keep up with."

Stolidly, with only the faintest note of disgust in his voice, Encerros said, "One of the crewmen has told us she is often in the
cabin of Señor Rosio. Much."

He did not seem motivated to say more than this, to press it to
a conclusion or weak accusation. For all the emphasis he gave it,
he might have been proffering it as mere gossip.

He said, "Respecting your wishes, I did not ask Miss Keefe of
this matter."

The shape of the accusation was there—listless, profitless, torpid as a reptile on a hot rock. The dumb bastard thinks I did it
because I'm jealous, Cooley thought. That she flew to Miami for
a rendezvous with her lover that I was conspiring to get rid of.
No. Encerros had no such belief. Yet it fitted the *macho* notions
they equip all cops with when they give them their badges and
guns. Near the end of cleaning up the inconvenient odds and
ends scattered out by last night's sputtering sensation, the lieutenant had come on a piece of dogshit and had lured Cooley to
step in it.

"Well," Cooley said with a reassuring laugh. "It's a matter of
life style. You know. Cosmopolitan people. You know. *Grown-
ups.*"

"Life style." It was as good an answer as any. Meaningless.
But the sullen, resentful Indian eyes had been set to note how
the master of all this elegance and dissolute life style would
twitch when his foot hit the stuff and began to skid in its slippery nastiness.

Get used to stepping in dogshit that the jokers plant for you
and you learn to handle it without any twitch at all. You feel one
foot slide so quick and far there's not a chance in the world you
can stay upright, but all they see is how you keep on walking as
if the *firma* was the same *terra* they kept their brogans on. They
hear your good-natured and tolerant laugh. "Hey. That's a good
one. Look, you ought to follow this up. I sure appreciate your
feelings not wanting to ask Miss Keefe about this kind of thing.
But with her life style she's not going to be embarrassed. I know
you've got to report, and I've found in the business world it's
damned important to look ahead and scan *all* the possibilities. A
little thing that most people would ignore, some *outside* chance

of an explanation anyone else would laugh at. By God, that's what you have to watch out for. Every time it'll be the thing that makes you say 'nonsense' that turns out to be *the* answer to the whole thing. Look, when do you want to talk to Miss Keefe? I can send for her right now. You'll want to wrap this up. You've done a damn fine job so far, and you can question her tonight. Or maybe you ought to question everybody that was on board the *Evita*. You could call Rosio, too. We can reach him in New York. Did you know he was there? I'm just as eager as you are to get to the bottom of this."

Lieutenant Encerros blinked. He said he appreciated Señor Hoyt's views. He saw no need to speak with the lady at this point in time. Her obligations as hostess he fully appreciated.

He ran his hand through his hair before he offered it limply for Cooley to shake.

Cooley left him, thinking—shaping the thought once only before he flung it savagely from his mind: Maybe it wasn't dogshit I stepped in. Maybe it was my own. Whichever it was, he was moving too fast now to hit the ground when his feet went out from under him.

2

There were many more or less separate parties going on to-night. Cooley headed for Page Fentress's suite, expecting to catch up with Charlotte there. Page had wangled himself the biggest suite on the premises next to the Monarch Suite.

It was tucked high on the rock slope, near the high wall that paralleled the beach. You had to climb the last part of the way on a zigzag stone stairway. As Cooley went puffing up the stairs, the odors of jasmine and night-blooming hibiscus overpowered the other smells in his nostrils. He trusted his nose. When the brain got baffled he fell back on what his nose told him. As he came out on the level of the patio, his sense of smell was distinguishing more and more separate smells of promise, the way many instruments can be distinguished in an orchestra when the brass ceases to dominate. Again for a while he would be distracted from what he had smelled with Encerros.

The first thing that caught his eye was Page Fentress himself. No one ever missed Page. The crazy fag was wearing a big, loose white . . . *dress*. The garment which fell to his sandaled feet was embroidered with a heavy masculine pattern of dark browns and blacks. The ruff of the collar looked like what men used to wear in the old paintings. An antique detail done in an ultramodern way. That was Page.

And what Page had set out on his patio as the focal point for people to look at and move around was a Moroccan shoeshine stand. That's right. It must have cost him all of thirty dollars and the air freight must have been nearly fifty times as much and he would probably sell it to someone here with a hundred percent markup. There were a lot of people clustered up to admire the damn thing—like people crowding up to an altar. Maybe you were supposed to offer up a shoe to some god that nobody had heard of before.

Cooley looked past it for Charlotte. The sliding doors of the living room were open to the night. The interior space was continuous with the tiled space outdoors. The inside was more brightly lit, but he could not get a glimpse of Charlotte inside or out.

He smelled a very youthful perfume and his eyes came to rest on a pair of fine satin buttocks. They locked on the buttocks with rage. He was sure he would have handled Encerros better if Charlotte had helped him get his nuts off, one style or another. Everyone here looked like they had been fucking before they arrived, and they smelled like they had done it to each other with flowers.

"Ooooo! Now I know you! You have tried to keel us."

The girl with the blithe buttocks had turned. It was Maette Mornay, slithering to him and grabbing the sleeve of his jacket.

"Naaaah," he said. He wouldn't kill her on a bet. The thing to do with such stuff was put her on Page's shoeshine stand and polish her off.

"Yezz!" she insisted. "On ze golf course. Under ze palmetto. You sleeng a golf ball at Helmut, dear Inge and me. Only zen am I told your name. Herr Hoyt. Remember? We were on ze beach yesterday morning and I do not know you are heem."

"I slung it for a joke," Cooley said.

She shook her head deliberately, smilingly, stupidly, her left hand still clinging to the goods as she swung on his white sleeve. "I have seen ze hate in your eyes."

"That far away?"

"Eet ees true ze ball have not reach us. Eet rolls to our feet. *Sérieusement,* I have seen hate. Ooooo! Now I see eet again!"

She might have. For he remembered she had been with Riordan, and Riordan looked happier out there in the green field than he had any right to be. I'm the only son of a bitch in this place that can't get screwed. Riordan would screw a snake if someone held its head. Probably so would this one if what they said about her was true. If not in broad daylight on the golf course, she would get to Riordan in some broom closet.

She was tugging his arm and he went with her. "Come. You muzz come in to see Page's Rothko," she enticed.

The featureless red painting reminded him what a Rothko was. He'd once had some money in a bunch of Rothkos that were being hidden out in a Casablanca warehouse to keep them from the heirs of the painter. A fast deal on which he'd come out all right. He could legitimately brag to Page that he'd once owned several Rothkos.

He was bragging of that very thing to dear Inge Suwe when Maette surprised him by bringing him a drink.

"I theenk you like zis, Herr Hoyt," the girl said mischievously. She offered the drink with a curious, spine-curling bow that seemed to offer everything. "Eet calls itself margarita."

"I don't dreenk," he said. His accidental mimicking of her accent seemed to put him at a disadvantage before Inge Suwe. Her laughter was downright scornful.

"Herr Hoyt is not old enough," she said.

He took the cold glass in his hand. He closed his eyes on the chance that such women could read the hatred in them at any range and even in poor light.

"*Mister* Hoyt," he said, trying to sound gaily mocking.

Inge Suwe was not German, she was Danish. She was not fat, she was richly endowed with flesh. Whatever the other women here were wearing, she was plainly wearing a corset, and it did marvelous things for her. It supplemented the authority of her sex, and she knew how to belittle any man with that authority.

"Herr Hoyt is a *pure* man," she explained to Maette. Her Danish eyes were as pale as an acetylene flame. "He is not a man to tempt. He will throw golf balls at you. Helmut would not come to dinner or here, Herr Hoyt. His feelings are hurt—his *feelings*—that you should throw the golf ball."

"I apologize," Cooley said. "I thought old Helmut knew how fond of him I am. Did I really throw it hard? I saw you, and . . . it was a way of saying hello."

"Yes," she said, refusing his apology with the peremptory syllable. The odor of her perfumed flesh within its corseting chastised him.

He drank from the glass because his mouth was so dry. She did not notice.

"Yes," she said, "if we were doing something against the rules, a word would have been sufficient."

"Honey, there're no rules here," he boomed.

"Explain to me so I may explain to Helmut what we have done wrong, please."

"Ha ha ha. Anything goes. Do any nutty thing. Far from the maddening crowd."

"If I could explain to him, he might leave his room again. Tomorrow. He will not pack if I explain to him," Inge insisted. She took Cooley's left hand and gave it an urgent squeeze. Her hand was soft, wet and deep, but its strength sent shudders up his arm. He saw the adoration in Maette's stupid eyes as he drained his glass.

He could not get away from them. The two of them were still pressing him ferociously when Charlotte came, though by this time Inge had worked out a formula for forgiving his rudeness on the golf course. She was explaining that Helmut, who had been too young for World War II, passioned himself on visiting its battlefields. North Africa was his great hunting ground. They had retraced every movement of Rommel's troops from Libya to El Alamein and back, taking many souvenirs and photos.

Charlotte was upset. She hardly smiled at Inge before dragging Cooley among an overgrowth of palm fronds at the corner of the patio to have a word with him. She did not look at Maette Mornay at all.

"Coo, I didn't realize for a while you'd gone to see the police chief. What did he want at such an hour, for heaven's sake? Is it word of Victoria? I've been at the suite and the offices waiting to catch you, and . . . ah, love, you've been drinking?"

He had had only one and it had sobered him.

His eyes burned on her steadily as if he had not seen her clearly for a very long time. She understood it was a glare of rebuke, but she would not admit she knew what for.

Steadily, in a low and perfectly controlled voice he said, "I told you once. I tell you again. Every prick here gets taken care of but me. Go to the suite and strip off and lay down and spread it out. I'll be there . . . when I'm ready. Warm it up for me. You know how."

He saw the fury shake her. Her eyes narrowed and opened again as if she had not heard—could not, would not believe she had heard him.

"Was it about Victoria the police had word? Tell me if she's all right, then go wallow in your drink for all I care. *Get your hand off me.*"

"Ssssshhhh!"

"I'll *sssssshhhh.* Asshole."

His fingers scraped slowly across his forehead, as if confirming with solid evidence that his skull was perfectly intact. He knew what was inside it was intact, perfect, clear. Sure, he could feel the drink. It had cleared out some cobwebs that had been gathering there—ah, all his life.

"I don't care if they hear us, and if you don't . . ."

"Why should I? Turd!"

"Fuck Rosio all the way through the Canal, and when I want it . . ."

"Shout your filth for all to hear," she dared him. Her passion had not raised her voice above a whisper still, but now she called, "Page! Page, darling, come here and listen to this, will ya?"

Again she whispered to Cooley, "You tell the man, since I don't know at all what you're saying. Page!"

The beautiful man came to them through the crowd of his guests. Some of them, of course, had heard the wild tone of her summoning him and turned to stare a moment to see what hilarity now was afoot.

Page circled each of their shoulders with his bare, braceleted arms. There was a honeyed smell from his skin. "My sweet ones," he crooned. "And shor if ye'll name it, me storeen baun, ye'll hae it on the instant. Command me, Titania, Queen . . . !"

But he knew there was bad trouble. He had heard it in her shout, seen it in her fateful posture, the broken, skew expression on her face. "Anything," he offered them in a discreet, compassionate voice.

"Cooley'd like a word with you," Charlotte said. "Tell him your great discovery. Speak, man."

"Beloved!" Page chided her. "Give the man a chance. Shall we take a walk, all three? If you'll give me a second to speak to someone we can all three go out on the water, if you like. To the end of the night. Was it not lovely on our island today, Char?"

"Stay with your party," Cooley said. "I have nothing to say to you. Stay with your boy. I hear you threatened to cornhole Tino before he gets away from here. Countess say you could?"

Charlotte made a sound of retching. Suddenly her fine-boned cheeks were awash with tears. She freed herself from Page's arm laid on her shoulder. She patted his chest fondly. "Thank you, Page. Come on, Cooley. We'll go to our place. Nighty night. It's home to bed for us, Page. Thank you, thank you."

It was unthinkable that she and Cooley should touch each other as they walked in fierce silence down stone stairways, up and around the cobbled lanes amid the gaily painted walls toward the Monarch Suite. When they were inside, Charlotte still had not uttered a sound. She flung her light mauve scarf down on the tile floor beside a shaggy rug, but gave no other outward sign of anger.

She sat, half huddled, in a tall-backed chair that she and Page had found together last year in Venice. So smart. So comfortable. Even the smell of the wood came through its outward varnishing like a reassurance from courtly times.

Her face was dry now. There was a kind of feverish zone of red across where the tears had been beneath her eyes. Her bare arms hung to a point of contact across her lap. A tendril of her hair had fallen loose and tickled her nose. She blew at it twice as if unable to raise a hand and brush the tickling away.

At last she said, " 'Spread it out. Keep it warm.' I knew it would come to this."

She counted on pity and love to break him. He loved her with all the ghastly cold in his heart. He pitied her from the baffled ocean of pity that had often come near drowning him in his dealings with women. He was too terrified to break.

"Then what've ye heard?" she burst out, fury spreading the red from under her eyes all down over her cheeks. "Don't you know that people like these will say anything? Was it that Inge? Why not? It could have been anyone. Did someone say I spread for Rosio? On the yacht? Speak, man. Ye've a tongue of your own, have ye not?"

"Lieutenant Encerros. . . ."

"Ah, the policeman was there dangling over the side to the portholes or kneeling at the keyhole. I wondered what the sounds were in the passage! I thought it was more than mice, but the man would niver get off me to see. . . . The police gave the story to Cooley Hoyt, the great thinker, and he thought . . ."

"*I'm* asking you."

"Asking me what?"

"It's a simple question."

"And a simple answer ye'll have. Yes. We was at it in Panama when the Coast Guard came alongside to take him away. There. Ye're happy now."

"You . . ."

"Don't call me names now, mind! Ye wanted the facts, ye deserve the facts. Tit for tat and a fair trade, for we're partners, yis we are. No secrets! None! Here, I'll get me a pencil and write down all the names for you."

She scurried into the bedroom, her skirts swishing stiffly as she skipped, and came back with stationery and a gold pencil. Now she went to the writing table by the massive drapes that hid the glass doors.

He saw her scribble swiftly. He did not count the number of times she moved the pencil down the page to add to the list. He saw her pause and rub the side of her nose with the little golden shaft.

"Lotty," he said.

"Don't interrupt me," she commanded gravely. "I'm thinking, for I must be totally honest in keeping my books. Or how will the poor accountants know what they've been dealing with, hey?"

"You don't have to . . ."

"I have to. I was commanded to. Tell the whole truth, he siz."

He saw her quickly make two additions to her list.

"It's all in the way of business," she called. "My business with Hoyt International. Or should you like the names before as well?"

"Quit it," he said levelly, oh, very soberly.

She heard him moving toward her as if he meant to take her pencil. She spun swiftly in her chair and pointed it at him like a dagger of gold. "Touch me and I'll put it through your eye," she said.

He turned on his heel and went out into the flower-smelling night.

He went back to Page's party and abducted Maette Mornay from under Inge's vicious blue eyes.

She wasn't hard to abduct. She was pliant and floppy as a wet mop. All he had to wait for was a moment when Inge wasn't watching.

He led the girl through lanes and terraces and galleries of dark and bright flowers, through aphrodisiac shadows and glamorous blossoms of light on stucco arches.

He was soaring high on an uprush of sweet flames in the belly and an angry sense that he was doing justice to everyone who had meant to cheat him.

He closed the door of a small bedroom behind them.

His stiffly clawing fingers were on her buttocks and his furious thumbs were prying her legs apart while the sound of the door latch was still in their ears.

Yet when he had her clothes off and she was spread wide on the bed and he was growling on all fours above her, he was not ready to perform. He didn't want to.

It was Charlotte he wanted, and this knowledge angered him further.

"Lie there!" he snarled. "I'll get me a drink. Don't move! I'm going to fix you, bitch!"

"Feex?" she piped dreamily. She only moved with the limp, wavering undulations of pale seaweed in a warm tide while he stood beside her, glowering and draining three little bottles of gin snatched from the well-stocked refrigerator.

"Fix! Fix! Fix!" he shouted as the heat mounted in his stomach and loins. He shoved her back with a forearm under her chin when she writhed around to approach his loins with open mouth. "I don't need any help."

And then he proved he needed no help at all. He did not need the help of her legs entwining him like seaweed to sink and drown and rear and plunge like a reborn sea lion as he fixed her and fixed her and fixed everything wrong with his goddamn world. . . .

When the sun rose for him the next morning, it rose over a flickering fringe of jungle beside a highway that seemed to go on climbing forever as the little car took the curves. He had a bottle of gin—a big one—between his knees. The girl was driving. It seemed they meant to go somewhere to let him sleep off the gin.

It wouldn't do for him to be seen around El Dorado until he was fully sober again.

There were too many people who would try to take advantage if he slipped.

IX

1

"Where is he?" Bob Pardon said. "He can't just disappear in a puff of smoke. Not even smoke. It's been three days now. Naturally people are speculating. Some of it is pretty silly. He's off in the Mideast. He's been captured by terrorists. He's run off with one of John Halvorsen's pets. Ridiculous stuff. But, dammit, he can't pull this on us. This is the time he ought to be here, reaping the harvest. I've got the Canadians to deal with. I've got to have some decisions. . . ."

"Or here enjoying himself," Charlotte said with a compassionate laugh. "Who else in all the world with such things going on—that he's worked for himself—would not lie back and get some good of it?"

"Whatever the reasons. We need him here."

"No," she said. "We've needed him too much. Wherever he is, I'm content, as long as he is with that fox. And I hope she is fucking him silly. It might be a good way—a good time—for him to die. In the saddle, as they say."

This had been her theme since the first morning after Cooley dropped out of their sight. On that morning Bob saw her more worn and grave than he would have thought possible. He knew her age, but she seldom showed it. The day before she had still been the Irish Kid, mascot and empress of the enterprises. Now she was playing the widow.

"I've run the man too hard. We all have," she said. "You know I woke up praying this time he was gone for good." She had a gold pencil in her hand, gesturing with it as she explained what she knew. It was the gold pencil that Cooley ordinarily wore in his breast pocket and whipped out to initial memos or jot down those random figures that were his most private and serious attempts at bookkeeping.

She rubbed the red mottling on her neck with the pencil and said, "You know, it's for his sake I hope he'll not come back. Down under it all—all he shows—there's always so much grief. And now that Victoria . . . such a worry to him, and now the disappointment. I could shoot her."

"Grief?" He was not denying it. It was only that he did not suppose that going on a binge, running away with a trivial piece of fluff like the one Charlotte described, was Cooley's chance of keeping the grief at bay. It was his private notion that money, the successful maneuvering among financial quicksands, was Cooley's necessary sedative. And now that the investment here was showing symptoms of promise, it seemed weird to him that Cooley would—as he apparently had—sulk away from it.

But he was not going to follow Charlotte into the depths where, he figured, she tried to be just to the impossible man. Like her, he had stuck with Cooley a long time—for reasons beyond any gain he might expect. But with him it was closer to fascination than to the fondness—or why not call it love?—that he attributed to Charlotte. He was, he told himself in times of great aggravation, a bookkeeper at heart. He wanted to stay around until he saw where the bottom line was drawn on Cooley Hoyt.

"Grief then," he said. "And I don't suppose he's told you much more than he's told me what it really comes from. So let him hide out with it and see what he can make of it. We'll get along without him."

"Have you never thought we'd do better without him?"

"Sure." He'd thought that, too. Never expected the day to come when either of them would put it in words. But he saw now, in her speech and the vivid way she kept things moving through these days of festival, that if she was going to be a widow, she was going to be a worthy one.

Cooley was gone. There might have been a hollow place at the center of all this luxury and splendor.

No one noticed it.

Look! At the pretty boats and those bodies, young and old turning to perfect bronze.

Feel! Those bodies warming and yielding to the sun and to each other. To the caress of breezes and spray flung from the painted prows of boats.

Taste! Doesn't it taste expensive!

If there was a vacancy, a hollow at the center of this enchanted frolic, how would you ever guess that as long as the sky was so blue and by night the music went on until dawn?

2

As Bob Pardon admitted, it was not to him or to the angels drawing up legal briefs for the Last Judgment that Cooley Hoyt was likely to make his grand confession. It was to Maette Mornay, who understood little and cared less.

He was in the girl's hands. She was almost as drunk as he when they left El Dorado. Yet she had a better idea than going to sleep off their drunkenness on the beach. Maybe she had some notion that she had snared a prize. She had a man of importance. Maybe he would get her out of her bondage to the Suwes.

At any rate, before the day was over she drove him all the way to Puerto Vallarta. There they rented one of the cottages at a beach hotel. Like many of the hotels on this gracious coast, it was a very charming place when they walked into it.

They turned it into a foul dive before the confession ended. On the cottage floor—at one time, and one time was hard to tell from another—Cooley was lying with his face in a shaggy rug. He stared down the length of his arm to where a giant thumb, probably his, pressed the curve of a barrel-sized glass holding something yellow.

Teeth which were probably the girl's were nibbling his hairy body.

"I sold her," he said. He began to cry again. The sobs plopped out of his mouth like something that might leave a permanent stain on the rug. The girl stopped nibbling long enough to ask, "Who?"

"You know," he said. But she probably thought he meant Charlotte, and Charlotte had said he sold her to that crooked Rosio. And many others, as listed with her pencil. Which was a reversion of the truth and punishable, since he did not care if she fucked Rosio, being grownup and able to consent an adult, and did not necessarily believe her anyhow, since she would say anything to hit him back if he hit her first, which he would admit to having. Done.

He meant Mary. "And the little child," he said. "I both them sold. Li'l Victoria."

"Ees not so good," Maette Mornay said, stretching up from him like the most beautiful alligator he had ever seen naked with such neat little tits, if she would only not try to keep sticking them in his mouth, which got dry even when she put something wet against it.

She took the yellow glass from him. It looked incredibly smaller in her small hand. "You cannot zell womens," she said judiciously. "Once upon a time. No more. No, no!"

"'F you know how," he corrected her solemnly. "I sold them. Greatest salesman. 'M the greatest salesman all time. Greatest."

"Muhammad Ali," she said.

When Cooley began to cry again, it was not so loud as before.

Maette Mornay started to nibble at him again. "Don't theenk about'm," she said.

But he thought. Here, drunk, he remembered it all. . . .

Merle Finch had taken a great shine to Cooley when Cooley worked for him at Southern Utilities. Merle Finch was the father of his best friend at prep school, poor Kerry, who'd never be an athlete like Cooley because of his asthma, Kerry living in Greenwich Village trying to be an artist by the time Cooley moved Mary and the baby to Atlanta.

"You'll like old Merle," Cooley said, the first weekend he drove Mary out to Skelton Duchy, the Finch estate. And on the way back, Sunday evening, Mary had clucked dryly and said, "You told me I'd like Merle. Why?"

"Why'd I tell you?"

"No. Why should I?"

"Why . . . why . . . why . . ." Young Cooley had choked on

his disappointment. He had no selling tricks with Mary. He had honestly thought she was enjoying herself. There'd been university professors and a Utah congressman among the weekend guests. The kind of people she admired. She'd taken a lot of pictures of Victoria in the pony cart Merle had been thoughtful enough to have harnessed for them. He'd given Victoria a Japanese doll in a glass box—an authentic antique—as a parting present.

"I like him for liking you," Mary said.

"That's not the point."

"He was generous with Victoria. In his way."

"What does that mean? In his way?"

"Maybe I just don't like rich people."

"Come on, now. That's a mean thing to say."

"It's not his fault he's rich? All right. I didn't much go for the way he talked about Kerry and Kerry's paintings. 'Little bit queer, aren't they?' 'My son among the Village fags.' I must have heard him say that kind of thing to a dozen people."

"Hell's bells. He's got Kerry's paintings *up*. Even in the big hall. Right with his Rubens and people like that." The fact was that Kerry Finch's paintings made Cooley uneasy, too. Not that they weren't very slickly done. "Magic realism" was the label for them. But all the people in them looked . . . "queer" was the right word for them. It just was.

"Okay, okay, okay," Mary said. "I suppose he's basically shy and therefore defensive about Kerry."

"Maybe he's shy with you, but, boy . . . !" Cooley said. "He's associated with some of the top people in the country, and he takes no crap from any of them."

He was glad to let it go at that. Yet he had been aware from the first that Mary had been ruffled by his older friend, the man placed to do him a lot of good. He thought shrewdly that Mary might be a little jealous of Merle and Merle's influence on him. He planned ways to show her that it wasn't a total influence. He wasn't Merle's yes man under any circumstances, business or private. Merle would have caught on quickly enough to that trick and it would have backfired, damn sure.

"You're a crazy son of a bitch," Merle told him once in his first year off the road and working in the Atlanta office. There'd been a battle royal on the executive staff about whether they were going in on a consolidation plan with Niagara and Florida Edison. Cooley had come up with an alternative for refinancing with a West German chemical combine that was already doing business with Russia, Hungary and Rumania. The upshot was only a winter of wrangling and office intrigue that postponed any decision at all until spring, when Southern Utilities' position had improved enough so the top brass decided they could stand pat for the next two years at least. In that winter there'd been weeks on end when Merle wouldn't speak to Cooley coming or going from staff meetings, but finally he called him in and said, "You're a crazy son of a bitch with the tact of a genuine redneck. We'll never know if you saved us from being eaten or if you ruined the chance of a lifetime. I reread your memos last night. They're hogwash. They're illiterate. But, damn you, Cooley, I think you were on the right track. One other thing. Your ass would have been on the street in January if I'd let Sawyer and Townsend read the memos you dropped on me. They're gentlemen. Don't thank me for that. Just make sure we have a long talk the next time you get a brainstorm. A nice, quiet talk in front of the fire, or preferably in a moving vehicle."

He'd have liked Mary to know that if there was a coolness between her and Merle—and he had to admit finally that there was; Mary's real feelings didn't change noticeably no matter how much they partied at Skelton Duchy; quite often in the second year of Cooley's being with the home office—then there was certainly nothing personal in it.

It went with Merle's life style and the fact that he'd never remarried after his wife's death. He liked women and he claimed to respect them, but certainly not for their brains or character. It was these two things in Mary that made him uneasy with her. He spelled his convictions out to Cooley that year in long talks in front of the fire in his study or in the billiard room.

"Courtesy is what they really want and what they really deserve, Cooley. It disturbs the natural order of things if you consider them as your equals. It took me too long to learn that. It cost me my son."

Heatedly Cooley had said that was just talk. Merle'd be proud of Kerry yet when Kerry was as famous as Rubens.

"My wife made him soft, and I let her," Merle said. "She was quite an intellectual, too, my friend. Kerry's not going to be famous—except eventually as a soft touch for his fag friends. He'll end up running a gallery or publishing a goddamn literary magazine. And it was Daphne's doings. She talked well. She believed in freedom and youth and *creee-ate-if* things. You know, she always hated my Rubens. She said I bought it because it looked like her. It did, too. A luscious woman. But they'd got hold of her mind, the goddamned fags who are running the ahts and the education in this poor pitiful country, and persuaded her that what she had down there wasn't what counted. It was what was *up there*. That's what she bought. She thought I ought to respect her because she'd been to Vassar College with the Yankee girls. God help me, so did I.

"She thought Kerry was going to be a scientist when he wanted a microscope for Christmas and a violinist when he wanted an expensive Stradivarius one year. I said fine, fine, fine. Fine, I said. I went along all the way, Cooley. That's why I'm talking to you this way now."

Cooley, with warming gin in his system, feeling his oats and knowing he must not be a yes man, said derisively, "I appreciate you are, and you're full of shit, sir."

"Why I talk to you at all escapes me," Merle said. "Your ignorance fascinates me. My people were schoolteachers. Never mind. The point is, I never understood until too late that the fags and the perverts had an agent in my own house in that woman. No—I have a right to talk this way, Cooley. You know it's a grief to me that Kerry is up a blind alley. His mother sent him there. You know what I believe? I believe even his asthma was something she talked onto him, confusing what was natural in him. He's a natural businessman like me. Never mind the athletics. We didn't give him the physique for that.

"My point is that it's my own fault for not seeing early enough that my gorgeous bride was just exactly that. She had just enough brains to fool me into thinking her brains counted. Cooley, I have you sized up as a cunt man."

"I've done my licks."

"I thought you had. Now, young fellow, don't make the mis-

takes—I see you making them—with your Mary that I made with
Daphne. You trust her character. Her intelligence."

"The German-Rumanian thing was her idea." Not quite true.
Mary merely believed that trading with the Iron Curtain countries was better than Eisenhower's Cold War. It was Cooley who
had the hunch that it was a frontier for venture capital, a nice
grab if things went right. But when he was with Merle he pic-
tured her in terms Merle would have to respect.

"Now I see it's a good thing we didn't get into it," Merle said
with tolerant irony. "She reads more than you do and talks to
clever people, and you suppose that's all there is to it. You kneel
down to worship her intelligence when the only justification for
that posture is to lick her pussy. Ha! You're blushing, my boy. I
can't believe you've never tried that."

"Don't hanker for it," young Cooley said in a useless denial of
his naïveté, wondering nevertheless what he had missed. "I'm
not prejudiced about it."

Cool in the advantage of his years, Merle chuckled and
claimed the point he had won. "Ha! It's an expression of the
gravest courtesy, young fellow. Makes them feel complete.
Therefore I'm prejudiced in its favor. Trust in technique, young
man, but don't trust their fundamental character. When you find
yourself in awe of their character or brains, it's time to consider
the whip and bridle."

Poor, slow, determined Cooley—he had tried to *convey* the
sense of Merle's declaration to Mary with the undimmed hope of
building understanding between them. He edited out what he
knew would offend her, of course, and ended with his evaluation. "Thing about Merle, he's been hurt by women, I know, and
he feels he went wrong with his wife, the way Kerry's turned
out."

"So he had a luscious, Rubens wife," Mary said. "And he got
his warped ideas about women from living with her. But I'm not
luscious."

This last was an arguable point. Anyway, she was all that
Cooley hoped for in a wife, in spite of some shameful lapses
when he had been on the road and lonely drunk. It was in the
spirit of making sure she was totally provided for that he got

himself intentionally high one night and tried Merle's prescription for the ultimate courtesy.

When she realized what he was up to, she pushed him away with the whispered endearment, "You're too clean for that."

Then Kerry Finch killed himself. There were hints about the reasons and circumstances that Cooley just did not want to follow up. Kerry had been summering in Vermont with an older friend, a poet whose work Mary had admired. The Atlanta newspapers reported Kerry died of asphyxiation. Only the rumors said he had pulled a plastic bag over his head, like some unlucky infant. If there were any suicide notes to the father he had loved, Merle never mentioned them. There was no obligation to assume a man was a fag just because he was an artist.

But Merle, more stubborn in his pride than he had been in Kerry's life, acted as if all the world knew for sure what his son had become. For one thing, he took down all the haunting paintings of Kerry's from his walls. As if now any of his visitors would have the clue as to what they really meant. He still entertained as many friends, politicians and business associates at Skelton Duchy as ever. He still bullied the board of Southern Utilities with his sharp ironies. Those who had feared and respected his "steel-trap mind" found that its jaws still gripped with the same precision. But Cooley, who had an eye for such things—who was born with a knack for reading faces—saw that Merle's smile looked more and more like a fresh saber scar. A slash that had come within a hair of the big arteries.

"I want you and Mary to come live with me at the Duchy," he said eventually to Cooley. "I know that Mary doesn't much care for me."

"She thinks she doesn't much like rich people. She's always enjoyed the university people—journalists and people like that—she meets here. Her only friends in Atlanta are ones she met here. That's the truth."

"I believe she doesn't like rich people!"

"It'd be pretty great for Victoria to live out here. She's the age when she'd like to be a princess. You know, this house, the whole damn estate—especially the barns—that's funny, but especially the barns—have always been just really enchanting to the kid."

Merle had no comment on that.

"Well, hell," Cooley said in a fluster, pushing his voice to the limit of its register of sincerity, "hell, you know how great it would be for me. The dream's always been—what I tell Victoria —and I mean it!—that some goddamn time if I work hard, well—*I can give her a place like the Duchy.* I don't mean with the southern tradition and all, but with this . . . *nobility.*"

He could play tricks with his voice. That, with his knack for reading faces and body signs, was his special asset as a salesman. But this time, maybe, his voice played tricks with him. Hearing himself talk about the nobility he planned for his daughter's future nudged him that extra inch into the real quicksands of sincerity. Over his head. He had named something holy. A vision.

And as soon as he had named it, he saw with stunning and absolute clarity that Merle had a stunning and absolute contempt for this kind of sincerity . . . unless it came coupled with the steel determination to make good on it at any cost. He just didn't give a shit for the feeling.

They were up on a high turret of the mansion at Skelton Duchy when this conversation took place. It was a late-autumn afternoon and the sky had the look of a soot-smudged ceiling in a slum apartment except for a few liquid rivulets of color streaked in the west. There was still a menacing, somber green in the pastures and the bare elms and willows that bordered the fields seemed to huddle over something they were hiding. A wind from the north kept flapping the collar of Cooley's jacket against his jawbone with a regularity that seemed like a code trying to get a message through to him.

He shivered in the wind and nodded his big, handsome head as if he might be sincerely considering Merle's proposition and trying to make his mind up about it. He took a sip from the glass of bourbon he had brought when he and Merle had climbed the antique ladder to get up here.

His mind was already made up. Shit. Might as well say that the wind had made it up for him. He saw the noble mansion and barns of Skelton Duchy, the stone and the heavy beams and the graceful, massive carving of the carriage shelter below them standing indifferent to any wind or winter either. Three floors below there was a carefully groomed wood fire in Merle's study and right now while they were up here one of the servants was in tidying up the ashtrays and positioning the leather chairs in immaculate order.

"That little old girl of mine would really shine if she lived out here in a place like this," he said.

He knew that Merle didn't give a shit if Victoria drove her own pony cart down to the brook, snapping the waxed leather reins and closing her eyes with the proud magic of it. Or scaring the swans up from the pond where the little Greek temple had stood since slavery times. Merle didn't give a shit if here Mary could issue her own invitations to the professors and reporters who seemed to like a background of aristocracy for their cocktail-party meditations on the state of the world.

Merle was just plain testing him to see how much he wanted these things for his women. Testing his salesmanship—maybe only curious to see if he was up to selling Mary on the idea.

There was no use in his trying to con Mary. She knew him by loving him. She might not have his knack for reading the faces of strangers. Hell, her drawback in that department came from expecting them to be as scrupulous in their motives as she was, while he knew something nasty about the simplicity of mankind in general. What he watched for in faces was the yes or no signal of greed when everything was right and the trigger went *click*. Not everyone could see that, and most intelligent people, except Merle, spoiled their chance to catch the all-important signal by too much analysis.

Mary, predictably, hit back hard as soon as he passed along Merle's offer to take them in as "family" at Skelton Duchy.

"You know," she said, with grim sobriety and tired pity in her voice, "it wasn't Kerry's mother that made him gay. Set him on the path. It was Merle, wasn't it?"

"Come on. Come *on*. Don't get into that, Mary. Screw Merle, then. We're all right in this apartment. After Christmas we'll start looking for our own house. Whatever you say. But don't bad-mouth Merle because you don't want to move to the Duchy. The man is hurting. Bad."

"I know he's hurting," she said. "He'll hurt you, too, Cooley. People do that when they hurt."

"That's not fair. Sure, I know how screwed up it all is, and you're going to say he wants to run my life as a replacement for whatever went wrong for Kerry. But he does not want to hurt me."

"I know he doesn't want to hurt you," she said, sounding like a judge pondering over a death sentence. That heavy and grim. "He didn't want to hurt Kerry, either. Or Kerry's mother. Poor Daphne. Now I see what happened to her. Merle just wants to suck your big cock and is too roundabout to admit it."

"Jesus Christ!" he bellowed. He clenched his whole body to calm himself. Levelly and quietly he said, "That's cheap, Mary."

She smiled a little and said, "I'm sorry. It is, isn't it? I've been thinking about Merle an awful lot. Ever since we came here. He's my adversary in your life and it's lousy cheap to simplify that by saying he's hot for your body just because I am."

"Well, Jesus Christ," Cooley said with trembling laughter. "Finally the girl lets me know."

"You'd always have known if you wanted to."

"You mean I'm queer, too?" It was astonishing how calm he could be and how he could chuckle over this little bit of rotten meat that had to be chewed and swallowed—because he had just heard the shutter click and knew he had her. "Come here," he said hoarsely. "I'm going to show you how queer I am for you. Come sit on my manly knee. And then you know what I'm going to do to you?"

She did not stir from her chair, though he kept patting the knee he wanted her to sit on, bearish, boyish and lovable.

"You're going to tongue me," she said. "I suppose that suggestion came from Merle, too. The expert on women."

Cooley got to his feet then. His fists clenched and slowly, deliberately he loosened them. Finger by finger. He had never hit her and he never would. He might have hit a woman. He could be a real shit. But he would not hit Mary.

He began to cry instead. "How goddamn dirty," he said, trying to push the words out distinctly through the sobs. How goddamn dirty, how goddamn dirty, how goddamn dirty. "Your shit-eating intellectual friends know all about how a man feels. To his friends. Goddamn dirty intellectual *shit!*"

"Cooley," she said. "Oh, darling, forget it, please. Please,

please, please. It's not what I think. It's just what I've thought *of*.
It's not easy being married to a man like you. I know you're
bigger than I am. Please, please, please. Please? It was dirty of
me to say those things. Oh, goddamn. We've waked Victoria."

She came across the rug to him, Victoria. Not to her mother.
That was another sign to him that he had won.

She came and grabbed his hand and held it to her cheek.

"Daddy, don't go," the little girl said.

"Goddamn soap opera," Mary said with a broken laugh.
"Daddy's not going anywhere, honey. Mama said some stupid
things. Mama thinks she's so god*damn* smart sometimes. Let me
fix us all a drink. Not you, Victoria. Get back to bed. It's all right
now, honey. All quiet on the Western Front. Bourbon, Coo?"

With his head bowed and teeth chattering, Cooley grunted his
refusal. He stood there in the middle of their rug motionless,
while Mary went with Victoria to her bedroom, said a little
prayer with the child and came back with slow steps. Her voice
still had a tone of prayer in it when she repeated her invitation.
"Drink, Coo?" She took several breaths and controlled herself.
"Will you drink with me, my lord, so we can talk things over? Or
did I spoil everything?"

"Nothing can spoil us. We're going all the way, kid. Look. I
didn't mean a thing I said about you."

"I was the one with the dirty mouth."

"Aw. Forget it. Yeah, we got to talk. But not tonight, huh? I
guess I'd feel better . . . get calmed down . . . so I wouldn't say
anything else I'd regret, if I walked around the block. Maybe
had a drink at Andy's to think about what you said, you know.
Okay?"

"Okay," she said.

How long had it taken him to come home from Andy's
Bullshot Inn?

Six days.

Came back on his own legs, didn't he?

The legs were his, sure enough. Maybe the guts and all the
other working parts inside were replacement parts for what he'd
burned out in his biggest binge so far. He came back feeling
clean, though. Clean from the Turkish bath that had sweated the

last of the booze right out of him. Clean from the bath of dirt and defilement he'd wallowed in to prove Mary wrong, wrong, wrong in some of her accusations. Clean and pure except for a taste in his mouth that scrubbing his teeth would not totally erase. Taste of perfume and soap and the reek of the lion's cage in the zoo, from proving to himself he could eat pussy if he had to.

A party girl who said she was from Toronto, heading south.

Mary had no reproaches for him that afternoon when he let himself into the apartment, smelling for her of talc and shaving lotion and all the other decent odors he could put between them. She did not offer to kiss him, though, and for this he was glad.

"How y'feeling?" she asked. He looked at her face with great tenderness. There was reproach enough in seeing that she seemed to have lost almost as much weight as he had during his absence.

"Pretty shaky," he said in a voice that he did not allow to shake.

She nodded and led him straight to the bedroom and turned down the covers for him, offering her shoulder for support while he got his shoes off. His teeth began to chatter and she shoved him into the bed fully clothed and pulled the quilt up over him.

She brought him soup and spooned it into his mouth when his trembling had subsided enough for him not to slobber it out.

"You'll have the whole weekend to get your strength back," she said. She told him it was Thursday, but he needn't think of going back to the office on Friday. "I've been in touch with Merle," she said. "I told him—thought I'd better—what I supposed you were doing. He agreed we wouldn't get the troopers looking for you. Not until next week anyhow. I've been by the phone. . . ."

"I got your message," Cooley said, grabbing her hand and clinging. "You brought me back from hell, girl. You brought me back."

Her hand was limp in his grasp but she wouldn't meet his eyes. "I've been in touch with Merle. I told him it was very generous of him to ask us to live at the Duchy."

"Forget about that!" Cooley said.

"I told him we'd say yes before he had a chance to change his mind. When you got back I said we'd talk about when to start packing."

Soon after that Victoria came in from playing with the neighbor's boys. She climbed on Cooley's chest and sat astraddle in spite of Mama's protests that Daddy couldn't stand to be fiddled with.

"Did Mama tell you?" she asked. "We're going to live with Mr. Finch at Skeleton Duchy, aren't we?"

"Skelton. Skelton Duchy," Mary said. "Not Skeleton."

"Won't that be nice?" Cooley asked.

"It will be nice in the spring," Victoria said. "And in the summer. Also in the fall."

"In the winter? Won't the winter be nice?" Cooley prompted.

"Best of all," Victoria said. "Daddy, I knew you'd come back."

Cooley had strength enough to wink at her.

"I knew," she chattered to him. "But Mama didn't know you'd *ever* come back."

"I knew," Mary said.

3

How soon after they'd moved in with him had Merle started screwing Mary? Not right away, probably. Probably not earlier than Cooley's trip to Japan that spring. He had never believed that Mary would start it with him right there under the same roof.

And when he'd come back from Japan, proud of the agreements sealed with the handshake of Mr. Kaminoko's son-in-law himself, there'd been nothing at all to signal anything unusual had happened in the gracious rooms or the blooming, May-lovely acres of Skelton Duchy. Mary had put on a little weight and was sporting a handsome tan from being outdoors so much with the child. If anything, she welcomed Cooley back with more tenderness and warmth than he was accustomed to when he returned from his selling trips, even right after they were married. She truly was hot for his body. Always had been. Even more so now. In that department perfect, though their minds weren't always in sync.

She was going to organize a Southern Folk Music Festival.
From time to time during the next months she would be traveling herself, and there would be, from time to time through the
summer, some people in the house that he might find pretty odd.
That was all the real news she had to tell him on his return, and
he had been glad to find how inventively she was adapting to
the new situation that Merle had made possible for them. Country music was better than the ballet. . . .

Victoria was thriving like the flower beds so numerous on the
lawn and along the drives of the Duchy. Pretty as a goddamn
painting. The servants adored her. She was turning them into
slaves, Merle said, her very personal slaves, and if this kept up
he could stop paying them wages. She was turning the Duchy
into a genuine fairyland, Cooley thought, watching her run
down the lofty, vaulted corridors or cross the shiny wax on the
floor of the ballroom. A damn little Scarlett O'Hara, for sure,
bringing the old days back before their very eyes.

If there had been any sign of what was really going on, Cooley
would have expected to snare it from Merle, from Merle's face.
The tone of his voice. His jokes about his Rubens nude. The degree of his satisfaction with what Cooley had pulled off in Japan.

Nothing of that sort.

By now Cooley wasn't really working for Southern Utilities
any more. He was working exclusively for Merle, though he still
drew his salary and his bonuses from SU and his Bigelow was
still on the office floor at the SU home office. Not even the execu-
tives of Kaminoko, Ltd., knew just when Merle was going to
make his break and trade his block of SU stocks for stock and
options in what he called jokingly the "new co-prosperity
sphere" in Southeast Asia.

When he saw what Cooley had brought home in his briefcase,
the market surveys, the projections, the labor statistics and rec-
ord of patents for Kaminoko, Merle said, "If Eisenhower had the
guts of a yellow dog . . . you and I would be on the plane back
to Nagoya tomorrow morning early. The grinning son of a bitch
just never could make up his mind about the Pacific Theater.
We'll have to wait until fall and see how much he's going to let
them kick us around in Diem's bailiwick. You can spend the time

reading up on Uncle Ho, my boy. Now if Ike had *his* guts and brains . . ."

And over their mint juleps Merle had given him a pretty shocking history lesson about American business with the French colonies in Asia going back into the twenties and running through World War II. All with the kind of malicious delight that was his personal tone in talking about the business world. ". . . They amortize plant development in *one year* out there, Cooley. It's the greatest rape since Attila the Hun. Let me list the companies that have owned their production capital clear in that little time. . . ." There were many occasions when Cooley heard him talk in terms that radical professors would have shied at.

But . . . no sign that Mary was any more than, say, a daughter-in-law to him. Nothing then.

Nothing before fall, when some of the major SU stockholders began a suit against Merle to harass his divestiture moves. "They haven't got a case," was his judgment, "but they'll tie me up two, three years unless Judge Appleton sees what they're doing and throws it out this week or next." The situation was touch-and-go for a while. Kaminoko was pressing for at least an initial commitment to their Burmese branch to show the Rubicon had been crossed. Something on paper and something in the bank—or at least a favorable ruling from Judge Appleton to make Merle's proposals credible. Kaminoko's son-in-law was in more or less permanent residence at Skelton Duchy during these times. One crisp fall night while he and Cooley were walking near the Greek temple on the pond, the Jap came very close to proposing that Cooley, too, cut his ties with Merle and join the effort to raise financing elsewhere. "Come up to Washington with me," he said. "On Tuesday. You'll see. Meet my friends."

Cooley got the hint and reported it back to Merle—as maybe he was intended to. It made him feel good to suppose the Jap had sized him up as someone who knew what loyalty meant. Merle knew, too, and said, "Good. I can guess who he's been talking to in Washington. I'll give you five to one on who it is. Maybe you should take him up. I'll tell you frankly this evening I don't know if I'm going to swing it or not. 'When the great

wheel runs downhill, let go your hold.' I thought I'd taught you
that, by now. I'll be a little disappointed if you and your yellow
friend are still here on Tuesday."

"Maybe Kaminoko's only trying to put a fire under you."

"Want to bet on that?"

"I do," Cooley said.

Because he had no sign then that his friend and benefactor
was double-crossing him with his wife.

Or only this—which wouldn't stand up.

A night in late summer when all the bedroom windows were
open since Mary didn't like air conditioning—and he was loving
her up in a nice relaxed way. Fingering her a little to get her
ready, just about ready himself to put the wood to her and coast
along to an ideal mutual orgasm that she set such store by.

He felt the fingers of both her hands rest on his lightly sweating shoulders. At first he thought it was just a caress, a bit of
tickling. She used her hands a lot.

She's pushing, he thought. And he damn near came right then
when he understood the downward pressure on his shoulders
was intentional. When his cheek slid down over her small left
breast, he felt the hard nipple touch his ear like a bony finger.
Never that hard before. He paused to graze a minute with his
lips on the round softness of her abdomen. And to catch his
breath. The palms of her hands curved on his collarbone, not
pushing hard, only telling him something.

His tongue was so dry it seemed glued to his teeth, immova-
ble. It was like tearing it to thrust it forward until it tasted his
sweat on her skin. But then, sighing affirmatively, recognizing
the message received, she withdrew the pressure from his shoulders and folded her hands behind her head.

He was willing to give her now what she had finally asked for.
All too willing. The willingness itself was his glory, his joy, his
shamed fulfillment.

"Aw," she said, echoing his disappointment. Pitying him, trying swiftly to cover for him and make it seem another of the
successes he counted on. "You were too tense," she whispered.
"It's all right. We've got lots of time. Let me help you. I want it.
You know I want it. Let me help. . . ."

It would have been insane to ask where she learned to help him the way she did then. All married women always know; it's only whether they're willing or not.

Judge Appleton found no merit in the briefs filed by the stockholders trying to keep the Finch money wired into SU, where it had been since the thirties. Merle was free to sink his capital in the Asian quagmire if he wanted to. He certainly wanted to. Eisenhower couldn't last forever. Someone would come along who would get the country off dead center. . . .

Merle Finch was happy—and his tongue was as sharp as ever, his view of the world twice as bitter as anyone else's. Once Cooley overheard part of his conversation with a man named Dunker, one of the "yeomen farmers" who managed the livestock and cropland at Skelton Duchy. Dunker was very apologetic in reporting that rats had got into some of the corncribs at a far border of the estate. The stables and other buildings near the mansion were in pretty good order, as far as Dunker could tell, but it shamed him that he'd lost a grip on any part of the land or buildings entrusted to him. He promised Mr. Finch that he wouldn't rest now until he had poisoned enough rats to say he had them under control. "Though ya cain't never git rid'm all. That's why they call'm rats, I guess, ain't it?"

"Mr. Dunker, let them *feed*," Merle said. "In my riper years I see clearly that rats are better than people. It would be very wicked to exterminate those superior beings."

Dunker laughed and winked and slapped his knee. He knew a joke when he heard one. Cooley joined the laughter halfheartedly. He was learning more and more of what Merle's happiness was foundationed on.

Still—they were all happy that fall. The Jap went home happy, with documents signed and sealed in his briefcase. Merle and Cooley shot quail together over some of the best dogs in Georgia. Evenings they listened to banjos and fiddles and twelve-stringed dulcimers around the huge walk-in fireplace of the great hall and drank quite a bit of mulled wine while they swapped stories with the musicians and planned their trip together to Nagoya after Christmas. Mary was right busy with her folk singers and had learned a lot about the techniques of recording them. A pretty little Amish girl had been hired as Victoria's governess, a girl of fine character who didn't mind slapping the child around a bit when she got too smart.

And Christmas Eve in all this baronial splendor. Cooley would never forget the grand, simple beauty of it—just the family and the servants, who came in to join them singing carols in front of the head-high flames in the big fireplace. Drunk on "silent night, holy night," Cooley had said, "Merle, I figure I know you about as well as I am ever going to know another human being. And I figure you're about as hard as a diamond drill. But now, admit it, you don't really think rats are better than people, do you?"

"Did he say that? Did you say that, Merle?" Mary asked.

"I hope you two know me," Merle said, sipping slowly from his glass. "Cooley, tonight—just for tonight—I believe people may have a teeny edge."

"Teeny-weeny?" Victoria piped up.

"Teeny-weeny," Merle said, hugging her. "And no 'Bah, humbug.' Not for tonight, at least." He kissed the child very tenderly on the forehead. Cooley felt the tears begin to wet his cheeks.

In Nagoya they were happy with what they found. Merle had taught him never to make the big trips, the dynamite agreements, without accountants right by your side, day and night. So they had brought four accountants with them, including one who had served in Japan in the days of the Occupation and knew Japanese. Cooley knew the accountants were excited. Really strung up like dogs in heat. You could get the whiff off of them, he told himself, and later was to trust that more than anything. Take an accountant who sees the *possibilities* beginning to show up among the snow mountains of paper and all the adding-machine tapes and it does something to their glands. All these chaps lacked to take the plunge themselves was balls and money. Their glands didn't really include the ones that are supposed to hang between the legs. The glands in them that money excites are more like sweat glands.

But he knew what they'd seen, though he gave up, after two days, even trying to follow the arithmetic. With Merle he was there to size up—one last squint—the big picture. He didn't even

have to trust the arithmetic, or even the faces of the men they
talked with, as long as he was on the scent. And he was on.

"It's going to be a big thing. A hell of a big step," he said to
Merle one night when they were eating alone at an interna-
tional-style restaurant. "Hell with 'going to be.' You've got it in
the bag now. I'll drink to that."

"You'll drink to anything," Merle said touchily. "Nothing is
ever in the bag, young fellow. And I've been thinking it would
be a very good thing if you stayed over here awhile. Stick with
your admirers in the Kaminoko office. Go with them to Seoul and
Rangoon and Saigon. I told you you ought to get to Hanoi while
you can. I'm damn well pleased with the way you've performed,
and you're right if you think this is going to be a big ride. Win,
lose or draw, in the next ten years it's going to be big." He
laughed and dabbed at his mouth with a napkin. "Go West,
young man, and keep on going. That's still the great advice. I'm
too old for it. For the big ride. But if I were you, Cooley . . ."

If I were you . . . Now Cooley saw in the older man's face the
sign he would think he had been waiting for all along. A sort of
naked ghastly envy, surprising in its openness, repulsive in its
hunger. It was like knowing someone else was fumbling around
over your body, trying to find a place to enter it and throw you
out, so he could claim it for himself. He would not have been
more stricken if he had felt Merle's hand on his knee under the
tablecloth, inching up toward his crotch. Merle hadn't wanted a
son to carry on for him. He wanted more than that.

If I were you, Cooley . . . Those were the words with which
the bargain was struck. There wasn't any question, though, of a
bargain being offered him, to decide on and reject it if he chose.
It was a bargain already signed and sealed. And then Cooley
with sweat on his forehead knew how it had been sealed.

He's been me. Maybe ever since that drunken binge when I
found the girl from Toronto. Maybe mine has been his body ever
since then.

"If I were you, Cooley, I'd look for an apartment here tomorrow. Don't stint yourself. You're going to be rich out of this if
any of us are. You've got my word on that. No use ever telling
yourself again you didn't have the same chance as your rich
friend Kerry. You've got it now, Cooley."

The knowledge of all that Merle meant had come then. The words to go with it wouldn't come—as if the knowledge of something so big as what was happening would automatically disguise itself without any more necessity to plan the lies that covered it.

Cooley laughed appreciatively and chugged his drink. "I do thank you, sir. I certainly do. I know you mean me well. Of course, my first thought is I ought to talk this over with Mary. I don't know how she'd feel about moving Victoria over here. If I just hung out here six months, why, I guess she'd divorce me. She's a girl don't like to wait around for me. Know what I mean?"

Merle's cold eyes said he knew it very well. He said, "It would be ridiculous for her to come here. If you can control your drinking problem, she's not ever going to divorce you, Cooley."

"My drinking problem. Goddamn, Merle, I feel like tying one on right now. Now we've got everything in the bag . . ."

"Don't do it. Don't throw your chance away. Don't fail me, Cooley. The next few months are going to be your test. You do understand that?"

4

He had not failed Merle. His very own fairy godfather Merle. Merle, who'd had his eye on him since the times he used to go home from prep school to Skelton Duchy with Kerry Finch, deceased.

No yellow man ever saw him drunk in the next five and a half months. He saved his drinking for the times he flew home to Atlanta for a few days with his people. Curiously enough—it would seem damn curious later; be tucked away with other curiosities that had to be forgotten if he was to move along—he had not failed Mary, either, and had saved his screwing for the times he was in bed with her at the Duchy, though he knew for sure now that she took care of Merle while he was away.

It was just that certainty that made him cunning in avoiding any approaches or any occasions that might have permitted it to be mentioned. He let it go on because it had begun, but he was frightened of its coming into the open. He told himself it must never be mentioned because Victoria must never know about it. (He and Merle and Mary *understood* it, he supposed sometimes. No one else would.) But, hell, probably Victoria already knew about it, and certainly the servants did, and maybe all of Atlanta. It was absurd, but he did not want it ever talked about, and he relied on Merle's tact to keep silent about it. On Merle's authority over Mary, now.

It was an endurable situation. Sometime it would have to break, of course. Perhaps Merle would die. He was nearly sixty-three now. Cooley did not believe Merle would let their peculiar arrangement fall apart or break up into outward ugliness. Their loyalty to each other had been proved and tested.

Then it was October again, and Cooley was home for what was supposed to be a longer stay. He would be at the Duchy until after Christmas. There would be time for him and Merle to get in some shooting in quail season. After all, the investors in SU had found some loose strings left over from Merle's years with the corporation, and Cooley might have to testify. Nothing very menacing.

There would be time for him to get acquainted with Mary and Victoria again. He had done pretty damn well with business in the Orient, and he wanted to bask in the knowledge that the wealth and power of Skelton Duchy depended on his efforts almost as much as Merle's.

After his labors he came home as the Conquering Hero—and goddamn, he felt like it after his first night in bed with Mary. Tender, yes. Loving, yes. But the truth was that he demolished her. In the rage of that night he could feel, bit by bit, whatever estrangement might have formed between them give way and dissolve as he mastered her, claimed her.

It was his wedding night. She was his bride. Whatever she might have held back from him he took, knowing he was taking it, knowing she knew. In a rage of gentleness he denied all other claims on her good body.

When they first rested she murmured teasingly, "You must have been practicing up this time over there."

"No."

"Saving up?"

He would not stand this remaining irony and clove her again to erase it. And at last she was moaning, "I love you. Oh, I love you-u-u-u-u"—a long-drawn cry of utter abandonment.

He lay finally beside her wishing that Merle might have been listening at their door. He fell asleep with the conviction that he needed no such vengeance to balance the accounts.

The three of them dined alone the next night. Dinner was fairly late. The two men had been hunting in the afternoon. In their happy fatigue they sat quite a while with their bourbon before going to change clothes for dinner. Victoria had come to kiss them all good night before the first course was served.

Merle was yawning over his brandy when they had finished. He patted his yawning mouth with the back of his hand, saying, "We had a great day in the field, Mary. The dogs were simply elegant. They seem to know when they can trust the men who're backing them up. Cooley was in great form. You didn't miss a shot, did you, my boy?"

"One," Cooley said. He could see it against his eyelids as he leaned back in the studded leather chair, relaxing in the comfort of the splendid food, shelter, the sniff of brandy rich in his arching nostrils—saw the furious, zinging body of the quail make for the line of brush beyond the rail fence, its dark silhouette suddenly, miraculously indistinguishable from the darkness of the terrain a split second before the over-and-under bucked against his shoulder. "I let both barrels go and missed," he admitted, with a yawn of his own.

Mary said, "I'm going to sleep with Merle tonight, Cooley."

He did not jump or jerk when he took in what the words meant. He leaned forward very slowly as if he meant to put his head down on the tablecloth and sleep. "Why?" he said.

"Why, because this is what it's all about, isn't it?" she asked with a shrill rasp of hatred. "I'm going to sleep with Merle. That's what I do."

Then none of them said anything until the clock struck eleven. Eleven elegant booming notes in perfect order and harmony like everything else in this noble house.

"Go on up, Merle. I'll be up in a little while," Mary said.

Merle seemed to bow in a courtly old-fashioned way before he left the dining room.

Then Mary said, "No fuss, no noise, if you don't mind, Cooley. It's the way things are and you know it."

He shook his head.

"You've always known it. You wanted it and you've got to take it the way it is."

"I didn't."

She got up from her chair with deliberate precision and half turned to follow out the door by which Merle had left. But she had a little more to say, in tones that would certainly not alert any eavesdropper to her passion.

"Unless you'd rather go up and give it to him. I told you that's what he really wanted."

Told him? Before anything at all had happened she had taken a wild shot of prediction about Merle's motives. Did nothing change? Did nothing that had happened since change her mind one inch from where it had set at the prospect of their moving out here?

"I wasn't cheap," she said with lingering sorrow. "After all, nothing you want really comes cheap, does it?"

"I guess it don't," he said. He wanted to object . . . that she had never protested before. He had never given her the chance. A worse woman would have made her own chance. "I thought you loved me," he said.

"I love you. I guess that's what you'll have to think about while I'm up there with him tonight."

Was she giving him another chance by deliberately going through every step of this horror? Or was it all some crazy playacting that she had to get out of her system? Could a woman feeling the way she claimed she felt really go up there and strip down to creep under another man? There would never be an answer for any of the questions that were suddenly and eternally there on the soiled dessert plate from which he'd eaten with such appetite. Never in all the years ahead.

But this much he would know and live with just the very best he could: that if she had given him another chance that night, he pissed it away, too.

A better man would have grabbed the chance, would have jumped to his feet and knocked her out with a clean, honest punch. He merely sat there and let her walk out to the stairs. He could hear her shoes on the oaken steps and he didn't hear them faltering.

A worse man would have done what he did. Get enormously drunk and create a hullabaloo through the noble rooms of Skelton Duchy such as had not been seen there in this generation at least. He worked up on it for the next two hours, going into Merle's study, where he knew he would not be observed by any servants, and drinking from the decanter of bourbon on the sideboard.

Two hours? Three, four? Who the hell would know how long he kept his part of the bargain in quiet before he raced out and started breaking things? The glass in the front door must have been among the first things he broke. He would vaguely remember putting his fist straight through it, the monstrous punch he should have given someone else.

Then room after room, flailing his arms and kicking at everything that stayed still. Most of the rooms were dark by now and he was far beyond finding any light switches. Furniture or people, whatever got in his way, he ran at. He must have done some of the breakage with his head.

It wasn't clear to him, of course, just when people began to mix in with the furniture, nor whether his arms were tangled by falling drapes or by someone grabbing for him.

Voices—that was it. That was how he could tell there were people trying to stop him now that it was too late.

5

Well, what can you ever say of a rampage when there's so much you can't remember? That not being able to remember puts it in a class with all the other most important things in your life—birth, becoming a man, falling in love, selling out what you love? There are usually some details that stick in the mind. Some of the rest can be reconstructed. But the whole thing, the real thing? It never stands up like a monument in the memory, though you know it is there—fatal and entire—a monument in the secret life that memory can't grasp except in glimpses that change with the years.

It would be nice to say that tearing up Skelton Duchy was his last drunken binge of those years. At *least* it would be nice to say that it marked a clean termination of his marriage and the involvement with Merle, a break decisive and abrupt as a cliff edge with a fall going down to the bottom of a canyon. The memory of anything clean would be a help.

He would know that he had been about to hack up Merle's Rubens painting when he was brought down by Mr. Cutler, the housekeeper's husband, with a kick in the back of his knee. Merle told him that. "You had the pendulum of the clock in your hand for an ax," Merle said, smiling icily, as he would not have smiled if actual damage had been done to the painting.

Merle had told him this in the hospital. It took an astonishing number of stitches to close the gashes in Cooley's skin caused by all the broken glass. He had broken three toes by kicking something or other.

"Mary's gone," Merle said. "We've lost her. And it was all unnecessary. She'd said things deliberately to test you. If you'd come up to your room from dinner, you'd have found her there waiting for you."

Both men knew it was a lie—the essential part of it was a lie, at least—but it offered a means of salvage. Like the other lies they had chosen, it was better than the truth.

"I'll get her back," Cooley said. "Go somewhere where no one knows us. Make a new start."

"That might be best," Merle said.

It might have been. There was a grave and tear-slobbered reconciliation between him and Mary at her parents' home in Springfield. He and Mary took Victoria to Eugene, Oregon, where Mary registered in the university to complete her B.A. and Cooley got a job selling Chryslers and Plymouths. They could afford a neat little house on the edge of town. They bought Victoria a Shetland pony. There were good times when they went out to the coast and walked the beach looking for the colored glass floats for fishermen's nets that drifted here all the way from Japan.

Cooley wrapped a dealer's Plymouth around a pine tree. The coed with him was badly scarred. Cooley was lucky not to be stuck with damage suits that would have kept him in debt for his foreseeable life.

Mary told him to go. He said he loved her and was going to make it right for her. She said love wasn't enough for that. "We're not kids any more," she said. "Love is for kids. It doesn't *have* to mess them up."

Cooley went to Singapore.

He quit drinking, and with his drinking problem out of the way he did very well.

Merle Finch died. He left Mary one hundred thousand dollars, which seemed like a very precisely measured figure.

John Fitzgerald Kennedy became President and got the country off dead center, where it had languished in the Eisenhower years. Cooley Hoyt did very well in Latin America, where the earth-moving equipment manufactured in Nagoya by Kaminoko, Ltd., helped bring a better life to the oppressed masses.

He was still in Singapore when he learned that Mary had been pregnant when he ignored the highway curve and sent the Plymouth hurtling down a shale slope into a grove of pines. He learned this from a letter announcing Paul's birth. He sent her a check for three thousand five hundred dollars, which was all he could afford then.

He came damn close to falling off the wagon again when he learned that she had been carrying his child when she told him love was not enough. There was a rush of typhoon and sandstorm in his head when he realized how much a lie her silence on that point had been, and he knew just how much he needed a drink to sober him up from that confusion. And from remembering that she never had told him, all the while they were in Eugene, whether she really shagged Merle that last night at Skelton Duchy.

In the month when he was fighting hardest to stay away from liquor he got sick with Japanese river fever, which his doctor said was rare, and by the time he had his strength back from the fever, the need for alcohol had almost gone.

He knew he was an alcoholic and he knew he had the strength to stay away from the stuff. He was free.

After that his real success began.

X

"You've got to be fair," Bob said to Charlotte. He saw that as the days of Cooley's absence kept piling up her attitude was evolving—changed from her first compassion.

"Ah! Fair! When was I not?" She was going to be wonderfully fair. But in her own way. When she saw clearly what that must be.

"You understand he's been afraid of losing you? For a long time. He's never let that show to you, maybe. You have to take it into account."

"I don't add one thing to another as you do," Charlotte said. "I trust what I know in my bones. It's him who's left me. I didn't leave him to make good on this party by himself."

"We don't know where he's gone."

"But I know. . . . Bob, he's let go. I know in my bones he wants to be finished. To quit all this that he was never at home with. Ah, ye'll say he wants one thing *and* another. What do you say he wants most?"

Bob meant to answer this very seriously. Wanted to be as fair to her as he asked her to be to Cooley in his time of retreat and disorder. With a little laugh at the hopelessness of the contradictions Cooley had to battle, he said, "I suppose he wants most that his 'firestorm of publicity' will pay off here."

"Then . . . ! Hasn't it?"

"It's a terrific spectacle," he admitted. "It's just what he had his heart set on. Yes, but . . ."

"And haven't I stood on my feet and seen it go the way it should?"

"And enjoyed every minute of it," he said—still fretting about her conscience, when he should have known she didn't operate by conscience.

"That's my way of being fair to him. It would have been a terrible cheat on him all these years if I had not enjoyed it so much, for he couldn't."

With his patient smile Bob accepted this. He might not feel the truth of it in his bones as she did in hers. But, finally, it made as much sense as the cautious bookkeeping of conscience which was his specialty.

He would trust her though he worried about her more than about Cooley. Trust her . . . but would never guess quite how Cooley triumphed in her playing the role he had made for her. In those days when she queened it over the beauty, wealth, lasciviousness and luxury of this place, she never lamented that Cooley was missing what he had paid so much for. As long as she was there for him, he wasn't missing a thing.

The President of the Republic came on schedule with his crew of security people and uniformed guards inundating the grounds. Functionaries of FUNATOR, the tourist agency, ate, drank, swam and ogled with every sign of approval.

There was a fly-past of military jets while the President stood beside Charlotte on the platform above the yacht basin.

The roar of the aircraft shaking the palm leaves before they blasted up in a shrill scream into the heart of the sky—arrogant as if they would overcome the sun itself—spoke to the wise, womanly part of her that would never be clouded by conscience. It told her that she had taken Cooley's dream and faithfully made it live.

With truth and lies she had been faithful. She had, as a matter of fact, lied to him about Rosio. She had never let that wily, eager old rooster climb onto her. She was wilier than he was and had been leading him here with tricks she would never tell to anyone. Yes, she had been naked in his stateroom. Yes, her savage and promising language had made him tremble with delighted anticipations. As ruthless old men will, he had admired her all the more for the courtesan maneuvers with which she evaded him as she led him on, for he understood sex might be a game as deadly and beautiful in its rituals of delay as any *corrida*.

She respected Rosio . . . and felt he would have approved what she was now doing for Cooley. More than that, it would have made the old conquistador hot as fire and cold as ice if he had known what she felt when the jets roared over and soared up . . . in a power untempered by quibbles about right and wrong.

"Charlotte, you must come to our suite. Yes, you must come. I've brought Maette home." It was Inge Suwe and she sounded very smug.

When Charlotte arrived she found the girl sitting very stiffly on a straight chair while Helmut and Inge Suwe confronted her.

"Maette's very much ashamed of what she has done," Inge said with a gloating smile. "Maette has to be punished. Since she was with Herr Hoyt, I wanted her to tell you she was sorry and that we will punish her."

"I am veree sorreeeee," the girl said in a zombie voice, without raising her eyes.

"Go right ahead," Charlotte said with cold fury.

Now Inge's round blond face colored like a pink peony. "Helmut, take down her clothes."

When Helmut had finished the spanking, Inge was panting uncontrollably. "You wish to strike her? Also?"

Charlotte stared at her with icy contempt and walked out. She did not condescend to asking them for any information at all that might lead to Cooley.

The Suwes obviously had lots of ways of getting their satisfactions from the girl. It would have neither surprised nor interested Charlotte to know if Inge had come while her narrowed eyes watched Helmut's hand redden the girlish buttocks. She did not look to see if Helmut's trousers were stained when he pushed the girl off his knees and onto the floor.

She had felt something far more satisfying than either of them could know . . . something that the inner heart feels at a beheading. A sense of justice beyond their fleshy sexuality . . . a tremor of the bones.

She felt so absolutely, perfectly fair to Cooley that a related proposition bubbled into her mind—now was the time for her to split from him, while the accounts between them balanced.

She talked to a fervent young Corsican film producer. He was intent on drawing her into a partnership. Of course, he had the idea that Cooley would provide the money for their ventures and that was a hurdle between his enthusiasm and reality. Still, the pattern of the future he sketched could be fulfilled in a variety of ways. It was a challenge to her inventiveness, her resources.

What if she stunned the Corsican by leaving with him in a day or two after the special guests had cleared out and the strangers, tourists and paying guests took over again? The photographers and special entertainers would all be flying to other assignments and the temptation to go with them came on her strongly.

Without the need for direct explanations, Jovan understood how she was feeling. Jovan brought her a splendid dildo, made for her by a Belgian couturier, heavy with lace and ruffled elastic straps, so when it was buckled on it was both ornamental and fierce. Jovan brought her a girl one night, a soft, enamored twenty-year-old Hungarian who had come here with the dream of making Charlotte's acquaintance.

The girl was exquisitely sensual, eminently teachable, a soft bud unfolding moistly to the hands of experience. She trembled uncontrollably when she saw the dildo added to Charlotte's strong and imperious female body, and in her melting eyes Charlotte saw the image of the completeness she had achieved. She handled the girl as a man would and only a woman could.

It was a night of surrender after surrender to her, a night of power and infinite tenderness. The tenderness unfolded like the petals of a blossom pushed from a green stem driving out of the earth toward the sun. She exhausted the girl utterly in fulfilling them both.

"Take me with you," the girl pleaded, lying in her arms in the morning. And Charlotte thought in happy wonder, Yes, she's right, she knows; I'm going . . . somewhere.

The girl's swollen young breasts lay against Charlotte's ribs soft as the flesh inside a shellfish. Her nipples were like tiny, unresistant mouths, like the tendrils of a vine seeking attachment, mute and delirious as they were stirred with the virile thumping of Charlotte's heart.

"I have no plans," Charlotte said. But as if this were the moment of a decision and a vow, she reared over the girl, pressed her head deep into the pillow and gave her a long kiss on the mouth.

"If you ever need me, find me and take me," the girl said.

Charlotte was certain from that moment she was leaving Cooley. Ah, not because he had let her down by pigging away with that little piece of fluff, nor because he had failed this party just when he should have taken command. At her best, she didn't do things for reasons. She was moved by profound realities, and there were times when she knew what those realities were—as anyone can feel on his skin the change of seasons, the fateful difference between summer and the spring that came before it.

She knew this: Cooley had abandoned that eager and ruthless passion to have and make things, the passion that had kept him skipping ahead in spite of clumsiness or crudeness or all the traps the world set for him.

It was her fashion of being true to him to leave now before he had the chance to dim and take from her what he had squandered out of himself.

"I'm calling for Señor Rosio," she said, caressing her ear with the phone. Then she said, "I'm well aware that it's early morning there in Cannes. You must wake him." After a minute more, while she ignored the explanations of his servant, she said, "I promise you he will want to be wakened. Do as you are told."

She was quite right. Ortiz Rosio found her reasons for waking him exhilarating indeed. "I'll be on the Côte d'Azur in a very few days," she said. "Three, four, maybe five. I can't be hurried. You know some of my friends there. Ask around and you'll find me."

He was getting the message and he asked, "You have finished there? With him?"

"It was you who did not see it through. A sniff of danger made you turn back."

He sighed in good humor. "And if I had persisted?"

"You'd have been dazzled. Ask! Anyone who was here will tell you it was a great success. We were living at the peak. It will be remembered."

In his courtly way he expressed regret at not seeing her on such a summit. Then, not without his own kind of chivalry, he asked a brutal question about her intentions toward him.

With her kind of chivalry, she answered brutally and heard him yelp as only Latins can when they see the flash of a sword driven home and the incredible color of blood gleam in sunshine.

"We will do well together," he said. "You were too much woman for that foolish Hoyt. That foolish American."

Then she called Page Fentress. "Page, I see now what you and I must do. I've got such schemes. Never mind the details. It's things you and I must do together, for we know how. What we did here was a good start. The world needs brightening everywhere. And we'll go do it, shall we not? Well, it's not marriage I'm proposing, you fool. But don't you be like the rest. Money is no problem, as you'll hear. It never is, do you think?"

BOOK II

I

1

I'm going to cut my hair. I'm going to cut all my hair off, Victoria thought.

She had tried to run and they had hassled her into a cage. They might call this a motel room and not a cell. Every time she stretched her tall body out on the bed and listened to the monotonous thrumming of freeway traffic come muffled through the walls, she knew it was worse than a cell.

She had tried to breathe. They left her stranded in this mechanical, air-conditioned cubicle.

She had known what she was good for. Oh, she really and truly had. Firing the guns in the green mountains, breathing rich and full and bravely, she had known exactly who she was and what she was good for. She had *tried* to tell them what she had been told. What the guns had said. She had believed that Bunny was listening to her as she had listened before to him, straining to get at the real thing beyond the words, giving up everything to listen and believe what she heard.

But he had not heard her, either. And now it was Benjamin Bunny Stewart with his big mouth that would never stop who had led her right around the circle to this air-conditioned cage by the freeway in Los Angeles.

And this afternoon while he was somewhere in the city talking, talking, talking to his so-called comrades, he had left her here by herself. Before he left he had said with his unbearable sweet patience, "It's time you called your mother. You can't let it wait any longer. Now that it's over and we're back safe. . . . You've been out of touch with her too long. Please? Victoria, she cares about you. Call her so she can stop worrying."

Victoria had not promised. She was lying stiff on the bed when he went out, with her arm over her eyes. She only wanted him to go away so she would not hear him constantly explaining, explaining, explaining. Then when he had taken his explanations away, she wanted the sound of traffic to stop so she could hear, in the silence, the brisk, fine crash of gunfire in the mountains, the only sounds her heart trusted from all the turmoil they had come through.

"I won't be too long," Bunny said. "You'll be all right, won't you? You're not feeling too bad this afternoon, are you?"

Please, just get out, she said, without answering him aloud.

And he went, but instead of the silence she needed, she kept hearing him all afternoon long.

Bunny talking to Stella Franklin:
"Stella, I'm trying to make a contribution. Victoria and I have the advantage of having seen some things with our own eyes. You and I have known each other for a while. You ought to listen to me. You ought to help me straighten out what I've seen so we could all see where we went wrong. Because if the Movement is going to succeed, we have to be realists. Really, Stella, what seems to dominate your mind is the question 'Does Bunny still *believe?*' You should have been a Spanish Inquisitor if that is all that concerns you. You won't quite admit that anything beyond faith is essential to effective action, but I tell you . . ."

Bunny talking:
"I believe in the Movement as much as ever. Might as well not believe in the law of gravity or Planck's constant. The Movement is a historic necessity. But how do we make our individual contribution? How do we fit? Simple faith . . . or constant self-criticism and assessment of errors? That's why I need some time to think and write about it. . . ."

Bunny talking:
". . . make you see how much our blundering and naïveté contributed to failure. You only emphasize the viciousness of repressive forces. I *know* that cops are bad down in Mexico, just as

they are up here. *Why* do we have to go over that ground again and again?

"But we have to learn how to take *responsibility*. Victoria and I might have tipped off the police so they could set their ambush. When we got word Rosio was not on the yacht we did our best to call things off. We panicked and began to think maybe there was a big screw-up and we had to get word to our people. It seemed like there wasn't much time and we probably blew the cover by going to ask in the barbershop and pool hall. I think we may have given the password away to someone . . . or in the *barrio*, where anyone we approached might have gone straight to the police. Don't you see? I don't think it's what you call 'reverse heroics' or 'infantile feelings of personal guilt' to run it through, talk it over, and see the weak spots."

And what was he saying now—to Stella or some of the others who were supposed to be activists—while Victoria lay in the motel room trying to get something out of the plastic air the air conditioner worked over?

Using her as an excuse—naturally—while he kept on adding up explanations of why they had failed to storm into El Dorado and finish off that son of a bitch on his yacht.

She knew that perfectly well because Bunny trusted her and wrote things in his notebook that went beyond anything he said to Stella's face or to any of the other people he talked to here or in Stella's apartment.

"They translate everything I say to make it fit their slogans. They also feed on the megalomaniac phrasing that is blinding us everywhere and for which good men keep dying. S. brings our people together to hear Victoria and me for 'debriefing sessions' and V. is more exciting to them than my sober reservations and doubts. They feed on her emotions. For that too I am guilty. At least I brought her home safe. A couple weeks' rest will bring her around."

It showed how much he trusted her that he would leave his notebook lying around for her to read that. How much . . . and in what way.

He trusted her to be his excuse. And that was what completed the cage into which he had led her now.

"Mother?" she said into the phone, lying on her side on the bed and talking into the instrument as if she were yelling down into a hole in the ground. "Mother? Of course it's Victoria. Who else do I sound like? Of course it's been months and it would be pretty rotten if you didn't just say you were glad to hear from me and, I mean, start asking ridiculous questions when I thought we had all that straightened out as between mature individuals. . . .

"Of course I'm with Bunny. Have been all this time. And he's well, too. He's in really good shape since we got back, and don't ask a lot of questions about that because I didn't call just to answer questions. I called to say I love you. I love you and I love Paul, and Bunny sends his love. He really respects you, and it would be too sickening if we talked like he was a son-in-law, wouldn't it? But he thinks he has got started on a book. He's doing a lot of writing and he's out this afternoon gathering material, I think, because that's what he's been doing on our so-called travels, he's been *gathering material*. . . .

"What? Of course that's what he's supposed to do and if I made it sound funny I wasn't trying to make it sound like a joke. I wasn't trying to make him sound like a joke, either, and if I sound sour that wasn't why I called, to sound sour, I mean. We are truly all right and there aren't any details to tell you, and why I really called is to tell you that whatever you hear in the next few days or maybe few weeks we're going to be all right, and, Mother, when you think that over, *please* understand that you're not to tell *anyone* that I called to tell you this. Now that's the message, and that's all for now, Mother."

Then as soon as she hung up, she dialed again and asked for a cab to come and pick her up. She went outside to wait for it, hoping to get more air into her lungs than she could get in the motel room, even if the air was just what it was famous for being, full of the cancer-breeding stuff they poured out every day all over the land of the free.

2

On the day of their return to the United States, Victoria had gone to sleep within minutes of their takeoff from Guadalajara.

When she woke there was nothing to be seen below the plane but an ugly gray plateau of clouds, like a prison mattress. There was nothing under the mattress, she felt. Mexico wasn't down there, six miles below the gleaming wings. It was in her. From just below her breastbone on down to her crotch there was a burning turmoil, as if she might be pregnant with reptiles and stones. As if her pills hadn't worked after all when something monstrous had crawled on her in the night, as if it were a dream but had left seed in her anyway.

Beside her Bunny had spread a silly little spiral notebook open in his lap. He had a yellow pencil in his hand but the first page of the notebook was totally unmarked.

He hadn't written anything for weeks. Not since they met Bull Timmerman on the highway north of Guadalajara and transferred the suitcases from his Continental Mark IV to their VW bus. In preparation for that action Bunny had carefully burned all his notes and journals. There had been no time for him to write anything since. He was probably scared to write now, until they had passed customs at Los Angeles.

With all his tan Bunny couldn't look pale. But he still looked scared to her. The little sign he flashed to her with his fingers when he saw she had waked was so timid it was only a confirmation of how terrifically scared he had been, especially on last night's drive through the mountains to Guadalajara. At one point she had been sure he would crash them off the road. That was when she was in the back of the bus tossing away their grenades and revolvers and the other things they were supposed to carry to their room in El Dorado. He was about ready to let go the steering wheel and climb back, to be near her, while the VW found its own way across canyons and high, narrow bridges.

That might have been all right with her. Except there would be no revenge in sailing out into space in the VW and hitting the stream-bed boulders with a kamikaze crash of noise and flame. The scalding in her gut was rage at having been trapped and frustrated at the police barricade back there. And someone was dead. One of her men. She did not know who. She would never know for sure. But she had slept with Raúl and León and Tomás while they were getting the attack ready. ("You've got to say yes to men who say no to the system," Professor Stewart had taught her, before they ever came to Mexico.) Sleeping with anyone made him yours.

Bunny had not taught her that. She was woman enough to know that by herself. Maybe Bunny had not taught her anything she knew for sure, though he had provided the words, the explanations, the slogans for a couple of years now.

The pigs had got her men and she was running from them. Flying from them now in the Friendly Skies of United, among tourists with their bright straw bags full of pottery and plated tin. But worse than that, deeper than that, hardly a thought that came near being put in words—she was cut off from her father again.

Bunny would never know her secret dream of having her father see her lit up by grenade explosions and the fires set in his expensive shrubbery while their frogmen blew the *Evita* out of the bay.

You'll see, Daddy. . . .

She must have learned that when she first learned what it was to be female and have to wait at home. When he used to go away so long from that place she still thought of as Skeleton Duchy.

It was a formula she had always called on in the worst times. When she was ten and very sick with peritonitis, a huge toad had come to her in the swirling melodrama of her fever dreams and announced she was going to die. *You'll see,* she said. When a horse threw her against a stone wall at school, she heard the bones grating in her leg as she got up on her knees by herself, telling the heaving, puke-smelling rocks of the wall that they'd *see.* She had never gone to a hard quiz at school or college with much confidence in her intelligence. Just, *you'll see.*

In field hockey or tennis or rock climbing (when she had hung on the pitons eight hundred feet above the stream in Eagle Gorge, when she really had known that with one little push she could take the guide and her brother Paul all the way down with her, wanted to) she'd looked right at the blue sky and made it take back the temptation to get it over with.

When she had tossed the last useless, unused grenade out of the VW and had to crawl back up beside the driver's seat to ease

Bunny's fear, she hadn't been able to say it. There seemed nothing to say it to.

"Want coffee, Victoria? The stewardess is coming."

"I don't want coffee, Stewart-ess."

"I want coffee. Are you feeling all right?"

"No."

"Do you want something besides coffee?"

"No."

"Why don't you go back to sleep again? We've got another hour before we're in."

"No."

"What's this Stewart-ess bit? We don't have any reason to be ashamed of anything. I'm not ashamed. Can't win them all."

"Sssssh. Someone might hear you. If you have any thoughts, write them in your notebook, if you want me to sleep."

"Then go to sleep if you want."

"No."

She closed her eyes when the stewardess leaned across her to give Bunny his coffee. She took a small revenge on Bunny by thinking what he did not know about her. He knew she had slept with Raúl in the barn the second night after they had delivered the suitcases. He did not know she had taken on León out in the jungle, stripping for him first, then helping him off with his boots and going down dog-fashion for him in gratitude for letting her train with the guns, to let him know she recognized he was chief of the band.

Nor did Bunny know about Tomás. Bunny agreed she should say yes to men who said no, but he wanted to be told about it—before, if possible, and certainly afterward.

In fairness to Bunny she would have to admit that he had been more help than her mother ever had in thinking clearly about her father. Bunny corrected a lot of her childish views. He had said, "What's your old man done but carry American business methods out into Third World countries and operate on them the way the Harrimans and Rockefellers and Du Ponts operated with the American settlers in Nebraska and California? It's all the same. You can say Cooley Hoyt—as a man, don't be too harsh on him, Victoria—is as much a victim of the system as anyone."

Which had impressed her until she thought it over. Yet it was good to know that a Maoist like Bunny could have so much intuitive sympathy for anyone in her father's role. A glove fitted a hand, you might say, and Bunny also said, "The apple never falls far from the tree"—which might or might not be one of Chairman Mao's thoughts. In the old days Bunny had even talked about reconciling her to her father's image, and he had been disturbed more than he would let on that they were actually going to attack her father's resort with guns, though Rosio had to be taken care of.

Bunny was the only human she had ever told about her last gruesome meeting with Cooley Hoyt.

It had happened the year her mother had finally remarried. Mary McAlister Hoyt Rossiter had very sensibly decided that Victoria, fifteen then, might profit from a summer in Europe while the newlyweds got some privacy in the Wellfleet house where Victoria and young Paul usually stayed with her.

So it came about that Victoria was in Rome with her best friend, Nell Jean Barker. Victoria learned her father was there at the same time. She learned it the way she usually learned about any of his business activities. Someone had tried to hide the information from her.

Nell Jean's father had been sitting at a café table with the girls, reading the financial pages of the *Herald Tribune*. Mr. Barker had been very cool about it, folding the paper carefully and putting it in his raincoat pocket and telling them to hurry with their sangria because it would be hard to get a cab in the rain, though the opera matinee didn't begin for almost an hour. Victoria had caught his look—between amusement, outrage and anxiety—that she recognized as a signal her father was up to something she ought to be spared. Usually it was some cheap magazine spread that showed him as a "swinger." In the pictures, batches of girls in bikinis would be perched on his sports car or fondling the horses at some château he'd rented for the season. She didn't expect to find that kind of spread in the back of the *Herald Tribune*.

When she got herself a copy of the paper later, it only had his head-and-shoulders picture with a story saying he was in the Eternal City for meetings with finance ministers from two of the former French colonies in Africa. As far as she could make out, they were all there "seeking means" to save from bankruptcy a chain of fertilizer plants that had been originally financed from a German bank said to be controlled by the Hoyt Associates. There was nothing in the story to suggest why Mr. Barker might have chosen not to let her see it, and she supposed he had operated on purely personal grounds, sparing her the knowledge that her father was so nearby when he was supposed to be out of her life for good.

It was in rebellion against such fussy protectiveness that she went to her father's hotel and up to his suite without any advance arrangements. She didn't even call up from the desk. There were two very black, blue-black, gentlemen asking for directions to Signor Hoyt's floor, and she, thinking they might even be the finance ministers she had read about, simply rode up with them.

They got a little nervous when she followed them right to the door, but one of them had already knocked before they realized she meant to come in with them. When a woman she later identified as her father's mistress, Charlotte Keefe, answered the knock, and the two black men began a rapid-fire parley in French that seemed to concern her, Victoria spoke up—"I'm just his daughter"—and the upshot was that Charlotte had let her in and had turned away the two black men. "Pas maintenant. Il s'occupe des autres affaires. Téléphonez ce soir, après huit heures, vous comprenez?"

The black men had tried to push into the suite anyway and there was a little scuffle between them and two big Italians who seemed to have been right behind Charlotte when she opened the door. After the black men were shoved out into the corridor, with one Italian strong-arming them back toward the elevator, Victoria saw her father in a tableau that altered all she had ever thought about him.

He looked desperate. There were men sitting on seven or eight of the chairs available in the parlor and they had pulled the chairs up in a kind of loose circle around the desk, where Cooley

Hoyt stood in his shirt sleeves with a phone in his hand. His right hand was upraised as if he were taking an oath. And what he was saying was: "You make *sure* Kettelring knows it has got to stop with him. They're his books and nobody else but him put his signature to them. And if he's in for twenty years his wife and kids will be taken care of. But make him understand it won't be twenty. Five . . . three . . . two . . . two years at the most. Tell him to remember Zuckel! Call me back when you've got to him."

Then Charlotte whispered to him and he turned—red-eyed and dazed, trying to grin at Victoria. He came around the desk to hug her and kiss her on the forehead, evidently surprised to find her already nearly as tall as he. He introduced her to no one there. In fact, he hustled her out, sliding swiftly into his jacket and pulling his tie straight. He took her downstairs again to the restaurant and there, amid a great embarrassed shuffling of enormous menus, they each ordered a cup of coffee.

"We're trying to save a bank," he told her with a hobbled shrugging gesture that was supposed to explain everything going on upstairs in his suite.

"I shouldn't . . . you shouldn't . . . you didn't *have* to come out with me. I only . . ." She was dizzy with embarrassment for him.

"Aw!"

The way he looked at her when he uttered that gravelly, groaning—and really pretty pitiful—syllable made an image that would last in her mind as if he had appeared to her in a dream, some great, awkward, wicked baby before he learned to talk or a broken old man after he had forgotten how.

Aw . . .

It would have to do instead of all the things she had expected he might answer to the questions she had expected she might ask. Because most of the short time they spent together there at the restaurant table he wasn't really aware there was anyone with him. Or that he had really left his telephone up there on the seventh floor.

She was in the midst of explaining painfully to him how she happened to be in Rome right at this time, and just happened to hear that he was too, when he broke in, out of his trance, to say, "Be proud that you're big."

"Huh?"

"I mean, don't ever let them tease you for being so tall. You be proud of it, hear?"

3

Four years after that farce she told Bunny, "I hadn't realized he could be a victim of the system until, probably, then. He *couldn't* talk to me. He kept sucking for air all the while we sat at that crazy table. Literally *sucking*. Like I'd disconnected him from his oxygen by dragging him away from his phone."

She *had*. That was exactly the right image, Bunny confirmed. She had cut off the air hose that keeps "men like that" going. Men like that have to be recognized as merely the single organs of this monstrous organism that has telephones and cable lines for windpipes and blood vessels and uses creatures that might be men the way men like that use others farther down the line.

It wasn't fair to say that Bunny's thinking did away with hatred or blame for individuals. It concentrated hatred on the *roles* and *acts* rather than the men. Which made it reconcilable with her mother's and her grandfather's Christianity. And made it just barely thinkable that Cooley Hoyt needed rescuing from the system that was choking the breath out of him.

It was her mother's role as a Christian activist that had probably steered her into Bunny's life and his pad, if you came down to it. Sex had to be somewhere. And linked up with other values. It wasn't always straight or good, sex wasn't, but it made no sense at all if you tried to separate it from other idealisms.

The first time anyone had given it to her was at the time of the Cambodian Incursion. The girls at her school had a spontaneous candlelight ceremony to mourn for what had happened. There was nothing else girls could do, they felt. There'd been that jock from Exeter visiting, who carried his candle and bowed his head while Chaplain Dorkin talked very sadly and quietly to them and afterward they sang "Where Have All the Soldiers Gone." After that the Exeter jock screwed her on the grass beside his

Porsche. He was gross and while he was messing her up she had lain there thinking, *You'll see.* She wouldn't have been surprised if he'd smashed the Porsche into a light pole before he ever got it back to Exeter.

Bunny, her teacher, very gentle and experienced and nine years older than she, had to straighten her out on a lot of sex matters as well as other values. He helped her get rid of a lot of body taboos. When she was quiet enough to feel gratitude, she always felt grateful to him for that.

Like her father, he told her she should be proud of her strength and her size and of her body generally when it was used in the right way.

She had discussed the incident in Rome with her professor, her lover. She hadn't mentioned the letter that came to her in the fall after she last saw her father.

> Baby,
>
> . . . whatever prompted you to come in just when you did, you were truly my good angel. You saved me from doing something I would regret to my dying day. It's hard to understand how just a few minutes to think things over will save a person from what he should know will never work. . . .
>
> . . . sorry we had no time to get acquainted. We will sometime when all this is over. We might even like each other quite a bit. I'll bet you are not quite so shy as you seemed with me.
>
> . . . I remember your saying you "wanted to soar." That's just what a lovely, wonderful, smart girl should want, and here is something that will help you soar right up amidst the clouds. . . .

He had included a check for ten thousand dollars in the letter and that had spoiled it all. She had to think it was money he had got from those scared black men she had seen in the elevator. Or it made her into some kind of rabbit's foot for a *deal* that he thought he might have fumbled if she hadn't interrupted him just as she did.

She tore the check up. It was the only money she had ever refused from him. But then, it was the only money he had ever offered her directly. The rest came sanitized by the formality of being paid through Hoyt International.

Another thing that Bunny did not know as he rode beside her in the plane—starting its descent toward the Los Angeles airport —was that she had put in a threatening call to Bob Pardon from Guadalajara. Bunny would probably never learn of that because she was already bitterly ashamed of it. If she was going to threaten, she should have threatened her father, directly. She had chosen Mr. Pardon because she knew he could be hurt by her language and her savagery. He had shown himself vulnerable. She was not sure she could have hit a chink in her father's armor.

She was also ashamed of making a threat when she had no way of carrying it out. But this part of the shame only heated up her fury and the great thirst to make them all *see*.

She and Bunny were going through the customs line at the airport when she scared him again. The customs man had made her turn everything out of her bags and was pinching his way through her expensive clothes, probably alerted by some hunch that she might be carrying drugs. He was taking a long time. Maybe he was just stalling while someone watching from the glass offices above was checking her and Bunny out.

She said loudly, "I've got something you can write in your notebook, Bun. The reason I went to Mexico and through with it all."

Suddenly his neck stiffened with the impulse to give her a warning shake of the head. His head wouldn't shake. He was frozen with indecision. The customs inspector was listening hard.

Victoria was giggling so much it was nearly impossible for her to choke the words out. "Nell Jean," she said. "The last time I saw Nell Jean she tried to get me active in a campaign against *aerosol cans*. She's convinced if we don't ban aerosol cans everyone will die of skin cancer in twenty years. She pointed out that Mother was very active in ecology and she wanted me to run a mimeograph machine to let people know . . . how much . . . danger . . . they're in."

The customs inspector began to laugh. He stopped pinching the seams of her clothing as thoroughly as he had been pinching them.

"It'd be awful not to have any ozone," he said. "My kid's worried about it, too. Made me start buying shaving cream in the tube again."

Then Bunny chimed in with the observation that science hadn't yet *proved* aerosol sprays would destroy the ozone layer.

"They've proved enough to scare me," the inspector said. "Gamma rays are nothing to fool with, kids." He motioned for Victoria to repack her bags.

And they were home safe.

That was what Bunny thought. He only said it once, as far as she could remember. And she couldn't accuse him of saying it without irony. She knew very well and very fully how he felt about Fascist America, the land of pigs and oppression. It was just that irony meant nothing to her, one way or the other. All his ironies were, when you came right down to it, little indulgences for his private gratification, like some of the little fancy things she let him do in sex. Really she ignored them and was glad if he enjoyed them selfishly. No part of their sex together had ever meant very much to her. She had followed him as she might have followed any man, for what he could lead her to, and when she got there she had forgotten all the ironies in his talk or his little finger-tongue manipulations.

"Home safe," he had sighed as they sank into the back seat of the taxi carrying them from the Los Angeles airport. He winked at her and suggested all they had to worry about was whether they had enough actual cash left to pay for the ride to Stella Franklin's apartment at the top of Benedict Canyon.

They didn't have. They had to borrow from Stella as it turned out. But the counting of money in the cab had led to Victoria saying, "I'll phone Mother for money."

"If it wasn't so late in the semester, your mother would haul you right back into college somewhere," Bunny said, enjoying the relief of being defeated, though he would go on complaining about it.

"Or else I'll get the money from my father," Victoria said.

"Mr. Pardon told us he had how much?—forty *million?*—invested in that ugly hotel."

The taxi driver shuffled in his seat when he heard the mention of forty million dollars. He was carrying a passenger whose father was worth forty mill . . .

Victoria saw his rodent's eyes flick to study her in the rearview mirror. Avaricious, frightened, stirred to life by the only thing that could stir them. . . .

That glimpse of his eyes may have been where she got her idea of having herself kidnapped and held for a ransom of forty million dollars.

II

1

It was a sick idea, Bunny said. "Literally. How could we have known we'd have these shock effects afterward? I'm almost afraid to go to sleep myself." He was angry, besides, that Victoria had first mentioned her plan in front of Stella instead of examining it privately with him.

"So drag me to a shrink," Victoria said, threatening tears. "People who know what we do can't go to shrinks."

Stella said, "It depends on which one."

"I wouldn't go to a shrink. They killed our men and they better pay for it. They'd *better*."

"Your father doesn't *have* forty million dollars. You don't understand money and credit. Even if there should be that much invested in El Dorado. . . . Do you think he drove up with a truck full of pesos—or gold bullion—and said, 'I'll buy this'? Victoria, be reasonable."

"If he could raise that much, he could raise . . . a lot," Stella said.

Victoria said, "Why do you keep picking at me? I need to rest. It doesn't have to be that much. Maybe five or ten. Will you let me go sleep now? Please?"

Stella Franklin had expected little more than an added risk from Victoria when Bunny brought her to the apartment. Stella supposed she was under surveillance, though she had nothing substantial to prove it. She rather liked the idea of being watched by the FBI and of having to keep her wits sharp to detect possible stool pigeons.

She did not think Victoria Hoyt would be a stool pigeon. A girl with a background like that and at her age would not have the conflicting pressures that made stool pigeons. Stool pigeons were those who had been clubbed all their lives until their spines turned to jelly. She thought that if Victoria Hoyt was pliable enough at her age to go wandering through Latin America with Bunny it was because Bunny knew how to dominate her. Bunny was very clever and quick-witted. If the girl had been his student he must dominate her intellectually.

At first Stella had to be reassured that Victoria was not just a spoiled, erratic product of too much money and permissiveness who might endanger the Movement by her whims. And, at first, Stella was inclined to agree with Bunny that the whim of arranging her own kidnapping was a freak plan. A happy-dust dream.

"Another one who burned out her brains from drugs," she said sadly to Bunny when Victoria went to get some sleep in her bedroom.

"It's not that," he said. "I didn't foresee what the aftereffects would be. They're terrific. Victoria was very cool while we were up in the mountains with the men. She learned to follow orders." He took a very deep breath of the night air that was coming in from Stella's open kitchen window, and he took a drink of safe California water before he poured himself scotch from the bottle on the table. He grinned his charming college-boy grin. "Hell, Stella, you don't know what we've been into. I didn't foresee how it was going to happen. It just seemed to happen. One thing led to another. I thought we were through when we picked up the gun stuff and delivered it. Two weeks before I wouldn't even have let Victoria in for that."

"I want to hear everything," Stella said. "Val and Don ought to hear it, too. I could probably get them here in an hour and a half for a debriefing."

"Not tonight. Please, not tonight, Stella. What I've got to tell anybody will keep. I want some time to think it over. Tonight we deserve a rest." He put his stocking feet up on one of Stella's kitchen chairs and sniffed the scotch in his glass before he tasted it. After he tasted it, he peered into the glass and licked his lips.

"Good," he said. The glitter of more than relief was making his eyes sparkle and she knew he meant to talk even if he was too tired to face any tough questions from Val and Don or any other men who had some experience with revolutionary action.

He sprawled and said, "Stella, why do we kid ourselves that we're part of an organization when there's just a lot of loose nuts and bolts rattling around? There *isn't* any organization of the Left. If the CIA knew what they were chasing they'd shit their pants. *They've* got to believe we're organized. But if they only knew . . . !"

It flustered Stella to hear him talking so irreverently. She thought he deserved to unwind. She tried to be patient as she listened, but it disoriented her from the beliefs she leaned on. "You two have seen the real thing," she said. "You got guns to our people."

His Adam's apple went up and down like a yo-yo on a short string as he gulped his scotch. It looked very fragile under the translucent fluff of his beard. "Let me tell you about this one kook. It's an Air Force colonel, no less, retired, and I guess supplementing his retirement pay by hauling stuff back and forth across the border in his—get this—big blue Lincoln Continental. Who would figure such a car is loaded with heroin? Ah, and what's heroin got to do with the Movement? I tell you, we're contacting people who wear a lot of hats. This time he crossed the border his principals told him, 'Now we've got something heavier for you to haul'—since guns are a little heavier than the money he's used to carrying home to Chapala."

"How do you know all this?" she asked sharply.

"That's another thing I'd just as soon keep between you and me. I'm a clever lad, Stella. But should I know this—in case I'm picked up and they put the pliers on my testicles? Certainly not. That's what I mean about our so-called organization. We're full of holes like me. The truth is, I was goddamn reluctant to get Victoria involved in any of this. So I had only Colonel Timmerman's description and the car and the license plates so we can rendezvous with him and get the stuff. From that I had time to get a name through a girl in the Embassy. He lives in Chapala country. We drive to Chapala. Old buddy of mine is into ceramics there. Also dealing in a small way. 'Timmerman?' says he.

'Oh yes, Wild Bull Timmerman, the Korean ace. Yes indeedy, the Wild Bull himself.' Then he gave me the rest of it. It's crazy. One thing after another seemed to keep popping for us. I thought, the luck she is running good. So we played the cards as they dropped. Right up to the bad stuff at El Dorado. And I thought, hey, here's little Victoria riding it all cooler than I. I should've seen that all the cool in her wasn't a good sign. She's been wounded, Stella. That kid's in there trying to sleep off a bellyful of shrapnel that we can't see. She'll come around in a few days. I hope. But, please, please, don't say a single damn word to encourage her in this loony notion of being kidnapped.

"By whom? Who's going to figure the details? *She's* not smart enough. I mean, she thinks *fine* about some things. But . . . ! Besides, who knows that prick father of hers would pay a dime for her carcass?"

"I heard that," said Victoria from the doorway.

It was a great pity she had. Bunny conceded that. To himself and all concerned. Feeling safe and sound, back in the good old U.S. of A., land of the pig, the motherfucker and the fascist, feeling smug with a little scotch in his bloodstream, he had said something awfully foolish. Now he had to get the ball in play again from behind his own goal line.

"But the fact you *couldn't* sleep—tired as you admit you are, and Stella can see it, too; you didn't hear all we said—is just evidence that we've got to take time to unwind before we can even discuss it rationally."

"I didn't think you'd said anything offbeat, baby," Stella said gently to Victoria.

"Humor her, then!" Bunny raged. "Shit!" He went to the window and slammed it down in case there were eavesdroppers out there, too, who would certainly get an earful if this got loud. Pleadingly he said, "Stella, Victoria. Let's *not* try to make sense of it tonight. Have you got any sleeping pills for her, Stella? I'll come to bed with you, Victoria."

"Like hell you will," she snarled.

"Well . . ." Stella began.

Bunny was standing with his feet widespread in front of the

girl. "Suppose you got the ransom? Any part of it. What would you do with it?"

"Give it to the poor."

He clapped a hand to his forehead. "Haul it over to Watts in a truck? With a pitchfork throw it out on a street corner?"

"I've got some cocaine," Stella said.

"No," Bunny said decisively. "Seconal? Nembutal?"

"Yes," Victoria said.

"Look," Bunny said, "if I agree to talk this over seriously tomorrow . . . In the morning. Whenever we get up. . . . I might sleep the clock around. . . . If I promise, will you not take the cocaine? Forget about it. She's never had it, Stella."

"That's what I told you," Victoria said. "So my father's a prick. Isn't that a good reason for taking him?"

"Not tonight, darling," Stella soothed her. "Ssh."

"Come on to bed," Bunny pleaded. "We'll sleep on it. We'll sleep. We've got to sleep so we can think it out right." He put his arm around Victoria's shoulders and she let him lead her back to the bedroom.

Bunny was sick when he finally got up the next day. Stella heard him in the bathroom before he came to join her in the living room. He plumped down in her ragged leather chair with a game grin and doubtful shake of his head.

"Diarrhea?" she asked. "You didn't have that much scotch last night."

"A touch of it," he admitted. With an even more anguished attempt at a smile he said, "Pussy-whipped. Might as well admit it. I wasn't expecting her to . . ."

The term offended Stella very much. "Is that what you learned in the land of *machismo?*" she asked.

"It's just a word."

"It's a very ugly word. Will she be getting up? Don and Val ought to be here in a minute. They'll be as eager to hear from her as from you."

"I know it's an ugly word. While Don and Val are here I'll refer to her only as Miss Hoyt."

"You've got a very sharp tongue, you know."

"A thick one. Mind if I just don't say anything to Don and Val?"

"There's no use in dragging your cynicism out for them. They've seen a lot more of the seamy side than you have."

"Buster," he said.

"What?"

"You should have called me 'buster.'"

They heard Victoria in the shower then and let the minor squabble trail off. There was no sense in old friends making an issue out of offensive terms. When Victoria came out to join them she was dressed in a white linen suit that made her look awfully young. She seemed rested and calm.

While the men Don and Val were with them she said nothing about kidnapping. The topic did not come up. Don and Val thought her occasional quiet descriptions added a lot of "color" to Bunny's report. They could hardly believe that this bright, deferential girl had faced the police across their barricades with a .38 revolver in her suitcase, along with a detonator and several grenades. They could hardly find words to express their admiration.

Bunny was shaken by her effect on her listeners. What he took to be her hysteria dovetailed all too well with the appetite of those who came to Stella's place needing the glamour of heroic fables to bolster what they wished to believe about their political fortunes, about the ultimate triumph of the oppressed.

When he and Victoria left Stella's apartment and moved miles away to the motel, he believed Victoria would calm down. When she lay fully dressed and stiff on the bed without saying a word for hours on end, he believed she was resting. When he understood she was reading his notebook in secret—though she had sniffed at his offer to look at it while he was there—he believed that this was a means by which their most serious dialogue went on, and that the essential terms of it were not changed.

He did not really want to challenge her wild proposals outright, because he wanted her to go on with him, serving the cause they had set out to serve after they could get a new perspective on it by drawing on what they had experienced. He meant to wean her gradually to some reasonable notions of their future.

He was not changing his colors. He wanted everyone to know that. He was clever. So he kept coming up with ideas of how the kidnapping *might* work. The more he convinced himself it was an impossible, improbable fiction, the clearer were his thoughts about how it could be managed.

The motel room they were occupying was an ideal point of departure. A little fracas staged here—maybe a couple of shots fired into the air as the kidnap car whisked away into the late hours of some night . . . The police could easily confirm that they had been here. "We'd better have both of us kidnapped. It's not so good if I'm around to be questioned," he said.

It was his notion that the best tactic would be for Victoria to tape a whole batch of appeals for ransom at one sitting. Then she should go and hide out somewhere while he and Stella would arrange to have the tapes doled out one at a time, at intervals, in various parts of the country. It would be good to give the illusion that the kidnappers were not only moving around the country freely, but also that they were *able* to move so freely without the pigs being in a position to corner them in any one part of the country.

Timing was of the essence, Bunny foresaw. Certainly he and Stella were unable to arrange the distribution of the tapes by themselves. That was why he wanted to run up to San Francisco with Victoria and talk to some wise heads he had known since his student days at Berkeley. Find reliable helpers.

"Why don't you think and not think so *much?*" Victoria asked. "We've got to do this *now.*"

"Why?"

"You'll chicken if we wait."

"Do you really mean that *you* will?" Bunny asked—professor to student.

"I think the sooner, the better," Stella said. "I'm not sure the ransom money is the main thing. On the 'Today' show this morning they were saying there's a new demand to get Mr. Hoyt back to testify for that rat Hogben. Now, could we make it a ransom demand that he come back and give himself up? I don't fully understand how you feel about your father, Victoria."

"How should I feel after what he's done to my life? Not to mention my mother," Victoria said. Her angry question had no ring of sincerity to Bunny. He saw that the anger was a pose intended to influence Stella—and this observation comforted him again with its assurance they were concocting a scenario with no purpose except to air their wishes. It was a sort of psychodrama, an amateur variation of primal-scream therapy.

He saw himself as the therapist, the only one who could play the essential double role of the man in the middle. He encouraged, he participated, he slowed them down by calling to their attention the obstacles they would encounter, the alternative considerations that had better be stated before anything rash was done.

Turning to Stella—intending Victoria to hear his caution sifted through the other woman—he said, "If we give the kidnapping a political coloration—I guess that's what it's all about—there's going to be a lot of heat on lots of our people—good, progressive people we all care about. The pigs are going to use it as an excuse to break down a lot of doors. Have you thought that through? It all sounds feasible while we bat it around ourselves, but . . . Stella, I'm not sure you're taking this seriously. Why didn't you bring it up while Don and Val were here? Aren't they wise heads? Shouldn't we have them behind us if we're going to move?"

"Not them," Stella said. "Not them," she said vaguely.

2

"He won't do it," Victoria said. "He wants to wait until summer. He wants to go to San Francisco and see his Berkeley friends. He wants to write a book about it."

"Bunny has courage," Stella Franklin said. "I saw him in Chicago in the Days of Rage."

"Don't think I haven't heard all about that," Victoria said. "The police clubbed him. Did he club any policemen?"

Stella laughed breathlessly. "You didn't see it. I did. I was on the street, but no one hit me. It took a kind of guts. A great deal. Bunny's thinking it over. We need his kind of mind, too."

"Men won't do what they have to," Victoria said.

"Men are part of it. We wouldn't get anywhere without them."

"We have to do it now or I can't do it. It can't be done without me. Can't you persuade Bunny?"

"I thought you could if anyone could."

"I persuaded him a couple of things. You know, he thinks we may have tipped off the police by trying to find Raúl and León that day. But we didn't. There was no way to find them by then without help. I said, 'Go to the barbership where Rafael was supposed to be or we could get word to Rafael at least.' After the barbershop maybe we should have gone out on the side roads and tried to find someone. . . .'"

"You don't need to go over it again," Stella said. "The police always have their informers. Always, always. But we have our resources, too."

"Have you talked about the plan to anyone besides Bunny? To Val or Don or . . . what was his name? The red-haired guy who was here when we came from the airport."

"Hughie? I wouldn't mention it to Hughie. Yes, I talked it over with someone else. He thought it was too wild."

"A man?"

"We've got to have men."

"There must be the right men. Bunny might come along if it got started. I've told him I wouldn't go to San Francisco with him. He wanted to go yesterday. He feels so safe now that he's back here."

"There's someone else I can talk to," Stella said. She took a very heavy breath, as though mastering a long, persistent fear. "There's always someone who'll do anything."

"I could talk to him, too," Victoria said. "There's always ways to persuade men."

"Some of them," Stella said. She got up and crossed the linoleum of her kitchen, where she and Victoria had been talking. She went to the window box, where her geraniums were thriving in the California sunshine. She watered them from a watering can, carefully, with the measuring hand of an expert gardener. "We could persuade him if he needed persuading."

"Bunny?"

"Not Bunny," Stella said.

3

It was past dark the next night when they drove out into the Valley in Stella's Plymouth. All three rode in the front seat as far as Carson Avenue, where they picked up Mike Lane and Rachel Dennis at a bus stop. Then Bunny got in the back seat with them.

"What's afoot, Stella?" Mike asked when they were rolling again. Mike appeared hardly more than a high school boy in spite of his dense black beard. There was an odd scar on his upper lip, as if it had been burst once with a blunt weapon. "Stella's very cloak-and-dagger with her phone calls," he explained good-humoredly to Bunny. "'Meet me at the bus stop,' said our gallant leader."

Stella was driving carefully, observing the speed limit and stopping for yellow traffic lights.

"We're going to see Nat," she said, keeping her eyes on the road. "Bunny and Victoria are just back from Mexico. They've never met him."

"Ah, we're going to see old Nat," Mike said. "I haven't seen him in a coon's age. Talked to him last week. Said he had some dynamite gold."

"We're not going for the gold," Stella said.

"Why'd you come back, man?" Mike asked Bunny. "Rachel and I wanted to go for the bullfights at Easter, but I traded off the Toyota."

"It's a long story," Bunny said.

"Tell the story, Bunny," Victoria said.

"It's all right. You can tell them," Stella said. "Mike's older than he looks."

"I'm a ninety-year-old midget and Rachel is a certified belly dancer. CBD, aren't you, Rache?"

"I'm only seventy-five. Will Herman be there, Stella?"

"If Nat asked him. I didn't," Stella said. She braked alarmingly as a black poodle darted into the road in front of them. The poodle stopped in a panic and went back onto the curb from which he had leaped.

"Ah, you've seen one tourist resort you've seen them all," Bunny said. "Miss Hoyt and I stayed at the best places. Can Cun, Acapulco, Playa Azul, Mazatlán, Las Hadas, El Dorado. You name it. Victoria got a splendid tan and brought back many quaint souvenirs."

"Are you really Victoria *Hoyt?*" said Rachel. "You think they'll get your father back to testify?"

"I'm Victoria. I don't use any last name."

Mike chuckled. "Save the punch line, man. There's nothing I like better than punch line interruptus, hey, Rache?"

"You mean saving it?" she asked.

"Save it for Nat," Mike said. "He likes to hear how the white folks live. Stella, is this the first time you've been to Nat's new house? He says this is the first place he's had where he can set his equipment up."

"I haven't seen Nat since summer," Stella said.

"Nat's a bug," Rachel said to Bunny. "He's a true bug about his equipment. Cameras mostly."

"Tape recorders?" Bunny asked.

"That sort of thing, too," Rachel said, and turned her face to the car window as if to count the streetlights passing.

Nat Fraser's house was a nondescript white bungalow in a neighborhood of big yards. They parked on a gravel drive beside a hedge that their headlights showed bounding his yard on two sides. The headlights shone into open garage doors. Inside there were two or three motorcycle frames. There were used tires and disassembled parts hanging everywhere. Then there was a labyrinth of unidentifiable metal frames, cables and ropes sloppily hung on the walls.

"Nat's a bug for *anything* mechanical," Rachel explained as they got out to walk to the house.

There was almost no furniture at all in the house they entered by the back steps. There were pathetic and filthy curtains at the front windows, over the drawn green blinds. There were two kitchen chairs in the kitchen along with a graying refrigerator. For the rest, the floors were littered with old and new toolboxes, wires, dust, bits of food and food wrappers. Blankets had been kicked into piles in the corners. Here and there magazines had been dropped.

There were electric cables and wires of many colors snaking among the chassis of tape recorders and battered television sets. Nat Fraser had been watching a giveaway show on an indifferently functioning set when his visitors arrived. He did not turn it off or turn down the volume of sound at their arrival nor when they all took places seated on the floor amid the sour colors projected out from the TV screen.

Nat was a plump black man, wearing bib overalls and a denim shirt. His quick smile was as precise as if it were tripped by some spring-loaded mechanism and limited against some pawl that he had adjusted with his own wrenches. And above his smile his eyes gimbaled tirelessly from face to face, wire to wire, calendar to calendar, button to button, toolbox to magazine to toolbox. And yet he was attentive to what was happening on the screen. A woman from Laguna failed to win three thousand dollars, but won instead a Shelvador refrigerator and a Sunbeam jet iron. As she shrieked and wiggled and waved her hands above her head, Nat remarked, "That mama gonna keep it all so cool." Rachel giggled appreciatively.

When the commercial came on, Nat got to his feet, hiked up his bib overalls and went to his kitchen. Over the voice that cackled the great savings at Hailey's Used Motors they heard him wrestling with a stuck drawer. He came back with a small mayonnaise jar half full of white powder. "Gonna have a loooooong talk tonight. Just as well be comfortable."

"No, thanks," Bunny said when the jar came around the circle to him.

"Yes," Victoria said. "Please." She watched Rachel sniff a pinch from the back of her hand and did the same.

"Now then, Stella. To what may one attribute the honor of your call?" Nat asked.

It was late, late before they got to the basement to see Nat's equipment. By then Victoria had spoken and Bunny had told a sterile version of their "Mexican hayride," as he now chose to label it. He was using his own sort of professorial irony to mock the luster of the design aimed at executing the South American oppressor, but Stella, listening from the optimistic drowse of the cocaine, remembered how many ingenious details he had contributed to the scenario and put aside any worries about the staunchness of his faith. When he was between ironies, there was the old familiar boyish eagerness in his voice. He had not slipped from his anger at the poverty seen along the mountain roads of Mexico. He seemed almost wheedling before Nat, eager to impress him as one who had committed not only himself but his woman to the rising wind of violence that would sweep down the rotten façade of capitalism.

Yes, in the right combination, Bunny was going to serve.

But Victoria . . . of course, the girl was the catalyst, the shock, the surprise, the bolt of lightning that started the fire. It was her moment.

It was her moment and she was rising to it fast—as if she recognized them as they recognized her. She was a leader because they gave her the power of their frustrations and their rage at the impotence to which they had been condemned.

"I don't care!" her voice rang. "I don't care what Bunny says. Or you say. It'll be a start! If we *move* . . . ! So maybe my rotten father wouldn't pay a nickel for me. If he wanted to, he might not be able to raise the money. We might not be able to collect it. Let's get started and work it out as we go. You won't even start!"

"We started."

"Let's go. Forty million *sounds* good."

"Send them a message. Hoyt's done us a favor with all his publicity. Let's use it."

"I don't care if we can't be sure in advance how it will all work out," Victoria said.

And little by little, cycle by cycle of talk, everything was stripped from the intelligible rhythms of verbiage except that repeated, stubborn, fierce "I don't care."

"I don't care!" the girl said.

It was their voice. It was the voice of the moment, of this night.

As it kept striking like a bloodied fist, as it pounded through levels and layers of quickly darting reasons, they all heard something answering—a sort of hollow and resonant laughter, like the sound made by blowing into a jug, a booming, faint at first and then percussive. It was the booming of Nat Fraser's laughter. A sound like a shadow responding to the white light of Victoria's "I don't care."

For a while it rose like a duet—proposal and acceptance, a yes and an amen, soprano and bass, a cry and an echo. And when they had all heard it rise dominant out of the discord of their chatter they were silent, and the two who had silenced them became quiet as well.

"I applaud," Nat Fraser said at length. His eyes flicked from face to face and to the doors and calendars and the action still visible on the TV screen. There was a detective film rolling now. A couple in a white convertible were racing along a curving road near the edge of steep cliffs. "High time we send them a message," he said. "Now you all come down to my basement and see my etchings." He got up from his squatting position on the floor and put out his hand to help Victoria rise.

"No," he said. "Leave the TV burning. Helps convince the neighbors I am a desirable tenant."

4

The basement was as crowded with gear as the rooms above. But in them the overwhelming impression was of clutter and slovenly disorder. The basement was his workroom. There was an outlandish, exotic precision in the placement of his pieces of photographic equipment, a placement that seemed logical until the eye realized it was tricked, that the odds and ends fitted together as in a dream of an attic or storeroom. Cameras, enlargers, projectors bulked here and there like the reassembled discard of a civilization barely remembered, as if all these antique and archaic mechanisms might have been committed to uses inconceivable to the civilization above ground level.

"That little ole coal bin inna corner's my darkroom," Nat said. "It will suffice. It will suffice. Found me this from an ancient press photographer. Says he lug it all the way from Amsterdam Avenue."

He was pointing out a nineteenth-century bellows camera on a massive, polished wooden trestle. The woodwork, brass and steel shone with polishing. "I am a bug for the dark, mysterious chamber in which we behold the image of man emerge," he said to Victoria. He showed her how the bellows extended and retracted on two rods of gleaming steel. "Put your head under this hood, my girl, and you will see how vastly superior the old craftsmen were. On the glass you will behold more clearly than life. . . . Here, turn this big knob for focus. Rachel, take a pose, give our Victory girl something to focus upon."

"She's got a gun," Victoria said from inside the black cloth at the rear of the camera. There on the frosty, transfiguring glass she saw Rachel holding across her chest a hunting rifle with a telescopic sight.

"Is it *per*fectly in focus?" Nat Fraser asked. His hand that had guided hers to the milled-steel wheel controlling the length of the bellows touched her strong-boned fingers again, encouraging her to perfect the image only she could see within the curtains around her head.

"Strike different poses, Rachel," Nat commanded. "Here." He tossed her a beret and on the frosty glass the girl pulled it on low across her forehead. She caught a strand of her long black hair from her shoulder and pulled it under her nose to make a mustache. "Dream, girl! Do not mock! This is a very solemn moment."

Victoria felt his guiding hand close on her wrist. Her breath dimmed the wonderful glass momentarily, and then it was clear again. She saw Rachel snarling and pointing the rifle at the camera lens, her feet spread wide as if she were positioning a bayonet. She felt the easing movement of Nat's legs as he sidled between the division of her buttocks, leaning his plumpness onto her as she felt more weight in the hand gripping her wrist.

Now Rachel was holding the gun over her head in both hands, in an ecstasy of triumph. Victory. The shape of her slender figure was as explicit as a word painted in giant letters on a *barrio* wall. *Venceremos!*

"Take that picture!" Nat said. Again his hand guided Victoria's to a mechanism somewhere on the front of the old-fashioned camera. His forefinger pressed hers until a tensing spring released with a deadly little click.

"Rachel saw the birdie. Victoria saw the birdie. Brothers and sisters saw the birdie," Nat warbled as he pulled the halves of the patent-leather hood from around Victoria's long hair. "Now you can come out and breathe. Take a big breath, Sister. Fill your lungs with freedom's air. Ain't she nice? Breathe it! Oh, breathe it!"

And truly beyond the cocaine—beyond anything she had ever felt as her own before—there was a separate intoxication of the air she breathed now, at his command. It *was* freedom. She had to do what she did now.

So easy. Beyond the fuss of restraints. A comradeship without the nervous talk of comradeship.

She strode around the bulking, beautiful legs of the old camera and took the rifle from Rachel's hands.

How majestic, royal, the hard precision of the bolt as she jerked it open for inspection. She saw the gun was loaded. The tilted, shady copper color of the bullet's tip was ready to be slammed into the chamber. She saw it rise as she pressed the bolt forward.

"Easy," Nat said. He moved very quickly to catch the barrel in his hand and keep it from pointing at any of them in the room with her. "It is dangerous. I perceive that *you* are dangerous."

"Oh yes."

"Now, Sister, you have seen what I am baddest bugs about," he said. "You really like these boon companions." He eased the rifle back and forth through her loosening hands, a kind of ritual, a kind of caress.

"I love them," she said.

"You love them?"

"You, too?" she said.

"I could *make* love to them beauties. Want to see the rest I got?"

"More guns?"

"I got plenty more guns. For you I get them out."

There were fourteen weapons, all told, packed and hidden in various parts of his basement studio. Five rifles, a Thompson submachine gun looking almost as old-fashioned and stately as the big camera on its frame of polished wood. Two revolvers. And the rest were automatic pistols.

He spread them out on a blanket unfolded atop a flat worktable, finding them one by one, kneeling to lift the submachine gun from its rag wrappings in an orange crate, skittering on bent knees to a pile of cardboard cartons from which three Mauser carbines came, reaching into a hole in the brick foundations to pull out a musty leather hatbox that stored all but one of the handguns.

He was showing them off to all his visitors, and all of them were caught up in the magnetic field of his excitement and the pride of his ownership. The lines of magnetic force flowed to them intensified through Victoria's dazed enchantment as the guns came one by one onto the table.

When he had found them all, Nat was breathing hard. He ran a big hand over the stock of one of the carbines and said, "It is an exquisite collection. Which one you like the best, Sister? Which one you *choose?*"

"I . . . choose that one," Victoria said. She reached for one of the pistols. Nat was quicker than she. He had it first.

"*Yes,*" he exulted. "A Colt's. Forty-five caliber. Regulation army model. Big, black, and ain't she ugly? This one. Ah-eee-ess. The sister chooses this one. Issued to the sister in the name of the Rebellion. Sister, come in the darkroom with me. We make it yours. Come in de dahkrum, we finda nahs holstah for'm. Come in. Come in. I give it *to* you."

"Victoria," Bunny said. He had said nothing for a very long time, hardly anything since they came down to the basement. The pulse in his throat was so heavy, strangling, dense that he was not sure she heard him now.

He moved to catch her arm as Nat guided her toward the darkroom door.

Mike Lane was in front of him. Mike Lane had a pistol pointed at his face.

"Let her go," Mike Lane said. There was wild laughter in his eyes.

He put the muzzle of the pistol against Bunny's forehead. "Rachel," he called. "Bring some more happy dust for our friend here. Then we'll turn out all the lights."

Bunny Stewart forgot there had been a gun at his head when he sniffed the white powder from the back of Rachel's hand. He forgot many things while the basement was in darkness. He thought he might have been lying for a while in a girl's embrace, not Victoria's. It must have been Rachel who eased him onto the floor.

They must have been listening for something. They lay so still there. Listening for the guitars playing far across the wide Missouree, where all his beautiful loves were humming and bidding him join them for the westward trek. He heard a long-drawn cry of some bird lifting out of the marsh at dawn. Rachel said, "Sssssh!"

He heard the bird cry, "Yeh—ussssssssssss. Yeh-usssssssss," as its long, awkward wings lifted it into the pink and gray. The wings became more graceful as the bird rose and went toward the reddening horizon, finally becoming a tiny speck. Then lost.

"Yes," Rachel said. There was an automatic pistol between their faces. Someone was holding it between their faces as they lay in a loose clutch on the floor. Rachel was sniffing the gun barrel, taking the smell which was not of oil or steel only, but also of the sea marsh from which the lovely bird had risen. "Do you smell it, Bunny?" Rachel asked.

He forgot if he answered. He forgot what he had been asked. There was a weirdly distressing smell in his nostrils when he woke and saw there was light in the room again, a sinister hybrid smell of flesh and metal, as if he might be tasting the slight decomposition of the fillings in his teeth. He was lightly nauseated by it, yet supposed if he went on sleeping it would fade. But Stella was shaking him to keep him awake.

"Come," she said. "Help load the cars."

He turned his aching neck to see a light far away at the head of the basement stairs. In silhouette someone marched up the stairs to the kitchen carrying a cardboard carton. In a minute or two he realized there were more people coming and going than had been here before. The newcomers were all blacks.

"Sick," he said. "Sleep here."

"No."

"Take us back to motel?"

"Can't you stand by yourself?"

"Sure. Can. Back to your place?"

"We're not going to my place. It's begun."

"'S over," he said, thinking she had said the Civil War had begun. A kind of merriment and horror sloshed like unmixing water and oil in his mind. He was sick and didn't care much if it was beginning or already finished. Then as he stood up and realized how frail and long his legs were, he got dizzy and the waves of nausea were too strong to master. He leaned against a wall and began to vomit on it.

"Help me get him in my car and I'll take him home with me," Stella said. "I'll catch up with you later."

"I've got a better idea," Mike Lane said.

"No," Rachel said. "No, no, no. Mike, he's one of us."

With a dawning terror, Bunny started to protest that he was intellectually committed to the liberation of all oppressed groups, minorities and individuals. The only sound that came out of his raw, bile-scalded throat was something like: Ahrew-come-aw—lib-peep . . .

"He's sick," Rachel said. "He can't even tell us what he wants. Mike! Don't do something crazy before we get started."

Mike said, "I wasn't going to do it here. But doesn't he look like a man who would protect Miss Hoyt from the black fiends who carried her off? The last full measure of devotion and all that? Pip, pip."

Rachel said, "No, Mike, no!"

"What are you two talking about?" Stella said. "I'll take him home and then we'll catch up. . . . Where's Victoria?"

"Victoria's going with Rachel and me," Mike said. "She's in the car."

"Where's Nat? I don't understand," Stella said. "Now you tell me why I can't take this sick boy ho . . ."

"Go home!" Mike said to her with a squeal of scornful laughter. "We've got a message to get through! Stewart can ride with Nat's friends. *Somebody's* got to be kidnapped. Somebody's got to be a hostage, no? Go home, Stella. Keep your mouth shut."

When Stella was gone and Mike Lane began tapping him—not hard—in the chest with a pistol, Bunny tried to explain how necessary to the plan his intelligence was, his analytical mind, his conception of the major principles of insurgent action.

"May-rin in-act," he said.

"Yes. Yeh-uss. You bet your bottom dollar," Mike said. "Now you come on and ride with these gentlemen who understand all about that. Rache, you come with me. I want to be down there and help shoot up the place."

It astonished Bunny that he could climb the basement stairs under his own power. It astonished him that human hands reached out to drag him into the back seat of a car parked in the yard and it astonished him more when the hands pulled what must have been a pillowcase over his head. He could breathe through it—what he was doing must have been breathing, though he could feel no expansion or contraction of his lungs.

He started to say that this was surely for the best, and that he realized he must submit to the authority of those who had taken responsibility for this revolutionary action, but . . .

The car started with a jerk and his head was thrown against the back of the seat. It was astonishing to him how soft the blow against his head was. The darkness to which he submitted was astonishingly sweet.

They were sending a message to all the oppressors of the world. That was about all that was perfectly agreed on.

By midmorning the first installment of the message was on the local radio stations. It took only a little longer for it to get to El Dorado, a thousand miles to the south.

BOOK III

I

1

Except for Charlotte Keefe, nearly everyone at El Dorado took the first word of the kidnapping with some degree of skepticism. "Why shouldn't it be a hoax?" Bob Pardon said to her. "She's a Hoyt, isn't she? The whole thing has a fishy odor. No one ever asked for such a wild amount of ransom. You've got to think of the company that girl keeps, Charlotte."

"Now I'll tell *you* to be fair," she said. "No one knows it's a hoax. I tell you, if it is, or it isn't, there's something terrible going on."

"Well, I'd count on you to stand by Cooley when there's trouble, but . . ."

"I wasn't," she said with the humblest frankness. "I was set to leave him. As you must have guessed."

"Then leave! Leave!" he said. "Cooley's girl is nothing to you. You're right, it's going to be terrible. But not in any straightforward way."

He wanted something finally to be straight in this kingdom of zigzag, and Charlotte's flight from it was the only straight possibility in sight.

But she—who had known since Cooley's disappearance how complete her freedom was—discovered all at once that freedom only allows you to choose where and how to take on bondage and commitment again.

He gave her his best reason for doubting the authenticity of Victoria's kidnapping. "I never told you she threatened—very emphatically—to come back and have another try at Cooley. I thought until now she was just badly upset when she threatened. But add it up. You have to believe there's *something* in it."

Charlotte didn't have to believe anything beyond her own visions. With wide eyes she told him, "I had me a dream of a baby. Cooley's and mine. On Los Colombes I dreamed it. The little thing was hungry and could not be nourished of me."

"All right. You had a dream." He meant by his tone to ease her out of trusting the feelings that went with dreams when, as he saw it, those feelings were not going to be reciprocated by either Cooley or Victoria Hoyt.

Still she said, "I mean, we shall have the child back from her kidnappers. Cooley must not haggle about what it costs. Nor us. Get ahold of that John Halvorsen and tell him to buy this place if he wants it."

She gave him no chance to explain that only women and kidnappers still seemed to believe that money came in large bundles that could be simply passed from hand to hand.

Nor explain that John Halvorsen had already been heard from. He has been one of the first conveyors of the bad news from Los Angeles. He called in case they hadn't yet heard at El Dorado what the Los Angeles radio was putting out. "The rumor here is that Cooley's kid is going to be released on stage in Las Vegas—and marry one of the kidnappers in a topless ceremony!"

"You know that any publicity is good," Bob said with the heartsick joviality that had settled on him now like any other loathsome habit.

That made the Sun King cackle instead of scoffing at the cliché. The point being, merely, that any publicity is good for *someone*—not everyone—and he already was feeling himself the beneficiary of this new sensation.

But the effect of the sensational events was not much different on the new team of journalists, who were presumably here to emphasize the dark side. The fashion reporters had flown away with the celebrities they had come to celebrate. The new gang was snapping for bloody shreds instead of sunbaked delights. From being the town crier, Bob had gone over to a game of hide-and-seek.

He pointed out to the new team that day by day he heard

more from them than he had to give in return. "The action is on
the other side of the border now. Why don't you fly back at least
as far as El Paso and hunker down in front of a nice cool television set? Don't you see that reality has all become electronic?
What do you care about the living, breathing Hoyts—we haven't
got any here anyway—when you've got the *name* of Hoyt to
stitch everything together with?"

Still, most of the reporters were a good lot and they took his
ranting as part of the time-killing repartee that went with the
pleasures of the place—the sun, the flowers, the handsome
women, the superflux of service—that made life good while they
waited for something ghastly to write about.

It was only the fat boy who said he meant to write for *Rolling
Stone* who claimed he took Bob seriously in his diatribes against
the media's part in the kidnapping. Along with Karen Steiglitz,
the fat boy was the only holdover among the journalists from the
spectacular days of the opening.

Still unable to produce any signs of accreditation, he simply
assumed the privileges of a veteran. Whether he still entered the
grounds by climbing over the wall or not, he began to haunt
Bob's days and nights—seeming to materialize like an overweight
and insinuating genie when Bob relaxed at poolside for a drink,
or when he stretched in the reclining chair on his own balcony,
supposing he had stalled the reporters for another day.

"I like your angle on reality," he would say to Bob—easing
alongside, easing into philosophic contempt for his hypothetical
brethren of the press. "It *is* electronic. Reality. It's the age of the
meta-fact. Who gives a shit, really, if there is a Victoria Hoyt or
if there's forty million dollars left in the world? *It* says so. And
all these yahoos hanging around—what are they ever going to
write except what each of the other of them writes?"

Bob felt no temptation to bounce with the fat boy on such
waves of meditation. It exasperated him to hear himself echoed;
it angered him to be patronized. "I thought it was your ambi-
tion . . ."

"To be a journalist? Right. But not one of them. They're part
of what I want to write about. Include them in the picture. I've
got thousands of words that weave back and forth between sen-
sations and impressions and my personal orientation."

"I'd like to read them," Bob said, keeping his eyes shut, neither smiling nor frowning.

"What I admire about you is, you wouldn't. Karen Steiglitz read some and tried to give me some pointers. I'm not after pointers. I'm after the total reality. That's why I value my talks from you. I figure you see it the same way. Multi-level. Multi-moralistic. Multi . . ."

"Yes," Bob said. "Multi everything. Now if you'll excuse me . . ."

But no matter how often or how successfully he excused himself from the fat boy—whose name he refused to learn—each time the boy eased up again it was with an air of intensified spiritual kinship, as if their dialogue had not been interrupted at all by Bob's attempts to withdraw from it, and as if in the thousands of words being written nightly, one supposed, by the ambitious boy, their mutual insights were extended until they wrapped every aspect of the mystery in a multi-dimensional web of prose. When Bob woke at night (and his sleep was fretful now) he would sometimes involuntarily imagine he heard the clack of the fat boy's typewriter, a machine of the future putting words into his mouth and pulling words out of his mouth that he intended never to utter to anyone.

That semi-hallucination was one of the worst parts of these days of waiting. He felt he had been invaded by a virus, felt himself not so much sick as turned into the helpless host of a sickness that might spread from him in an unlimited contagion.

Yes, the boy had got to him in some fantastic way, and before he knew just what he was anxiously listening for, he knew that he was beginning to receive a message from the fat boy's loquacity. The message of a generation and its ways that he had tried to immunize himself against.

For somehow he believed the fat boy was tuned in to the way Victoria and her fellow conspirators must be sending out the impulses that could hopefully be translated into reasonable action.

"As you say, Mr. Pardon, they *aimed* it right for the evening news, whoever set this up. Don't think the underground haven't got their connections with the networks and don't know what buttons to push to get on prime time. That being the villainous low state of journalism in these freaked-out times.

"Like—how would you translate out the amount of ransom they're asking? I mean, it's very unprofessional, even for the New Left, to ask for a ransom of that magnitude. *Unless* it's a jerk-off they mean to follow with a serious figure later on, when and if the negotiation settles down to getting Vicky back. Care to commentate on that?"

"No. No. No, thank you."

"All right. And you still shouldn't mind my prose, which I got to use when I talk to you. But in the new journalism I'm going to write it will be mostly the way it is to be poolside here with you, sprawled out watching that South American—or is she Spanish?— cunt over there oiling her long legs while we're having a margarita and I'm sensing your integrity among finks and then I ask you: Mr. Pardon, you know very well that Vicky Hoyt was right on the grounds here the night the greaser police shot up the local *cuspidores*. And what does that mean? How does that add in?"

"It sounds suspicious," Bob said. It sounded as if information he wished to keep from certain ears was seeping roundabout—as information always did.

The fat boy went on, "I speculate they are the ones who got her and that they are opening a branch office in the States and maybe Papa Hoyt is one of them, too. Does that grab you?"

"It passes the time."

"Then, please, try this one, Mr. Pardon. I know some of the same type *cuspidores* in the L.A. scene. There're a lot of crazies there. *Genuine* crazies and mean sons of bitches. Smart-ass little left-wing maiden gets talking to them, says, 'Why don't we fake a kidnapping, rip off my pig daddy for a little bread for the Movement?' They say, 'Ho-ho. What a great idea.' Then they rip her off for real. Then? Next? They let the hoopla spread. They know how to heat it up in the media. *But.* They know they're not going to take Hoyt for that kind of bread. So. When the figure drops to *one* million even—you would know it was the boys talking to you right out of the horse's mouth. Comment?"

The sense of talking to someone in a dream—of having been coached and prepared to understand a foreign language—came

to a peak in Bob's mind. Never mind the daylight around them.
For this minute they were in another land altogether.

Bob reached steadily down to pick up his margarita glass
without shifting the bulk of his torso from the towel spread over
his beach chair. He tasted it and set it back down.

"Are you telling me that is it? What we are to pay? *One* million? Is that the figure you are actually asking?"

"Ho-ho-ho," the fat boy said. But this time it was he who
broke off the conversation. At that point.

It was not perfectly clear, or convincing, to Bob that this was
the first contact made by the kidnappers. As he watched the fat
boy traipse clownishly around the perimeter of the pool and go
out of sight in the shrubbery bordering the path to the snack bar,
he was only convinced—by all he remembered since the day of
the fat boy's appearance—that he had seen part of a design that
might be central.

And yet if the fat boy had finally given him a peep at the
cards to be played, the real threat that had to be appeased, the
means by which the message had been conveyed to him was
more hallucinatory than the inner voices that came to Charlotte,
preparing her for what was to come.

Late in that day, Bob saw her come wading in through the
shallow water off the beach. His eye picked her out from the
other bathers by some unnamable quality of isolation about her—
as if she not only paid no attention to anyone else bobbing and
splashing and cavorting in the delightful surf but counted on
being invisible to them, too.

He hobbled off to intercept her. But when he came on her on
one of the cobbled paths leading to the Monarch Suite something dejected about her posture quickly decided him to keep
still awhile longer. They were all too vulnerable now—too prone
to overreading suggestions and even fantasies that could betray
them as much as anyone who intended them harm.

"I'm tired," Charlotte said when he caught up to her. "I swam
all the way in from the islands. I seem to need to be in the water
now."

"Listening to the voices of the deep?"

"Don't make fun of me. It's true, they say, that in others' trouble we see what's been wrong with us."

"There's nothing wrong with you. Except you're tired."

"Much more than that," she said. "I see what I have to atone for."

"Now, don't go religious on us. Not you."

"No. No. But I must think it all out again, what is right to do. It's not enough to be fair. Or it is for you. Not me."

She took him up to the suite for a drink. They sat outside, of course, for the beauty of early evenings here was constant though everything else—even the heart—was corrupted by knowledge. These structures on their jungle promontory were an altar built for the moment, the radiant present instant that the senses know. And his heart had never resented more that the treacherous mind would open the gates to the hostile past and future—for in this majestic light Charlotte seemed more than ever the priestess of that altar.

"You've come to tell me we must do something about Cooley. I know, I know," she said.

He admitted it reluctantly. "At least take steps to find him."

"Ah, I know where he is." A wondering smile stretched her sad mouth but her eyes were fixed on the deep water where she had gone for counsel. "That fool Encerros! The police are good for *something!* They've kept him in sight. God knows what for. When the poor devil deserved at least to do his business with no one peeking. This morning I talked to him on the phone—if you can call it talking."

"Still drunk?"

"I wouldn't say. . . . I couldn't say, since I've never seen him so. Bad hit. Bad hit by too many things at once. I think no one else could have made out what he meant at all."

"He knows about Victoria?"

"Who can make it out? I suppose he's heard less gabble than you. But it's made him wild thinking of so much money. Forty million! He'll break a blood vessel in the shape he's in. At such a price, says he, the girl is no kin of his."

"Well . . ." Bob gave a little gesture of fatigue. "Are you surprised? And when it comes down to it, I think he's right. It's not a very noble position for him to take. It's not his duty to be noble when—probably—the girl has contributed so much to whatever mess she's in."

"But still, that's just what his duty should be. If you're left no choice of being anything else, I'd want him to be noble. And want something like that for myself. Never too late, what?"

The gravity of her tone was developing into something else. "I'm a barren woman," she said, saying it as if she were repeating a sentence of death whispered to her when she had swum so far, offering her body to the deep, fecund waters of the bay.

And he thought he saw then what she was trying to make out of this grimly garbled confusion. "You want to claim Cooley's daughter for your own? Make the man act like a father even if he never has been one? But don't you see . . . ?"

"You're too quick for me and I cannot always understand your thinking. No. The girl could not be my daughter. Yet . . . I've begun to understand her. Yes, I have."

And then he thought: No. Charlotte was not angling for a chance at nobility or at being the good woman, either. She was the one who knew so well the uses of glamour and its fine satisfactions. And when she said she understood Victoria now—what could it mean except that she was challenged by the glamour of ruin? She was Charlotte and she was not going to let a snit of a girl play at death and destruction and attract all eyes while she was neglected.

It seemed to him then while so many of his fixed assumptions collapsed that now he understood for the first time why she had attached herself to Cooley in the first place. Not because Cooley gave her a chance to create or build—though he had done that, too—but because someday he would give her the chance to shine with the glamour of pointless sacrifice.

"You should have got out before now!" he raged. For that moment he was angered at all women. How could anything ever go straight in the world, or grow, or be at peace while they nourished such contradictions in themselves?

Then, all at once, he and Charlotte were grinning at each other. "By God, all right," he said. "We'll have to stick with him in this, too. Of course, you'll go fetch him and stiffen his spine again. You'll try. But between him and that girl they'll tear your wings off."

Cheerily she said, "I'm strong. I've proved that. But I'm a barren woman and women are not strong for that. Tear me? Isn't that what a woman is for?"

2

The police were not much inclined to take Victoria's kidnapping at face value. Probably they would have been little involved if it had not begun to blossom in the realm of public entertainment. What baffled everyone from the start was that the reliable line between reality and report had been capriciously erased. What good are police routines in tracking a girl who has been transformed into an electronic ghost, a voice in the air? It was like playing three-dimensional chess on a two-dimensional chessboard.

From the motel room in Los Angeles luggage had been hastily but thoroughly removed in the late hours of a Thursday night. The only witness was a candy salesman from Sacramento, wakened from his sleep in the adjacent room by the itch of chronic psoriasis. He had heard voices in the room of Mr. and Mrs. Benjamin Stewart—not including any distinctively feminine voice—before he heard the shot that blew the lock off the door. He had been reckless, itchy or thoughtless enough to expose his face at the window and had seen "a light-colored car, either a Chevy or a Plymouth," depart at great speed while someone with an arm out the window fired two shots in the air.

Inside the room on a bed that had not been slept in, there was a note declaring Victoria Hoyt had been "taken hostage" and would be held until forty million dollars in "war reparations" was paid by the "colonialist exploiter" Cooley Hoyt, her father.

It was a shabby and unconvincing beginning, and if the name Hoyt had not had a journalistic currency even the local radio stations in Los Angeles might have been discreet enough to postpone any report. Over the weekend the matter simmered. By then fingerprints in the motel room had established beyond question that Benjamin Stewart had been one of the occupants. From arrests in Chicago and others following demonstrations in Washington his fingerprints had gone into federal files.

"So they've established—the finks—that he's a radical and therefore—what's the verb?—is involved in the snatch," Karen Steiglitz said, keeping it all orderly under the palms and blue skies of El Dorado, spending a guessable three hours a day on the phone with the "news headquarters" in New York City.

"Watch the verbs," Bob said. "Many missing persons have disappeared forever in the semantic funhouse where cops and journalists store their verbs. And as for that bearded academic renegade being 'involved in the snatch'—as a feminist you should beware your choice of nouns. The great viewing public cannot adequately sympathize with a snatch, nor the sisterhood empathize."

"Anyway . . ." Karen said.

Anyway, that media event known as the Hoyt Kidnapping had simmered over the weekend. On Monday night a disc jockey in Boston had played a tape which had been "delivered" to him. On that tape a girl who said she was Victoria Hoyt spoke briefly and almost intelligibly. She said she was being treated well, that her captors were "determined men and women." She ended with sobs and then a clear appeal to her father to meet the ransom conditions. "I don't want to die," she said.

In nearby Cambridge, Victoria's mother missed the playing of the tape. Mrs. Rossiter did not listen to programs played by disc jockeys. But if Mary Rossiter did not have the notoriety of her first husband, she was known locally for her participation in the Anti-War Movement and other liberal-to-radical manifestations. The reporters there had an additional incentive for calling it to her attention. Naturally the reporters had asked if she knew anything of her daughter's voluntary participation in a maneuver to unhook Mr. Hoyt from part of his worldwide financial holdings.

The stunned woman only admitted that she had had a recent phone call from Victoria in Los Angeles. Mary Rossiter had gone into Boston to listen to the tape after hearing part of it played on the telephone and being unable to recognize the voice as her daughter's. She did not know, until the reporters told her, that Victoria had recently flown from Mexico to Los Angeles. But she could not believe the girl had been in contact with her father there.

The Boston disc jockey gave the police little useful information about the origin of the tape. He only told them that he had found it on his desk when he arrived at the studio the afternoon before he played it. The note taped to the can merely said: UR-GENT, HOYT KIDNAP. An office girl said she had noticed the tape on the desk as early as 2 P.M. Perhaps someone had left it there when most of the staff was out to lunch.

For reasons that had not yet been traced onto Karen Steiglitz's situation map, Mrs. Rossiter had urged the Boston police to urge the Los Angeles police to question a Stella Franklin about Victoria's presence in that city.

In Governor Hogben's state the leading newspaper front-paged both the story of the governor's trial and a headline reading:

HOYT'S DAUGHTER: I DON'T WANT TO DIE.

Victoria's second tape was delivered to a radio station in Detroit. "A pattern of blacks is emerging," someone said, as if all were explained by the fact that the tapes were relayed to black intermediaries for broadcasting.

The single copy of the tape sufficed because now the essential —the slogans, the indoctrinated emotions, the headline stuff—was amplified across the country in reproductions made by the major networks.

Victoria—if it was Victoria—said in a sad voice that the people who held her hostage were dedicated and experienced revolutionaries "supported by the wretched of the earth in our country and in all lands." They were willing to die if necessary after killing her. She was young and had lots to live for. She said she understood their motives. Great wrongs had been done to the people they represented. They were the pioneers of a revolutionary movement that would soon sweep from America the corrupt bankers and politicians and oilmen as Nixon's men had been swept out by Watergate. But though she understood their motives, their methods were wrong. They saw themselves as being like John Brown, who had fought the slaveholders in the South before the majority of the people were ready for the Civil War. She understood that they had taken her hostage because she was a member of the exploiting classes, but she did not want to die.

HOYT'S DAUGHTER UNDERSTANDS KIDNAPPERS

VICKY WANTS TO LIVE

POLICE SEE PATTERN IN VICKY TAPES

VICKY BRAINWASHED?

VICKY'S MOTHER: PLEASE!

In her third tape, broadcast a day after the second, Victoria lamented to the American public that she had grown up without knowing her father. She believed, though, that he loved her too much to let her be executed. "Dad, if you hear this I'm going to say something so you'll know it is me. Now. Do you remember the Christmas Eve at Skelton Duchy when Mr. Finch sang 'Silent Night' with us? Now do you know it is me, Dad?"

On the same tape Victoria declared that the network of revolutionaries who had taken her captive was far larger than anyone had suspected. The FBI and police could not possibly find her because she was moving constantly on the "underground railway." But as soon as her father had met the ransom demands she hoped to see him and "get to know him and make up for all the years apart." She said she was being treated with "the greatest consideration" by the revolutionary guards who were escorting her from one part of the country to another. "I am allowed to say I saw mountains this morning," she said.

A male voice came on after hers and denounced Cooley Hoyt as a pig exploiter who had gone from "interior colonialism" to ravish the underdeveloped countries around the globe. The American people should demand that he be brought to justice in American courts. But since the American legal system was too corrupt to do this necessary cleaning up, the revolutionary cadres had devised this method for returning to the people "some small part" of what had been stolen from them. The entire ransom, when it was paid, would be distributed among progressive groups who fought for the rights of youth, women, blacks, Indians, the aged and those of Hispanic origin.

One further condition would have to be met by the pig government that had launched Cooley Hoyt and his ilk to prey on the freedom-loving people of the world. A plane and air crew would have to be made available to the cadre of revolutionary guards now deployed to guard Victoria. They would have to have safe conduct to a Muslim country.

In a final passionate burst of oratory, the speaker promised that though he would have to take temporary sanctuary abroad, "I shall return. When the day comes. When the people rise!"

He announced that the next and final tape with Victoria's voice would be broadcast "from a people's station in Washington, D.C." Afterward Hoyt would be invited to secret negotiations. "The last chance."

It was sheer lunacy.

But whose, whose, whose?

If it were mine, Bob Pardon thought, I would know what to do. I would take a swim longer than Charlotte's. One man alone could always find the remedy for such disorder. Maybe Cooley had found it by his giant binge, and if so it was the greatest cruelty to disturb his peace by bringing him back.

But then, mercifully, he saw something with his own eyes that convinced him the insanity was limited and not an epidemic sweeping the world.

He saw the VW bus that had brought Victoria and Bunny Stewart here six weeks before. Getting out of it this time were Karen Steiglitz and the fat boy whose name he had never wanted to learn, the aspirant to *Rolling Stone*.

They had someone else with them, who got out of the VW last. A man about Bob's age, tall, with short gray hair. Pudgy, looking like a college athlete who has put on exactly a pound a year in the thirty-five years since his varsity days. Looking, in spite of his bright Bermuda shorts and flowered shirt, like a ranking member of the armed forces making an on-the-ground inspection to see if the premises were suitable for his own Rest and Recreation on government per diem.

Looking, as Bob said an hour later to Karen, every inch what he professed himself to be: Lieutenant Colonel Harold Timmerman, formerly of the USAF, now living in comfortable retirement in the American community near Ajijic.

Glumly Bob conceded Karen had sniffed out part of Victoria's track. "At least you found the car."

"The getaway car," she called it. But in her satisfaction she was willing to be modest. "You're the one who knows reporters never find anything. People who want something to surface bring things to them. Bull Timmerman's just been in New York."

"Bull?"

"I don't find him very appetizing, either, but . . . He was in my offices there, talking to Nick Sanders. I told you once Nick had heard there'd be an attempt to get Rosio here. It's pretty clear that Timmerman was our source. Why don't you say 'aha'?"

"Because every card in the deck is a joker. I don't know how to stay in the game. Unless you've been instructed to make me believe he's a CIA man with a thousand covers. Why would I be better off to think that?"

She swore that she had no such instructions, though she had been on the phone with Timmerman while he was in Nick Sanders's office. "He told us to meet him at the plane in Guadalajara. He turned up the car."

"Us? You and the fat boy?"

"Hubert Hollins. He's ambitious and has lots of theories. He thinks Bull is the kingpin in the drug business. They were talking about that as we drove down here. Wild! Hubert's attached himself to me. I guess he sees the Sanders Show in his future."

"All right. You've got the car and you've brought us in a paying guest—I assume he's paying his way here, or whatever government or news network he may be representing at this given instant in time—but where's Victoria? Has he told you or Nick Sanders that? I'm convinced I'll hear it first from you."

She shook her head, but she wanted him to believe that Bull Timmerman had come with some important contribution. "He's very anxious to see Hoyt. He says he can help. Maybe he can."

II

The gracious and comfortable tourist accommodations of Puerto Vallarta have been interwoven in the life of the city, farms and fishery without a perceptible shock of contrast. It is a resort that displays no more than normal flamboyance and a few of the beach hotels have long been recommended by travel agents to honeymooners who want at least some seclusion.

At a cottage in the grounds of one of these hotels Charlotte knocked briskly on the door.

The knocking sounded loud to her, as if all the sound might be bouncing right back at her. None of it penetrating the interior. As if the room beyond the door might not be continuous in time and space with the sidewalk bordered by flowers or the bright dazzle of light on the Pacific out beyond the sentinel palms.

"He's in there," said the discreet young man from the hotel desk. He had walked out among the cottages with her to point out the one in which Cooley was holed up, and also maybe to watch out for any trouble she might encounter or make. "Knock again. He might be sleeping. He sleeps much."

She did not knock any more. She turned the knob and stepped decisively inside. She closed the door just as decisively in the face of the discreet young man behind her.

The blinds of the room she entered were drawn down tight. In the dimness Cooley was sitting ramrod straight at a little table. He faced the door like a man facing the door of a cell in Death Row. The wideness of his eyes was a signal of something beyond terror or pleading, either. Some utter resignation that asked only for decorum in the process of execution. But it was not even the widened whites of his eyes that hit her hardest. His beard had been neatly shaved off and beneath the still robust tan of his forehead and cheeks his chin gleamed pale as the belly of a dead fish.

"Ah, they've been at you, old man," she said. She took three fast steps to reach him and pull his ruined face against her belly.

There was an antiseptic smell about him, whether it was something he had been drinking or a lotion with which the barber had anointed him, she could not tell. There was a glass half full of a clear liquid on the table in front of him. She tasted it. Water.

In a reflex of angry pity she looked around for something more merciful to put in the glass and hold to his mouth. Let the man drink his fill, since he had gone this far.

She went to search the kitchenette and cupboards for alcohol and found none. When she came back to him empty-handed he had finished the water in the glass. He was still licking his lips thirstily.

"Will you kneel and pray with me?" he asked.

She realized she had been waiting for his voice. In bad times his rich and somber tones had never deserted him. That crazy voice that seemed to have nothing to do with the confusion or downright panic he might be feeling in the hairbreadth situations he had talked his way into. It was the voice he counted on to talk himself out of traps that maybe should have held and broken him before now. It was the salesman's voice. He seemed to belong to it more than it belonged to him. And when he asked her to pray with him that voice almost persuaded her to give in. Why not?

"No," she said.

She had come here telling herself she would use whatever trick or duplicity she could command to get him on his feet again.

"I won't pray with you," she said. The request had startled her. She was ready to believe prayer was what he needed. Still her nostrils tightened as if they caught an unclean smell.

He was not ready to pray. No man was fit for prayer until he had used up everything of his own resources. If there had to be prayer, let it begin with the whimper of a body or soul broken beyond the possibility of saving itself. That voice of his was unfit for prayer. It was given him for use in the world, a kind of armor that had to be stripped off for love or salvation.

"It was always too late for praying," she said. "Never too late for us. Cooley, man, git yer damn feet under you. Stand, you big son of a bitch! Stand, I say. Stand!"

Her own voice was no better. It was like commanding him to have an erection. The idea of any sexual communication between them was as repulsive as the idea of prayer—the nerves themselves rejected it queasily. He had gone very far away from her, as if all the days he had spent holed up in this room with the girl and then by himself had been a continuous voyage farther and farther into a desert wasteland.

When he tried to speak to her he seemed to be excusing his frailty to some stranger. His pale chin was sunken against his chest and he didn't or couldn't raise it.

His eyes rolled up when he said, "You told them I was in Europe, yes? Board meetings to revive the IMTF. Essentially sound. Only minor refinancing necessary. I hope everyone was told that."

"No," she said. "No one was told anything, Cooley. You can explain as you like when we get back."

The idea—the mere mention—of going back to El Dorado seemed to terrify him further. Or even the idea of standing up. As if he had to remain seated to keep the mocking world from seeing how he had soiled himself.

"I'll get you back," she said. "You can rest. Think of what story you'll want to tell people about why you were gone. Be ready to help Victoria."

If he had been uncertain before, now he was not. He threw his head up and back with real ferocity. "She's punishing me," he said. "It's only something she and her mother have thought of to punish me."

"And maybe you deserve it," she said. She said it without heat, calmly, and her tone seemed to please him.

"I'll pay," he said. His mouth started to form some brag or

other, a brag of money. Then he began to cry. "I can't pay," he said. "There's never enough. Never enough."

Tears are not prayer, and when she had seen him cry before she had always taken it as a kind of mechanical display of the nervous tension he used to drive himself—a sort of garbage spilled from the reckless and spendthrift concentration on his objectives. She had never sympathized with his tears, and she didn't now.

But these, at least, spoke to her. The only language possible for what he had hidden from her as he hid it from everyone and even from himself. And her response was just as basic and uncalculated.

She shoved him from his chair, cuffed him out of it with a maternal vigor that might have got him moving again. She knew it was what he wanted and needed. But instead of rising onto his feet, he simply slithered down flat on his back on the floor. His lips were working, not for words or sobs, either.

And that communication reached her, too. She got down on all fours beside him. Not to see if he was really too sick to stand. In this moment of ugly tenderness she knew exactly what was happening and what was necessary.

She opened the top of her dress. She was over him like a lioness drooping her spine to offer a dug to some shapeless wriggle of fur and clutching paws, offering it drink so it can know what it has to be. Like the she-wolf of the legend, she fed him.

Fed him what she had probably always had to give. Not milk, nor anything as clear-cut as an idea of manhood. There was neither physical nor intellectual nourishment for his absolute thirst. But he knew her then as he had never quite known her in his lunging potency. She knew what he was taking. In the night she had mastered and exhausted the Hungarian girl she had learned something more of the way men may renew themselves from the nameless current that does not have to be called either male or female.

"Have it. Have it," she crooned to the suckling creature that hung on her with such weakness, such strength.

Afterward, of course, they rose as if they hadn't noticed what had taken place there on the floor. As if they were both so shamed by it that they must mutually deny it had ever happened.

But at least now he could move by himself, talk, contemplate what had to be done—and in general resemble the Cooley Hoyt who had finagled El Dorado into existence.

He was fussy and fragile, but all the way back on the short plane ride he worried aloud about how to handle "the Victoria mess." Evasiveness and bragging returned naturally to his manner as he reclaimed his strength.

And she didn't know what more she could do than match it. "There may be a break, we think. There's a man showed up who says he can act as go-between. A sort of army man who lets on he knows you. . . ." She was very leery of Colonel Timmerman, but it occurred to her that the man was not entirely unlike Cooley. And the two of them might, indeed, find some common and useful ground.

2

"I don't know how they forced your little girl to say some of what she put on those tapes," Bull Timmerman said. "You can bet she's scared. But don't be fooled by all this political hoopla they've got going up in the States. That's for the networks. You know how they gobble up any leftish propaganda. And it's what you could expect from that hippie professor who set this whole thing up. He's probably had this in mind for years, working out a smoke screen to cover it, and he's the one who's brought her back into Mexico, because this is where his connections are."

He was getting to the point with Cooley and Charlotte. He was doing so on a catamaran, sliding on a light wind four or five miles seaward from El Dorado. The colonel had indicated he had some qualms about talking in any place that might be bugged. ("I learned from folks around the city hall back in Arkansas that some things shouldn't even be said among friends except in a moving vehicle and preferably when people were wearing as little as the law allows.")

"But she's in Mexico again," he said. "You bet, she's in Mex-

ico. That's where Stewart does his business. The name of the
game is drugs. Spelled m-o-n-e-y. I suppose he led her around in
the name of idealism until the time came to go for the big score.
But now she knows this is for real."

"The colonel's in the drug game," Cooley said to Charlotte. He
was lying flat between them on the canvas platform of the catamaran. He was shivering with something like seasickness,
flinching at the occasional spray that touched his skin.

"Woop! Woop! Just a minute," the colonel protested. "If you
should have a recording of our conversation in Cuernavaca, I
don't believe you'll find it supports that evaluation. No, sir, I
don't believe it would."

Charlotte had seen Timmerman as a crafty, cunning games-
man—like Cooley in that way. But as she listened to him operate
she saw him more and more as a sniffer after carrion, a vulture
circling after the smell Cooley was beginning to give off. She,
too, had got a whiff of terminal decay—and nothing made her
wilder than to watch this man she loathed easing closer to
Cooley's undefended weaknesses.

She saw it was Timmerman's trick to offer straws, and her
greatest fear was that because the man had done his homework
and made part of his story plausible, Cooley would grab for a
straw.

Bull Timmerman said, "I believe I indicated I had some acquaintance with young fellows in the drug field."

"Fliers."

"Now you're on target, Hoyt. Information is my field. Intelligence. For whom it may concern, now that I'm out of the service
and on my own. I came over here thinking this concerned you.
And I'll tell you this. Stewart is in with these babies I mentioned
in Cuernavaca. You might say this is another way of their making the proposition I told you about then. I guess they'd like a
million dollars to get airborne. Go into the big time."

"You're saying Victoria's not a red. Or, you know, whatever
they call themselves by now."

"I'll tell you this, Hoyt. Your little girl's not much of anything
but a sucker. I reckon she played along for a while. You know,
there's been a lot of talk, in and out of the press, that this whole
thing is a phony. Uh-huh. Maybe it started that way. But it isn't

any more. Once they crossed back into Mexico, the guys who had it all lined out took over. I'm backgrounding you in everything I can so you'll know what you're dealing with when you get a phone call . . . just about anytime now."

"A million," Cooley said. "I can do that. How do I know . . . ?"

Gravely, and almost in the tone of a family counselor, Bull Timmerman said, "I expect parents always ask that. And have to settle it with their own conscience, what they are going to believe. Or trust. You wouldn't want to get an ear in the mail just to convince you, would you?"

"I can see why you wouldn't want this conversation bugged," Charlotte said.

The colonel didn't hear her. He didn't like her any more than she liked him.

"He's not alone," Cooley said. "I don't know who his connections are. When I talked to him that other time in Cuernavaca, I thought he could be CIA. Easing in on Rosio."

"He's got nothing to sell but your trouble," Charlotte said. "He's trying to sucker you."

"If I paid a million . . . I'd have done something."

"No!" She had to guard all the breaking points, all points where the shell had been cracked. Damn it all, he might throw money at the unknown horror and then wash his hands of the grim reality, his conscience laundered with nothing accomplished.

She did not trust Cooley to stand up to Bull Timmerman. They were too much alike. Both con men. But she knew which one suffered, grieved, hoped to do right. Which one was hers.

So she went to Timmerman's room that night for a showdown.

"You got to show us something," she said. "Or get out."

"Get out? I'm a paying guest. Enjoying myself. Trying to be of service." He was staring at her out of his unearthly blue eyes, not out of curiosity, or out of contempt. Certainly not out of any fear of what she could do to him. He played everything safe. He stared as if he couldn't quite believe her recklessness in mixing into what was not her business.

He gave her a glass of scotch. Not from hospitality, but as if it were part of a routine, like an anesthetic administered by a dentist before pulling or knocking out a few teeth.

"Show you something? And you wouldn't want an ear?" he said mildly. "I thought you'd come to show me something."

She almost snarled with impatience. "I have nothing . . ."

"What you showed Rosio."

"What . . . ?"

"Your cunt. Isn't that the way you and Hoyt do business? Poor Rosio still thinks you were bringing him up here to get him killed. But you weren't, were you? Only to make a little deal so Hoyt could branch out into heroin and soft stuff. I guess it turned out lucky for everyone that no connections were made."

She laughed at him. He was not impressed by her laughter. He had expected her to be tough. "It helps to know who wears the pants in any family. You don't want to show me yours? Maybe you'd like to listen to something."

There was a tape recorder lying atop the clothing in one of his gaping bags. He fished in another bag for a cassette. In a minute she heard her own voice saying, "I promise you he will want to be wakened. Do as you are told."

That was followed by a pause she remembered as well as the words she had said later to Ortiz Rosio.

"You can turn it off," she said to Timmerman. "But that's me. That has nothing to do with Victoria Hoyt, and you can't bluff me."

She was jolted anyway. Jolted to find what she had never quite found before—how vulnerable she was to the danger that threatened others; how vulnerable they were to her mistakes. She knew she had made a mistake in coming here, too, and it shamed her.

The worst of it was she felt his pale eyes measure with precision just how much he had shaken her. She rose to leave, simply afraid that if she stayed longer she would give more away.

He caught her near the door. Suddenly her right arm was twisted painfully up between her shoulder blades. Her face was shoved against the irregular plaster of the wall. He hooked a big finger in the back of her dress and tugged once, very lightly, to show he could have ripped it off then and there if that was his wish. And that she could have done nothing about it, having stepped over the line into the area where she was helpless. It was a sheer display of power, meant to humiliate her. He clinched it by whispering, "You can bring the money yourself. I'd like to have a look at your pretty thing."

Then, after all, he sent her back with what she had come to ask for. He gave her a sealed manila envelope. "Don't waste any time. Show it to Hoyt. There's no more time to waste."

In a rage of humiliation she carried it back as he commanded, because she could think of nothing else to do. It turned out to contain a photograph which—like everything else that came from Timmerman—stopped short of proving anything.

The photo, a six-by-eight glossy, showed a girl, bound and naked, forced to kneel by a gun held to her head by a black hand. There was a towel or scarf thrown over her head, so she was unrecognizable.

But Cooley groaned, "Victoria!" when he got a look at it. And it had been decided for them that the colonel was going to get his money.

They were with Bob Pardon, going over the prospects of getting together a million in cash, when the phone rang to spare them the payment and confront them with worse.

Bob answered, keeping his face imperturbable because they were both watching him so intently. "Yes," he said. "He's here. Put her on."

He lowered the pastel-colored phone to his side and covered the receiver with his palm. "It's Mary," he said to Cooley.

"Who?"

"Your wife. Mary. Mary Rossiter calling from Cambridge, Massachusetts. Do you want me to speak to her?"

"What's she need me for?" Cooley's eyes were rolling. He was stalling off probabilities he couldn't handle.

"Come on. You can talk to her. Come on, don't let her down."

"She . . . heard anything?"

"I'll talk to her if you don't feel you can."

"I'll talk to her, but, hell, I don't have anything to tell her yet. I don't want to get her hopes up."

They heard the faint, unintelligible, tentative reconstruction of a woman's voice questioning out of the phone. Bob grabbed Cooley's wrist and forced the phone into his reluctant fingers.

"Yes?" Cooley said. "Hello, Bright Eyes. Long time no see. Well, we didn't know how seriously you were taking this. Whether it was on the up-and-up. Well, of course I've been sweating. Kept the situation under constant review. All my best people working on it. We weren't in touch with the kidnappers until tonight. We're going to make the payoff. To that bastard Stewart. And we'll bring her here and . . . and . . . you just hang on tight, Bright Eyes, and remember, I'm doing what has to be done and . . . Who?"

Then the other two heard rapid syllables, muffled a bit by the pressure of his ear against the round of the receiver, but panicked and swift now, like a message coming from the bottom of a mine shaft, meaning disaster.

"They've killed *who?*" Cooley asked.

"Oh, Mother of God," Charlotte said. "Jesus, help me now, I beseech Thee. Oh."

"You've got that wrong, Mary. Bunny Stewart is down here waiting for the payoff. We'll get him eventually, maybe. Well, but, Mary . . . Yes. Yes. Yes. I see. Well, that certainly changes things, doesn't it? But you hold on, Bright Eyes, because . . ."

Bob said, "Let me talk to her, man." Cooley was still babbling and gesturing in the air when Bob pulled the phone away from him.

"Yes," Bob said presently. "No. He's not in good shape. Yes. He wants to do *anything* that can be done. Yes, come if you want to. Come."

At least, they told each other in the heavy inertia that followed the call, at least the colonel's story and his gamble had been blasted out of the water. For the freshly killed body of Bunny Stewart had been found some hours ago in Baltimore.

But Colonel Timmerman, whose sources of information seemed to be speedier than theirs, could not be confronted with his fraud. He had checked out and driven away two hours before Mary Rossiter mistakenly called for strength, information and support from the former husband who had so little of it to provide.

III

"It was all a horrid fairy tale until they—someone—killed Bunny," Mary Rossiter said. "Day after day we expected to hear from Victoria herself. We wanted to think . . . my husband and I were as open to one theory as another because anything might have been true . . . that she might be in some Third World country."

Bob Pardon had flown to Guadalajara to meet her and bring her in to El Dorado. On the short flight back he listened to two things—the mangled, persistent attempts she was making to rationalize the nightmare and below that the choking denials of a personal guilt that only a nightmare could have floated to the surface.

She had committed no crime. She had worked, fought, sacrificed for noble causes that her heart told her were more important than her personal happiness. Over the years she had hoped to set an example and a goal of liberty for her children. She had wanted her daughter to fulfill herself generously. "To follow her own drummer, as they said. To believe in the liberation of the human potential in herself and in all people."

But what if that unleashed potential wasn't a potential of good or evil, either, but only of endlessly capricious invention and destruction, a chaos multiplied and compounded out of the innocent chaos of the inhuman universe? Then there is guilt in merely being alive, that guilt compounded by bringing children into the absurdity of conscious life—compounded again by trying to love them in their uncontrollable passage here and there on earth.

The sob of that guilt was what he supposed he heard under the almost equally pitiful attempts to justify, to theorize, to fit together fragments of a puzzle that got worse scrambled by every attempt to solve it.

Up there in the reasonable environment of Cambridge, Massachusetts, Mary and her present husband had waited with imaginable anxiety for the dust to clear. Like other listeners who reluctantly trust the police and the news media, they were waiting for a "break." Because nothing better was available to them, either, they were waiting for the next tape carrying Victoria's voice. It was supposed to speak to them—to anyone who cared—from the nation's capital.

Instead that promised tape was found on a Baltimore street in a parked car. The can of tape was resting on the lap of Bunny Stewart. It might have been assumed that he was the courier on his way to deliver the tape to a radio station in that city or nearby Washington—except that the police had determined he was dead before he had been put in that car.

He was not the messenger. He was part of the message. Spelling authenticity to the consumers of news.

The tape itself was in character with those that had already been aired across the country. In the short portion that recorded Victoria's voice she spoke again of her wish to live and be on good terms with her father when he had paid forty million dollars to "the peoples' defenders." Again, her portion of the tape was surrounded by oratory denouncing the nation as a whole for its crimes against the young, the blacks, women, Latin Americans, the old and the poor.

But this tape had, according to the police, been worked over. An amendment had been dubbed in near the end. After a sound of malfunction, a new voice spoke, intended for Cooley Hoyt.

"You've passed up one chance. You know what we're asking. Repeat. You know what we're asking. The next time it will be your girl. Or an ear. The weather is changing. Repeat. The weather is changing."

"'The weather is changing,'" Mary said to Bob. She gave a frightened glance from the window of the plane—scanning the brutal mountains below them as if the terrifying scale of this Mexican landscape mirrored an expanding recognition of how much more she might be asked to confront. "Do you down here have an inkling what that could mean?"

"An inkling," he said, as gently and cautiously as he could. "We had an approach. It turned out to be . . . unreliable. A son of a bitch trying to cash in on your troubles." He was thinking it just possible that Colonel Timmerman might have had something to do with the dubbed-in portion of the tape. He was thinking anything was possible—except decency, order, faith or even sanity on a scale to match the losses already incurred. "I hope you didn't come all this way, Mary, expecting we—him—to have it all put together."

For once on their ride together she flared into an anger that seemed to him unnecessarily ugly. "I don't expect anything of him except that he has money to pay them off. Now it's clear someone is after money, isn't it?"

"No."

"Then . . . ?"

"I think you're all after . . . Well, if it turns out badly, as badly as it could, you mustn't destroy each other on top of all the rest."

The weight of his sober compassion got through to her. She gave a little nod and murmured, "Oh, I didn't come to claw at him. But . . . to see if he's forgotten he had a daughter. I couldn't be sure he'd feel obliged to do anything to save her."

"You'll see he hasn't forgotten," Bob said. It wasn't much. He didn't intend it to be. Most of all he dreaded the cruelty of false promises. He saw that his cautious assurance meant less to her than her first look down at the opulent spectacle of the towers and walls of El Dorado as the plane made its approach from over the ocean.

There it stood to her eyes—the visible and tangible sign of the power even she believed in, the power of money and celebrity, though she might have spent a lifetime protesting those things *shouldn't* count.

He shepherded her to her room, promising she would see Cooley as soon as she liked. From the terrace outside he pointed out to her the Monarch Suite and the siege set up around it by the media. Over there, across the compound, the sun gleamed on half a dozen microphones sticking above the balcony wall like the weapons of a revolutionary platoon come to guard or hang the lord of the estate. From two trucks television equipment and canvas chairs straggled out almost to the stairwell leading up to the glass doors behind which Cooley and Charlotte were secluded. In the chairs that were just now taking shade from the magnificent palms, half a dozen men and women were reading or playing backgammon.

Again, when she saw this concentration, he heard the note of helpless anger from her. "I see he's in his element still. Eyes of the world on him."

Bob groaned. "It's like the wishes in a fairy tale. All come true. The last wish has to be that the others hadn't been granted."

2

Charlotte had seen the man wrecked and trembling on the floor at Puerto Vallarta. She watched him reconstruct himself for Mary's arrival with a sad pride.

He prepared himself in the bathroom—showering, shaving, deodorizing his armpits, toughening and toning his skin with lotion. Hell, maybe he was putting together a body out of spare parts, arms and legs that would look like the real thing. He dressed up to look like the master of this place. A jacket with a subtle yellow sheen, a ruffled shirt of pale lavender. Pleated and cuffed straight-cut trousers pressed as sleek as a show dog's flank. A gold bracelet for his left wrist instead of a watch.

From time to time he felt his chin as if he had misplaced the beard. Had forgotten it was sacrificed in his debauch. No matter. His hands might betray emptiness, anxiety. Charlotte might know how artificial were all the gestures of command and authority he was rehearsing before he had the nerve to go over and meet the hurt woman who had been his wife. All these were better than nothing. Without the show she pushed him into . . . nothing.

She thought she could guess the first words he would offer Mary.

She was right.

"Don't worry about a thing, old girl. I've got some high-level things going. All we've got to do is keep the faith."

Mary stared at him with a disbelief that would have been sheer disappointment except that she *had* to trust this facile hypocrisy.

Cooley evaded her stare, but his voice went on as majestically when he said, "Someone told me once that men—and women—who can stick through the third hour of the bombardment are the ones who'll come out. Isn't that right, Charlotte?"

"Ah, it is," she said. "Mary, you've proved that you can take it, and it *will* come out right." She saw that Mary would not float or sink, either, on such glib pieties. She was sure enough that Mary had to see her as the bitch goddess Cooley had run off to follow and she was willing to play that part.

She didn't mind being misunderstood. If it helped the woman get what she came for, then let the illusion stand up as gaudy and convincing as ever it might be.

For herself, she trusted only the nature of things, and it was in the nature of things that good women like this one would sniff her out as a gilded whore. Fine. Such women weren't wrong. It was fine that there were enough women of all sorts to go around, for the world was bigger than anyone said, and in its griefs it needed all the kinds of women that might be.

So—she *would* show herself to Mary as the mistress of this whorish place they'd run up here for the fun and profit of people no better than they were created to be. Before the anxious day was over she would pretend nonchalance. "It never helps to sit and chew your nails. If you'll come with me I'll show you the greatest luxury of all." And she took Mary in a speedboat out to one of the delicious coves on the island of Los Colombes.

She saw Mary thought this a waste of time. The woman had come with some desperate notion of making Cooley serve to get the girl freed. And ah, what a pity, if she grabbed too fast and found there was nothing left of him but the windbag and the liar, with all his poses.

What a pity for all of them if that happened. Because Charlotte believed he was better than that. There was something

—some last strength left in him—that wasn't going to be easy to bring out. And sure to God, he didn't know himself he had it.

The tide was high when they got to the island and the miniature beaches were almost submerged. There was a shouting and carousing of El Dorado guests along the reef. A white pleasure boat had pulled in close to where they lay down to talk and was anchored almost within earshot. Strangers were diving from its stern in rotation.

Mary watched them through puffs of smoke from her cigarette. She could not trust herself to relax—as if her daughter's life might depend on this nervous vigilance. What Charlotte had no language for conveying was that Victoria's life didn't depend on them or anything they might do at all.

She said, "You found Cooley the same. I saw that jolted you."

At this moment it jolted Mary just as much to learn that she had been understood. "Well . . . obviously he's got what he wants now. All this."

"You don't believe that? What he truly wants? No."

"He wanted money. To be noticed. Paid attention to."

"You ditched him for that?"

"I didn't. . . . I suppose that's what made it impossible for us to get along. It doesn't matter. That's long gone. In another world by now."

"I wonder if it ever is. I'll tell you what I thought when I knew you were coming. That you were coming to take him back."

Mary gasped irritably. With an effort to keep their talk politely under control she said, "I want him to use his . . . resources . . . if it will help with Victoria. That's my only interest."

"I wonder if it ever is."

"I've made another life. It was going all right until Victoria got in this trouble. But I wish him well, too. I don't want him to suffer from this. If he is suffering."

"Don't you know?"

"I know he is." .

Charlotte laughed quietly. "The man suffers before anything happens. While it happens. And after. If it weren't one thing it would be another. You say he's got what he wants. Ah, no."

"I suppose he suffers. Why should he put on such shows to deny it?"

"I doubt they ever fooled either of us. Should we pretend to be fooled? Pretend to ourselves, I mean? If he must put on his shows, why then we must let him. He won't change. That's all he has."

"I hope not." Mary flung her cigarette at the water. It went out with a tiny hiss. "He has you. I'm glad of that. Because yes, it is true. He wouldn't have tried so hard if things hadn't burned him so much."

"He has me," Charlotte said. "I'm what he wanted. You're what he loved. Lives are like that."

"He told you that?"

"He doesn't tell much. To no one. I trust what I feel in my bones. You said he hadn't changed. I think he can't. You and I can change, for we're women."

"Men can't?"

"He's not a man," Charlotte said, running sand through her strong hands and letting it pile in a little white cone between her knees. "I'll tell you, he's what's left of a wish. Once upon a time a boy made a wish. Then the boy went away and the wish stayed. He's a wish."

Something in this whimsy made Mary frown and then say with a crooked, pained smile, "Then I'm glad he's got his wish. Got you. I only wish you hadn't said he loved me . . . once. That's a kind of accusation, isn't it?"

"I suppose it is," Charlotte said quietly. "I never accused no one. Not I. But if it's there, it's there, as things are."

But now what might have been frankness between them—if there had been time for it to germinate in this tolerant sun and shade—flickered away as quickly as the shadow of a leaf when the sun moves. Mary's face set in a tight, strained mask.

"Well, it is lovely out here," she said. "Really. But I'd like to go back now. You know I can't . . . Didn't come here to bask in . . . all you have here. No."

And then before they left she repeated, "It would have been easier for us to be friends if you hadn't mentioned his caring for me. That was cruel."

3

It was Cooley's great inspiration of that day to insist Mary should stand up with him to face the microphones and cameras of the news people in an appeal to the better instincts of the kidnappers. "Let them see the parents are united in this. If Victoria should see it—let her know we're together. Wouldn't that help her?"

He came miraculously alive in this appearance. His great voice throbbed with sincerity. "I'm ready to declare we'll do *anything* —in the realm of human possibility—meet any demands—go anywhere—pay any price we can—to have our beloved daughter back safe and well. We've heard her say her captors are treating her well. We trust their word that they are idealists, who are doing this for a cause. However mistaken their methods may be. We, too, hope for a better world. Someday. If you people who have our daughter hear this, we want you to know we have been listening respectfully to your ideas. And I think it is time that we —and all Americans—should do some soul searching and see where we went wrong that such a thing could happen. But we plead with you not to damage the cause you believe in.

"And, Victoria—my little girl, my big girl now—if you have the chance to hear this, your mother and I want to say simply: God bless you and keep you. Make His light to shine upon you. Remember—the man who can win is the one who can stick through the third hour of . . . who can . . . hang tough! It will be over soon. We can make up for our mistakes. We love you. We love you."

Hearing him among the rustling palms and the almost funereal abundance of flowers of this place, Mary had the dizzy feeling that she was seeing him already on the colored screen and hearing his voice come from a television speaker. She saw him as perfect for the medium, whatever he might be in the flesh. She was glad of that—and so moved by the organ sound of his voice she could only echo tremulously, "It will be over soon, Victoria. Hold on."

She remembered Charlotte saying he was not a man. Seeing

him win a sort of technical respect from the technicians of the medium recording his passion—seeing him rise to the reality of his role—she understood this better.

Charlotte saw no need to watch while he was being filmed. She knew what he did best and she was in a deep study pondering how to help him—and Mary, too; a woman she neither liked nor disliked; a woman whose deep trouble spoke to her. It was not clear what she could give them—except the fullness of herself, which was what she always gave when she wanted others to excel what they believed they were capable of. Really, she had no tricks. She had found they didn't help. Ever. Her magic, her authority came from relaxing into the simplicities of her womanhood. The Marquis had not taught her that. He only taught her that she already knew it.

It was without any clear-cut design or purpose that she dressed, bit by bit, fastidiously, up to the emeralds Cooley had given her. While the two others were praying to the lens of the TV camera, she was bathing, oiling, perfuming herself and glamorizing her body with every item of clothing she put on. She was a woman who dressed for her occasions and she felt the grotesque solemnity of Cooley's reunion with this woman who had been his wife. If she came on at dinner as an image of what Cooley had wanted and run after, let Mary see that with absolute clarity. For it was important now, all-important, that some clarity should come into the confusions of Mary's grief.

So when the curtains were drawn over the glass front of the Monarch Suite to shut out the view of the curious as well as the last of the winter twilight, they sat together as a family group, subtly rearranged. Clearly enough—no one had to say it; they all accepted it as if it were natural—Charlotte was the matriarch. Youngest of the three, she represented something older, the manners of a race and time these *Americans* (seeing them together reminded her keenly of what Cooley was) respected with just a little uneasiness. Jeweled, carefully made up—while Mary expressed her trouble by a rumpled dowdiness—Charlotte was still the most natural of the three. With her flawless bare arms, smoothly ripened shoulders whisked by her tawny hair, she dominated the conversation by her patience, her glowing silences.

The women had cocktails and wine. Mary was drinking as if she needed it. Cooley needed something, but it didn't take liquor to take him deep into the role of sentimental father.

He rubbed his eyes and said, "What got me worst on the tapes I heard . . . Vicky asked if I remembered when we sang 'Silent Night' back there one time at the Duchy."

"She hates to be called Vicky," Mary corrected.

"Victoria. Sounds like an old lady, but all right," he said. "Of course I remember our singing very well. And didn't the future look good up until about then?"

"I guess so," Mary said. "Yes. It did."

"That's what makes all this seem like . . . When we're here like this, I can't believe it's happening. Like she's still somewhere in school. But . . . school! That's where she got mixed up with that bastard professor. Sorry. He's dead and I shouldn't . . ."

"Oh, you wouldn't have liked him," Mary said, with a note that said she had—and that was another of the light-years of distance between them. "But in my opinion—then—they had a good personal relationship."

"Don't they even call it love any more?" Cooley said, wounded and grinning. "Sorry. He was her . . . choice. I admit she had a right to her own choice. But, hell, with all she could have had . . ."

"I suspect she had a lot," Charlotte said.

"She wasn't exactly underprivileged," Mary said. "Too much, she thought. She thought she had too much. From the money you sent."

"I shouldn't have," Cooley said. He was not grinding his teeth, but his jaws kept moving back and forth as if he *might* have been grinding them if he wasn't on good behavior.

"I guess accusing ourselves won't help," Mary said. "But I meant you wouldn't have liked her ideas any better than you might have liked Bunny Stewart. And if you want to blame anyone, of course I'm as much to blame as . . ."

"Ideas don't matter," Charlotte said. "I wish people had no opinions. Which they get from politicians anyway. They mean us no good."

"Well . . ." Mary pondered. Then she decided to agree. "If all the world could live in a climate and a place like this, no, there would be no need for politics."

It occurred to Charlotte that Mary was drinking too much, or at least more than she meant to. After the cocktails she was washing down her food with wine when the servants brought their dinner in. And yet it was closer to her mood to think "much" than "too much." Careful measures were not only pointless but a little shameful. Let them be as awkward or as graceless as they must, she prayed, only don't let them be small.

She wanted them to pray, as she would, to the god of battles and trust the outcome, win or lose, instead of setting too much store or hope in unctuous appeals made for television. If they ended up rolling on the floor, clawing at each other's faces with their nails in a fury of blaming each other for what had gone wrong, that might be better than calculated evasions. If Mary got drunk and Cooley, too, they might settle great things between them though they could not make everything right.

Still, Cooley's great effort at tolerance for things he could not sympathize with would do for beginners. Since the bastard professor who had corrupted, screwed and maybe helped kidnap his daughter was dead, Cooley was going to try to be kind to his memory. When Mary, swinging out on the alcohol, went on justifying herself, Cooley's teeth still did not come together to make a sound of grinding.

Mary was saying, "I guess you know—but how could you by that time?—I was active from early on against the Vietnam War. That's like a dream now, too. Back in the sixties we felt we had to be ready to put our bodies up against the Establishment bayonets. You can say those are slogans . . ."

"I don't know," Cooley said earnestly. "I didn't say . . ."

". . . but they didn't seem like slogans when that horror was going on. When the monks were burning themselves. And a poor troubled boy I talked to once burned himself later. With gasoline. The media has forgotten him now. Whatever we say now, the need seemed real then."

"I didn't say . . ."

"And Dick Rossiter and I took Victoria to Washington with us at the time of Nixon's so-called Cambodian Incursion. We even took young Paul, though I was afraid to have him with us in the streets for the actual demonstration."

"Ah, you were wonderful!" Charlotte said. She reached to caress Mary's pale arm. The candlelight flickered in her eyes. "You done that well!" she cried, in praise and astonished envy.

Mary could not stand praise from her. She broke into tears at this and had to have a cigarette to quiet herself, though her plate was hardly touched. "I'm not repenting. Not anything that may have overstimulated her. You never know where things will lead, though. That's where they've got us."

"They have not," Charlotte said.

But Mary was not talking to her—and probably not to Cooley in this crest of feeling. She was answering the mocker who lived in her own head. "I'll *never* admit I'm sorry we stood up then. It had to be done. To stop him and his mad bombing. It had to *be*."

That was the cry Charlotte had been listening for, though she could not have predicted it and though she didn't pay much attention to the words or certainly not to the circumstance they referred to. Mad bombers came and went. Always. They went because somewhere, in the crotch and in the heart, was the fierce and absolute will to refuse their domination.

She heard what Mary believed herself capable of—and she understood then how this evening ought to end. Still she made no tactical moves to shape it. The design that was working out was not hers, though in her bones she understood it as neither of them could. Approved it as neither of them would.

She thought they were over the hump now, and as the servants brought dessert and coffee, she led Mary to talk more of what Victoria had been. "And all she got, though Cooley thinks she got nothing since she missed our party here."

He flared in anger and disappointment at her. "I never said that!"

"Tut!"

"You ought to take that back."

"I never take things back. As you should know by now."

Now, though the discord was not big, it was Mary's turn to pass over it. A subtle shift of relationship was beginning to take place. Cooley didn't understand it at all, but both women did. Now it was Mary who was being wifely.

She surged into the occasion. "Cooley, I wish there was time! You have the idea that Victoria's life was all . . . well, militance. But she had a lot of things. Friends in school. Camping. Mountain climbing. She has talents—though not for singing and she's too big to be a dancer. We have a house in Wellfleet and every summer she was very active on the water. Skiing, surfing. She's a fine scuba diver. Fearless. She crewed on a ten-meter boat the summer she was fifteen. Up there she had a new crowd of friends each year."

"Then what made her . . . ?"

Mary shook her head in impatience. "You keep going back to the same question and if I haven't made you see, you won't see. And I said it *might* be my fault—if you've got to call it that. But it was in her nature, too, to go the way she went. Most liberals, when they hear about injustice, say, 'We *ought* to do something about it.' Victoria says, 'I will.' Don't you see? And it would shame her to deny her that right. However it has come out."

"Yes!" sang Charlotte.

Mary raced on. "One time when we were at the Cape the word came on the radio there was a boy buried in a landslide from one of the dunes on the Truro beach. She wanted to go up and dig for him. I told her there was no use going. She'd only be another spectator or in the way of the men trying to rescue him. But Victoria ran out, and, goddamn it, wouldn't you know, the state cops caught her for speeding and then assaulting an officer just as she turned off the Pamet River road two miles from the beach. She was heartbroken and blamed herself. I couldn't get through to her to convince her that was the way things happened. I couldn't make her understand it was beyond human help."

Slowly Cooley's lower lip began to curl. His shoulders bent and trembled. "She . . . ?" He put his head down in his hands and began to sob. "She was gonna . . . ?"

The noise was awful. He blubbered. He blew his nose. He tried to grin and it was hideous.

"She was gonna get . . . that boy out?"

The women sat and watched him, bonded in a compassion that could not last, that did not need to last.

"Do you see what I'm saying?" Mary asked, her own voice tearful now. "Is it getting through to you finally? Any of it?"

"Ah," Charlotte said. "Yes, yes, yes. It comes through. Will you take him for a walk, Mary? It will do you both good. You both must have your cry, for tears are needed, too."

"Won't you come?" Mary asked, and when Charlotte refused, Mary said, "Yes. I need a walk. I've drunk too much."

It was past one in the morning and the first-quarter moon was far down over the black, silver and purple ocean. There was still music from the discotheque down by the yacht anchorage. A few bathers drifted or stroked in the main pool like weightless shadows between the overhead illumination and the lights under the water.

"She's like that sometimes," Cooley said to Mary. "She's not heartless. But she doesn't need anyone. I mean, comments like implying all I cared about was whether Victoria got to our big shindig here. Jesus!"

Mary said nothing. They were walking now on the big stones of the breakwater. With Cooley holding her elbow lightly to make sure she didn't trip, they went all the way out to the point at which it bent and angled toward the far shore of the bay. They were very much alone out here, wrapped in the scented warmth of the night, but still completely aware of the glamour and the dimming sounds of pleasure behind them, the muted percussion of a rock guitar.

They picked their way over a gap in the boulders. The chop of the ocean beyond flung a random spray. He tightened his grip on her arm and spun her to face the spectacle of lights and half-lit walls and the sparkling dark filigree of palms. For a moment of hushed breath they listened to the music of carefree happiness. They could not move from here to mingle with the dancers or move to the music of this moment. But it was as if they could look back over years to some wondrous possibility that had seemed easier to reach then than it seemed now.

Melancholy and near—the festival of lights and gaiety that had

to be bought with a currency they did not have in their youth
and which they had squandered by now.

"Goddamn it!" he said. He flung up his arm in a clutching gesture, as if he meant to claw his way back across separations and
time. "Goddamn it, if Vicky only *could* have been here for the
party. We had big people here! Names everyone has heard of."

For once she understood him perfectly. The hugeness of his
yearning. The crooked generosity that had ruined them all.

She kissed his cheek.

"You meant well," she said.

He was twitching with melancholy tenderness when he got
back to the Monarch Suite. He came in on tiptoe, supposing
Charlotte must be asleep. He felt a small guilt, on top of all the
others, for having been out so long with Mary. He was sharply
aware of how carefully Charlotte had dressed for dinner. He
supposed she had made herself so attractive out of a sense of
competition with Mary. Women were always in competition, he
thought, and the thought increased both his melancholy and his
compassion for what he put them through. Had always put them
through, though he hadn't intended it that way.

He did not turn on the bedroom lights. He only switched on
the small bulb in the dressing room but its beam slanting
through the doorway showed him Charlotte's naked back, so
golden against the cool gray and blue shadows of the bedclothes.
If she was wearing nothing else in her sleep, she had not taken
off the emerald necklace. He saw the single jewel and silver
filigree of the pendant clasp peeping from under her hair.

His eyes were fixed on her back as he dropped his pants. Then
as they slithered around his ankles, he felt a pounding, twanging
vibration as if someone were hitting the floor from beneath with
a sledgehammer and the jolting shudders were running through
all his bones and particularly up his spine. And his hard cock
seemed to be a branch of the spine sharing the almost unendura-
ble vibrations of the shuddering bone.

It was his first erection since he had run off drunkenly with
that brainless French twit. She had ruined him. Revolted him—
sucking away on him by the hour, indifferent to his limpness,
while he lay there with a drink in his hand, welcoming her only

as part of the torment that kept his bad thoughts from being even worse.

Only . . . as he stripped off the rest of his clothes and pranced toward Charlotte it flashed into his mind that it wasn't the glimpse of her nakedness that had given him this terrific erection.

It was Mary's kiss on his cheek, out there on the dark breakwater, while he had been yearning toward the lights and music from shore.

His fingers found the hot moistness between Charlotte's thighs before she rolled partway around to face him. Then he saw she had not been asleep, for with the motion of turning toward him she reached up and flicked on the reading lamp above the pillow.

She was not refusing him. Her body was there for him . . . and would open like a velvet purse spilling treasures . . . if that was what he must have tonight. She let him nestle his weight between her raised knees. He could feel the quickening pulse of her belly against the hammering in his chest. To move upward and in was almost as easy as falling. He had only to let go. To let everything go in the miracle of release.

But her clear, questioning eyes held him. What do you have to have? they asked.

"Sorry I woke you," he mumbled.

It was not the moment for apologies. His cock knew that, if he didn't. He felt it bend and droop and said "Sorry" again as if apologizing to it for abusing it with his mistakes.

But she made that all right, too. With exquisite gentleness she cherished him between her knees. Her palm curved to caress his cheek with an overwhelmingly maternal reassurance that he was not alone in his bewildered quest.

"I was not asleep, you good, crazy man. I was trying to guess what Mary told you that took so long."

"Nothing. You heard everything she has to say. Poor kid came to us because she didn't know where else to turn. I was showing her . . . what we built. You and I. To keep her mind off things."

"Ha!" Charlotte said. And now she did force him away from her. She sat up and put both hands against his shoulders. "Think, man! Damned if she come here just to hang around. And it's not money she wants to be sure of neither. Can you not force her, at least, to come clean and spill it?"

"I guess not until she's ready. But what . . . ?"

"I don't know *what*. But, go back to her. For once in your life *make* her come through."

"How?"

"Go on! Get dressed, you fool. Go!"

IV

1

"What was the very, very, very, *very* greatest moment in your life?" Victoria Hoyt had asked her mother once.

"That isn't easy."

"I don't care if it's easy. Do you want to sleep on it before you tell me?"

"I'd better sleep on it."

It had always seemed important to encourage Victoria to sleep on things, because her enthusiasms had always come with such violent certainty, before there was any chance for her to weigh them as she ought to. And when you slept on a childish question, very often you forgot it and got up the next day already concentrating on the daily routines. Silence is innocent. You were innocent if you didn't answer the very, very, *very* most important questions.

But that time, she remembered, Victoria kept on heckling for an answer.

So her loving mother hugged her and said, "You could have guessed easily enough. The most important moment was when you were born. You first and Paul second. You first—because you were my first child, and children count more than anything for a woman. You'll see."

Victoria hugged her right back for giving a sweet answer, but Victoria was disappointed. Suspicious of its innocence.

The questions of children can always be taken as innocent ones. But the innocent answers are false and they satisfy only half of what children want. The true answers always have a tint of terror and perversity in them, and children know this and turn away from their parents looking for the whole truth at any cost.

The truth was that the greatest moment of Mary's life had come when she heard Cooley smashing glass and furniture downstairs that night at Skelton Duchy. When the first sound of it reached them in the bedroom upstairs, Merle Finch had tried to withdraw from her. It was her climaxing triumph to know that he could not—that his ruthless will could be captive to the rage in her, so she could have her revenge on him and Cooley both for their exploitation of her.

She had known that power once only. She suppressed the memory of it because, consciously, nothing was more hateful to her than revenge. She hated the idea that any person could dominate the conscience of any other. She hated all personal oppression. And violence.

And yet—since the first public word of Victoria's kidnapping came to her there had been moments at the threshold of sleep when some rebel part of her nature had rejoiced in it as an act of vengeance against Cooley. She had wanted him to pay; more secretly she had wanted him to feel a torment of anxiety and shame. Not even Bunny's death had quite erased the sly, lurking, unspoken intimation that justice was being done.

When Cooley returned to her door that night, she was just at the boundary point between waking and sleeping where the indecent underside of her motives could rise shadowy and be entertained. She was resenting the probability that right now in Charlotte's bed he was grunting, lunging—forgetting—the ghastly responsibilities that lay on top of her like a stinking corpse.

Tonight was not the first time she had experienced how the potent emotions unleashed by Victoria's danger spread like a brushfire into areas that should have been immune to them. Anxiety and fear of loss should not—in God's name—in God's name, never!—have made her as hot as she had been the night she kept Merle from quieting Cooley's rampage.

Yet—shamed by her jealousy of him and Charlotte—shamed as if she had soiled the luxurious bed in which she was lying and found the excremental soiling an even further luxury—she let herself visualize Charlotte's nakedness and Cooley kneeling before it with his tongue extended.

And with it came the sleepy, rotten thought: If Victoria is dead tonight, he deserves it.

He knocked then. At the sound of his knock she knew she was going to be punished for her guilty wish. Bob Pardon said: "The last wish has to be that the others hadn't been granted." Something like that froze her mind as she leaped from the bed. She went to the door as if running for a high window from which she could jump.

The blind velocity of her rush carried her against him. He caught her to hold her from falling. His arms closed behind her back while she smeared his face with a helpless gush of tears and pecked at his jaw with swift, pleading kisses.

"Aw," he said. "Aw, Mary."

He lifted her and half stumbled to put her at rest on the bed. Her arms were around his neck, her nightgown fallen from her thighs. There was an overwhelming clumsiness as he shuffled on top of her.

"Ah . . . no! Cooley, no. I've got too much guilt already. No, no. Please!" But a sense that this guilt might be great enough to smash the others out of the way seared through the dark inside her skull. Her arms did not let go their drowning grip on his neck, and when he entered her, she said, "It's *you.*"

He was not taking pleasure. He was not gentle with her. He rattled her flesh and bones as if her body might be the pouch in which his stolen love had been hidden from him, and he meant to have it from her or kill her. She could not remember how he had used her when he had made her pregnant twice before. *She* couldn't—but her stinging bowels remembered that piercing while her mind struggled to protest its consequence.

She began to sob helplessly, writhing from side to side in anguish, but when he slowed in uncertainty and fear of hurting her, she said, "Don't stop. Don't stop. Give it to me."

Her arms let go their grip on his head. They fell back on either side in an unpremeditated caricature of surrender or crucifixion. Her head was thrown back over the pillow as if her throat had been offered to a knife.

They were voiceless now except for the hiss of their breathing, but when she had felt his seed leap into her they seemed both to hear a shriek of victory—as if their eardrums had been shattered by the impact before the nerves could translate it into sound.

He lay inert on her, feeling the pulse of her abdomen beat against his ornamented belt buckle. He shifted his weight, whispering, "That'll hurt you."

Everything he had done for more than twenty years had hurt her. None of it, he was trying to say, had been intended to. It was this hopeless incongruity that fired her bitterness as her mind came fully awake. "I'm so ashamed," she said. "Of both of us. Does . . . your woman . . . know where you are? Can you never be square with any of us?"

"She sent me."

"To do this?" For a moment a wild and vicious impulse to laugh ran its dirty course through her mind. The simple way he put it invited shameful derision. Yet now she trusted Charlotte's goodwill. She tried to cling to her trust of the man as she had known it when his stubborn cock was opening her—but as that thrust eluded her, her waking thoughts were making a desperate reassessment. "They try to help us and we spoil it. You. Me. Never mind. Now we know we're capable of anything. Creeping, crawling monsters. Rats are better."

"No."

"Merle taught us. We're his product. Don't you remember? He knew us. It's taken us all this time to prove it to ourselves." She jerked her naked leg from under him and rolled so he had to face her back.

"He was wrong," Cooley said meekly. "Don't you remember once we made him admit he was wrong?"

"He could say anything at any given time. So can we. So can we. So do one favor for me, for old time's sake. Tell me this didn't happen."

He licked his lips and said very meekly, "We did it, all right."

"Oh, my God. 'We did it, all right.' That's what you said—exactly—the night Victoria got conceived. I thought you'd put a rubber on and you thought I'd . . . Then you said, 'We did it, all right.' Why in *hell* won't things change?"

"We got to be what we are"—said the man who had spent his life mistrusting that truth. Then he said beseechingly, "I was glad afterward I'd knocked you up. Wasn't I? You can't say I wasn't."

He thought she was crying then. He heard no sobs and was afraid to ask or otherwise intrude. He sat beside her, stiffly upright on the bed as if any movement might knock over something very fragile. He might have cried himself, but felt he had no right to do so after so many failures to make good for those he had wanted to love.

She was not crying. She lay in the dense heart of the night and the charm of darkness, trying to separate herself from it and speak in the voice of a responsible woman. She dared not trust the way her feelings and her thoughts dissolved in the flux of luxury and immoral sweetness that this place drugged her with.

At last she said, "There's one thing you've got to do."

"I'll do anything."

"Get on the media—the television—tomorrow and say in flat, simple words that you are not going to pay a ransom to anyone at all for any Victoria Hoyt. Why didn't you do that before?"

"But I *would* pay! What else am I good for?"

"No!"

"Why not?"

"That's what I'm going to tell you. I didn't come straight down here from Cambridge. None of us Hoyts ever does anything straight. . . . Well . . . ! I tried to tell you at dinner. . . . No, I was softening everything, sweetening it up. Now I better tell you more about people you won't—probably you can't—believe exist."

"I've known some rough types."

"But not these. They're in a different world. Really. For one, Stella Franklin. I stopped to see her in Los Angeles. What she told me will change your mind."

"Aw! No, it won't."

"But, goddamn it, it should. It should."

2

Mary told her story with plaintive emphasis. It was not a confession. She had no clear individual guilt to confess to him or to anyone. But the guilt of a generation—maybe of a civilization and its mistakes—tinted her thoughts like a dye seeping from one garment to another in the wash water. If she was not guilty, she was not innocent, either, and if she was talking about a woman named Stella Franklin, she knew all too well how that woman would have rationalized the motives that got her involved.

"The first thing to realize about Stella," she said, "is that by now she's nearly out of her mind with fear. She's opened Pandora's box. . . ."

"Pandora who?"

"Never mind. As she sees it, whatever she and her group, her friends—'the people in the Movement'—supposed they were starting, it's got far out of control. 'Propaganda,' Stella says. They wanted propaganda and publicity. And Victoria went along with them. They didn't really expect—or intend, Stella says—to get ransom money. They wanted to show the New Left isn't finished, isn't helpless. And, because you'd already stirred up so much publicity and your name had been given a kind of negative meaning in media shorthand . . ."

"That's my fault, too!"

"No," Mary said, "but however it seems to you, you're a perfect natural target. You're a cartoon."

"Yeah! It's true. I am. So why don't they laugh instead of hurting people?"

She did not mean to hurt him more, but she had to hold steady to make someone like Stella Franklin comprehensible to him at all.

"You're not only a capitalist, a money man, you're a corrupter of our government of laws, and a sort of panderer to the appetite of the parasites—like Ortiz Rosio. Some of the other questionables you assembled here and made so visible through the press. You're also . . . male. That's a crime now, too. I'm trying to tell you what ideas are in fashion now in certain circles. The way they talk to each other now. You've got to understand that a young girl defying her male parent is very tempting to use to exploit whatever cause you're trying to advertise. Don't you see—this is the way Victoria might think it out as well as Stella."

"Think it out! Jesus. Everybody's *thinking*."

"Yes. But the fear in her . . . part of the time I was with her it steadied me to feel someone with more shakes than I. Other times it would drag me nearer the edge than I'd be when I have to face it alone.

"A woman my own age, you see. A stranger, someone I'd never laid eyes on, though I knew about her from Bunny Stewart. He counted on her. I was sure as I could be that he would have been in touch with her if he was in Los Angeles and seeing any people in the Movement."

"Movement?"

"Don't ask exactly what it is. It isn't anything exactly, and that may be part of what's so dangerous about it in a lot of ways. There are people you recognize and have to take on faith because something clicks and you say, 'Yes, she's sincere.' Which I said when I got off the plane and she was waiting to drive me around in her car so we could talk. She's just about my age and in some ways it was like walking toward a mirror to walk down the corridor in the terminal and see this woman carrying the book on Impressionism that was to be the identification for me. I don't think I'd have needed that book. It was like seeing yourself in a dream, or seeing that part of yourself that is pure fear walking toward you with a human face. We homed in on each other and she said, 'Victoria's alive,' in a way that scared me as much as if she had said the opposite.

"'If you hadn't come I'd have gone to the police,' she said. She meant it, too, and that is a sign how hard she's been hit, because I am sure that turning to the police for anything, or with any information they could use, would seem to her like treason and the worst treachery in other circumstances.

"She drove me from the airport to a park. We sat on a bench under the palm trees. While she told me the rest we were in plain sight, *if* anybody was keeping an eye on us—which I doubt, because if they had trailed her to the airport where she met me, wouldn't they have grabbed me or at least approached me when she took me back to the terminal and I got on the plane to come down here?

"To sum up what she said: Yes, the whole scheme was Victoria's idea as much as or more than anyone else's. By now I'm sure Stella bitterly regrets that Victoria showed up when she did. Stella was born to sit around with 'like-minded people' and denounce the fascist pigs and the fascist cops in security for the rest of her life, and now she knows it, too late. It's her version of things that Victoria talked her into something—as Victoria has a way of doing."

Cooley growled out of the dark. The story he was hearing made sense to him only intermittently. But he had no uncertainty about where the guilt lay. With those who had misled his dream child. "They'll all try to blame her," he said with quietly murderous savagery.

"With some reason. That's what I hoped you would see. I love her. Don't misunderstand. Maybe because I love her I know what she's capable of. Why should you love someone you had no chance to know?"

They were floundering amid a vast debris of lost chances, chances flung away or never glimpsed until too late. Clawing down, down, down for any solidity left. For Mary that had to be the truth as far as she could see it now.

She said, "They were full of ideas about how to begin. After the phony shoot-out at the motel they spent a day somewhere in the Los Angeles area making all the tapes and taking some photographs that haven't surfaced yet, as far as I know, and then they were all going to scatter. The plan was for Victoria to stay in one place, hidden, while the tapes were going to show up all over the country to give the idea that she was always on the move. Maybe someone saw it all smelled too much like a hoax. So they killed poor Bunny to make it authentic."

"Who'd decide a thing like that? Wasn't he the mastermind? Calling all the shots?"

"Who'd decide? There aren't any masterminds. Just a lot of people hacking away at random for all I can see. Or maybe . . . Victoria might have told someone to do it."

"That's a hell of a thing to say."

"I know. I can't back it up. It's what scares me more than anything else. I had to say it aloud to someone. I never have until this minute."

"It couldn't be. He was her . . . whatever he was. She must have loved him, or she wouldn't be sleeping with him."

Thankfully, Mary knew she could not back up her conjecture with proof. Stella, frantic and afraid as she might be and looking for a way to get the spilled milk back in the pitcher, had done a little more than hint that Victoria might have fallen in love with someone else. The rigid stereotypes of Stella's revolutionary vocabulary had not softened because she was in a panic. For her, to know a black man meant to love him for the persecutions his race endured. Or else a fundamental prudery had moved her to tell Mary that now Victoria had found a black mate, one who was as passionate about "striking back" as the girl herself.

"Cooley, I'm going to let you have the whole thing. As much as I know. It seems there's a black man involved in this."

"I wasn't going to tell you!" he said. His reaction was so sudden and agonized that for a moment she was deluded into thinking he had heard from someone the same version she got from Stella.

Only for a moment. "The black son of a bitch may have . . . Mary, it's hard to tell what all they've done to her if they've gone and murdered her . . . her *guy*. I've said some awful things about this Stewart, but maybe he was killed trying to protect her from . . . We've got to face what . . . might have been done to her." Then he was bawling out his description of the photo Colonel Timmerman had given Charlotte. "The black bastard was holding a gun at her head. I thought it could've been a fake photo. Now what you've told me fits. It was the real thing, but I wasn't going to tell you. Believe me, Mary. I was going to spare you that."

The misunderstanding was too gross and painful to try mending now. Mary simply lacked the ruthlessness to correct what she saw to be Cooley's wishful error—not on the basis of Stella's interpretation.

"Not all black men are . . ."

"I'm not prejudiced," he swore. "But holding a damn gun at her head while she's blindfolded . . . ! That's how they made her say all that crap on the tapes, too."

"No."

"How do you know?"

"You still believe you know Victoria," she said uneasily.

"How'd you behave if some crazy nig . . . black person was jabbing a gun at your head?"

"We don't know that. . . . Never mind."

"Black or white, what the hell. What I think you're saying is that after starting all this, your Stella Franklin wants to get Victoria back to us."

"I think she'd much rather have Victoria killed," Mary said. "While we were sitting in the park there were minutes when I was *sure* she wanted to piece her information together with mine so she could arrange for someone to go there and kill her. Maybe she wasn't. As it came out I got hers and she didn't get mine. Cooley, I want you to believe I'm fighting with everything I've got. I don't want to give Victoria—you, either—to anyone."

"What?"

"Oh, she knew where Victoria meant to hide out. But not exactly. All she knew was it was somewhere in New Mexico. Cooley, it's that shack your father built up in the mountains. That's what I have to tell you. She's there—if we want to believe any part of Stella Franklin's story."

"She's *there*," he said with a roaring breath of relief.

"I think so. But you've got to think. Help me. It might be all a trap and they were trying to lure you into it. You might not pay for Victoria, but you might raise some to save your own skin."

"That's the way those shits would think," he said, refusing to think if it meant thinking like those he despised so much. Welcoming a trap, if that was what it was, that promised to end the uncertainties that fed on each other and kept multiplying.

"Mary, we'll go and fetch her out," he said, drinking the last illusion of a simple stroke, one great swipe that would clear the slate of all their botched cleverness.

"She's not alone there," she said. "They're armed."

Almost jovially he said, "The kid wouldn't shoot you. If she wants me, it's time we settled that."

3

"You can't," Bob Pardon said. "It's another pipe dream. Charlotte, make him understand this is the wildest goose he's ever chased."

"He'll do what he thinks he has to," Charlotte said. "Cooley?"

"I'll give it a whirl," he said, grim and solemn and desperately afraid he might appear to either of them to be the cartoon character Mary had mentioned. "I can't even tell you two the facts in my possession."

"You've got a secret plan!" Bob scoffed. "Once more I'll point out slowly that you don't even know if you can get into the U.S. If you should get in and this turns out to be a false lead, how will you get back down here? There are too many people waiting to nail you with subpoenas. It will be the end of everything. I know the kid's the most important thing. But we've got deals to close if we expect to have money to buy her out. If we have to."

"Take charge of the deals!" Cooley said. It was pretty late in the day to admit that Bob had been effectively in charge of business matters for a long time. "Take charge!" he boomed, still playing his phony, necessary part.

He told Charlotte, "You were right. Mary's brought me the key to the whole thing."

She did not ask to be told what that key was. She resisted being told, in fact, fearing that if she didn't believe or trust what she heard he would sense that and lose faith himself. "Then you must go," she said. "Ah, Cooley, whatever they say, remember you and I have done things no one else could have got away with."

"By God, we have."

"And made them all wonder how we done it."

"Sure!" he said, avoiding her eyes, steadying himself by remembering that—somehow—he had always kept his promises to her.

It was still early when he and Mary took off from the airstrip above El Dorado. The morning birds went silent in the jungle on either side while the pilot was warming up the chartered Cessna. The mingling of jungle smells with ocean air had never been sweeter or more luxuriant—never more careless of the troubles that were dragging them away.

Charlotte was calm and grave and lovely as the morning itself as she drove them up to the airstrip with their skimpy luggage. She had no advice or messages of farewell to utter. But her tranquillity steadied them, as if her placid acceptance promised them they were doing the right thing.

Before they stepped up into the plane Bob arrived in his jeep.

He had two envelopes of currency for Cooley. In one of them was fourteen thousand dollars of U.S. money, in the other a little less than seventy thousand pesos. It was the available cash on hand. Hardly a figure to match against the exorbitant fantasies of the kidnappers. The snub-nosed revolver in Cooley's suitcase was pitiful armament for an imaginable battle.

"I've talked to the bank in Mexico City," Bob said, wiping some morning perspiration from his forehead. "It's complicated. But they'll stand by with up to a million in cash if there's any firm contact from . . . In case you're on the wrong track." There was no need to explain that the spider web of Hoyt finances would be completely demolished if that much money had to be called up.

"Pay if you have to," Cooley said, in a last offhand, airy affirmation of his power to command.

Charlotte kissed Mary and held her a moment at arm's length, giving one small nod that must have meant they *could* trust Cooley—as long as they kept him pumped full of their strength and convinced him of their need.

Then Cooley and Mary were in the plane, the motors revving up as they settled themselves in the broad seats and buckled their belts. As the plane swung onto the runway and the crescen-doing roar of motors tugged them forward, Cooley set his jaw and bared his teeth. His expression was a cartoon of consummate and concentrated fury—as if for once in his life all his sly ene-mies and even the weaknesses within him had come out of the shadows so he could meet them face to face.

But as the plane climbed in a broad, slow circle his mood sof-tened into a melancholy gaiety. He pressed his face to a window to keep the towers and flowered walks of El Dorado in sight as long as he could. Then he crowed hoarsely, "Hey, kid, stick with me and maybe sometime we can stay at a swell place like that. They tell me a lot of beautiful women and rich men hang around there." He winked like the callow boy she had once decided to marry . . . before either of them knew much about the world.

Then it seemed to her, in a queer reversal of perceptions, that it was not the proud structures of El Dorado that diminished in scale as the plane carried them away. It was Cooley who seemed to be shrinking. If this kept up all the way to the border, he might disappear altogether.

As long as she had seen him inside the showplace of El Dorado, he had been a believable cartoon of will, cunning and the know-how that got things done. Of course it was Charlotte, too, who had done so much to make that image of him seem authentic.

For the moment, at least, it wouldn't come clear to him that their errand might involve life and death. Out of a musing silence he roused himself to say, "You know, Mary, we never could have imagined we'd be going back to that shack my crazy dad built."

His eyes glittered with a kind of thin delight at the sheer capriciousness of time and events. "Wouldn't it seem funny to old Harper L. Hoyt that it's worked out this way? I haven't remembered the old boy for years, but I bet it would make him laugh. You asked how I was going to get across the old Rio Grande. Well, I sure wish Harper L. Hoyt was here to tell me how it could be done. To tell me how Geronimo would have done it."

The mention of his father touched her. At least it was a twinkle of the genuine affections he had always been so anxious to disguise. She reached to take his hand and squeeze it. She felt the dampness of his palms, and that sign of his fragility also gave her an odd consolation.

"I know, I know," he said earnestly, apologetically. "It won't solve any problems to think of the old man's fairy tales. You got to leave it to me. I'll come up with a plan. Dammit, you've got to believe I'll swim the damn river if I have to. I *will*."

Mile by mile he let slip everything she had come down here asking him to provide—all the resources that added up to the paper tiger called Cooley Hoyt.

With those things shredding fast, he had nothing much to go on that he had not had as a boy. A boy with a most unpromising future.

BOOK IV

I

Early in his life Cooley had realized his intelligence wasn't good enough to get him very far. Even earlier he understood that (a) he must start with no money to pay for either education or counsel, and (b) he must come out ahead. He would have to use his faults the way luckier people used their talents.

These awesome truths were his major legacy from his father, Harper L. Hoyt, wildcat oil explorer (self-styled), real estate developer (intermittently employed for his glibness; intermittently fired for trying to finance his private deals with company credit), organizer of educational tourism and free-lance writer.

In this last irregular occupation his scant earnings were squandered by the wild imaginings set off by the very act of writing. If he scraped together five hundred dollars by writing about sunken treasure for the men's magazines of the day, that five hundred was committed in various multiples—borrowed, embezzled, wheedled from his wife or parents—to buying his way into an actual expedition sailing from Mexico or the Gulf ports of the United States to hunt the spills from the galleons on their way to Spain. When he wrote about sporting figures, his own prose seduced him into betting on the men or teams he had glorified for the magazines.

Under a variety of pen names, Harper L. Hoyt had also written stories about the West for the pulp magazines. The most profitable of these fictions was a series, published under his own name, in which a young American lieutenant of cavalry had matched wits with the legendary Geronimo. That lieutenant was called Frank Cooley, and for him Cooley was christened.

Since the characters of this popular series were fictional, except for Geronimo, there was no direct and tangible means by which Harper L. Hoyt could invest capital in the lost mines, the cargoes of bullion, the wagon trains of settlers, the smuggled opium, the kidnapped heiresses, the contraband rifles or the lucky homestead sites in fertile valleys of which he wrote.

In this frustration it was as if he had tried to bet his only son and his son's life on the wide-open possibilities with which his imagination romped.

Tried to bet his son on the losing side. What else?

True, he had named the boy Cooley in honor of the rugged, savvy young officer who always—according to the laws of popular fiction as they were then agreed on—interposed himself and his hard-riding platoon between Geronimo and unprintable disaster. But this was a trick, a deception worthy of the legendary chief himself, since Geronimo was the true and legitimate hero of the conflict. To Harper L. Hoyt it may have seemed that Lieutenant Cooley was a sort of son to the great wizard of desert warfare, tempered and instructed by pursuits and bouts of gunfire that left both of them intact through issue after issue of *Range Western* and its successor, *Holster Western*. Cooley was Cooley. Harper L. Hoyt was Geronimo, and the wisdom of the unbeatable and elusive warrior was what he wished to offer his son.

"Kid, this world is full of sons of bitches and you got to know how to keep away from them. It's not all sons of bitches, and you'll meet them you like, as well. Sometimes you'll meet them that you love and you'll know they are your own people. There are good women as well as bad, and it's when you got them to protect and depend on you, then's when you need to think like Geronimo.

"Listen. What was the old fellow's greatest trick? *To make himself invisible*. Kid, he was out there on desert country flat as a tabletop. The soldiers trailing him could spot a rattlesnake coming out of his hole for twenty miles in any direction, the air was so clear and there was so little to hide himself behind. Could he hide himself and his pony, let alone his braves and his women, behind some little boulder or stick of cactus here or there? And what about the dust clouds their ponies would kick up if he tried to maneuver out of the way of the cavalry or the Mexican bandit gangs? You see, there was *no way* for him to hide, was there?"

"No," young Cooley said.

"You can't guess where he learned to hide himself, how he evaded capture by all those who were trying to take him and probably show him off in a cage when they had him?"

Ten-year-old Cooley said, no, he couldn't guess. He had read some of his father's stories in the magazines by that time and was already beginning to guess there was some sort of fakery in the narrative that permitted the series to go on so long when there was so much powder and lead flying. He thought the old man always faked with words, but now he was listening with respect, at least, to the riddle that had got his father so excited.

"I'll tell you where he hid! *He hid in the minds of the people hunting him.* In the blind spots of their minds. Do you understand that?"

"I don't," Cooley said, suddenly restless, feeling cheated and at the same time a little sorry for the old faker.

"Somewhere back in their minds just about even with their ears. You can't see your own ears, can you, kid? Well, that's it. People have blind spots in their minds, even when they got a perfect field of vision for twenty miles. Everybody's got blind spots in their mind, in their thinking, that they can't cover. Geronimo knew about those blind spots, and you got to train yourself, kid, to be like him, because it's going to be tough all the way for people like us and you can't let them find where you are or which way you're going to move or they'll take you. It's sad but true. They'll take us if they can."

When Cooley, the boy, thought this over, it only convinced him that his father had blind spots in *his* mind. Cooley thought he was hidden in one of them, all right, and his father couldn't see him at all. Couldn't all the time make the common-sense distinctions between him and Lieutenant Frank Cooley riding his chestnut mare to the top of a butte, seeing puffs of smoke above the foothills and asking, "Now what's that old wizard Geronimo mean by his signals this time?"

2

Young Cooley didn't care much more for the true stories of his father's life than for the poorly paid fictions. The true tales had an even more flagrant smell of failure and dishonesty—though in them the faulty clichés appeared to come from the nature of things. From a world committed to shabby detours leading to disappointment, a world that used Harper L. Hoyt as shamelessly as he exploited Geronimo in his pulp fiction.

For instance: Harper L. Hoyt had "ridden with Pancho Villa" as he often bragged. It happened to be true. Left in that brief headline, without expansion, there was a truth both legendary and marvelous. An inspirational testimony that glamour and high adventure were as possible in the real world as in fiction. If Cooley had only heard the headline declaration once—on or near his twelfth birthday—he might have never repudiated his old man. In fact, he heard the whole grotesque verity in detail too soon and thought about it too late.

Young Harper L. Hoyt had been on the bum in San Francisco in 1914 when agents for Pancho Villa were recruiting mercenaries for the army Villa was building up somewhere in Sonora. Hoyt was buddying with "a college man" expelled from Stanford for "consorting with chorines." They talked each other into accepting the recruiters' offer of a dollar a day plus arms, ammunition, food and a tent to sleep in. Somewhere west of Nogales a Ford truck filled with Yankee recruits, "mostly derelicts," hauled the two young men across the border into what was supposed to be a legendary adventure.

They "rode with Pancho Villa" for six months. . . . The hell they did. They cooked and gathered wood and curried the horses. They did whatever chores the bullying troops required of them, including carrying great bundles on their backs as they ran afoot behind the mounted men. "By God, they made squaws out of us," Harper Hoyt said in one recounting of the tale to a drinking buddy while Cooley listened, squirming.

The college boy had been sodomized the first night south of the border. "He got to kind of liking it. He got to be a downright favorite with the noncommissioned officers. When they burned and looted a town they were apt to bring him back some presents—beads or bracelets, that kind of thing. Didn't do him a bit of good, though. He still had to fetch and carry and dig latrines right along with me and the other derelicts. See, the greasers thought of him as a woman, but they don't go light on their women. You want to know how I saved my own skinny-rinctum? Well, I did and doctors have certified that yours truly is *virgo intacto*, my friend. That first night a big fat garlic-chewing corporal came at me and I sliced an ear off him with a cooking knife I'd brought from the cook wagon. He sat right back down there on the sand, holding the place where his ear had been, and it was 'Mama mia' and 'Holy Virgin' loud and clear for a while. That fat canary was really singing. I can hear it now, as they say. His buddies were going to either drag me through the cactus behind a horse or just shoot me then and there, but an officer came riding up about then to find what all the blubbering and moaning was about. I can't recall all he said to them—my Spanish was elementary in those days, too—but it was fierce. He saw to it that I was given a side arm on the spot, and I was made a kind of majordomo over the derelicts. That didn't help me, either, though. I still had to be up before the sun to get the frijoles heated up. Hardest work I ever did in my life or mean to do. Or mean to do, you hear me?"

They never saw a penny of the dollar a day (U.S.) that had been promised them, though the paymaster for the Mexican troops kept scrupulous accounts of how much they were owed for their service. Sometimes there were enough horses for them to ride when the army moved from one encampment to another. Sometimes not. Except for the revolver given to Harper Hoyt for self-defense they were not armed, and Villa was too clever to let them go with the attack formations that raided across the border into the U.S.

"But one day we were all riding up toward Brownsville, which old Pancho had hit before. The talk among the troopers was that he was moving up to repeat past successes on the Brownsville merchants and bankers. But it seems for once the

U. S. Cavalry had its information straight, so when we hauled up across the river from Brownsville, by God there was about four companies of the Cavalry drawn up in formation right across from us. Pancho's army milled around the better part of the day, and back a ways from the river there'd be some firing of guns into the air—just to show the Yankees old Pancho was ready and waiting for them if they came over after us, I guess. Not a single shot from the Texas side, though now and then you could see the sun flash on an officer's saber which they had drawn and was holding to their shoulders.

"And in the afternoon I made it up with this college boy— whose name I will keep secret because he's married to a sweet little woman in Pasadena and has become a lawyer—that now was as good a chance as we would ever have to get back into the Land of the Free.

"We had horses and between us we carried a big oxhide full of drinking water down to the Mex platoon at our end of the bridge. Man, what a splash when we dropped that damn oxhide and I said, 'Yow,' and we dug in the spurs!

"Well, I'd figured the Villa boys would hold their fire for fear of drawing an attack from the Cavalry. No, sir. I could hear the bullets humming around my head like bees all the way across that damn bridge. Later the Cavalry was to claim that none of their people had joined in the shooting, but I think to this day it came from both sides, and the greasers were trying to ventilate us for sure. Look!" He unbuttoned his shirt and peeled it back across his collarbone to explose his left shoulder where the scar was. "See that? One inch lower and it would have hit bone. Eight inches lower, the heart! That's my little reminder never again to trust a man who won't offer me better than a dollar a day."

And yet that three-inch scar across his shoulder muscles had been a brand that certified Harper L. Hoyt. It was a confirmation that once, for under a minute, on a bridge hot in the afternoon sun, between two armies that both disclaimed him and had very probably both tried to kill him, he had brought together fiction and reality in an act of valor worthy of either. An escape? Sure. But what an escape!—as if in the drumbeat of hooves and sporadic musketry he had been the man his silly heart intended him to be, owing no allegiance to either fantasy or reality any more than he owed allegiance to Villa's army or the U. S. Cavalry, citizen of both as he was citizen of neither.

The scar was his passport to move in either fantasy or reality as if one had exactly the same laws and the same rewards as the other. That was the way he had lived, and when he died he had exactly no material goods to leave Cooley except for an unsurveyed and almost worthless scrap of real estate in a waterless canyon in the mountains where he had built a small cabin in his later years. He called the cabin "his study" and for all Cooley knew the old man probably wrote at least some of his pulp fiction and *machismo* nonfiction when he took the whim to go up to the cabin for days or sometimes weeks. It was no more a study than it was an outlaw hideaway where Harper L. Hoyt could sit tight and defy the world to smoke him out.

3

No. The accounting was unfair that said Harper L. Hoyt left his son nothing besides the nearly worthless cabin. The old man had been in the education game on the same precarious and marginal terms as he had entered literature. In his time he had promoted educational summer tours and camps. Throw in a few junior years abroad for those schools dedicated to the ineducable children of prospering families. He was an innovator before his time, before innovation became the shibboleth of high-priced schooling and the catch phrase for obtaining government grants.

Somehow he got wind of some other rare innovators who were opening a progressive school in the high country of New Mexico near Los Alamos. The school was founded by a group of idealistic teachers from New England. The reason they had taken over a ranch in the high country for their school buildings was that the founders of the school couldn't get the rich kids they needed to pay the big tuition unless there was a health gimmick thrown in. So the student body had turned out to be mostly bona fide asthmatics, though a few were supposed to have something worse with their lungs. Asthma Mater some smart-ass student called it.

But it was for damn sure that Harper L. Hoyt would never have wangled his son into a fancy progressive school if it hadn't been for that pinwheel compromise of noble intentions and makeshift compromise with economic realities. The headmaster, a fine old guy named Robinson, was determined to have some healthy students, so his rich kids could be reminded what breathing was like, so there were half a dozen scholarship students from the small towns and ranches in the area. That was where Cooley came in. His IQ was tolerable. His lungs were first-class.

Beyond that he had a great instinct for grabbing at life rafts, a mortal conviction that the school was his one and only chance to break beyond the poverty to which his father was committed without being reconciled. No one had to tell Cooley that to get along you had to go along.

He made himself liked at the school. He did favors. He worked hard. He respected the masters. He respected his fellow students according to reports of the wealth of their parents—and found to his not very great amazement that most of the other students did the same. In the beginning, at least, this honest and straightforward respect for his monetary betters was what attached him to Kerry Finch. It was common knowledge that Merle Finch had more money than the father of any other kid in the school.

In the beginning. . . . Afterward, it had been something like love.

Friendship . . . ? Oh, what the hell do you call it when words are so tricky and anybody can change his voice to make any of them as mocking as any others? What should you call it when you're stupid and young like everyone else is or has been and you see a person who is more than a person—a family and a name and a way of life and of looking at things that is as big for a country boy as the ocean when he sees it for the first time with the gold of the sun on it.

Years afterward, when Cooley was working for Merle Finch at Southern Utilities, he'd run into one of the guys from the school at a convention in New Orleans. They'd had a few drinks together and the asthmatic son of a bitch had narrowed his eyes and said, "Working for Finch and Southern Utilities? I always said it helps to marry the boss's daughter."

Bender . . . that was the asshole's name. The asshole knew that Kerry had killed himself. Still had to have his little joke about feelings he couldn't know anything about.

And there was his jaw, right under his nasty grin.

You know when you can take a man's head off with one immense punch. But they don't know it. They put their chin out right in front of you.

"Well . . . Kerry and I did have a little thing going," Cooley said.

To get along you've got to go along. With all the goddamn shit they will put on you. And on your dead . . . You've got to respect the way things are.

"That was pretty funny, Bender. We're getting along all right at SU. We're putting a little away for the proverbial rainy day. Nice seeing you."

Don't even call it friendship out loud, or they will shit on you for that. Now they will shit on you for anything.

Call it loyalty?

To what? Not even somebody. You can't hold on to anybody enough to claim you've been loyal to them. If he had been loyal to Kerry Finch and if he had been smart as the others they threw him up against, he might have stayed with Kerry.

Saved him.

How?

They didn't teach you that at Asthma Mater. Or anywhere else.

Loyal to what, then?

To a moment—a time—when you are a goddamn stupid kid with a father who is trying to make up something to you with a slick deal to get you into a school where you can get the advantages. And you get them. You see, for a while, that people can be so much bigger and better than anyone ever told you before, that they might be rich and wise and passionate and hold their places on the earth with nobility. . . .

Yeah. He had loved Kerry Finch. He had loved Skelton
Duchy.

The whole bright promise.

Once.

Somewhere.

His father still had a few more years to live in the times when
Cooley and Kerry Finch used to come up to the cabin from
school on fall or spring weekends. Three or four times they went
with other boys, driven up in one of the school cars and
shepherded by one or another of the adult faculty members. The
trouble with going in such a group was that there was no water
available in the canyon after the snows went in the spring and
when there was snow to melt for drinking water and washing, it
was apt to be uncomfortably cold. There was no way to heat the
cabin except for the fireplace, which had to serve for cooking as
well.

And though their progressive school was dedicated to the vir-
tues of "living from the land" and "making the connection between mind and nature," the brute fact was that most of the
boys griped irresistibly when they were uncomfortable. Without
flush toilets their bowels became as inefficient as most of their
breathing apparatuses. Shivering through a weekend with a gang
of constipated asthmatics was more than most of the faculty
would endure. So Cooley's one possible offering to his richer
friends was not a success.

Except with Kerry. Kerry liked the shabby little cabin and its
isolation very much. For him weekends up there were at least a
fair exchange for the visits he had offered to Cooley among the
luxuries of Skelton Duchy, back in Georgia. In his last year at
the school Kerry had a driver's license and a car of his own, so
they didn't have to depend on school transportation for the
three-hour trip up or back.

Once Kerry expressed the wish that after graduation he and
Cooley could take a year off before college, fix up the cabin and
live there together.

"I could paint and find out if that's really going to be my
field," Kerry said. "Maybe in a year I could get good enough to

convince Merle that I truly could be an artist. Mother's already on my side, I think."

"What would I do?"

"Well . . . hunt and explore and put in practice some of the ideas about habitat we've talked about at school." The scholarship boys had, by a sort of natural selection, fallen into the role of athletes and woodsmen among their frailer schoolmates. In the yearbook Cooley was described as "a mountain man; in the tradition of Kit Carson, whose place in history he will probably not take."

But Cooley had worked hard and sucked up to the masters for his college scholarship, and a year's delay was out of the question for him. "We might live here without a phone and lights," he said, "but it's crazy to talk about living here without water."

"Beer," Kerry said.

"Drink beer all the time? I guess we drink plenty." It was a time in their lives when drinking beer was very important, ceremonial. "But it costs money. I don't have a rich old man. What would you do, buy all the beer for both of us? Support me?"

Talk of money and of that difference between their situations made Kerry moody. And talking about fathers cut a little deeper than that. Cooley had seen him at Skelton Duchy very polite with his father, very smooth and witty, and it had never got through to him that Kerry feared and despised his father. On the other hand, Cooley made it a point never to talk about his own father at all. Once when they were drinking beer in front of the cabin fireplace Kerry called him on it.

"I get the idea you were born by a virgin birth. Or, if you were smarter, I'd think you just made up the fact you've got a father."

"I've got one. He built this place. What else do you need to know about him?"

"He's never come to see you at school. Okay. First he was in the CB's. But the war's been over for a while. Where is he now?"

"Working for an oil company. Venezuela. What do you have to know about him?"

"You don't need to get huffy," Kerry said. "Look, Cooley, every family has skeletons. That's why we live at Skeleton Duchy, as my witty old man likes to say. Cooley, I took you home and gave you a look at Merle. I'd like to meet your father. Anyone with the sense to build a place out here away from everyone must be someone I'd like."

With more emphasis than was quite safe—maybe the beer was getting to him and bringing down his guard—Cooley said, "D'you ever think when you were a kid there ought to be some way you could trade off fathers?"

If he had lowered his guard, Kerry for the moment had none at all. "That's a kind of terrible thing to say, Cooley. You've only seen the good part of Merle. You've only seen what he wants you to see. I think even my mother is fooled by him. I think I'm the only one in the whole *world* who knows what he truly is. He's evil, evil, evil."

The wind in the chimney made the flames whoosh upward and Cooley chuckled about that. "Talk about ghosts," he said. He opened another beer for himself. "Want another?"

"No. No, thanks."

Cooley swigged from the beer can and thoughtfully said, "Well, gee, Kerry, I guess you're right. Maybe all boys get the feeling that there's something wrong with their fathers. But . . . I never felt like talking about Harper L. That's really all there is to it." He felt philosophical now, sitting there listening to the faint mutter of the fire, taking the time to relish each mouthful of beer. "I'll admit I have a different perspective on Mer . . . your father than you have. I'll admit I think he's a pretty great guy. I look at it this way, anyone who's in a position like his who'd take time to play chess with me and go out hunting the day you were sick. I mean, someone like that taking an interest in me and telling me things I didn't know about business . . . Sure, I'm impressed, and if someone like you had seen Harper L. they might find a lot of good things to say about him."

He was still talking when he understood that Kerry was crying. His first impulse was to lay his hand on Kerry's shoulder, but Kerry shook it off the way he'd shake off a snake that had dropped on him from a branch. In the firelight his eyes and teeth shone moistly. "Cross yourself, Cooley!" he yelled in the midst of uncontrolled sobbing that drowned the low noises of the fire and the night noises around the cabin eaves.

"Cross yourself, cross yourself! We're not Catholics but I know about crossing yourself to protect yourself from evil. You better do it. I'm telling you!"

It was the first and only time he ever saw Kerry's gentleness break into hysteria. It was so shocking, so unexpected and so painful, when you came right down to it, that he felt a muscular impulse to gather his friend in his arms and rock him until he had quieted.

"All right," he said. He made the sign of the cross on his forehead, breast and shoulders the way he'd seen it done in the movies. "All right, I did what you asked. Now can you shut up and tell me what brought that on?"

Kerry's breath sounded as it did sometimes when he had an asthma attack. Cooley had been present for a couple of those. Through that wheezing Kerry said, "You did it, and now the Beast can't touch you." He went off into whoops of laughter almost as scary as his sobbing had been.

To quiet him down after the outburst it seemed like a good idea to leave the warmth of the cabin and go outside for a hike. Cooley suggested it and they climbed all the way up the canyon to the top where it led out onto a mesa. They came out of the dark labyrinth of trees and on the open mesa they saw the whole, uninterrupted spread of April constellations. The chill wind felt good. Kerry was breathing hard from the climb but his breath sounded normal.

"Awful damn silly of me to blurt out like that, Hoyt."

"'S okay, Finch."

"'S what Merle can't stand about me. It's my nerve, he says. Bang bang the bird killer. Haven't got the nerve. Can't face cold steel. Pip, pip, you know. 'It's who can stand up in the third hour of a bombardment, my boy.' How would the son of a bitch *know?*"

"Easy, Finch."

"Right, Hoyt. Still two hours to go, right? Pip, pip. It's what he can't stand about me and by God, Hoyt, he's never seen me break in front of him since I was five. You understand that?"

"Sure I understand."

"Gad, boy, I believe you do."

"You want to go back down now? Or we could hike some more."

"Back down. 'S all right now. Truly, as we Finches say. Only one thing you ought to promise me if you can. Well, silly. Forget it."

"No. I'll promise."

"Then promise you won't ever wish Merle was your father. You *got* a father. Maybe he's no good, but you got a father."

"Right."

"Shake on it, Hoyt."

"Shake on it."

Up on the mesa, in the April night, everything clear enough—like the bright constellations overhead—so you could make promises and shake hands on it.

After that . . . babble, babble, babble.

So you had to forget most of it. Try to forget all that wasn't useful to you.

When Kerry went off to be an artist and turned faggot—or gay, or whatever was the right thing to call it nowadays—and then killed himself, Cooley had to forget that very brief minute in front of the fire when he had meant to take his friend in his arms.

He neither quite forgot or paid any attention to his promise not to wish Merle Finch was his father. The issue never came up, Cooley thought. The dealings between him and Merle were always man to man. He would not just say that they had come out very lucky in the end. But, man to man. . . . It just wouldn't occur to Cooley to think Merle Finch was the Evil One. That sort of hysterical talk wasn't part of his vocabulary, either as a boy or after he got rolling in his career. He only came close to it in his alcoholic deliriums, and he had got himself out of the trap of alcoholism. More or less by will power. . . .

More or less by thinking what it was like to stand and take it "in the third hour of a bombardment."

"How the hell would the son of a bitch know what a bombardment is like?" Kerry had asked about a father who had never been to war and had picked the phrase up, probably, from his expensive library on the Civil War.

But men knew those things, and when they heard them they

recognized them. They latched on to them. Wore them like a lucky charm on a watch fob.

And maybe Kerry knew, too. *Still two hours to go, Hoyt.*

How could you tell what it was like for a suicide and why they quit before the third hour and you didn't?

Babble. Babble.

Geronimo is my father. They will not take me or my people.

4

When he was twenty-four and she was nineteen, Harper Hoyt's son had taken his bride to that cabin in the dry canyon, supposing he remembered it to be a good place for them to hide away from people for a part of their honeymoon trip through the West. It was a lousy place.

What required, after all, only a locked door, drawn blinds and a silenced telephone became almost a test of survival when they tried to enact it in a waterless, deteriorating, insect-ridden relic thirty-eight miles from the nearest town and fifteen miles from the nearest ranch equipped with a telephone.

He and Mary had stayed overnight there. They had made love on the barren floor in front of the chilly stones of the fireplace—some sort of homage to the romantic mania that had imagined humans could find habitation in such a desert place.

But they had not even stayed until sundown of their first full day there. They had spent the night in a Santa Fe motel where Mary showered off the pine pollen and ashes and maybe insect droppings from the floor before they made love again on a proper bed with Magic Fingers and a print of Old Santa Fe hung above it.

Morning came again before she regretted not having, at least, taken some snapshots of the mountain cabin. She remembered the shadows of pines on the rock wall of the canyon had been really beautiful. He regretted that they hadn't climbed up to share the view from the mesa above.

He had never seen the place again to this day. When he was in Tulsa in the mid-sixties with Charlotte he had played with the notion that there might be time to drive her over that way to

show her where he had gone to school and probably to fuck her
(as she chose to put that matter) on the cabin floor to reclaim
the premises after his break with Mary.

They never found time. But even so—maybe because he knew
so much money was going to come rolling in from his Vietnam-
ese contracts—he took the trouble to have a New Mexican contractor reshingle the roof, replace the long-broken windows and
make the place tight against animals and elements. The contractor also was to repair the road that led into the canyon from the
highway. The photos he subsequently mailed showed he had
done a good job on all assignments.

Six years ago Mary had come West with the children, Victoria
and Paul, so they could have a go at some real mountains to test
their climbing nerve and skills. Victoria had heard of the cabin.
She had also read the pitiful few of Grandfather Hoyt's western
stories that her mother had kept in her files all these years, the
pulp pages crumbling when they were bent now, the line illus-
trations of Apache and U. S. Cavalry battle formations almost as
foreign as the drawings of battle chariots in Egyptian tombs, the
name of Harper L. Hoyt almost as quaint as that of James Whit-
comb Riley or Gene Stratton Porter. . . . Victoria's comment on
the tales of Geronimo and Lieutenant Cooley was "Camp-EEE!"

But it was Victoria of the stubborn whims who insisted that
she and her brother and Mary take a day off to drive down from
Colorado and find the cabin. It was locked up tight, they found.
The contractor's padlock on the door was, in its turn, showing
signs of weathering. There were minor washouts in the road. But
the interior of the cabin appeared to be unaltered and
unchanged.

They only saw that unfurnished interior through the new window sashes the contractor had set in new two-by-six frames,
painted dark brown to match the older logs of the walls. Interiors seen in that way are tantalizing. There are mysteries and
promises in every locked house. In the blind spots that can't be
seen from outside the glass all sorts of spooks and bandit heroes
may be hiding.

It seemed to Victoria they had a right to accept that teasing
invitation. "Why don't we break a window and go in? No one

would know we did it. It looks like no one ever comes up this way. Why should they? I want to *be* inside."

Mary vetoed the suggestion. Absolutely they must not.

"It would be like robbing a tomb," Paul said. He wanted to go in almost as badly as Victoria, but he would probably not have broken a window to do it. "If we broke a window we'd have no way to patch it up," he reminded his sister. "The rain and snow would get in and ruin it. It's a neat place. I wouldn't want to spoil it."

"We could lean a board or a shingle up over the broken pane," Victoria offered.

"No," Mary said. "No, no, no."

She sat waiting for them in the car parked under the pines by the cabin while the two of them climbed up the canyon. From the top of the mesa their blood-curdling yells filtered down to her. When they returned to her, smiling the smiles of children who have been up to something more forbidden than breaking windows, she asked wearily if she might be told what the shrieking had been about.

"Geronimo," Paul said.

"His last battle cry," Victoria said. "Did you think it was us yelling, Mother?"

"Heavens, no," Mary said. "I recognized *him.*"

"And then he vanished in a puff of smoke," Paul said. "You can't take Geronimo alive."

"A puff of gunsmoke," Mary said.

"Don't you believe it," Victoria said. "I am in the mountains and when my people need me I shall return."

"Well, Douglas MacArthur," her mother mocked, laughing.

"*That* pig," Victoria said with a snort.

II

1

On the mesa above the cabin Harper L. Hoyt had built as a setting for his outlaw fantasies, his granddaughter was running. The broad, rolling crest was dotted with boulders and piñons, but Victoria's eye projected an oval track among them, like the one on which she used to jog with Bunny at college. She was running in the faded navy-blue sweat suit that was a twin to the one he used to wear. She had carried hers with her to serve as pajamas or work clothes on their travels.

Each morning since she had come here with Mike Lane and Rachel, she had set herself the task of running eight times around the track. It helped pass the time. It would keep her in shape—she expected some final terrible effort of endurance might anytime be demanded of her. But most of all the running kept down the swarm of recollections that crawled and oozed in her mind when she had to lie too long around the cold cabin. While she ran she felt clean. Even though each lap of running brought her right back past the spot where Mike sprawled in the spring sunshine to watch her go past, she felt she was going someplace. She had to have that or she would have cracked in pieces and let everyone down.

Because they had no word any more from the outside. For a few days they had, at least, the car radio. They had heard enough news broadcasts to know their plans were working. She was being hunted. The attention of the whole wicked country had been drawn to her, and maybe some would be jolted from their apathy by the message she had to send. She had heard part of one of her tapes played from a Denver station. The sound of her own pleading voice had moved her as if she were listening to someone else who was very far away, lost and in trouble. Listening, it seemed to her that at last she was identified with the miserable victims of oppression and war whose suffering had brought her here.

But one evening when Rachel was out at the car listening, the radio had gone dead. Since then, nothing. While there was still the incoming radio contact, the mountains around them had seemed like a marvelous curtain behind which they were hidden from the world. Now, day by day the mountains came to look like all the world there was. The snowy peaks and the long blue ridges went on into an everlasting emptiness where her breath, her voice, her existence would be lost without an echo.

This morning as she finished her eighth lap, she collapsed like a rag doll beside Mike, rolling to a halt with the momentum of her running. She lay with a blue-clad forearm over her eyes, feeling the rapid, healthy thump of her heart against the uneven gravel beneath her. She felt a light tugging under her left hip and realized Mike was pulling free the strap of his carbine. While she ran, Mike also kept her pistol belt and the holstered .45 Nat had given her. While she wore it, he had told her, she was his woman. If she let anyone take it from her, he would die. That was his superstition, and though she did not want to think she was his woman, she did not want him to die. He had told her she must always sleep with the gun between her legs—"to keep him from the cold" and to remind herself what he had done to her to change her into a true fighter. She had never done that because she could not bear a reminder. It was from the threat of such memories, edging back while she lay in the tomb-like chill of the cabin, that she had to escape by running.

That night in Nat's basement was like an image reflected in a pool of water. If you kept throwing rocks into the water, the image was always incomplete and fragmented—as it had to be if she was going to survive. She might have become too much afraid of the gun to keep it at all, and then Nat would die and her dreams would name her his murderer.

"Had enough?" Mike asked with his scoffing chuckle. Her insistence on running so much never ceased to amuse him, and though she kept saying he needn't make the long climb up the snow-clogged canyon from the cabin with her, he always trudged along.

"For now," she said. "Until I get my breath. In a hurry to go down?"

"For another can of stew? I'm not that hungry. I like it up here. Can't you tell I like it? You brought us to a pretty place."

"Then I'll run a few more laps. You think Bunny might come today?"

"I don't allow myself to think about what might happen. I follow orders," he said. The words and tone sounded funny to her, so she glanced out from under her sleeve. Behind his heavy black beard his face looked more childish than she had ever realized. This rugged landscape and the vastness of the sky made him younger, she thought. Younger than her classmates in college, as young as her brother Paul. And now with a flood of sisterly compassion she thought that the scar on Mike's upper lip made him look like a battered slum child given to her for protection. These impressions made her say, "While I was running I remembered the time my brother and I played Geronimo up here."

"Is that what we're playing now?"

"This is real," she said stubbornly, feeling giddily at the same time that only the sun and the mountains and the gravel rolling beneath her hips and shoulder blades could be counted on as long as they waited for news.

He snorted but said nothing.

"What do you mean? What are you thinking?"

His scarred lip stretched in a smile meant to be self-mocking. "It's real Sierra Club up here. I mean, it's a nice place for you and your kid brother to play Geronimo." As if to illustrate, he swung his carbine barrel down the ridgeline of mountains above the mesa, hunting for some popgun target. "Bang, bang. I don't think about anything any more. I gave it up."

"You do too."

"You think. But you get quieter every day. I keep thinking when Sister is tired of running we'll go down and get in the car and drive back home. I think this isn't air around us. It's glass.

And something's watching us through it. We'll never get out from behind the glass."

She sat up beside him now. It helped when she knew for certain that she and Mike or Rachel were getting edgy with each other. It gave her something definite to guard against. Most of the time they oozed around each other as if they were coated with oil, and she felt that nothing they said could be counted on, though they were nice to each other and always considerate. Still, it would be worse yet if they fell to quarreling. "I'm going to run some more laps," she said curtly.

She ran three more times around the imaginary track on the mesa. Both times she trotted past him she noted a kind of ferocity, like envy, as he watched her approach. Then, calmed by her weariness and laboring breath, she sank down again near him in the comfortable midmorning warmth. At last she said, "I guess you and Rachel would still be all right—back there doing your thing—if I hadn't come along. And Nat, too. Fussing with his cameras and radios and calendars. If I hadn't come along when I did."

"Nat wanted his war. Sis, you may not realize you were just what he was waiting for."

"But not you?" she asked with a deepening frown, as if he had to yield enough to let her comfort him.

"Nat had this thing about kamikaze pilots. You never saw all his collections. I'd go there sometimes and find him with this little Japanese flag tied on his head like a kamikaze. Once he was going to load his motorcycle with dynamite and ride it into a Nixon parade, or go to Washington and charge through the White House gate." He laughed with a peculiar embarrassment as he mentioned these secret wishes—as if they would sound not only weird but frivolous in this rugged outdoor environment and the keen, fresh air. But the added embarrassment inflamed him, too, as if he might be committed to vengeance on the mountains and sky that made his friend's secret shameful. "Shit, why not?" he said, gritting his teeth.

"But you?" she repeated in a pity that seemed to have no more right to be stated here in the open than his absurd thirst for vengeance.

"Me?" he asked. "Me?" He strained as if, truly, he could not understand what the single syllable meant. As if up here it would not even translate into any language he was permitted to use. "I guess I learned not to think about 'me' very much. I tell you, Sis, I think I learned that a long time ago. Not when it's a question of right and wrong and what they've done to us. You must know it just comes out clearer, what they're up to and what they've really done to all of us and our lives, if you use a black man like Nat to think with and see what they've done to him, what it's like to grow up black in America. Don't you think about him all the time?"

She might have tried to answer that directly if she had not so recently been running. But now her head was clearer than most of the time, and she bore down on Mike and what was right for him.

"Get out," she said. "You and Rachel take the car and get out now. They couldn't ever get you for anything real. Because it wasn't real. It isn't. You haven't kidnapped me. I know there's been a lot of publicity and maybe it will do some good, but there hasn't been any ransom paid as far as we know. Maybe, as Bunny says, it's crazy to think there would be.

"So you two get out! I'm not afraid of staying here by myself until Bunny comes. Are you afraid I'd tell on you? Afraid I wouldn't tell the truth if the police caught me?"

She thought what she said was reasonable enough, considering everything. And the stare Mike was directing at her was unlike him. He put his finger on the scar that spoiled his mouth, as if in deep meditation, toying with it, trying to make his mouth all whole again, she thought, so it would answer her generous wish straightforwardly.

"What *is* the truth by now?" he asked. He got to his feet, tossed her her pistol belt and gun and stalked away toward the canyon that led down from the mesa to the cabin.

There was still a lot of snow among the trees staggered down the canyon. There had been snow on the mesa when they came in and enough on the winding lane that led in from the highway so the car left tracks. But their luck had been good and the snow melted from the mesa and the lane within a day, so there were no tracks left to show any passer-by that a car had come in this way.

Only by night did they risk building fires in the fireplace, for fear that the smoke would be spotted—though they had no particular reason to believe anyone in this region would have come to investigate anyway. "The country is very big," Nat Fraser had said. "We're going to make it very hard for them to guess where in this big country to look."

But the canyon, still cold enough to keep snow, seemed to force the chill of its stone ledges and boulders into the cabin during the day. So for many of the daylight hours the three of them lay fully clothed inside the two sleeping bags that they had zipped together. The second sleeping bag was Bunny's. Like the sweat suit she ran in, it was one of the enduring mementos of all they had been through together, and surely of what it was all for. Among the smells of pine smoke and warming food, the ice-hard smell of rock and the winter that persisted around the little building, the smells of their bodies lying too close to each other in impatient waiting, she thought sometimes she could still make out Bunny's smell from the quilted cloth. If it was the smell of his sweat or lotions or semen or soap, it was one reassuring thing for her senses, her mind, to hold on to when everything else began to heave and twist and threaten to strangle her with the same question Mike had asked: What is the truth—of anything—by now?

This morning when she and Mike came down from the mesa, Rachel had heated coffee on their Sterno stove and offered to warm them one of the big cans of stew they had gathered in haste on their way here.

"I'm tired," Victoria said. "I ran some extra laps and I'm going to lie down." She kicked the remaining snow from her shoes and took them off. She crawled into the sleeping bags and pulled the cloth over her face.

"Is there anything left besides stew?" Mike asked. When Rachel started to check the stack of supplies he said, "Never mind. I'll eat something later. It's a long time until evening. I'll save eating for a while." He crawled into the sleeping bag, and Victoria could tell from the tugging that he was as far from her as he could get, that he had rolled to face the corner made by the log walls and the planks of the floor.

On some of the days when the three of them had lain in the bags so long for warmth they had talked a lot. They had said this was like being in a lifeboat together. They had learned a lot about each other until finally it began to seem that what they had to tell of their lives and what they had read or seen at the movies or what they believed and where they had learned it did not matter very much. All that mattered was the cold that came in so stealthy and slow through the walls so close around them. By this time there was usually not very much talking all day long. There was not even enough left to say to keep them talking when they crouched up to the fire in the fireplace by night.

After a while Rachel said, "Why don't you ball her, Mike?" She was still sitting across the single room from the sleeping bag, with her knees drawn up to her chin, her hands both curved around her coffee cup for warmth.

She repeated her suggestion—not so much lasciviously as with a desperation that came from both fear and boredom.

From under the cover of the sleeping bags Mike said, "Shut your mouth, you goddamn maniac."

Rachel went on as if she hadn't heard him, as if even the interval before she spoke again had nothing to do with his reply. "I thought about you up there. You say you go up to run. Don't you ball while you're up there? Don't you wonder why none of us have done it while we've been here? How many days is it now? How much stew have we eaten? But no balling! It's pretty damn ascetic of us and the Movement ought to see that we get a medal. I can understand why Victoria wouldn't want to ball. She's waiting for Nat to come and give her his enormous black cock. To suck."

"I swear I'll shut you up," Mike yelled. He jerked angrily at the cloth of the sleeping bag. Victoria, feeling her own body growing more and more rigid, felt him pulling his legs up so that his back bowed tightly against her elbow.

Now Rachel's voice was more a complaint. "While you're up there running, I lie here on these damned hard boards thinking about you and Nat, Victoria. How you open up for him and arch your back off the boards and take his glorious big swollen cock into you. Black, black, black! And the way you screamed that night in the Valley when he put it to you. And he shoots all this white, white stuff up into you, and you get down on your knees and beg him to let you . . . to let you . . . to let you . . . Why don't you ball her, Mike? We don't know when Nat's coming, Victoria. Let Mike have a little. Let Mike eat a little. A little, a little? I'll sit here and drink my hot coffee. . . . Don't we need a little relaxation? Don't we need a little for mental health?"

No one laughed at that. They heard. They didn't hear. Mike had said, even up on the mesa where the air was alive, that it was like being encased in glass. Like the horrid little figures in a glass globe that were engulfed in snow when you rolled it between your hands.

And Victoria Hoyt was in there, inside that glass globe, not knowing whether she heard the voice crooning from across the cabin or not, not knowing if she was awake or asleep, or whether it mattered, but hoping she was asleep because this was too bad, too bad, and sleep was worse than being awake. Since the night Nat had worked on her, sleep was so bad she had to run from it.

Even in sleep she had to run from sleep, trying with all her might to hold on and dream that she was up on the mesa running in her blue sweat suit, and if she lagged back just a little bit Bunny would catch up with her. Catch her elbow. Begin to explain things. As he always had.

2

Bunny would say she was sick. Bunny had told Stella she was sick after what had happened in Mexico. Her mother would say she was very sick.

So she was sick. She knew she was sick. They had told her the world was sick, and she understood she mustn't be afraid of sickness. Maybe she could drain the sickness of everybody into herself, like a sponge taking the pus out of the body of the world, taking all the guns and bombs and fire into herself and softening them and cooling them inside the woman's body that had been given her for something. Maybe that was what Nat had taught her, whatever he meant by his awful black sickness when he put the cold muzzle of the gun into her, murmuring, "You big. You don't know how big. You can take him. See, you big." And she had shouted as if her mouth had tasted steel and she was spewing splinters of steel and slivers of bone out into the deafness of the world that had never listened to her.

She wanted to be that sick, to prove once and for all—to whom? to nobody? to the deafness?—that you could be that sick and survive. But the thought, the memory of that incredible cold entering her body was too heavy for her mind. It kept crashing into ugliness and when Rachel let her ugly mouth talk about Nat and her, that made her sick with the wrong kind of sickness. Rachel was supposed to be her sister. Rachel understood her no better than anyone else ever had.

She slept.

In her hand there was a candle and around her, on either side, the sad girls of her college were singing. There were candles in their hands, for they were all in Cambodia. Around them there were tens, then hundreds and thousands of children running down a white dusty road while things kept buzzing over them with a monstrous swiftness that zinged past their heads and set some of them on fire as they ran. The sky and jungle were so dark they ought not to keep moving like that. Children ought to be home in bed. But they were all pale and she knew if she touched them they would be cold as that cruel coldness between her legs, pushing toward her. Then she made up her mind it wasn't right to fight it. She opened to take the coldness into her. That was the only way to stop it. To stop the children running as they burned like the candle in her hand.

"They'll see."

They would see that Victoria could stop it.

She could not sing as sadly as the other girls with candles in their hands. No one ever thought she could carry a tune.

There was a way to stop it. Only women had the way.

She felt it come into her and did not yell at the dreadful taste of steel and death. There was no farther for them to go.

And then it began to come out of her again, not cold now, but as warm as her blood which would follow it and flow down like a flowering of stars across the night.

You're sicker than anyone can be.

If she had a father he would know she was only as sick as she had to be.

But she had no father. So she fought for breath enough to scream.

"Now, stop it," she said.

Mike's hand was on her shoulder and with her eyes as wide open as they had ever been she saw his frail, bearded face leaning over her. "It's only a bad dream," he said very gently. His spoiled, scarred upper lip was drawn back from his upper teeth. She knew he was kind and he was smiling, but it didn't help.

"You said, 'Now, stop it,'" he chuckled. He was trying to be kind to her. People had always tried to be kind.

She fought at the top level of the sleeping bag, trying to roll free from Mike's hand and the confinement of the cloth. She was stronger than he, but someone seemed to have sewed the sleeping bag tight around her while she slept.

"To the car," she said. She pretended to relax. "Yeah. I guess I had a bad dream. I'm sorry. I just want to go out to the car and listen to the radio to see if there is any news."

"Broken," Rachel said from the dimness across the room. It was half dark in the cabin and Victoria, taking a deep breath full of confusing smells, knew she must have slept away most of the day. But Rachel was still where she had been before the bad sleep came. "You know it's broken."

"I'll try to fix it," Victoria said calmly. "You know there were those wires we couldn't figure out. The red one and the black one with those little copper clips on them. That looked like someone had jerked them loose."

"Yes, but . . ." Mike said patiently. "You remember we tried them on everything they would fit on. Every possible connection. And we know the battery is still okay. It isn't those loose wires."

"I think Rachel pulled the wires loose," Victoria said. "I've thought that since the day the radio wouldn't work any more."

Neither of the others said anything. Victoria sat upright so that at least the upper part of her body was out of the sleeping bag. Mike, beside her, made no move to keep her from sitting up.

"We're all getting a little kooky here," Rachel said pleasantly.

"It doesn't make any sense to say I pulled the wires loose when none of them were cut or anything. And we tried to fit the plugs back on anything they'd fit in case any of them had slipped loose. Don't you see, Victoria?"

"I don't know what you did to it," Victoria said. "I didn't want to make a fuss because we're all in this together. And I told you to get out, Mike. But you lied to me."

Now, for a long time, neither of the others spoke. The air in the small room of the cabin was colder than it had ever seemed before, as if the walls were not really logs, but the chilled stones of the canyon itself, of winter itself, crowding in. Moving by stealth and disguising themselves as wood or cloth or anything they had to use as long as it was not warm.

Finally Mike said, "There was some bad news, Sis. There's another wire you can't see on the radio. I twisted it in two. Rachel and I thought . . . We didn't know, you see. Remember! The pigs will say anything. What if it's a trick? We have no way of knowing how they're trying to trick us with what they say on the radio."

"You better tell me," Victoria said.

Again neither of the others seemed able to reply.

"Tell me what they said."

His scarred lip stretched in one more lying attempt to smile and be kind. Then it softened into a relaxed solemnity. "They claim Bunny is dead," he told her. "Wait now! I told you we'd be damn fools to trust anything they said. . . ."

She was out of the confinement of the sleeping bags before he got a grip on her arm to stop her. She knew where the car keys were and she was not about to stop to pull shoes onto her stockinged feet. "I'm going in to find out," she said, already heading for the cabin door, already with her hands on the two-by-four bolt across it before Rachel sprang and grabbed her around the waist.

Rachel was no match for her in strength. And if she had got through the door she might have had cunning, sense or just sheer strength enough to run down the long lane toward the highway instead of pausing to try to start the car. She could have outrun them both. Rachel had a foot against the door to keep her from tugging it open, now that the bolt was loose, but Rachel's grip was loosening.

Victoria was almost free when Mike caught her hard across the temple with the barrel of her pistol.

The blow did not knock her out. She was blinded and dizzy and down on one knee, flailing her arms groggily to drive away the cloud of rosy pain that kept her from thinking. It was her mistake to think that Mike was going to hit her again with the gun. He was only prodding her with the muzzle and begging her to give up.

"I'd have to shoot," he said twice. "I'd have to." Then he said wearily, "Tie her up, Rache."

When she was bound, Mike and Rachel made her as comfortable as they could in one of the sleeping bags in front of the fireplace. A little later, after it was too late for the chimney smoke to be seen, they made her a roaring fire and Rachel offered to feed her some of the beef stew that had finally been warmed. Victoria would not open her mouth for the spoon. She gave no sign of listening to them when they spoke to her.

For some hours Mike sat by the fire beside her and kept on trying to explain what he knew and what it meant.

"It was crazy of me to screw up our radio. It's all we have. Now we really don't know what moves have been made. I don't know what to do except wait. We can't wait forever. We've got to wait."

Later he said, more or less talking to himself—or perhaps to Rachel or perhaps to the cold granite faces of the stones that sat up the canyon walls like giant stairs behind the softer pines—"I don't think Nat would have killed Bunny. I don't think he would. I just don't see it. I don't see what there could be that he would think he could gain."

The bowl of beef stew that Rachel had fixed for him sat untouched beside his cheap, cracked boot. At one point he nudged it gently toward Rachel with his foot. "Why don't you eat it, Rache? Keep up your strength. You're going to need it."

But they were in no real dialogue. Now his dialogue was only with himself. "But then, I don't know what Nat might do, do I? Or his friends. Or me. They have suffered so much. Oh yes, brothers and sisters, say that again. And so they are crazy. They are insane. Oh boy, there isn't any doubt of that. And I am a-fraid. That is a big difference. That is a great big difference, isn't it, Rache?"

"Shut up," Rachel said.

"You don't want to hear my analysis?"

"We know you're smart," she said. "Smartest kid on your block. And that is why they broke your lip."

"I am not smart. Oh! I am *not* smart. I am imaginative. Victoria, you know how bad it is to be imaginative, though just a kid? It burns inside your skin. It makes your bowels itch. You have to do things. Yes. You have to do them. To see how they will come out. I am only smart enough to see this was never intended to work. Pure kamikaze. Sink a pig battleship. If you can."

The fire was still burning heartily after midnight when Rachel took a good draft of cocaine. Mike refused to share with her.

She said irritably, "Will you stop talking? No one is going to listen to you now. Can't we . . . ?"

"Kill her? I have been thinking of that while I have been talking. Because even if I am not smart I think of a whole lot of things. And now I am trying to imagine if there is a better place to kill her than this and what is to gain or what is to lose by killing her or not killing her. Victoria, are you listening?

"Because if you are listening I want to tell you I do not know who killed poor Bunny Stewart, but I know there are plenty of crazies in all this who would have done it if Nat did not. Or if Bunny is dead I do not know, since the pigs lie to us by television as well as radio. But I know that I am scared.

"Victoria, does it comfort you to know how scared I am?"

III

Mary was back in the United States of America because there, before her eyes, was Walter Cronkite. Another government had fallen. Once again there were refugees on another littered road. Some were at sea searching for a rescue fleet that kept withdrawing ahead of them. Yet Walter was confident there would be another "orderly transfer of power."

Walter's smile was intact. The world was intact. It was only the faulty color of this television set that gave the illusion he was decomposing. The yellow was brilliant as pure sulphur and bled off his hands and face onto the poisonous blue of his shirt. The red rims of his eyes, mouth and hands were out of register—like hairline incisions cut into the flesh of the screen itself.

There was another yellow-green Walter behind this scarlet and animated etching, saying the same things. Behind that an ashy-gray Walter with a face that seemed sculptured out of the mud of a dead planet.

And to Mary's eyes it looked as if his teeth had been filed down to points. It seemed as if the sulphurous yellow in which all the Walters were talking to her had spilled out onto the carpet of this motel room in which she waited and watched.

Then, just before Walter said, "And that's the way it is on this Thursday night," he told her gravely that there was what appeared to be a break in the Hoyt Kidnapping.

"Earlier in the program we saw the scene in the New Orleans airport where two men were killed in an attempt to hijack a plane bound for Bogotá. Those men have now been identified as Nat Fraser and Willis Gordon. The Los Angeles District Attorney has confirmed that both these men were being sought for questioning in connection with Miss Hoyt's kidnapping and the murder of Benjamin Stewart. This coincides with a telephonic communication received earlier in the day from the El Dorado resort in Mexico saying Cooley Hoyt had left there by private plane. He was thought to be carrying ransom money and may have been on his way to a rendezvous with the kidnappers."

A commercial came on to advertise a new restaurant opening here in El Paso, specializing in takeout Mexican foods.

Mary took three steps from her chair, intending to shut off the television set. Yet, when her thumb was on the nickeled button, something like a fear of sacrilege, a fear of being cut off from that yellow-lighted world where things "coincided" so fluently, kept her from the choice of sitting in silence and darkness while she waited for Cooley.

She retreated to her chair and learned that four people could dine on tacos, frijoles and enchiladas purveyed in yellowish cartons more cheaply than they could prepare the same meal at home.

After that a game show came on with the tormented screams of fat women with red, off-register mouths and filed teeth. One after another the women won their prizes and expressed ecstatic gratitude. Again and again the loud protests of anxiety turned to joy as wishes coincided with fulfillment. Mrs. Darlene Cranston won a two-week all-expenses-paid tour of the Caribbean.

That's the way it was on this Thursday night on the right side of the Rio Grande.

Mary was still in her chair when, finally, Cooley knocked on her door. The yellow light from the television colored her figure when she opened the door on its chain to make sure it was he and not the police bringing news of him.

"Thank God," she said. She caught his hand and pressed it to her cheek. Then she said, "You're not wet."

In fact, he had still been promising to swim the Rio Grande if he had to when she saw him last on the Mexican side of the border and drove across by herself in a rented car. She was to wait for him in this designated motel. He had not even given her an alternative course of action in case he failed to show up. They were too far gone, too nearly used up, to think of alternatives. This was the last gambit over which they had any control. If it didn't work, they had lost Victoria either to the authorities or to the nameless menaces outside the law, and in their extremity it did not matter much which of those landed on her first.

"Lucky I didn't try to swim," Cooley said—protesting now that he had not truly contemplated anything so absurd. He bragged that he still had tricks he hadn't shown her yet. She was supposed to take the mere fact that he had got across the border without being spotted or taken into custody by authorities on either side as a sign of more tricks still to come when they were needed. "All it took was money," he said. "Good thing you still have the U.S. currency. It took money and finding the right man."

Money was his trick—and along with it the nose to sniff out corruption, even on this short notice. He might not have the outlaw contacts that Colonel Timmerman supposedly had, and the money actually in his pocket was not at all what he would think of as big money, the kind that made things happen like wishes granted. But he was still the expert from the back alleys. They had taught him how to make whatever he had in his fist seem big enough to those whose help he had to have.

At four that afternoon he found his man in a barbershop near the river in Juárez. By five, in the scruffy apartment above the shop he had his deal. The man wanted fifty thousand pesos to guarantee him passage over the river and unobserved delivery in El Paso or anywhere within fifty miles of the city center that his heart might wish. Cooley understood this was twice the amount ordinarily asked for such a delivery. Hell, he trusted his man because the fellow had made such a quick and accurate estimate of his urgency. He was dealing with a total stranger and an utterly familiar corruption.

They had got along beautifully, these two. Cooley told him sweatily that he did not have fifty thousand pesos to hand over. Others had had to be paid to direct him to the barbershop. But if this present transaction went through with no hitches, there would be no problem in arranging to double the fee.

His man laughed—meaning he had understood that before he asked for the fifty thousand. He might or might not have recognized Cooley Hoyt's face. He wasn't saying. But as Cooley watched his man case him for later blackmail, figuring how easy it would be to find out what name this new client signed to his checks, Cooley's trust increased.

He and his man were not going to shake hands on the deal they concluded. Instead of this clincher, Cooley set himself up to be laughed at. He hitched nervously at his belt and said, "I guess I've got to take the chance you won't be on the phone to the Border Patrol the minute I drive off with your boy."

His man didn't even bother to smile at that. He knew the ploy. Good. It was better than a handshake—this confirmation that he was dealing with equal deviousness.

So money had been made to float him over the cold river he could not have swum. The paper raft. The ultimate act of faith. Nothing at all when men did not have faith in each other's desperation and greed.

The exploitation of such faith had produced a dark-blue Mustang that carried Cooley into El Paso from a downriver crossing in a rubber boat. That boat was rowed expertly by a faceless Mexican who did not understand money except as wages—no doubt higher for this type of work than for daylight labor. A quiet, polite collegiate type drove the Mustang into the city and dropped Cooley at a Texaco station. He got directions to the motel where Mary was supposed to wait and walked there as fast as he could. He found her room number written on a cardboard under the seat of the car they had rented in Juárez. He reached the door of her room on the second-floor balcony without running into anyone at all. So far so good, except he was late, late. The crossing had taken more time than he had wanted to allow for it.

She began rapidly to explain to him what she had heard on the evening news from Walter. Trying to ask him what it meant to them. But he said, "Damned if I can figure that, either. Talk to me about it while we drive."

2

Knowing what you have to do is something. Not much. Knowing that you have to retrieve the years when everything went wrong, though so much of it seemed to be working right. They said, the ones you listened to, *a little farther down the road you'll have it made, you'll see what it's all been for.* Knowing someone else has had the secrets you should have had and is watching you dig your own grave without even getting any laughs out of it. At least they ought to get some laughs out of it while they watch you flail around blind because you don't know how to do what you have to do.

"Why are you telling me now?" he asked.

There was no rage in his voice, but rage began to shake the speeding car, as if some soft, gigantic hammer or an invisible fist of darkness was beating irregularly against the front bumper. The tires stuttered on the pavement without veering quite enough to cross either the white center line or throw gravel from the shoulder. Then the rage seemed to be not only shaking their rented Impala but lifting it and carrying it along. The sound of the accelerating motor had no meaning except rage. The red line on the speedometer edged past one hundred.

"All right," Mary said wearily. "If you want to kill us both, I won't say we don't deserve it."

"Not us," he said. "Not us."

He wanted to kill . . . not Victoria, but that other Victoria who had been smuggled into the world to take the place of the darling kidnapped long ago by phantoms and never returned. Wanted to kill . . . no one. But to reach and strangle that horrible life his child had had instead of the one he had schemed to provide for her.

"You're not smart, Mary. If you want to get the use out of me —whatever the hell you think you're doing with me—you might've kept your mouth shut. No! Now you're telling me she was going down for this crazy, murdering black *lunatic*."

"I'm not telling you."

"You said . . ."

"I told you what I heard from Stella. I don't have any details. And it was Stella who called it love. Not I. . . . I told you how it might fit with what I heard on the TV a while ago. You're right. Why did I tell you?"

"You could have told me last night. When you were being so honest."

She could have. I could have. We could have. They could have. . . . Again the futile accusations hammered from side to side in his skull. But whatever had been beating the front of the car was slacking off now and the red line of the speedometer was shrinking reluctantly.

After a great gulp of air he said, "You were trying to spare my feelings, and I respect you for that. Not much we could try except what we're trying. It may not work. Maybe it's too late if those . . . those fellows were trying to skip the country. But we had to try."

"I was trying to be fair to you, too," she said miserably. "If I'd told you then what I've told you now, would you have stayed back at El Dorado?"

He wanted to say no. But he wasn't sure of that, either. And with all his options kicked to the winds he had no reason not to be honest. "Nothing to stay there for. Charlotte's through with me," he said.

"I don't believe it. I believe she's . . . she's a lot of woman, I think."

"That's why she's through with me." It was a huge relief to say it. To have someone to say it to. So he went on a little. "I've never known why good people put up with me as long as they do sometimes. Charlotte. Bob Pardon. Even you did. For a while."

She did not betray this rare and hard-bought honesty by any sentimentality. She did not say that they had all hung on, maybe, because they guessed, or only just hoped, that honesty would be ripped free from all the camouflage he had offered them, supposing only his disguises could be loved.

She said nothing, but there was a new sort of peace between them. A truce made at last.

They had no other truce. Whatever they might resolve between themselves had no bearing any longer on the dangers of this night.

He slackened speed, glancing again into the rear-view mirror to see if some late-roaming police car might have chanced on them and seen his extravagant violation of whatever speed laws they had here. He saw headlights a mile or two behind them, closing, then falling back a little and presently equilibrating to keep pace with him.

They were being followed all right, and it did not take his calming mind long to move from that realization to the next; they were in a web of surveillance. Mary had told him that all watchers of the evening news knew he had left El Dorado. He had let it pass then because she told him other things harder to come to terms with.

Now he believed that Mary's movements to El Dorado must have been watched. Probably her meeting with Stella in Los Angeles was known. By now it was very possible the police had Stella's version of that conversation—with whatever hedges the woman would make to protect herself.

I should have swum the damn river, he thought.

But what for? The only gain from such a venture was that he might have drowned, gone into the clean black emptiness without hearing any more tormenting things about Victoria.

It was not his man in Juárez who had tipped the police about the crossing. It didn't have to be. They had not been out of the net since the Cessna left the El Dorado airstrip. The alert would have been spread very quickly all along the Mexican border, no doubt all across the southern approaches to the country in case tricky Cooley Hoyt should have feinted and then made his real attempt at entry from a Caribbean or South American point of departure, or even from Europe.

His maneuvers in crossing the Rio Grande had been tolerated. Not for the amusement of his watchers. He did not think they were amused, only that they were smarter than he and more numerous and infinitely better equipped. They had probably been in the El Paso motel office a few minutes after Mary checked in there, waiting for him to show up. They had chosen

to leave Mary and him with the illusion that the entry was unde-
tected.

Now he saw that they were still trying to stretch that illusion.
He pulled into an all-night truck stop to refill with gas. The car
that had been following him across long empty stretches of highway roared on past. He saw there were four men in it.

When Mary and he went to use the rest rooms, he knew he
was being watched from the fluorescent-lighted glass cubicle of
the station. No use trying to guess which of the men lounging
there had been stationed to report his progress. Now that he was
sure they were in a net, he felt a degree of relief like that he had
always felt in turning from the bafflement of his life with women
to his business affairs. He could even tell himself: I wanted them
here. They've taken my bait. It was a good move to cross the
river as I did, because it makes me look dumber than I am.

They knew a lot of things he didn't. He knew a few things
they didn't. They might be *altogether* smarter than he. He still
had the option to make them play on the terrain he knew better.

Hide in the blind spots of their minds. Now no other hiding
was possible.

After the truck stop, Mary drove for an hour while he slept.
He got to sleep with surprising ease. As if he had no more worries. . . . No, as if all the nightmares were outside him now, and
inside was a room left empty by the nightmares gone out to
prowl the real world.

He had a little dream of Charlotte—she was wearing the green
necklace he had bought her. Goddamn, the stones around her
pretty neck looked fine, green as little leaves with the morning
sun behind them, fringing them with cool green fire. Charlotte
was very pleased with them and that was all he could ask.

It was still dark when he woke with a questioning grunt.

"We must be less than thirty miles from Albuquerque," Mary
said.

There was a stripe of rosy light across the eastern sky, bright
enough to define a line of smoke low on the horizon. His shoulders and back were stiff—from the cold, he realized, surprised
somehow that they had come out of the comfortable tropics to
the country his skin and nerves found more familiar, after all this
time away. He felt a kind of pleasant hunger, trustworthy while
his mind was still empty and fragrant from his skimpy dream.

"I think we're being followed," Mary said.

He didn't turn to look behind them. "Yes," he said.

"If it's police . . ."

"It's police."

"I'm not sure. I wasn't convinced for a long time that car way back there was following us. See? He's more than a mile back. It *felt* like he was following us."

Without knowing why, he wanted to laugh at her anxiety. "It's getting tight, isn't it?" he asked. Then, as if to humor her, he turned for a lazy look at the gray Pontiac on the road behind them. At least it looked like a Pontiac in the early dimness as it came down at an angle toward the corner they had turned when Mary first spoke. The car still had its headlights on and he could only see its silhouette against the frosty hill behind it. But he was as sure it was a Pontiac as he was sure about his determination to do what had to be done. He was waking to a day he had been waiting for all his life.

"Don't you know what it means?" he asked. The note of gladness in his voice startled Mary into a quick glance at him.

"It means they don't know where she is yet," he said. "They wouldn't be following us like this if they had found her. They're counting on us to lead them to her."

"Oh."

"We could decoy them up into Colorado. Kansas. All the way to Kansas."

Mary said nothing, waiting to see if that was a decision. He knew then that whatever decision was made would have to be his. It was on his shoulders to decide what was going to happen to his child. It would hurt Mary too much now and in the times ahead if she decided and that decision turned out wrong.

"We'll have some breakfast in Albuquerque and then we'll see," he said.

3

His appetite was terrific. He was still hungry when he had finished scrambled eggs, sausage, hashbrowns and toast. He could have eaten another order of everything, but he settled for another cup of scalding black coffee.

Their waitress was a drab girl in a baggy orange uniform, but she had nice eyes and was very polite considering how busy she was serving the crowd of men in working clothes. Cooley liked her. He liked the place with its steamy clatter and the hard, wisecracking voices of the men around them as they talked about a Henry Martin who had just been run off the school board in a district election and about a blue movie a couple of them had seen in Denver.

Cooley left a five-dollar tip for their waitress and she came running after him to ask if he had made a mistake. "Aw," he said. "You keep it. Got to spread it around, you know."

"Well. Have a good day," she said. "Come back now, hear?"

He walked out to the car with Mary thinking, yes, it could be a good day. The little remnant of hunger after his big breakfast made him eager to get on with it. He felt as he used to when he was a boy setting out in the morning to go hunting.

The morning air was crisp over the parking lot. He looked around among the parked cars to see if he could spot the gray Pontiac that had been following them. It was not in the diner's parking lot, nor parked by the curb across the street. It did not occur to him that the pursuit had been abandoned. It only occurred to him to admire the efficiency of those who directed it, as if he had achieved a perfectly harmonized alliance with them, each counting on the other to act out his part without the need of further cues.

The sun was still not quite above the suburban housetops. There were streaks of frost on some of the lawns. The delicate sting of air in his nostrils made him hesitate a moment before he slid onto the seat of the car and closed the door. He had been born less than a hundred miles from here and he felt he was already home.

When he had backed deliberately from the parking lot and wheeled onto the highway again, he brought the car to a moderate speed and held the speedometer steady. He did not want to discuss with Mary what they were going to do. She did not push him to give his decision. She only said, "The tea came in a teabag. I couldn't very well read the tea leaves."

Then they were past the junction where they might have turned toward Santa Fe. She said nothing for another mile or two after they had passed it. Then she said, "You're right. No sense in trying to lead them off the track."

"No."

"It has to be ended."

"One way or the other," he said. "If Victoria's there we've got to get to her."

"No more moves left."

"They haven't closed in yet. I figure they won't until we leave the highway beyond Los Alamos. They may still hang back until I swing off the blacktop by Hindeman's old ranch. You remember that?"

"No. Maybe I'll recognize it."

"And if they haven't made any move until I'm off the blacktop I'll have to try to outrun them all the way in to the canyon. I think we can do it. If there is no snow on the road. I've been looking as we drove. Very little snow left. Only a few patches. If there are no rocks down in the road. If I can hit all the curves without slowing too much. If we have a few minutes to talk to her—for you to talk to her—before the police get there. Or . . . we'll do what we can."

"It has to be ended but I don't want anyone hurt."

He ignored the latter part of her statement. She had yielded the decision to him and he had to do his best.

"Reach in my suitcase and get the gun," he told her.

She hesitated, but then reached over the back of the seat to open the zipper on his bag. She slid back into her seat holding the short-barreled revolver in her hand as if she could not believe its actual weight and shape. She had accepted the idea of death but this was death itself, the weight and hard-edged shape that her senses refused to tolerate. "I said we were capable of anything," she reminded him pitifully. "I don't want anyone else killed."

He promised her nothing. How could he make any promise in this moment of total uncertainty? Only, he wanted her to trust him, to leave the resolution and the guilt to him. He wanted to claim that much back from all that had been squandered.

In a minute, with no more discussion, she half turned in her seat and dropped the gun in his jacket pocket.

"I hope to God she isn't there," she said. "But we've come all this way, and it's got to be over."

IV

1

A better driver—even a driver with no more skill but better luck —would have made it. The lane scratched out across the foothills, and only graded or filled where it had to be, ran for nearly seven miles from the county blacktop to the pines that hid the cabin. When Cooley left the blacktop he was almost two miles ahead of the yellow sedan that had followed him up from Albuquerque. He had the advantage of surprise. He was accelerating across the first mile of jolting, rising single tracks while the men in the following car were still wondering how to interpret this move—and no doubt reasoning that he was running toward a dead end, so there was no hurry in catching up.

It was never to be clear to him that the pursuers even tried to close in. They didn't have to. He had no luck this morning.

In a badly washed, climbing curve still almost half a mile short of the cabin, he lost control. The curve was passable. He simply tried to take it too fast. He heard the fenders screech on rocks piled beside the ruts. The steering wheel jerked out of his grip as the left front wheel sank and the bottom of the car dragged in a loose mixture of pine needles and dirt. The car made a sick, collapsing twist to the left and he saw the windshield suddenly marble in front of him as a pine snag hit it. He shut off the motor, thinking, We can still make a run for it.

His door would not budge. He hammered it with the heel of his hand. Then he reached across Mary and was pushing her door up at an angle, shoving her out ahead of him, when the

shocking bray of a bullhorn in the lane behind them said, "STAY
IN YOUR CAR." He let the door sag shut as two men came running up with drawn revolvers.

"Hoyt?"

"Yes."

"Mrs. Rossiter?"

"Yes."

"Climb out. Take it slow. We're here to help you if you'll cooperate."

"Fine," Cooley said.

Of course, they confiscated his gun right away, frisking him
efficiently and then checking Mary's purse and the bags inside
the car. The man who told them his name was Harris said, "All
right. Let's have the trunk key." The other man unlocked the
trunk and they all peered into its clean, impersonal emptiness
like archaeological diggers who have thought they were opening
a tomb only to find themselves looking into the excavation for a
suburban basement.

"The money . . ." Harris said. It was not quite a question, but
a little more than the transposition of his thought into sound.
Cooley was about to answer that Mary had what was left of the
cash they brought from El Dorado when he realized that wasn't
the money the police were concerned about. As usual, they were
partly right and partly wrong in their surmises.

"Then you already made the payoff?" Harris asked. His face
did not show disappointment or come close to admitting his cal-
culations might have been faulty. There was only an almost
ironic squint as he conceded Cooley might have decoyed them
away from the point where the transaction was made, the ransom left. "Bad business to let that kind of money get to the kind
of people we're dealing with. Come on. Get in our car and we'll
go back to Albuquerque."

"No," Cooley said. "No, we couldn't do that." For a flashing
instant he had seen the possibility of pulling them all back from
here and going on with the improvised game while there were
still possibilities of deception. He had been wrong and the police
had been wrong about why they should follow him and Mary.
But there was nothing except delay to be gained by any more

deceptions. The funnel was narrowing. "No. There hasn't been any ransom paid. Isn't going to be. We've been told our daughter's being held just over there. There's a cabin up the road a piece. We sure appreciate your showing up when you did."

"She's here?"

"We think so. You can't see the cabin from here. Get around the next curve and you can probably see it back in the pines."

"You were going to walk in—without money—and . . . ?"

"Negotiate. Or I'd take her place as hostage. Or whatever they wanted."

"Or shoot it out? You know we have a report that your daughter may be armed and dangerous."

"We don't even know for sure she's here," Mary said. "Please just cooperate with us a little. If we could only get it straight whether she's here or not . . . and please don't go in there shooting."

Cooley said, "From the curve ahead we might be able to see if there's a car in there. I doubt if many people find the place. Not this time of year."

He and Harris climbed another hundred and fifty feet on the road to where it broke over a small ridge. From this point on again the road was nothing more than lightly worn car tracks and a faintly detectable stunting of the brush across a swayback meadow to the stand of trees at the canyon's edge. As Cooley remembered, the cabin was just visible from here, though his father had not intended it to be easily spotted from any direction. They made out the corner of a roof, a few regular lines that were not the lines of nature. A glimpse of stone that must be the chimney. The car parked near it was easier to make out than the cabin itself. It was a blue 1970 Plymouth.

"Well," Harris said. "Maybe your tip was good. Want to tell me more about it?"

"I want to go over there. If you would give me my gun I'd go over and see who's there."

"I'm not sure you do," Harris said. "I didn't want to go into this in front of the girl's mother, but there's new stuff coming in about Victoria Hoyt. The Mexican government would like to get hold of her, too. Armed and dangerous. You wouldn't want to shoot it out with your own daughter, would you?"

"There's been a lot said."

Harris nodded to admit that. But then he asked brusquely, "Is there any way out besides the road we came in on?"

"Not another road. You can climb the canyon to the mesa up behind. I suppose they might have already gone out that way. They could have heard the cars. Or the bullhorn. If you fellows would just stay out of sight until I walk over there. If it didn't work out you could do what was necessary."

"Why were you so anxious to get there ahead of us?" Harris asked. "Never mind. We'll go back to the cars and talk this over. We had better figure how to do it right."

By the time they got back down to the cars there was a gray Pontiac parked in the road behind the yellow sedan. There were four more men in business suits. Two of them had pump shotguns and two had rifles with telescopic sights. Harris sent the men with rifles up to the higher curve to keep an eye on the cabin.

One of the new men said, "I've called in more cars. The first ought to be here in ten minutes. I'm going to call for copters from Los Alamos to put men up on the mesa there. They can get a good look down the canyon. I doubt if there are roads down there to send our cars down."

He and Harris were still busy figuring the terrain when two state police cars came in and took their places in the crooked line behind the Pontiac. The uniformed troopers were also carrying rifles besides their side arms. From far off, probably as far as the blacktop, they heard a siren cut on and hold for a long minute, the sound very distinct in the morning air—arrogant, patient and violent as it rolled up the rocks and wooded slopes around them. They all felt a battle was being prepared.

"I don't need the gun," Cooley said to Harris. "Let me walk over there and see who is in the cabin. It could be hunters . . . anyone . . . not the people we're looking for at all."

Harris listened to this thoughtfully. Shook his head. "It will be a little while before the copters come up from Los Alamos and we're not going to make a move until we have our fellows in place."

Or if they would let me walk over there with a grenade, the pin pulled so if I got inside and she was one of them, I could let the handle go and it would save the taxpayers a lot of money. . . .

Cooley didn't make the offer aloud. Yet somehow he seemed to know the same thought was in Harris's mind.

They saw the helicopter hovering for a while over the mesa, looking from the road to be higher than the snowcapped peaks of the Sangre de Cristo beyond. The morning sun made a bright disk, like a halo, of the whirling blades. The halo of light rose and fell like a spot of light on the surface of an ocean swell, a great invisible tide flowing over the continent, merely rippled by these local mountains. The copter was scouting the mesa and the branching arteries of the canyon that ran down from it before it picked a spot to land and disembark its load of sharpshooters.

Watching the disk of light, Cooley felt his eyes water and strain. He had an impulse to rub them, as if he could erase that deadly flaw in the bright blue sky and leave it as immaculate as it used to be when he came up here with the boys from school.

But even if he blindfolded his eyes that disk of light would still be there. It was like the hallucinations that had tormented him during and after his bout with alcohol. Something gone wrong inside his head, something wrong with the wrecked circuits of nerves, some final terror of death and the beginning of decomposition. What had healed him of that?

Now he could only remember that Charlotte had come. She had made him know that if you held fast for long enough the unbearable hallucinations would go away.

He grabbed Harris's arm and whispered, "I've got something to tell you. You said this had to be done right."

But the time for misleading or persuading Harris had slipped past, like all the other times when one wise or honest or open exchange between men and women with different obligations might have eased them past the collision of guns against guns. "Let's hear it," Harris said with calm professionalism. But he was already committed to doing this thing right according to his training, according to his clear duty and the decent, deadly requirements of the society whose sworn defender he had to be. "Let's hear it, Hoyt. The last thing I want is any bloodshed. If

you know how to do this without bloodshed, speak up, man.
We're not going to make a move until we have to."

"I didn't say without . . ." Cooley's great thirst to see this
right wouldn't even pause to consider physical pain or destruction. It was almost as if he saw this field before them and the
cover of pines across from them as the terrain where some boy's
game of battle could be acted out with yips and yells and all the
killed who pitched down dead getting up again when the playing was over—and still feeling passionately that how they
behaved and what they learned would matter all their lives
thereafter. Almost as if this was still the game he had started
when he first came up here with his father and played all alone
with only the mountains judging him.

"We don't even know who's over there yet," Harris said with
professional patience. "We're not going off half cocked this
time."

                                2

They knew soon enough. The trained men, the armed men, the
men who had studied how best to handle such a situation were
all supposed to be in their assigned places when many of them
heard the shattering of a glass window in the cabin and then a
single shot from a carbine.

"Come on in and get us, pigs!"

The voice ringing out over the meadow was so boyish, excited,
it could have been one of Cooley's buddies from old times, up
from school for a weekend holiday.

The shot did not sound very loud or threatening, either, but
the sun-warmed silence over the meadow sounded ghastly after
the reverberations of it died away. Now the sun was well up and
the gray-green mottled meadow was like a bowl of warmth—still
as only a mountain meadow can be on a sweet spring day. A day
when death seems not only intolerable but very near.

Cooley twisted to look at Mary's face after they heard this
shot. No one had seen where it struck. But Harris, with a sweep
of his arm, had commanded them all to drop flat.

Cooley saw that Mary was going to endure the signal shot and whatever the silence meant. As best she could. He saw she had dug her right hand into the pine needles and gravel on which she lay. She would hold on like that if the earth flipped over and that was the only way to hang on, with nothing below her then but the everlasting emptiness and the blue sky to fall through. When she fell, she would still be holding on to that handful of pine needles and gravel.

A uniformed man with a walkie-talkie crawled up behind Harris and said, "McConnell says he's ready to rush it if he has to. Or he can put tear gas through one of the windows."

"Not yet," Harris said. "We've got all day and I don't want any bloodshed. By anybody. Tell him not yet. To keep his men well back."

Cooley said humbly, "I know you've got all day. So if you would listen to me now. If we could go down to your car and talk a few minutes?"

He had a voice that a great many people had believed against their better judgment and common sense and even the evidence of statistics when the meaning of those statistics was uncertain. The voice of Moses, Bob Pardon had said, telling the people that just because there is a desert ahead of them there must be a Promised Land on the far side of it. A voice, at least, that spoke to the last cherished crumb of hope that the universe is not a closed corporation, that the ends of life are not foreclosed by whatever has happened before—not by all the massive weight of generations and centuries of history piled like a mountain of dirt beside a mass grave already dug and ready.

A voice always perverted and misused to sell the façade and sham of the American dream, because that was the easiest part to sell and sell out. Because there was money in it. Because the dream of El Dorado would always and always speak to the weakness of people who would not be happy when and if they got there, nor even sure that they deserved to be if the place matched perfectly the hungers that made them claw and deceive on their way.

A voice deserved neither by him nor by the people he had fooled or failed because it had never spoken the hard words, the necessary words it must have been intended for until this morning.

"You're going to get bodies," the voice said to Harris as the two men sat for a while together in the front seat of the unmarked police car. "If that is what is needed, then all right. Sooner or later you are going to get bodies. You know that because you—we—have already got some. I guess you know more than I do about who killed them—Stewart and those two black men who tried to get out of the country—and you may know why. I might not understand why if you kept trying to explain it to me from here on in. I'd say I did, if you told me. I might say anything. That woman up there waiting isn't going to say she understands. She's got a girl over there and you say the girl is armed and dangerous."

"May be," Harris quoted from what had been quoted to him. He was a decent man. He did not want to make judgments, because to judge was the duty of other men in the system whose servant he was. "Your daughter may be a victim. But . . . maybe she was the one who took a shot at us. I know your feelings and Mrs. Rossiter's, Hoyt. I swear to you again, I'm going to avoid bloodshed as long as I can. There's a good chance we can get them out without killing anybody."

"No. You won't admit how much they hate."

"Who? Hate who?"

"Me. America. The way things are. How much they won't have it. I don't understand, either. When there is that much hate, doesn't it stand to reason there are going to be more bodies? Doesn't it stand to reason you are going to be blamed for them? I don't know you from Adam. I believe you don't want bloodshed. If you could just tell me how you're going to stop it. If you could just tell me how you're going to convince that woman up there that it is not your fault. She's not a crazy. I know her. I know she always wanted the best and you couldn't buy her off it or fool her for very long. You can't add it all up and come out right by asking how many votes Mary Rossiter controls. She's going to think this out and go on thinking this out and people like her will have the votes or guns or whatever it takes to get rid of whoever it is that has killed their children in the mess we have all made.

"You are going to have bodies, and if you want people like Mary Rossiter to say it is your responsibility, then you will just hang on and keep the situation frozen until you have them. They've got to hate somebody, because they know something has been done wrong. That is true. Something has been done wrong. Somebody has got to be blamed, so if you would just let me have my gun and go over there, it might not be on your head. It might not be the pigs that did it this time. Don't you see that?"

The voice might get to Harris, the temptation to believe that there was a way out, not specified by any instructions or training or supported by a common-sense appraisal of his sworn duty to the institutions he believed in and served. But the words roused his skepticism if not his suspicions or contempt. He had heard them before—or something enough like them to make him refuse to credit them.

He was glancing sideways at Cooley with a mixture of sympathy, doubt and calm that amounted to refusal. "I certainly understand your feelings," he said. "Look, I've got to get back up there and keep an eye on things. Relax. I'm not going to make a move until I have to."

They had walked almost back to the bend in the lane from which the meadow fell away toward the cabin when he slapped his chest to feel the pockets there. "Damn," he said lightly. "I meant to get my sunglasses while we were in the car. Well . . . it's getting bright. Would you be kind enough to go get them for me? I'd better talk to the men up on the mesa. Keep them cool."

The sunglasses were exactly where he said they would be, in the glove compartment in a brown leatherette case. Beside the case was Cooley's snub-nosed .38.

When Cooley gave him the sunglasses, Harris wiped them carefully and put them on with unhurried deliberation. "Appreciate that," he said.

He ducked a little to stay under cover and went to the three riflemen who were watching the meadow and the trees beyond. He spoke briefly to them. Then he came back and began to speak into the walkie-talkie. "McConnell? Tell everyone to hold up. Mr. Hoyt is going to walk over there and try to have a talk with them. I'll give you twenty minutes to pass the word. Absolutely no shooting and no tear gas until he comes back. No. I'm not telling you to cover him. In any way. It's his decision and he's going unarmed."

3

It was very good to be walking. The sun felt good on his head and through the cloth of his jacket as he started across the meadow. Everything smelled good.

Do you know what you are smelling, Hoyt?

I think it is the world, he said. He had been alive all these years and he had never thought before that the world had a smell just a little different from the nice smells of women and money and food and tobacco and the ocean on a warm day when the breeze caught it and you could even think you smelled the islands, the faraway islands. It occurred to him now that people like Charlotte who really loved the world had learned how because their noses were good enough to catch its special scent, beyond all the others. He felt very good about Charlotte as he started his walk, though it was not at all as if she were with him now. He felt good because he was alone and understood what she had wanted him to understand.

The first part of his walk across the meadow was downhill, and then the other part, which sloped up to the edge of the pine woods, was not steep at all. He thought he remembered running across this same ground in years past, getting velocity on the downslope and still feeling the momentum as he passed the low point and started up again. But he had no specific memory of other times or of other people. Whatever of them was left was altogether transformed and altogether his and part of what was happening right now.

He came at an easy walking pace through the edge of the pines and made out the California license plate on the blue Plymouth parked beside the cabin. He took a healthy squint at the cabin's chimney and thought it was a kind of miracle that no gung-ho cop had yielded to the temptation of tossing a tear-gas grenade into it. The cabin made a poor fort—provided all you had to do was capture it. As he came close to the door and saw that the padlock and hasp had been pried off, he realized he hadn't seen a single movement up in the woods or seen any police behind rocks as he came across the meadow. They had some time left and were leaving it up to him for now. Surely by afternoon they would have tried closing in.

The only two windows in the cabin faced the same direction as the door. As he came across the space between the parked car and the one log step that led up to the door, he thought he got a glimpse of a girl's face bobbing down from the one window that was still intact. She had probably been watching him all the way across the meadow. He thought it was not Victoria, but he had a poor idea of what she looked like, didn't he?

They could have shot him if they had wanted to. He didn't suppose they had any plan or tactics at all. Amateurs and bunglers to the end, acting on the spur of the moment, armed and more dangerous than professional criminals because it was only their feelings, their hate that told them what to do.

When he stood up very close to the door on the split log that served for a step, he knew he could not be seen from either window. He put his hand in his pocket then and took proper hold of the butt and trigger of the revolver. He knocked lightly with his left hand and said, "I'm Victoria Hoyt's father. Is she here? Victoria?"

"Say hello to your father," a male voice said. "Say hello, Comrade Victoria. It may be your last chance."

"Hoyt the pig," a girl's voice said. He thought it wasn't Victoria's voice, but he didn't know, really, what her voice sounded like.

"Whatever you want to call me," he said. "I don't care. There's still time to talk about . . . what you hope to get out of this. That's what I came to talk about."

The girl's furious voice said, "Bring the money? Ha! You shouldn't have brought the fuzz."

"I didn't bring any. But we can talk about anything. Arrangements can be made."

The male voice—it sounded like a quavering teen-ager's—said, "First thing is to clear the cops out of here and give us safe conduct. Can you get us into Mexico? You fucked up, so . . . we got to take your girl with us."

"Maybe," Cooley said. "You'll have to let me in to make sure she's all right."

"We don't have to do anything."

"Victoria!" he called. "Can you answer me? Your mother's here with me."

"Answer him," the boy's voice instructed. "Goddamn it, answer him! C'mon, Victoria. Last chance. You had plenty to say before. Speak up. Rachel, the man wants to hear the voice. Yeah."

There was the sound of a slap. Pause. Another slap. Then a whole firecracker string of slaps and a sound of grunting.

"Stop it," Cooley said. "I believe you've got her. That's why I'm here. I tell you again I came over to discuss reasonably how we can settle this. It's never too late to make a deal." He took the revolver out of his pocket and scraped his shoe across the rough step to cover the sound when he cocked the gun. "Let me come in now. I'm coming in."

"Dad! Don't come in! They . . ."

Whatever was to be said to him was cut off by a sound he recognized too well—a boot hitting a skull. And the shock of hearing it almost tripped him into lunging at the door. He felt his weight move forward as if he had already left the balanced support of his legs. His shoulder was against the door and it was not yielding.

"Sure, you can come in," the boy said. "Nobody's got much choice, have they? Rachel, take the bar off the door and let the man come in and have a look. Let him come in and see we mean business. Come on in and tell her not to try any more funny stuff."

He heard the sound of the bar being lifted from the brackets, and he was glad that what was happening now was shifting and moving too fast for him to bother analyzing what any part of it meant. There was nothing to be outwitted now. He was cut off from any obligation to try.

He was still in time and all that had gone before must be continuous with what would happen now. But this was another kind of time. He was in a bubble of time that had a thin, tough shell around it, so that whatever happened had not been already poisoned, ruined, betrayed by his mistakes and crimes—but was there immaculate and whole and by itself.

He felt the sun on his back and knew he was already a little ahead of the sun, which is supposed to be the inescapable clock. For once he had got ahead of that mocking winner of all gambles. He was already in the moment to come when those inside and those across the meadow would see him move.

He knew everything that was going to happen inside that bubble of time. He understood why it had to be and why it was right. *You can't ask for any more than that. You don't need luck or anyone's approval when you know that*, he thought, with the last conscious awareness he ever had.

"Come in if you want to see your girl," the boy's voice urged.

He kicked open the door and went in firing. He had already seen the boy standing squarely in front of the door where he would have to be to take the best aim.

Feeling—after thinking had stopped—the ripping, stabbing, ball-crunching kick of the bullet that caught him in the belly as he pulled the trigger the second time. Seeing the bearded boy's face jerk back as if a rope under his chin had snapped tight. Falling among rosy waves of absolute fire that weren't coming up from the floor but from the agony in his gut. Still able, when he hit the floor, to see the boy flung back against the fireplace with nothing but blood above his beard.

Still able to roll and get the .38 up in both hands, tracking a figure still standing and swaying in terror from side to side. He heard a voice he knew well saying, "Dad, Daddy," through a gurgle of blood in the corner behind him.

He heard the standing girl say, "Please don't. Please don't."

What she asked made no difference. She was in the bubble with him, where whatever was going to happen had already happened. She was quite close to him and his elbows on the slippery floor were steady enough to support the gun.

"Please don't," Rachel said. "Please don't. We didn't mean . . ."

But it had already happened to her, just as it had happened to everyone in that cabin except his reclaimed child Victoria.

V

1

"He wanted me to soar," Victoria said. "He wrote me that once in a letter." It was the only thing she and her father had ever agreed on, and they never could have agreed on how it was to be done.

But there it was, after his death, like an imperishable sign exchanged between them. Like a confession of the reckless folly that smashed the common goodness life offered them as it was offered to anyone else. "People can't," she said. "We can't soar."

Her mother was driving her home to Cambridge after the funeral services for Cooley Hoyt in Albuquerque. After the slaughter in the mountain cabin. After the first onslaught of questioning by police and reporters. A kind of numbness had seen her through those things, a refusal of awareness, a kind of physical indifference to what the yammering world considered so sensationally important—as if her real self had retired deep within its labyrinth of nerves to nurse and keep alive a secret, a little flame, that was all that had escaped extinction.

That secret they could not take from her, and they got very little else, either. She had not lied. She had simply not responded to their hounding questions. They had her now. She could not run any more. Let them make what they could of their evidence.

It was as if she, too, had died in that swift cataclysm of gunfire, just as she used to foresee she would and probably should.

But had not quite died, because it was her strength and her

duty as a woman to preserve the secret meaning of what had been acted out in blood, even if her hurt mind and tongue would never, never be able to declare it.

Let them all—including her mother—stretch their necessary explanations and finish them off by judging her sick and treating her as insane if that was what they needed to keep their own sanity functioning. Oh, *yes,* she was sick and they would go on and on proving it in their attempts to believe that they were well.

Already as she drove with her mother into the monotonous spaces of Kansas, she felt her numbness beginning to lessen and everything hurt more. The right side of her face was one big bruise from being kicked by Mike Lane in his hysteria of defiance and panic. Her head ached and throbbed—no worse than the day before except that now she was aware of pain again. With the return of awareness that she still must live in her physical body, she began to understand that the worst was still ahead. And not just for her.

Now they were in the part of the world called Kansas, with the long, sullen roll of prairies still brown from the fallow months of winter, the insignificant small towns strung on a highway like an elastic that has been overstretched and discarded when its resilience is used up. Here and there they passed towering grain elevators standing luminous against the gray sky like temples of a religion no longer cherished or intelligible. And after Kansas, Missouri, Kentucky, Ohio, Pennsylvania, April, May, June, voices, questions and the terrible ticking of the heart like a clock with no hands to point out hours of either joy or clean and total despair.

"Shall I go to prison?" she asked her mother. "If I told them what they want they'd send me up for sure."

"No," Mary said. "No. I don't think so. We have to weigh everything. Find what we can trust. Go on hoping to find justice. We have to believe in justice. Your rights to a defense. We don't have to go into that until you've had a chance to recover."

She could hear her mother, but somehow her mother could no longer hear her. Justice . . . ? What was it except the things that had happened? Whatever had happened was justice, and that was the knowledge they wouldn't believe they were strong enough to bear.

There was the pity.

There was the beginning of pity, to know they couldn't bear what they said they wanted and wasted themselves to get. It was sick to know that. And in that sickness something began, something was renewed that must never be allowed to die.

"Yes," her mother said with a humble little laugh that might as well have been the sob she refused. "Your father meant to soar, I guess. That's as good a way as any of summing it up. Why, even at the end he had to kill instead of . . . I don't know. Maybe it had to come to that. But we have to learn to take one day at a time. We're only what we are. You're right, we can't soar."

Victoria pressed her hand to her aching cheek. Her mother was right. The world was right. Everyone agreed at last and waited for the end that proved how right they were.

No. Not everyone agreed.

No, no, no. If she had been all alone, she would have to agree, too. The secret would be lost because no one was strong enough alone to hold it.

But for a minute, while the car held straight and efficient and secure on the Kansas road, she knew it might have been otherwise. She was no more with the living than with the dead now and as long as she could remember the agony of their refusal she could feel the lift, the rising, the exultation of escape.

She could never tell anyone how strangely now she loved them all—Bunny, Nat, Rachel, Mike, her father. If she tried she would lose the assurance herself, and it was all she had.

"I want it *changed*," she said. "*All of it. Everything.*"

Her mother agreed as well as she knew how. "Yes, we want it changed."

2

"We should be scattering them as we fly," Charlotte said to Bob Pardon.

They were bringing Cooley's ashes back to El Dorado in the

Cessna. The small, discreet carton that held the modest urn was
a puzzling cargo for them. They had cared about the man and
tried to guess at the will that moved him so bewilderingly sometimes. They were still trying to guess when he had left so little
certainty.

Bob said, "I've been wracking my brain about what to do with
them. I keep thinking they're already scattered."

They were not sentimental people. They needed no more
ceremonies to appease their own feelings. But they knew better
than anyone else how hard it might be to dispose of the riddle
he still presented. He had pursued no grail but the Offshore Dollar. Owed allegiance to no flag or father and finally not even to
the women in whose name and for whose sake he had made his
grabs for wealth.

"I won't keep the urn. A nuisance," Charlotte said, counting
on Bob not to mistake her feelings.

"I'll dispose of them for you," he said. It seemed he was speaking to Cooley as well as to her, promising the Knight of the
Offshore Dollar that the ashes of his heart would offer no clues
to the hounds or jackals on his track.

Geronimo . . . gone!

They approached from seaward for the landing at the El
Dorado strip. They saw the beach and the turquoise waters
crowded and gay with catamarans and lounging bathers. The
parking lot was jammed with expensive cars. There would always be people with money, even in hard times. There would always be those who make money from hard times. To the eye
alone it was clear that Cooley's firestorm of publicity was going
to pay off. For someone. El Dorado was going to make money
out of money out of money out of a dream and the defenseless
generosity of a beautiful natural setting.

And there—no surprise—was John Halvorsen's Learjet parked
just off the runway. The Sun King was evidently here to sweeten
and tinker with his offers to buy. Eventually he would take over
at El Dorado. It would be added to the armada of luxury hotels
that went around the earth like the gunboats of a new diplo-
macy. The Sun King would own everything because his time had
come. It didn't matter much what rules or laws or governments

came and went. The Sun King could play by any set of rules and win. If the guerrillas came back again and seized this opulent playground in the name of the proletariat, they would probably name the Sun King commissar in charge of tourism and recreation.

"I don't want him to have it," Charlotte said. "I suppose there's no other sensible way, is there?"

"Whatever else is left of Cooley's companies is coming apart fast. It will all go with a rush. There was a kind of mystique in his name. People all over the world—those who should have learned their lesson long ago—business people with problems as bad as his—counted on him to pull a rabbit out of the hat. Even if it was finding someone to bribe they hadn't thought of. If you want the most you can salvage, we better deal with Halvorsen."

"I do," she said. "I've no doubt there'll be a mountain of legal fees for Victoria. I want there should be two or three of the crookedest lawyers in all the United States to wangle her out of the mess. They're not to have her ass if it takes every penny."

"The crookeder, the more they cost," he warned.

"I mean what I say. I'll get along." Then she grinned jauntily. "I mean, I want what I can git as well. For there's much I mean to do with my life yet. But I'm leaving it all up to you. I'll be out of here tomorrow. The next day at the latest. To join up with Jovan in Caracas and then ease over to Paris or Africa."

"To see Ortiz Rosio?"

"Ah, well, sure. He always likes my company. As others do. Don't think bad things of me, Bob, nor tell any gossip that might be understood."

"I adore you."

"You'll tell all the world that Cooley got his money's worth of me?"

"That he died ahead of the game because of you. Hell, Charlotte, when I say adore, I mean *adore*."

"You know—my mind is strange, as you know—I've thought these last years was like being married to *you*, and Cooley was our spoiled kid we had to make the best of."

Primly he said, "It was something like that. You'll have much to think of if you ever grow old."

3

After a morning with John Halvorsen and his lawyers, Bob had gone down to the main pool and found himself a beach chair in the shade. He, too, would be leaving very soon. It was time to go, and he would miss El Dorado. It would not be painful to leave it. He had done his best here, as he had done his reasonable best with his life.

The luxury of El Dorado was not an evil, though the wicked as well as the good took their pleasures from it and left their traces. He did not know who deserved it and who did not. He supposed it was not indecent to feel he deserved some hours of quiet here after so much turbulence.

So he drank his margarita and fell asleep.

He was wakened the way a deserving man should be wakened in a place that claimed to be a model of paradise. A young woman was tickling his foot. It was Karen Steiglitz.

"You thought I was gone for good," she said brightly.

"I thought your story had outrun you and you were back in the States trying to cut it down to manageable proportions. Neat parcels to fit the time slots."

"It goes on and on, doesn't it?" she said pleasantly. "You told me there wasn't any central thread to it."

"I abide by that opinion. The more it goes on, the more we will never know. Can you tell me who killed young Stewart or why?"

"I can even come close to that," she said. Karen was blithe and professionally unshakable. She had always been taught to have no more squeamishness than an undertaker. She had looked at corpses. She had seen mutilations, nastiness without any redeeming necessity. But she had her pieties. Vulnerability. There were shadows around her eyes and the smallest corner of her lip was caught an instant between the tips of her canine teeth before she said, "The blacks. I don't know for sure if it was Nat Fraser or the man who was killed with him. But Nat Fraser is a book unto himself. He spent a lot of time in an asylum. He wasn't a man you could reason with, I suppose. When things got rolling. . . . Anyway, the police are going to close the case by blaming Stewart on the deceased black men. It's possible. It's handy."

"You can still blame the blacks," he said. "Which doesn't mean they use razors only to shave with."

"An ice pick. On Bunny Stewart. Which does not exonerate Fraser any more than his blackness. But . . . suppose someone gave him the order, or what he thought was an order. Someone who would have a way of getting through to crazy Nat Fraser and telling him there was a way to do business after the initial foolishness of asking for forty million."

"Now you're getting ready to curl my hair," Bob said. "Who?"

The shadows flitted in her eyes. "I'm not sure of anything," she said. "I don't even want to talk about it down here. If you'll come to my room, I'll tell you what I'm not sure of."

Nothing he was going to learn at his age was going to embitter Bob. His hair simply wasn't going to curl at further exposures of what men are capable of. And yet he could still admit that below the bedrock cynicism on which his kindness was built, there were caves, holes, gaps and sheer vacuums where something kin to demons lived.

When Karen finished her story he still protested, "You haven't told me how or why he sewed this crazy quilt together."

"But at least I see his finger in every part of the pie," she said. "The one who'll keep the mischief going if he can."

Colonel Bull Timmerman, an ace left over from the Korean War, turned into a very wild card indeed. "He'll let it be inferred when it suits him that he's part of the CIA. I doubt if they know or he knows any more whether he's with them or on his own, though I have no more doubt they use him. The lines aren't all that clearly drawn after a while. From what I piece together he's into a little of everything in Latin America—smuggling, spying, intriguing with displaced people when it might be profitable, selling them out when he sees an advantage. Another freak of the times, like Cooley Hoyt. Old soldiers never die.

"I know now for a *fact* that it was he who tipped Nick

Sanders there was going to be an assassination attempt on Rosio here. I know he has some photos Nat Fraser took. But something slipped or someone began breathing down his neck and he passed the word to the police so they could spirit Rosio out of harm's way and ambush the terrorists here. The terrorists to whom the colonel had been funneling arms—just as he's into the drug trade and at the same time rationing out information to U.S. narcotics agents. A real joker, I tell you, the man who stands on the middle of the teeter-totter with one foot on each side."

He saw no better reasons for believing than for doubting this much of her thesis. He had no doubt that Colonel Timmerman was a very mean and nimble operator. He supposed Karen was in a position to get a reliable general view of the way the man operated. Reporters don't have to prove things. But just as no one could prove where the colonel stood—and make it stick—no one could say for sure just where Karen herself stood as she sat here at El Dorado accusing him.

Karen's mind seemed to be running along the same lines. "That's why I'm getting out this evening. I'll be on the morning plane from Mexico City. I'm thoroughly scared of him, and I don't know if I'm doing you a favor telling you this much. I want you to believe I'm trying. I think . . . we owe something to good people and I think you mean to be good."

"How little that counts."

She wouldn't quite accept that and in any event the rest of what she could now tell him might make a difference. She had just come back here from Ajijic, where she had spent a day with the colonel in his retirement villa. "We were talking about a book he wants me to write." At the core of this literary aspiration was the colonel's assertion that Victoria Hoyt was a full-fledged member of the guerrilla gang that came to shoot up the hotel. He knew she had run in guns for them. He wanted money either to tell his story or to keep it under wraps. His chief bargaining card was his insistence that he was the only person who could— or was likely to come forward to—prove what he was saying. If Nick Sanders didn't see fit to put up money for the corroborated story, or if the girl's family didn't pour in money to stop it—then Karen had his authorization to deal with book publishers in New York.

"Do you want to write the book?"

"I thought about it," Karen said. "No. I want this to stop. All of it. I'm not going to tell Nick anything about it—and he wouldn't put up the money the colonel thinks it's worth anyway."

He could only thank her for her good wishes.

He could not expect her or anyone else to come up with a reasonable plan for insuring Colonel Timmerman's silence. It was that impotence that curled his hair, for the man was a time bomb, out of reach, beyond punishment and beyond appeal.

"Because he seems to be the only one in the whole bloody sequence who never supposed he was trying to do something in the name of right or justice," he said to Charlotte. "Maybe that's why the rest failed and he can't be touched."

4

It would have debased his trust in Charlotte not to forewarn her of troubles threatening farther down the road. He wanted her out of here. He trusted her to make something fine of her life wherever she went. He wanted her departure to be clean.

And first she seemed to agree with him that it was an ugly thing to turn up, but beyond their power to settle.

Then she thought it over. She slept on it. From a distance Bob saw her the next morning as she sat alone on the balcony outside the Monarch Suite, sipping her coffee and watching the idle signaling of the palm fronds as they swayed between her and the tranquil loveliness of the ocean.

Later in the morning he knew she had gone alone in a motorboat to the offshore island she liked better than anything here. She was gone little more than an hour, though he had been convinced she was going out there to compose her farewell thoughts about Cooley and her years with him.

And then in the afternoon when he was sitting on the shaded side of the balcony in front of his room, he saw her on the cobblestone path below him, striding his way. She was wearing a very simple white dress, severe as a uniform, but so subtly tailored and chosen with such imagination that if it was a uniform it was one that should have been worn by a queen coming to review her troops. Charlotte always dressed for her occasions.

She played her necessary roles with a straightforwardness not intended to fool or cheat anyone. As soon as he saw her he thought he knew what she was coming for. She came toward him through the heavy lattice of shadows falling from the palm trunks across the sun-smitten stones of the walk. Her step was jaunty. Her neck was stiff.

"I want me a gun that can't be traced," she said.

"No—you don't."

"The truth of the matter is, I do. I have me heart set on it. I'm a woman who has always got what she wants. People have give it to me or I took it in me own ways. Bob, it would be tidier not to have to ask around, though someone else might oblige me. Will you get it for me?"

"I could."

"I thought you would."

"Charlotte . . ."

"Oh, what's the use of talking any more? I want what I want and will have it. Y'know, there were times—not many, I admit—when I thought I ought to have given Cooley a child, something to slow him down, something to have for his own, for heaven's sake, for I knew how lonely he was, even with me."

"Charlotte."

"And now I cannot. And still the man should have his child. That's an old Irish prejudice. He freed her, didn't he? The girl's in awful trouble still, but she's good. Or perhaps she's not. But she's his and the man will have his child."

"But . . . even if you could kill Timmerman and get by with it . . ."

"The brute will get her locked up with his mucking around. You doubted if there was any way to get at him, but there always is."

"Think!" Bob said sharply. "You don't have to persuade me what you *want*. Before all this is unraveled it may turn out that there are several people who can pin something on her. She's got money. Or will have. She'll have lawyers. Killing Timmerman won't guarantee her safety."

"You don't know and I don't. But I'd rather like the child to know she's not alone. In the bad times coming she ought to know she's not. In a war we have to do things without being promised they will win. Now it's all a war, isn't it?"

"Yes."

"It was always that for Cooley, and I'll not admit he lost it. Will you get the gun for me?"

"Charlotte."

"That's three times you've called my name and I've heard you," she said. She was a woman who knew well who admired her and who adored her. She was impatient with his fears for her. "Will you get it now? I'd like to be on my way."

He did not have far to go. The gun was in his bureau drawer, clean and reliable as it had been for the twenty years he owned it and kept it for whatever emergency beyond the reach of the law might sometime require it. It was as clean of identifying marks as it was of dirt. He unwrapped it carefully from the felt sack and let it slide into the purse she opened to receive it.

They went back out on the balcony so she could smoke a last cigarette with him before she left. While they sat there he said what he had to—the fourth try, and he got it all out this time. "Charlotte, you don't owe him anything. Leave Timmerman alone. Go straight to Paris. I'll have the maids pack your things. I'll stand by to handle Timmerman if it's money he wants. I won't ever say forget all this. You mustn't and you won't. But you don't owe the girl or her mother anything."

"I don't owe no one," she said airily. "What I do is for me. Will you give us a kiss, old man?"

She took the gray Mercedes, backing it with precision out from among the crowded limousines in the parking lot. She did not look up toward him, though he gave her a last wave of the hand. She was concentrating on her driving and she handled the car with perfect authority, gunning it on the curves among the palms, past the revolutionary monument that she and Page Fentress had found and brought here to soften what was modern and merely expensive. She accelerated up the long incline to the guard gate, the car rising like a fighter plane breaking from the deck of a carrier.

She was out of sight. Driving toward Ajijic in the afternoon sun.